Br
H
re
ob
w
E
ce
U
sp
si
ar
S

MRS HUMPHRY WARD

HELBECK
OF BANNISDALE

EDITED WITH AN INTRODUCTION AND NOTES
BY BRIAN WORTHINGTON

PENGUIN BOOKS

Penguin Books Ltd, Harmondsworth, Middlesex, England
Penguin Books, 625 Madison Avenue, New York, New York 10022, U.S.A.
Penguin Books Australia Ltd, Ringwood, Victoria, Australia
Penguin Books Canada Ltd, 2801 John Street, Markham, Ontario, Canada L3R 1B4
Penguin Books (N.Z.) Ltd, 182–190 Wairau Road, Auckland 10, New Zealand

First published 1898

Published in the Penguin English Library 1983

Introduction and all editorial material copyright © Brian Worthington, 1983
All rights reserved

Made and printed in Great Britain by
Richard Clay (The Chaucer Press) Ltd, Bungay, Suffolk
Filmset in Baskerville

TO THE MEMORY OF

Q. D. LEAVIS

CONTENTS

BIOGRAPHICAL NOTE
9

INTRODUCTION BY BRIAN WORTHINGTON
13

FURTHER READING
27

HELBECK OF BANNISDALE
33

NOTES
391

APPENDIX: ROMAN CATHOLIC RECUSANTS
394

BIOGRAPHICAL NOTE

Mrs Humphry Ward was born Mary Augusta Arnold in Hobart, Tasmania (then called Van Diemen's Land) in 1851, the eldest of eight children. Her mother, Julia Sorel, came of Huguenot stock and her father, Thomas, was the second son of Dr Arnold of Rugby. An Oxford First, he had forgone academic life in order to become a farming settler in New Zealand, but having no such aptitude he took up the post of organizer of primary education in Tasmania until 1854, when his conversion to the Church of Rome forced him to resign and return to England. A period of struggle, privation and constant anxiety for his wife and family resulted and he taught briefly at the new Catholic college in Dublin, then with Newman at the Oratory in Birmingham until 1865, when 'a strong temporary reaction' led him to renounce his new faith for eleven years. In 1876 he finally returned to Rome, to the despair of his wife and the destruction of his resumed career at Oxford. The education of his children had followed the custom by which the boys attended Catholic schools and the girls were brought up as Protestants.

The happiest feature of Mary's childhood was holidaying at her grandmother's house, Fox How, in Westmoreland; it and the surrounding countryside influenced her throughout her life. Frequent visitors included her uncles, Matthew Arnold and William Forster (initiator of the 1870 Education Act and First Secretary for Ireland a dozen years later), the poet Arthur Clough and the biographer Arthur Stanley. A special memory from her childhood was a visit to Wordsworth's widow. Her formal education at a series of boarding schools was rudimentary, but was most effective at Ambleside, where the headmistress was Miss Anne Clough, later to be the first head of Newnham College, Cambridge. At Oxford (where her father had become a Tutor in Anglo-Saxon) Mary, in her own words 'a self-conscious bookish child', delighted in the Bodleian Library, 'which became to me a living and inspiring presence', and in the stimulus of friendship with brilliant dons like Jowett, Mark Pattison, Bywater, T. H. Green and Pater. She met George Eliot and William Gladstone, becoming well informed of the current religious and political controversies.

Although women were not allowed to be members of the university, she applied herself with remarkable success to that intense academic study which Mark Pattison had recommended to her: she became an authority on Spanish literature, researched into the nature of biblical testimony, and was commissioned to write the lives of early Spanish ecclesiastics for the Dictionary of Christian Biography. Later she made history by becoming the first woman examiner of men at either university, and she was the first secretary of Somerville College. The social and recreational life of Oxford also delighted her, and one of her own modest contributions was to help found the Croquet Club.

She married T. Humphry Ward, Fellow and Tutor of Brasenose College and editor of the five-volume *The English Poets*, and in 1881 they moved to London on his appointment as leader-writer on *The Times*, of which newspaper he eventually became the art critic. His wife wrote reviews, a children's story called *Milly and Olly* (1881), an influential translation of Amiel's *Journal Intime* (1884) and, the same year, her first novel, *Miss Bretherton*, which interested Henry James and may well have sowed seeds for his own novel about an actress, *The Tragic Muse*.

It was, however, with *Robert Elsmere* (1888) that she achieved fame and success to an astonishing degree. Having as a young woman decided that Christianity could be revitalized by discarding its miraculous element and emphasizing social mission, she translated that lifelong belief into novel form. Tolstoy called her 'the greatest living novelist', and James described the work as 'the most serious, most deliberate and most comprehensive attempt made in England in this later time to hold the mirror of prose fiction up to life'. Gladstone reviewed it at great length in the *Nineteenth Century*, claiming that she tried to undermine Christianity by putting forward only one side of the argument, and 'that in proposing a substitute for traditional faith reached by reduction and negation, she was dreaming the most visionary of all human dreams'. She vigorously answered the charges but must have known that such serious attention could only add to the novel's commercial success: in England over 70,000 copies were sold in its first year, and in the U.S.A. between a quarter and half a million. There being no copyright law (as Dickens had known too well), the author received a mere £100 from America, and that injustice furthered the passage in Congress of the Copyright Act from which she and other writers subsequently benefited.

Robert Elsmere shows a young clergyman sacrificing his living in favour of active social work in the name of Christ, and its author put her precepts into practice by helping to found the University Hall settlement in Gordon Square for popular Bible-teaching and simplified Christianity, as well as the general social and educational improvement of poor children. In 1897 it was funded by the philanthropist Passmore Edwards (who had been inspired by *Robert Elsmere*) and named after him; it is now known as Mary Ward House and is in Tavistock Square. The settlement was the first to set up a scheme for educating crippled children, and by 1918 Mrs Ward's propaganda in favour of facilities for physically handicapped children had helped to bring about statutory provision for them.

Despite uncertain health and, oddly, the most intense agony from writer's cramp – even so she refused to follow Henry James in working by dictation, a practice she blamed for his elaborate later style – she maintained an enormous output of novels and a full social, intellectual and charitable life, her most contented times being spent at family homes in Surrey or the Lake District. She was a notably successful and influential woman (in 1920 she became one of the first female magistrates, and she was awarded an honorary LL.D. by Edinburgh University), but she and a number of other influential ladies, including, surprisingly, Beatrice Webb, founded the Women's National Anti-Suffrage League in 1908, and later a Joint Advisory Council of Members of Parliament and Women Social Workers to bring the views of women to bear on the legislature without the aid of the vote.

She maintained an enormous popular success as a writer, moving from socially concerned novels like *The History of David Grieve* (1892) and *The Story of Bessie Costrell* (1895) to glittering upper-class tales like *Lady Rose's Daughter* (1903) and *The Marriage of William Ashe* (1905). As late as 1911 she returned to the theme of her greatest success, showing in *The Case of Richard Meynell* an 'Elsmere' who remained inside the Church of England to practise his new faith.

Significantly, it was *Helbeck of Bannisdale* (1898), which had made the quietest initial impact in terms of mass sales (a mere three editions in its first year!) but had received striking approval from other writers and thoughtful critics, that maintained its appeal and slowly established itself by the time of its author's death as her one fine and lasting major novel.

Mrs Ward's success in the U.S.A. and her visit there and to Canada in 1908 had an unforeseen result. During the First World War she was commissioned to bring home to the American people the efforts and successes of the Allies, first in *Letters to an American Friend* for the press, and then in three books, beginning with *England's Effort* (1916). In addition, like her friend Henry James, she worked tirelessly for the war effort.

In 1918 she wrote *A Writer's Recollections*, which concentrated on the first part of her life and gives a fascinating picture of academic and intellectual life in the late nineteenth century. She was still writing novels, though her extraordinary success was past, until her death in 1920. She was survived by her husband, a son who had been a Conservative M.P., two daughters (one the wife of G. M. Trevelyan) and, one of many nephews, Aldous Huxley.

Her reputation was such that the following telegram was sent by King George and Queen Mary:

Their Majesties believe that Mrs Humphry Ward's distinguished literary achievements, her philanthropic activities and her successful organizations to promote the health and recreation of children will endear her memory to the hearts of the English-speaking people.

PUBLISHED WORKS
OF MRS HUMPHRY WARD

Milly and Olly or a Holiday among the Mountains (1881)

Miss Bretherton (1884)

Amiel's Journal Intime (translation; 1884)

Robert Elsmere (1888)

The History of David Grieve (1892)

Marcella (1894)

The Story of Bessie Costrell (1895)

Sir George Tressady (1896)

Helbeck of Bannisdale (1898)

Eleanor (1900)

Lady Rose's Daughter (1903)

The Marriage of William Ashe (1905)

Fenwick's Career (1906)

The Testing of Diana Mallory (1908)

Canadian Born (1910)

The Case of Richard Meynell (1911)

The Mating of Lydia (1913)

The Coryston Family (1913)

Delia Blanchflower (1915)

Eltham House (1915)

A Great Success (1916)

England's Effort (1916)

Lady Connie (1916)

Towards the Goal (1917)

Missing (1917)

A Writer's Recollections (1918)

The War and Elizabeth (1918)

Fields of Victory (1919)

Cousin Philip (1919)

Harvest (1920)

INTRODUCTION

Mrs Humphry Ward asks in her commentary on *Villette* by Charlotte Brontë: 'What may be said to be the main secret, the central cause not only of her success but, generally, of the success of women in fiction, during the present [nineteenth] century?' Hitherto women's range of materials in the novel had been necessarily limited, but 'the one subject which they have eternally at command, what is interesting to all the world, and whereof large tracts are naturally and wholly their own, is the subject of love, love of many kinds indeed, but pre-eminently the love between man and woman ... But it is love as the woman understands it.' She goes on to say that, with few exceptions (such as Richardson),[1] English novels by men are not as a rule studies of love, perhaps because of 'the development of the Hebraist and Puritan element in the English mind, so real, for all its attendant hypocrisies'.

Helbeck of Bannisdale (1898) is proof that she spoke with the authority of a fine novelist who had called upon her deepest resources as a woman of feeling and intellect to create a work that set 'the love between man and woman' against their passionately held personal beliefs, to culminate in the inevitable and intolerable catastrophe which is tragedy. What special power of imagination and intensity of conviction enabled the hitherto successful social and argumentative novelist to reach such heights, once and once only?

It was *Robert Elsmere*, written in 1888 deliberately in the tradition of novels of religious or social propaganda, such as Froude's *Nemesis of Faith*, Newman's *Loss and Gain* and Kingsley's *Alton Locke*, that brought Mrs Ward international success by touching on the nerve of late Victorian life: the challenge offered by rational investigation and learned textual criticism to a literal belief in the Bible, not only Genesis (in the face of Darwinian theory) but also the New Testament with its stress on the divinity of Christ and His miraculous powers, which were subjected to a sophisticated investigation that cast doubt on the very nature of biblical testimony. The fact that a long novel on such a substantial theme sold widely to people of all classes in England, Europe and the U.S.A. says much for the intelligence as well as the concerns of the age, but to a modern reader a great deal of the novel fails because its characters are too theoretically conceived, being thinly fleshed bodies for abstract ideas: the woman of fervent traditional Anglicanism; the doubting young cleric; the Puseyite fanatic; the dry intel-

1. Mrs Ward edited an abbreviated edition of *Clarissa* and must have been struck by the heroine's tragic fate.

lectual Scholar-atheist; the 'new woman'; the Paterian don. Nevertheless, in what was only her second novel, Mrs Ward wrote with skilled organization of material, life-like dialogue that could successfully incorporate intellectual ideas and themes, and a narrative gift that was never to leave her. And late in her career we find in *The Case of Richard Meynell* (1911), whose hero chooses to fight for his *Elsmere* beliefs within the Church of England, a readable, professional and less wordy book, but one in which the feeling has lost its Arnoldian nobility and the fire which had excited readers of *Robert Elsmere*. The author's command of her medium has become assured to the point of slickness; she manages the story and holds the attention with ease, but the price is high: belief is registered too much as a token and love is only conventional romance.

Mrs Ward kept her audience in terms of numbers despite the dying down of her artistic flame, but she lost the respect of discriminating readers, except in the case of one work, *Helbeck of Bannisdale*. To quote the laconically elegant words of Sir Edmund Gosse, it was 'her culminating book, so good in fact, that it might seem to a reader that Mrs Ward was, by dint of determination, slipping into the ranks of the creators'.[2] Nearly sixty years later we can vouch for her standing in those ranks through the writing of a work that refutes the charge that she was by nature a critic, not a creator.

Its origin was deep in her own life at its most sensitive period, for her childhood and adolescence were scarred by her father's conversion to Roman Catholicism after six years of matrimony with a wife for whom conversion was out of the question. She and the other children were obligatory witnesses of a basic incompatibility in the home, the more poignant for Mary in that, reared in her mother's abhorrence of Catholicism, she was drawn by instinctive love and sympathy towards her father, whose scholarly tastes were her own. In her autobiography she writes feelingly of 'that great controversy in which from my youth up I had been unable to follow him, without in the smallest degree chilling the strong affection between us which grew up with life, and knew no forced silences'. And of her mother's reaction to her husband's unlooked-for conversion she wrote:

My poor mother felt as though the earth had crumbled under her. Her passionate affection for my father endured till her latest hour, but she never reconciled herself to what he had done. There was in her an instinctive dread of Catholicism ... It never abated. Many years afterward, in writing *Helbeck of Bannisdale*, I drew upon what I had remembered of it in describing Laura Fountain's inbred and finally indomitable resistance to the Catholic claim upon the will and intellect of men.[3]

The scene was set for tragedy for everyone involved, and the marriage did in effect break down in the sense that Mrs Arnold became an invalid and her husband spent more and more time away from home; this, however,

2. Sir Edmund Gosse, *Silhouettes* (Heinemann, 1925).
3. Mrs Humphry Ward, *A Writer's Recollections* (Collins, 1918).

was in the second period of his conversion. Mary and her sisters were indoctrinated with a revulsion for Newman himself as the cause of their troubles, and kept away from their father's Catholic friends as from a contagion. Later, from her position of detached married woman, she was the go-between with the painful duty of trying to reconcile where no reconciliation was possible. After his wife's death Thomas Arnold married again, this time, of course, a co-religionist; his sons did not, however, remain in their father's communion and his daughters did not join it.

The materials were thus abundantly at hand for the novelist that Mary Ward had become: tragic situations, serious themes and her own emotional involvement. From her childhood she had taken naturally to writing stories, with a first novel at seventeen. *Helbeck of Bannisdale* was written when the Arnold tragedy was over, with her mother dead. There was obviously a great personal involvement: though the problem was her mother's and not her own, there is something of herself in Laura Fountain. However, Laura's situation is not in fact that of Mary Ward's mother, and Alan Helbeck, a cradle Catholic and the head of an old Catholic family in the north of England, is not her father. The novel is therefore not autobiographical like, for instance, *The Way of All Flesh* or even *Father and Son*, and the theme, the impossibility for someone brought up with an open mind of accepting the authoritarian form of religion, is treated schematically without the restraint of being tied down to history. Mrs Ward took some pains to free herself from prejudice as far as she could, and to cut out her inevitable personal indignation. She wrote to her father that she had greatly toned down the first version of *Helbeck* 'for your dear sake'. One would have liked to compare the two versions. So anxious was she not to offend her father that the proofs were sent to him in Ireland and received his approval, ample justification for her having said to him: 'I won't do it if you dislike it, but though of course my point of view is anything but Catholic, I should certainly want to do what I had thought of doing, with sympathy, and probably in such a way as to make the big English public understand more of Catholicism than they do now.'[4]

In addition to her father's approval came the satisfaction of reading among laudatory reviews an accusation that she had made the ancient Catholic faith too attractive! Then a judgement from within the Church, Father Clarke's denunciation of the novel as a caricature of Catholicism (in the *Nineteenth Century* magazine), was answered by another, from Mr St George Mirvat, which was a vindication of Mrs Ward's absolute fairness to the faith.

The truth is that the novelist had conceived the main plot out of an imaginative sympathy with the fortunes of the ancient Catholic family who had lived in Sizergh Castle, near Kendal, and a comparable sense of

4. Mrs G. M. Trevelyan, *Life of Mrs Humphry Ward* (Constable, 1923).

history in nearby Levens Hall, a handsome Elizabethan house. Differently treated by time, the two houses were imaginatively made to fuse into Bannisdale Hall, with its mixture of ancient dignity and faded splendour. The writer confessed that she was never more compelled by a subject and, significantly enough, she began writing it in the Lake District, at Levens Hall itself, which she had the good fortune to rent for a time. Westmoreland had been from childhood her happiest home and she knew its language, customs and people with an inwardness that was to prove a fundamental strength of the novel, set at the boundary between Lancashire and Westmoreland.

Her success in representing English Catholicism at its late-nineteenth-century stage of development is dependent on the artistic balance with which she manages the paradox she herself expressed: 'Catholicism has an enormous attraction for me, – yet I could no more be a Catholic than a Mahometan. Only, never let us forget how much of Catholicism is based, as Uncle Matt would have said, on "Natural truth" – truth of human nature, and truth of human experience.'[5]

The balance is achieved partly by means of the range of Catholic types she portrays and partly through the reactions to them expressed by members of other communions or, as in Laura's case, of none. Laura's stepmother, Augustina, had recoiled from the sternly demanding new Catholicism of her brother, Alan Helbeck, and married a fervent Cambridge sceptic chiefly in order to escape to a more interesting way of life and avoid becoming an old maid. The pull of her upbringing proves so strong, however, that, once widowed, she must return to Bannisdale to be restored in the eyes of her brother and the Church. For her the comforts of inane chatter with the local priest, the fussy attentions of the sisters and the simple pieties of relics and confession prove all-important, and Laura respects the benefit which her stepmother receives from her observances while detesting the religious and their doctrines. (With tragic irony, she does, however, come to appreciate the concentration of the Catholic minds upon the dying of Augustina, seeing it as 'the faith to die in ... It is a work of art'.)

Father Bowles is a character through whom Mrs Ward answers the charge that she has no sense of humour; quickly and neatly drawn, he is substantial in himself and represents the old priesthood that is being replaced by more learned and sophisticated men of the post-Newman era:

He was a priest of the old-fashioned type, with no pretensions to knowledge or to manners. Wherever he went he was a meek and accommodating guest, for his recollection went back to days when a priest coming to a private house to say mass would as likely as not have his meals in the pantry. And he was naturally of a gentle and yielding temper – though rather shy.

5. *Life of Mrs Humphry Ward* (see n. 4, p. 15).

The novelist does not condescend to him or disguise his inadequacies. Helbeck himself treats him with aristocratic breeding and impersonal respect, but the easy and polished Jesuit Leadham, a convert and ex-Fellow of Trinity, Cambridge, can hardly hide his disdain and regrets silently that 'the older Catholic priests are as a rule lamentably unfit for their work' as he hears Father Bowles's 'purring inanity' about the undoubted truth of the miracles at Lourdes. Leadham (the name's resemblance to 'lead 'em' suggests a proselytizer) seems to be analogous to Thomas Arnold, only from Cambridge and able to take up a career straightforwardly in the Society of Jesus and the general academic world by virtue of having been converted long after the reinstatement of the Catholic hierarchy and the Orders and after the death of his wife and children (as in the actual case of Cardinal Manning). He displays intelligence in his analysis of Laura's position but cannot overcome a complacent condescension: 'You see, she is alone. There must be a sense of exile – of something touching and profound going on beside her from which she is excluded . . . She has not a single thought in common with you all. No: I am very sorry for Miss Fountain.'

Laura, by contrast, sees the priestly will in him as a 'living tyrannous thing . . . developed at full proportion to, nay at the cruel expense of the rest of the personality'. She recoils from his 'sacerdotal pride' and 'that horrible egotism of religion that poisons everything', so that in her last desolate attempt to accept Catholicism her request that Father Leadham be her teacher indicates both her respect for his power and skill and the hopelessness of her real expectations.

Perhaps the most strangely striking of the Catholic figures, other than Helbeck himself, is Teddy Williams. Through him the author presents the terrifying Jesuitical demand for self-denial: he is not allowed to visit his dying mother (a suppression of human feeling that appalled Laura when she heard the child's story of the saint in Book I), nor is he allowed to practise his art of painting except by permission of the Order. (How similar this seems to the case of Gerard Manley Hopkins.) Yet he is strongly individualized, and in an intriguing way: he has an 'ambiguous voice' and 'a womanish cheek' and an embarrassing attachment to Helbeck, whose engagement he takes morbidly to heart and tries to prevent, apparently on religious grounds. He resents and avoids women at Bannisdale. A Victorian novelist could not have been more outspoken in showing that element in High Church or Roman Catholic rites which holds an attraction for homosexuals. Williams's conversion from the traditional Protestantism of his countrymen and family is a tribute to the magnetism of Helbeck but also highlights the antagonism felt towards Papism – 'the accursed thing' – by the rest of the neighbourhood. He ends up as the nastiest thing of all, a prating aesthete.

The Protestant peasantry is presented magnificently in a richness of speech and acuteness of observation that challenge comparison with the rural scenes in George Eliot (the Catholic housekeeper Mrs Denton is a similar achievement), and the grim energy of the family at Browhead Farm is described in a way that is reminiscent of *Wuthering Heights* but is no mere pastiche. The piano scene between Laura and Hubert anticipates D. H. Lawrence, and Mrs Ward is not afraid to describe the young man's sexuality: Laura notes to herself that she 'must try to keep him shy'.

The grotesqueness and narrowness of Elizabeth Mason's Protestantism does not prevent her from reaching points of dignity and deep feeling. She speaks of Laura's staying in a Catholic household in terms that echo Bunyan or a Ben Jonson Puritan: ' "It's aw yan" – she said, stubbornly. "Thoo ha' made a covenant wi' the Amorite an' the Amalekite. They ha' called tha, an thoo art eatin o' their sacrifices!" ' To her Helbeck is 'nobbut a heathen'.

The vindictive anti-Catholic discussions she holds with the fiercely evangelical parson, Mr Bayley (a type to make us nowadays think of Ulster), equal the cosy gabblings between Father Bowles and Augustina or, more shockingly, the shaming sarcasms against Protestant missionaries that Helbeck exchanges with Williams. Yet, in a moving scene in Book V, she apologizes to Laura in words of poetic compassion: ' "Mebee A've doon wrang. – We shouldna quench the smoakin flax. Soa theer's my han, child – if thoo can teäk it." ' Her children, Polly and Hubert, show a more offhand and modern attitude to religion but cannot shake off their inherited hatred of Popery.

It is the family's 'Methody' farmhand, Daffady, who embodies the best of the English peasantry and Dissenters. He himself is a skilful, devoted farmer and an unpretentious itinerant preacher, to whom the very idea of a priesthood is doubtful in scripture, though he commends the Christian aims of all churchmen, an attitude as old as Queen Elizabeth or Oliver Cromwell and as new as ecumenicalism:

'I've allus thowt mysen,' he said hastily, 'as we'd a deäl to larn from Romanists i' soom ways. Noo, their noshun of Purgatory – I daurna say a word for't when t'minister's taakin – for there's noa warrant for't i' Scruptur, as I can mek oot – bit I'll uphod yo, it's juist handy! Aa've often thowt so, i' my aan preachin. – Heaven and hell are verra well for t'foak as are ower good, or ower bad – bit t'moast o' foak – are juist a mish-mash.'

He instinctively takes to Laura in her misery, though he cannot sense the import of the words quoted above for a girl who is on the point of suicide.

In Dr Friedland (a transmutation of the influential Oxford historian T. H. Green – dedicatee of *Elsmere* – into a Cambridge don) may be found the strengths and weaknesses of the liberal mind. He shows unrealistic optimism and a shallow knowledge of human nature in his attitude to Laura's dilemma:

'How can there be any possible doubt what I should have said to her?' said the doctor, slapping his knee.

' "My dear, you love him – *ergo*, marry him!" That first and foremost. "And as to those other trifles, what have you to do with them?" '

But he also embodies the progressive point of view shared by Mrs Ward herself and most educated people of the later Victorian Age:

'At present what one sees going on in the modern world is a vast transformation of moral ideas, which for the moment holds the field. Beside the older ethical fabric – the fabric that the Church built up out of Greek and Jewish material – a new is rising. We think a hundred things unlawful that a Catholic family permits; on the other hand, a hundred prohibitions of the older faith have lost their force. And at the same time, for half our race, the old terrors and eschatologies are no more. We fear evil for quite different reasons; we think of it in quite different ways. And the net result in the best moderns is at once a great elaboration of conscience – and an almost intoxicating sense of freedom.'

The Friedlands are a refuge for Laura and her sole link with the world of her father; Dr Friedland's humane presence is seen to be more impressive than his learned and reflective maxims and he is given the last word on the tragedy, in tones that echo the best Hardy in spirit and expression.

However, the presence that asserts itself most insistently on Laura's conscience and outlook on the world is that of a man who died before the opening of the story, her father, Stephen Fountain. She has had only him to love and respect and she has been formed by his prejudices without (as Friedland puts it) knowing the reasons for them – except that as an atheistic heretic he had been blocked in his academic advancement at Cambridge by religious orthodoxy (an interesting similarity with Mrs Ward's father). Her father's memory obliges Laura to keep faith with him; she is frequently prompted to ask herself what he would have said or done, and at the end when she is determined to try to be converted she hears him saying, 'You cannot do it.' She prefers extinction to disloyalty towards either love, her father or Alan Helbeck.

Impressive as the presentation of these characters and themes is, the glory of the novel and the final ground for claiming it as a work of distinction lie in the nature of the love and conflict between Laura Fountain and Alan Helbeck. The latter's name ('holy stream') suggests his ancient lineage and purity, and the love of the fells and river valley which unites him in feeling with Laura, for whose father just such a love had been a Wordsworthian near-religious devotion. At the beginning of the novel Helbeck is conscious of feeling 'more alone than he used to' and his house typifies himself, being 'of singular character and dignity'. Its architecture is a historical growth but 'the whole structure seemed still to lean upon and draw towards the tower; and it was the tower which gave accent to a general impression of austerity'. This we learn before knowing anything about the man; it arouses the reader's expectations about him and outlines what he is to become. In front of the house 'were neither flowers nor shrubs

– only wide stretches of plain turf and ground; while behind it rose a grey limestone fell into which the house seemed to withdraw itself'.

This is both a metaphor and symbol, as is the later description (in Chapter 6) of the garden behind Bannisdale: 'all dark like the Tudor house that stood before it and the sun', with only tortured yews and box 'ranged along the straight walks'. This is a symbolic setting for the Helbecks, laid out 'according to a plan unaltered since the days of James II . . . Only from the high stone walls that begirt this strange and melancholy pleasure-ground, and in the "wilderness" that lay on the eastern side, between the garden and the fell, were Nature and the Spring allowed to show themselves . . . Otherwise all was dark, tortured, fantastic, a monument of old-world caprice that the heart could not love, though piety might not destroy it.'

That grand yet remote nature in Helbeck shows a chink of lightness and humane feeling as he tries to obey the injunction to remain in the world and not turn Jesuit (which is finally seen as a living death), but it is pride, which he shares with Laura (she calls him 'proud as Lucifer'), that immediately arrests her interest in him. His aristocratic absoluteness has overcome his piety in that he resists the Bishop's pressure on him to go out into the Protestant world (except to a token extent) and he believes 'Extra ecclesiam nulla salus'. The deadly irony is that love and marriage are seen (even by him) to be his health but he loves a woman who is outside the Church. Also, Father Leadham, who deprecates Helbeck's hermit-like piety and withdrawnness, has to face the mockery of finding that the godless Laura Fountain has become Helbeck's life outside the Church and in the world.

Helbeck's personal dignity and charm, 'that seemed to emerge momentarily' from under the absent hermit-manner of his ordinary life, 'enliven Laura to resentment and fascination'; 'her wild pagan self' awakens him to love, with the result that 'the blast of human longing, human pain, was hard to meet – hard to subdue', but in time the passions of love and faith in him subtly merge: '. . . where others saw defection from a high ideal and danger to his own Catholic position, he, with hidden passion, and very few words of explanation even to his director, Father Leadham, felt the drawing of a heavenly force, the promise of an ultimate and joyful issue'.

That sense of life-enhancement which rises out of his and Laura's declared love is not, even so, allowed to obliterate the deepest realities of their nature. When Helbeck confesses the story of his soul (in Book IV) and emphasizes what is an awesome truth to him – 'Sin and its Divine Victim, penance, regulation of life, death, judgment – Catholic thought moves perpetually from one of these ideas to the other' – Laura can only recognize the unbreakable intensity of his faith, and 'in her some spring was broken'. For her the overriding sense of Sin in Catholicism is a source of horror, and its attendant attitude to women as inferior and works of the devil (shown particularly in the story of St Charles Borromeo in Book IV) a cause of disgust as well as indignation.

In that lies the tragedy, and it is traced with delicate psychological insight and the subtlest ordering of plot that never suffers from the excesses of arranged coincidence that mar Hardy's attempts to achieve tragic inevitability. Book III, with its visit to the industrial town of Froswick, is an impressive demonstration of character and event ironically shaping each other.

Early in their acquaintance Laura tells Helbeck, 'There are some ways of life that are too far apart', yet she feels herself invaded 'by a force that at once drew and repulsed her'. Mrs Ward depicts with extreme delicacy the yoking of attraction and resistance between the lovers' characters and beliefs, and finally expresses the tragic wisdom, the true insight which makes *Helbeck of Bannisdale* an important work that achieves what is rare even in major novels:

How sharp was the clash between the reviving strength of passion, which could not but feed itself on the daily sight and contact of the beloved person and those facts of character and individuality which held them separated! – facts which are always and in all cases the true facts of this world.

Laura Fountain, whose name is unobtrusively symbolic, and particularly so when we remember how she is associated with the river and the metaphorical waters of emotion and fate, has 'always had a most surprising gift of happiness', a disposition independent of any religion or theory, in contrast with Helbeck, who is without the gift of happiness and whose religion is not of a kind to supply the lack of it, hence Laura's irresistible attraction for him as she 'gives her heart' to the 'wildness of the austere fell' (a prefiguration of her love for the passionate inner life of Helbeck). When visiting her bigotedly Protestant kinsfolk she feels 'here surely was something more human – more poetic even – than the tattered splendour of Bannisdale' because on the farm 'generations of human beings had fought with snow and storm, had maintained their little polity there on the heights, self-centred, self-supplied'. Her sympathies are acute and her sense of values is spiritual, yet the Jesuit pities her and looks forward to converting her because Helbeck tells him 'that she has had no training, moral or intellectual'. But in fact he is wrong and she has had an unconscious training in the conditioning by her father which has rendered her immune to the arguments of priests and even the emotional appeal of a rigidly Catholic lover, so that although she felt isolated during the chapel service at Bannisdale 'her whole nature leapt in defiance. She seemed to be holding something at bay – a tyrannous power that threatened humiliation and hypocrisy, that seemed at the same time to be prying into secret things.' As well as intellectually rejecting 'intolerable superstition', she reacts in her feelings and 'a wave of the most passionate revulsion swept through her'. She is 'steeped in denial and cradled in doubt – and knowing well why she denies'. Helbeck learns and has to admit that. Consequently the conflict between them becomes self-generating. 'At the touch of resistance in him her own will steeled'; she tells Helbeck, 'There is something in me that fears nothing – not even the breaking of both our hearts.' When he is with his Catholic friends and talks of matters sealed to her, 'it roused in her that jealous half desolate sense that was becoming a habitual tone of mind'. She sees the final truth with sudden despair and will not face 'the chilling reality that was waiting for her in the dim corridors of life'. Her death has echoes of Ophelia's, but she is not mad and her generosity of spirit is such that she arranges the drowning to appear accidental in order to avoid hurting her lover still more.

The novelist's triumph is not only to have presented love 'as the woman understands it', but to have conveyed the love of both sexes, along with the experience of faith, especially in Catholicism, which through personal contact and considerable study she came to know sufficiently to describe it from inside and outside, its appeal and its horror.

The literary history of which *Helbeck of Bannisdale* is a part is a largely unexplored area (for a detailed discussion see *Novels of Religious Controversy* by Q. D. Leavis, to be published by Cambridge University Press). The development of the Catholic–Protestant controversy in the nineteenth century and later may be traced in the work of our novelists, and was most successfully dealt with by women novelists. The theme appeared first in the late eighteenth century in Mrs Elizabeth Inchbald's *A Simple Story* (1791) and had its most brilliant treatment in Charlotte Brontë's *Villette* (1853) and *Helbeck of Bannisdale*, though it is admirably and variously presented in such works as Benjamin Disraeli's *Lothair* (1870), based on an actual case, in which animus is replaced by amusement as, with characteristic wit, the author documents priestly manoeuvres to court the aristocracy; *Mount Music* (1919) by Somerville and Ross, in which a power-seeking Catholic priesthood as well as family life are vividly described; and *Frost in May* (1933) by Antonia White, whose semi-autobiography gives gripping evidence of the claustrophobic atmosphere of a convent school and its attitude to a convert. Ironically enough, in 1899 it was another Mrs Ward (Josephine) who tried to answer from within the faith her namesake's novel with *One Poor Scruple*, which was hailed by part of the Catholic press as a refutation of *Helbeck of Bannisdale*. Alas, Josephine Ward, being conditioned to accept the system from childhood, could provide only propaganda that begged all truly moral questions in favour of a correct theoretic answer, thereby endorsing the case made by outsiders against that way of life. *One Poor Scruple* exhibits a religion that consists in keeping to the rules; the mere questioning of them is sinful.

On the other hand, the author of *A Simple Story*, though a practising Catholic from a long-established Catholic family, manages to show sympathy and understanding towards both the priest, Mr Donniforth, and his

Protestant ward, Miss Milner, investing them with life and a credible attraction towards each other, portrayed against the background of eighteenth-century manners and in the presence of three Catholic types, old Mrs Holton, who is not unlike Augustina Fountain in her unthinking piety, the charitable Miss Woodley and the largely hostile Jesuit, Mr Sandford. The lively and independently minded heroine is very much an outsider, but asserts her personal freedom at the risk of ruining the possibility of her marriage to a Catholic.

In that novel, as well as in *Helbeck of Bannisdale* and *Villette*, the Catholic lover requires the woman to accept the role his traditions impose upon women. Each heroine, however, insists as a right on the freedom of thought, speech and action in which she has been reared. Lucy Snowe in *Villette* refuses to accept the good woman's life history as shown in the sequence of pictures which her lover, M. Paul Emanuel, directs her to fix her eyes on; she insists instead on looking at Cleopatra. Laura Fountain, having had the lives of Helbeck's mother and grandmother set up for her as models, decides such a life would be intolerable for her. Miss Milner despises Miss Fenton, a pious and coldly dutiful Catholic young lady, who prefers a convent to an earthly bridegroom.

Charlotte Brontë's anti-Catholic case is in some ways so similar to Mrs Humphry Ward's that it might be thought that the latter had acquired hers from *Villette*; in fact her account is independently based and reflects a more knowledgeable and inward recognition of Catholicism. When Charlotte Brontë, with her sister Emily, experienced life in Brussels, her English puritanism was outraged by the apparent lack of perspective and the hypocrisy she found at a school where 'lying was no cause of shame but rebuke and penance were meted out to anyone who missed going to mass or read a chapter of a novel'. The heroine, Lucy Snowe, is unmoved by the accusation that, in not responding to Catholic doctrine, she lacks devoutness or spirit of grace, faith or self-abasement, and sees that it is useless to argue with M. Paul Emanuel, who can at first find nothing Christian in her and sees her, like many Protestants, as revelling in the pride and self-will of paganism. When persuaded to read a volume of Catholic apologetics, Lucy's scornful response is stirring in its display of character, but its sarcasm comes across as polemical compared with the shifting and confused resentments of the unbeliever Laura Fountain:

> I remember one capital inducement to apostasy was held out in the fact that the Catholic who had lost dear friends by death could enjoy the unspeakable solace of praying them out of purgatory. The writer did not touch on the firmer peace of those whose belief dispenses with purgatory altogether: but I thought of this, and, on the whole, preferred the latter doctrine as the most consolatory.

Even after experiencing the psychological power of the confessional and the temptation to yield to Catholicism in order to satisfy her lover, Lucy emerges fortified by the confidence 'that the more I saw of Popery, the closer I clung to Protestantism'. Charlotte Brontë then makes M. Paul Emanuel – surely improbably as a pupil of the Jesuits – tell Lucy that indeed she must remain a Puritan, as he is convinced by her account of her religion. Such yielding would scarcely be possible to a sincere Catholic, whose desire would be to convert his wife and bring up their children in the faith. The novelist must have known that, but suppressed it for the sake of a happier love story, though she ends the novel on an equivocal note: the ambiguous conclusion, in which M. Paul Emanuel may or may not die. This may have been done in order not to desolate her father, but the implication of the novel strikes many readers as properly tragic because of the incompatibility of the lovers at a deep level.

The lovers in *Villette* and *Helbeck* are convincingly shown to be attracted by opposite and respected qualities in each other, but Mrs Ward's novel moves more inexorably towards tragedy. Its powerful scenes are not arguments, but make up a drama of truly novelistic action, dialogue and feeling. Even Dr Friedland's monologue in the opening chapter of Book V is only an open analysis of what has been implicit because established dramatically by all that has gone before. The author's direct comment is brief and poised, the novel has excellent narrative form and is varied in style of description. Landscape is evoked with Wordsworthian grandeur and at times with the exultant delight of Gerard Manley Hopkins's notebooks:

> Overhead, great thunderclouds kept the sunset; beneath, the blues of the evening were all interwoven with rose; so, too, were the wood and sky reflections in the gently moving water. In some of the pools the trout were still lazily rising; pigeons and homing rooks were slowly passing through the clear space that lay between the tree-tops and the just emerging stars ... Even in this dimmed light the trees had the May magnificence – all but the oaks, which still dreamed of a best to come. Here and there a few tufts of primroses, on the bosom of the crag above the river, lonely and self-sufficing, like all loveliest things, starred the dimness of the rock.

In Book III, the visit to Froswick is described with a caustic insight into character and an immediate evocation of setting that equal the best in Arnold Bennett, and the episode of the terrible fate of the steelworker not only shocks Laura and the workers in the yard to a realization of the arbitrary closeness and power of death, but also shows Laura's instinctive truth of feeling and womanliness as she cradles the orphaned girl. As a result of her selflessness she misses the last train to Bannisdale and is put at the mercy of her amorous cousin and of local slander. The account of her escape from him to the quarry and her delirious wandering back to what she now regards as home is a masterpiece of ironic coincidence, acute psychological observation and moving evocation of scene and mood. Running through the whole novel is the delicate symbolism of the Romney portrait of Helbeck's grandmother, wife of the man who drowned in the Greet and dignified reminder of an earlier age of the Helbecks (and of English Catholic families in general), as well as an implicit measure of Alan Helbeck's need to choose between Laura (and the preservation of Bannisdale Hall) and Catholic good works.

Mrs Humphry Ward herself seemed in retrospect to recognize how uniquely and passionately she had risen to the pitch of tragedy: 'Yes, it was a good subject and I shall hardly come across one again so full both of intellectual and human interest.'[6]

A contemporary judgment on *Helbeck of Bannisdale* epitomizes the novel's appeal and its distinction, which is all the more impressive today when time has tested the novel's quality: 'It is her best book. It is a true tragedy, because the clash is inevitable. This is not so easy in Art as many may suppose.'[7]

PUBLICATION HISTORY

Helbeck of Bannisdale was published in 1898 by Smith, Elder & Co, London, and later in the Westmoreland Edition (1911). It appeared in Nelson's Sixpenny Novels in 1904 and Nelson's Library in 1911 and 1918, and in the Daily Mail Sixpenny Novels.

In the U.S.A. it was published in two volumes by Macmillan, New York (1898 and 1899), and in the Garland Reprint Series (Harvard) in 1975.

6 *Life of Mrs Humphry Ward* (see n. 4, p. 15).
7 ibid.

FURTHER READING

LIFE

J. Stuart, *Mrs Humphry Ward: Her Work and Influence*, Walters (1912)

Stephen Gwyn, *Mrs Humphry Ward: Her Work and Influence*, London (1917)

Mrs Humphry Ward, *A Writer's Recollections*, Collins (1918)

Mrs G. M. [Janet] Trevelyan, *A Life of Mrs Humphry Ward*, Constable (1923)

Enid Huws Jones, *A Life of Mrs Humphry Ward*, Heinemann (1973)

CRITICISM

Henry James, *Essays in London and Elsewhere*, Macmillan (1893)

Letters of Henry James, ed. Leon Edel, Vol. III, Macmillan (1980)

Sir Edmund Gosse, *Silhouettes*, Heinemann (1925)

J. Chapman, *The Victorian Debate*, Weidenfeld & Nicolson (1968)

Emile Legouis and Louis Cazamian, *A History of English Literature*, Dent (1971)

Donald D. Stone, *Novelists in a Changing World*, Harvard University Press (1972)

Robert L. Wolff, *Gains and Losses: Novels of Faith in Victorian England*, John Murray (1977)

Q. D. Leavis, 'Novels of Religious Controversy' (to be published in her *Collected Essays* by Cambridge University Press)

RELIGIOUS HISTORY

J. Aveling, *The Handle and the Axe: A History of Catholicism to the Nineteenth Century*, Blond & Briggs (1976)

Facsimile of the title page of the first edition, published in 1898

HELBECK OF BANNISDALE

BY

MRS HUMPHRY WARD

. . . metus ille . . . . Acheruntis. . . .
Funditus humanam qui vitam turbat ab imo

LONDON

SMITH, ELDER, & CO., 15 WATERLOO PLACE

1898

TO

E. DE V.

IN MEMORIAM

CONTENTS

BOOK ONE
33

BOOK TWO
133

BOOK THREE
185

BOOK FOUR
239

BOOK FIVE
311

BOOK ONE

CHAPTER ONE

'I must be turning back. A dreary day for anyone coming fresh to these parts!'

So saying, Mr Helbeck stood still – both hands resting on his thick stick – while his gaze slowly swept the straight white road in front of him and the landscape to either side.

Before him stretched the marshlands of the Flent valley, a broad alluvial plain brought down by the rivers Flent and Greet on their way to the estuary and the sea. From the slight rising ground on which he stood, he could see the great peat mosses about the river-mouths, marked here and there by lines of weather-beaten trees, or by more solid dots of black which the eye of the inhabitant knew to be peat stacks. Beyond the mosses were level lines of greyish white, where the looping rivers passed into the sea – lines more luminous than the sky at this particular moment of a damp March afternoon, because of some otherwise invisible radiance, which, miles away, seemed to be shining upon the water, slipping down to it from behind a curtain of rainy cloud.

Nearer by, on either side of the high road which cut the valley from east to west, were black and melancholy fields, half reclaimed from the peat moss, fields where the water stood in the furrows, or a plough, driven deep and left, showed the nature of the heavy water-logged earth, and the farmer's despair of dealing with it, till the drying winds should come. Some of it, however, had long before been reclaimed for pasture, so that strips of sodden green broke up, here and there, the long stretches of purple black. In the great dykes or drains to which the pastures were due, the water, swollen with recent rain, could be seen hurrying to join the rivers and the sea. The clouds overhead hurried like the dykes and the streams. A perpetual procession from the north-west swept inland from the sea, pouring from the dark distance of the upper valley, and blotting out the mountains that stood around its head.

A desolate scene, on this wild March day; yet full of a sort of beauty, even so far as the mosslands were concerned. And as Alan Helbeck's glance travelled along the ridge to his right, he saw it gradually rising from the marsh in slopes, and scars, and wooded fells, a medley of lovely lines, of pastures and copses, of villages clinging to the hills, each with its church tower and its white spreading farms – a land of homely charm and comfort, gently bounding the marsh below it, and cut off by the seething clouds in the north-west from the mountains towards which it climbed. And as he turned homewards with the moss country behind him, the hills rose and fell about him in soft undulation more and more rich in wood, while beside him roared the tumbling Greet, with its flood-voice – a voice more dear and familiar to Alan Helbeck perhaps, at this moment of his life, than the voice of any human being.

He walked fast with his shoulders thrown back, a remarkably tall man, with a dark head and short grizzled beard. He held himself very erect, as a soldier holds himself; but he had never been a soldier.

Once in his rapid course he paused to look at his watch, then hurried on, thinking.

'She stipulates that she is never to be expected to come to prayers,' he repeated to himself, half smiling. 'I suppose she thinks of herself as representing her father – in a nest of Papists. Evidently Augustina has no chance with her – she has been accustomed to reign! Well, we shall let her "gang her gait." '

His mouth, which was full and strongly closed, took a slight expression of contempt. As he turned over a bridge, and then into his own gate on the further side, he passed an old labourer who was scraping the mud from the road.

'Have you seen any carriage go by just lately, Reuben?'

'Noa –' said the man. 'Theer's been none this last hour an more – nobbut carts, an t' Whinthrupp bus.'

Helbeck's pace slackened. He had been very solitary all day, and even the company of the old road-sweeper was welcome.

'If we don't get some drying days soon, it'll be bad for all of us, won't it, Reuben?'

'Aye, it's a bit clashy,' said the man, with stolidity, stopping to spit into his hands a moment, before resuming his work.

The mildness of the adjective brought another half-smile to Helbeck's dark face. A stranger watching it might have wondered, indeed, whether it could smile with any fulness or spontaneity.

'But you don't see any good in grumbling – is that it?'

'Noa – we'se not git ony profit that gate, I reckon,' said the old man, laying his scraper to the mud once more.

'Well, good-night to you. I'm expecting my sister to-night, you know, my sister Mrs Fountain, and her stepdaughter.'

'Eh?' said Reuben slowly. 'Then yo'll be hevin cumpany, fer shure. Good-neet to ye, Misther Helbeck.'

But there was no great cordiality in his tone, and he touched his cap carelessly, without any sort of unction. The man's manner expressed familiarity of long habit, but little else.

Helbeck turned into his own park. The road that led up to the house wound alongside the river, whereof the banks had suddenly risen into a craggy wildness. All recollection of the marshland was left behind. The ground mounted on either side of the stream towards fell-tops, of which the distant lines could be seen dimly here and there behind the crowding trees; while, at some turns of the road, where the course of the Greet made a passage for the eye, one might look far away to the same mingled blackness of cloud and scar that stood round the head of the estuary. Clearly the mountains were not far off; and this was a border country between their ramparts and the sea.

The light of the March evening was dying, dying in a stormy greyness that promised more rain for the morrow. Yet the air was soft, and the spring made itself felt. In some sheltered places by the water, one might already see a shimmer of buds; and in the grass of the wild untended park daffodils were springing. Helbeck was conscious of it all; his eye and ear were on the watch for the signs of growth, and for the birds that haunted the river, the dipper on the stone, the grey wagtail slipping to its new nest in the bank, the golden-crested wren, or dark-backed creeper moving among the thorns. He loved such things; though with a silent and jealous love that seemed to imply some resentment towards other things and forces in his life.

As he walked, the manner of the old peasant rankled a little in his memory. For it implied, if not disrespect, at least a complete absence of all that the French call 'consideration.'

'It's strange how much more alone I've felt in this place of late than I used to feel' – was Helbeck's reflection upon it at last. 'I reckon it since I sold the Leasowes land. Or is it perhaps –'

He fell into a reverie marked by a frowning expression, and a harsh drawing down of the mouth. But gradually as he swung along, muttered words began to escape him, and his hand went to a book that he carried in his pocket. – '*O dust, learn of Me to obey! Learn of Me, O earth and clay, to humble thyself, and to cast thyself under the feet of all men for the love of Me.*' – As he murmured the words, which soon became inaudible, his aspect cleared, his eyes raised themselves again to the landscape, and became once more conscious of its growth and life.

Presently he reached a gate across the road, where a big sheepdog sprang out upon him, leaping and barking joyously. Beyond the gates rose a low pile of buildings, standing round three sides of a yard. They had once been the stables of the Hall. Now they were put to farm uses, and through the door of what had formerly been a coachhouse with a coat of arms worked in white pebbles on its floor, a woman could be seen milking. Helbeck looked in upon her.

'No carriage gone by yet, Mrs Tyson?'

'Noa, sir,' said the woman. 'But I'll mebbe prop t' gate open, for it's aboot time.' And she put down her pail.

'Don't move!' said Helbeck hastily. 'I'll do it myself.'

The woman, as she milked, watched him propping the ruinous gate with a stone; her expression all the time friendly and attentive. His own people, women especially, somehow always gave him this attention.

Helbeck hurried forward over a road, once stately, and now badly worn and ill-mended. The trees, mostly oaks of long growth, which had accompanied him since the entrance of the park, thickened to a close wood around till of a sudden he emerged from them, and there, across a wide space, rose a grey gabled house, sharp against a hillside, with a rainy evening light full upon it.

It was an old and weather-beaten house, of a singular character and dignity; yet not large. It was built of grey stone, covered with a rough-cast, so tempered by age to the colour and surface of the stone, that the many patches where it had dropped away produced hardly any disfiguring effect. The rugged 'pele' tower,[1] origin and source of all the rest, was now grouped with the gables and projections, the broad casemented windows, and deep doorways of a Tudor manor-house. But the whole structure seemed still to lean upon and draw towards the tower; and it was the tower which gave accent to a general expression of austerity, depending perhaps on the plain simplicity of all the approaches and immediate neighbourhood of the house. For in front of it were neither flowers nor shrubs – only wide stretches of plain turf and gravel; while behind it, beyond some thin intervening trees, rose a grey limestone fell, into which the house seemed to withdraw itself as into the rock, 'whence it was hewn.'

There were some lights in the old windows, and the heavy outer door was open. Helbeck mounted the steps and stood, watch in hand, at the top of them, looking down the avenue he had just walked through. And very soon, in spite of the roar of the river, his ear distinguished the wheels he was listening for. While they approached, he could not keep himself still, but moved restlessly about the little stone platform. He had been solitary for many years, and had loved his solitude.

'They're just coomin', sir,' said the voice of his old housekeeper, as she threw open an inner door behind him, letting a glow of fire and candles stream out into the twilight. Helbeck meanwhile caught sight for an instant of a girl's pale face at the window of the approaching carriage – a face thrust forward eagerly, to gaze at the pele tower.

The horses stopped, and out sprang the girl.

'Wait a moment – let me help you, Augustina. How do you do, Mr Helbeck? Don't touch my dog, please – she doesn't like men. Fricka, be quiet!'

For the little black spitz² she held in a chain had begun to growl and bark furiously at the first sight of Helbeck, to the evident anger of the old housekeeper, who looked at the dog sourly as she went forward to take some bags and rugs from her master. Helbeck, meanwhile, and the young girl helped another lady to alight. She came out slowly with the precautions of an invalid, and Helbeck gave her his arm.

At the top of the steps she turned and looked round her.

'Oh, Alan!' she said, 'it is so long –'

Her lips trembled and her head shook oddly. She was a short woman, with a thin plaintive face and a nervous jerk of the head, always very marked at a moment of agitation. As he noticed it, Helbeck felt times long past rush back upon him. He laid his hand over hers, and tried to say something; but his shyness oppressed him. When he had led her into the broad hall, with its firelight and stuccoed roof, she said, turning round with the same bewildered air –

'You saw Laura? You have never seen her before!'

'Oh yes; we shook hands, Augustina,' said a young voice. 'Will Mr Helbeck please help me with these things?'

She was laden with shawls and packages, and Helbeck hastily went to her aid. In the emotion of bringing his sister back into the old house, which she had left fifteen years before, when he himself was a lad of two-and-twenty, he had forgotten her stepdaughter.

But Miss Fountain did not intend to be forgotten. She made him relieve her of all burdens, and then argue an overcharge with the flyman. And at last, when all the luggage was in and the fly was driving off, she mounted the steps deliberately, looking about her all the time, but principally at the house. The eyes of the housekeeper, who with Mr Helbeck was standing in the entrance awaiting her, surveyed both dog and mistress with equal disapproval.

But the dusk was fast passing into darkness, and it was not till the girl came into the brightness of the hall, where her stepmother was already sitting tired and drooping on a settle near the great wood fire, that Helbeck saw her plainly.

She was very small and slight, and her hair made a spot of pale gold against the oak panelling of the walls. Helbeck noticed the slenderness of her arms, and the prettiness of her little white neck, then the freedom of her quick gesture as she went up to the elder lady and with a certain peremptoriness began to loosen her cloak.

'Augustina ought to go to bed directly,' she said, looking at Helbeck. 'The journey tired her dreadfully.'

'Mrs Fountain's room is quite ready,' said the housekeeper, holding herself stiffly behind her master. She was a woman of middle age, with a pinkish face, framed between two tiers of short grey curls.

Laura's eye ran over her.

'*You* don't like our coming!' she said to herself. Then to Helbeck –

'May I take her up at once? I will unpack, and put her comfortable. Then she ought to have some food. She has had nothing to-day, but some tea at Lancaster.'

Mrs Fountain looked up at the girl with feeble acquiescence, as though depending on her entirely. Helbeck glanced from his pale sister to the housekeeper in some perplexity.

'What will you have?' he said nervously to Miss Fountain. 'Dinner, I think, was to be at a quarter to eight.'

'That was the time I was ordered, sir,' said Mrs Denton.

'Can't it be earlier?' asked the girl impetuously.

Mrs Denton did not reply, but her shoulders grew visibly rigid.

'Do what you can for us, Denton,' said her master hastily, and she went away. Helbeck bent kindly over his sister.

'You know what a small establishment we have, Augustina. Mrs Denton, a rough girl, and a boy – that's all. I do trust they will be able to make you comfortable.'

'Oh, let me come down, when I have unpacked, and help cook,' said Miss Fountain brightly. 'I can do anything of that sort.'

Helbeck smiled for the first time. 'I am afraid Mrs Denton wouldn't take it kindly. She rules us all in this old place.'

'I dare say,' said the girl quietly. 'It's fish, of course?' she added, looking down at her stepmother, and speaking in a meditative voice.

'It's a Friday's dinner,' said Helbeck, flushing suddenly, and looking at his sister, 'except for Miss Fountain. I supposed –'

Mrs Fountain rose in some agitation and threw him a piteous look.

'Of course you did, Alan – of course you did. But the doctor at Folkestone – he was a Catholic – I took such care about that! – told me I mustn't fast. And Laura is always worrying me. But indeed I didn't want to be dispensed! – not yet!'

Laura said nothing; nor did Helbeck. There was a certain embarrassment in the looks of both, as though there was more in Mrs Fountain's words than appeared. Then the girl, holding herself erect and rather defiant, drew her stepmother's arm in hers, and turned to Helbeck.

'Will you please show us the way up?'

Helbeck took a small hand-lamp and led the way, bidding the newcomers beware of the slipperiness of the old polished boards. Mrs Fountain walked with caution, clinging to her stepdaughter. At the foot of the staircase she stopped, and looked upward.

'Alan, I don't see much change!'

He turned back, the light shining on his fine harsh face and grizzled hair.

'Don't you? But it is greatly changed, Augustina. We have shut up half of it.'

Mrs Fountain sighed deeply and moved on. Laura, as she mounted the stairs, looked back at the old hall, its ceiling of creamy stucco, its panelled walls, and below, the great bare floor of shining oak with hardly any furniture upon it – a strip of old carpet, a heavy oak table, and a few battered chairs at long intervals against the panelling. But the big fire of logs piled upon the hearth filled it all with cheerful light, and under her indifferent manner the girl's sense secretly thrilled with pleasure. She had heard much of 'poor Alan's' poverty. Poverty! As far as his house was concerned at any rate, it seemed to her of a very tolerable sort.

In a few minutes Helbeck came downstairs again, and stood absently before the fire on the hearth. After a while, he sat down beside it in his accustomed chair – a carved chair of black Westmoreland oak – and began to read from the book which he had been carrying in his pocket out of doors. He read with his head bent closely over the pages, because of short sight; and, as a rule, reading absorbed him so completely that he was conscious of nothing external while it lasted. To-night, however, he several times looked up to listen to the sounds overhead, unwonted sounds in this house, over which, as it often seemed to him, a quiet of centuries had settled down, like a fine dust or deposit, muffling all its steps and voices. But there was nothing muffled in the voice overhead which he caught every now and then, through an open door, escaping, eager and alive, into the silence; or in the occasional sharp bark of the dog.

'Horrid little wretch!' thought Helbeck. 'Denton will loathe it. Augustina should really have warned me. What shall we do if she and Denton don't get on? It will never answer if she tries meddling in the kitchen – I must tell her.'

Presently, however, his inner anxieties grew upon him so much that his book fell on his knee, and he lost himself in a multitude of small scruples and torments, such as beset all persons who live alone. Were all his days now to be made difficult, because he had followed his conscience, and asked his widowed sister to come and live with him?

'Augustina and I could have done well enough. But this girl – well, we must put up with it – we must, Bruno!'

He laid his hand as he spoke on the neck of a collie that had just lounged into the hall, and come to lay its nose upon his master's knee. Suddenly a bark from overhead made the dog start back and prick its ears.

'Come here, Bruno – be quiet. You're to treat that little brute with proper contempt – do you hear? Listen to all that scuffling and talking upstairs – that's the new young woman getting her way with old Denton. Well, it won't do Denton any harm. We're put upon sometimes, too, aren't we?'

And he caressed the dog, his haughty face alive with something half bitter, half humorous.

At that moment the old clock in the hall struck a quarter past seven. Helbeck sprang up.

'Am I to dress?' he said to himself in some perplexity.

He considered for a moment or two, looking at his shabby serge suit, then sat down again resolutely.

'No! She'll have to live our life. Besides, I don't know what Denton would think.'

And he lay back in his chair, recalling with some amusement the criticisms of his housekeeper upon a young Catholic friend of his who – rare event – had spent a fishing week with him in the autumn, and had startled the old house and its inmates with his frequent changes of raiment. 'It's yan set o' cloas for breakfast, an anudther for fishing, an anudther for riding, an yan for when he cooms in, an a fine suit for dinner – and anudther for smoakin – A should think he mut be oftener naked nor donned!' – Denton had said in her grim Westmoreland, and Helbeck had often chuckled over the remark.

An hour later, half an hour after the usual time, Helbeck, all the traces of his muddy walk removed, and garbed with scrupulous neatness in the old black coat and black tie he always wore of an evening, was sitting opposite to Miss Fountain at supper.

'You got everything you wanted for Augustina, I hope?' he said to her shyly as they sat down. He had awaited her in the dining-room itself, so as to avoid the awkwardness of taking her in. It was some years since a woman had stayed under his roof, or since he had been a guest in the same house with women.

'Oh, yes!' said Miss Fountain. But she threw a sly swift glance towards Mrs Denton who was just coming into the room with some coffee; then compressed her lips and studied her plate. Helbeck detected the glance, and saw too that Mrs Denton's pink face was flushed, and her manner discomposed.

'The coffee's noa good,' she said abruptly, as she put it down; 'I couldn't keep to 't.'

'No, I'm afraid we disturbed Mrs Denton dreadfully,' said Miss

Fountain, shrugging her shoulders. 'We got her to bring up all sorts of things for Augustina. She was dreadfully tired – I thought she would faint. The doctor scolded me before we left, about letting her go without food. Shall I give you some fish, Mr Helbeck?'

For, to her astonishment, the fish even – a very small portion – was placed before herself, side by side with a few fragments of cold chicken; and she looked in vain for a second plate.

As she glanced across the table, she caught a momentary shade of embarrassment in Helbeck's face.

'No, thank you,' he said. 'I am provided.'

His provision seemed to be coffee and bread and butter. She raised her eyebrows involuntarily, but said nothing, and he presently busied himself in bringing her vegetables and wine, Mrs Denton having left the room.

'I trust you will make a good meal,' he said gravely, as he waited upon her. 'You have had a long day.'

'Oh, yes!' said Miss Fountain, impetuously, 'and please don't ever make any difference for me on Fridays. It doesn't matter to me in the least what I eat.'

Helbeck offered no reply. Conversation between them indeed did not flow very readily. They talked a little about the journey from London; and Laura asked a few questions about the house. She was, indeed, studying the room in which they sat, and her host himself, all the time. 'He may be a saint,' she thought, 'but I am sure he knows all the time there are very few saints of such an old family! His head's splendid – so dark and fine – with the great waves of grey-black hair – and the long features and the pointed chin. He's immensely tall too – six feet two at least – taller than father. He looks hard and bigoted. I suppose most people would be afraid of him – I'm not!'

And as though to prove even to herself she was not, she carried on a rattle of questions. How old was the tower? How old was the room in which they were sitting? She looked round it with ignorant, girlish eyes.

He pointed her to the date on the carved mantelpiece – 1583.

'That is a very important date for us,' he began, then checked himself.

'Why?'

He seemed to find a difficulty in going on, but at last he said:

'The man who put up that chimney-piece was hanged at Manchester later in the same year.'

'Why? – what for?'

He suddenly noticed the delicacy of her tiny wrist as her hand paused at the edge of her plate, and the brilliance of her eyes – large and greenish-grey, with a marked black line round the iris. The very perception perhaps made his answer more cold and measured.

'He was a Catholic recusant, under Elizabeth. He had harboured a priest, and he and the priest and a friend suffered death for it together at Manchester. Afterwards their heads were fixed on the outside of Manchester parish church.'

'How horrible!' said Miss Fountain, frowning. 'Do you know anything more about him?'

'Yes, we have letters –'

But he would say no more, and the subject dropped. Not to let the conversation also come to an end, he pointed to some old gilded leather which covered one side of the room, while the other three walls were oak-panelled from ceiling to floor.

'It is very dim and dingy now,' said Helbeck; 'but when it was fresh, it was the wonder of the place. The room got the name of Paradise from it. There are many mentions of it in the old letters.'

'Who put it up?'

'The brother of the martyr – twenty years later.'

'The martyr!' she thought, half scornfully. 'No doubt he is as proud of that as of his twenty generations!'

He told her a few more antiquarian facts about the room and its builders, she meanwhile looking in some perplexity from the rich embossments of the ceiling with its Tudor roses and crowns, from the stately mantelpiece and canopied doors, to the few pieces of shabby modern furniture which disfigured the room, the half-dozen cane chairs, the ugly lodging-house carpet and sideboard. What had become of the old furnishings? How could they have disappeared so utterly?

Helbeck, however, did not enlighten her. He talked indeed with no freedom, merely to pass the time.

She perfectly recognised that he was not at ease with her, and she hurried her meal, in spite of her very frank hunger, that she might set him free. But, as she was putting down her coffee-cup for the last time, she suddenly said:

'It's a very good air here, isn't it, Mr Helbeck?'

45

'I believe so,' he replied, in some surprise. 'It's a mixture of the sea and the mountains. Everybody here – most of the poor people – live to a great age.'

'That's all right! Then Augustina will soon get strong here. She can't do without me yet – but you know, of course – I have decided – about myself?'

Somehow, as she looked across to her host, her little figure, in its plain white dress and black ribbons, expressed a curious tension. 'She wants to make it very plain to me' – thought Helbeck – 'that if she comes here as my guest it is only as a favour, to look after my sister.'

Aloud he said:

'Augustina told me she could not hope to keep you for long.'

'No!' said the girl, sharply – 'No! I must take up a profession. I have a little money, you know – from papa. I shall go to Cambridge, or to London, perhaps to live with a friend. Oh! you darling! – you *darling!*'

Helbeck opened his eyes in amazement. Miss Fountain had sprung from her seat, and thrown herself on her knees beside his old collie Bruno. Her arms were round the dog's neck, and she was pressing her cheek against his brown nose. Perhaps she caught her host's look of astonishment, for she rose at once in a flush of some feeling she tried to put down, and said, still holding the dog's head against her dress:

'I didn't know you had a dog like this. It's so like ours – you see – like papa's. I had to give ours away when we left Folkestone. You dear, dear thing!' – (the caressing intensity in the girl's young voice made Helbeck shrink and turn away) – 'now you won't kill my Fricka, will you? She's curled up, such a delicious black ball on my bed – you couldn't – you couldn't have the heart! I'll take you up and introduce you – I'll do everything proper!'

The dog looked up at her, with its soft, quiet eyes, as though it weighed her pleadings.

'There,' she said triumphantly. 'It's all right – he winked. Come along, my dear, and let's make real friends.'

And she led the dog into the hall, Helbeck ceremoniously opening the door for her.

She sat herself down in the oak settle beside the hall fire, where for some minutes she occupied herself entirely with the dog, talking a sort of baby language to him that left Helbeck absolutely dumb.

When she raised her head, she flung, dartlike, another question at her host.

'Have you many neighbours, Mr Helbeck?'

Her voice startled his look away from her.

'Not many,' he said, hesitating. 'And I know little of those there are.'

'Indeed! Don't you like – society?'

He laughed with some embarrassment. 'I don't get much of it,' he said simply.

'Don't you? What a pity! – isn't it, Bruno? I like society dreadfully – dances, theatres, parties – all sorts of things. Or I did – once.'

She paused and stared at Helbeck. He did not speak, however. She sat up very straight and pushed the dog from her. 'By the way,' she said in a shrill voice, 'there are my cousins the Masons. How far are they?'

'About seven miles.'

'Quite up in the mountains, isn't it?'

Helbeck assented.

'Oh! I shall go there at once – I shall go to-morrow,' said the girl with emphasis, resting her small chin lightly on the head of the dog, while she fixed her eyes – her hostile eyes – upon her host.

Helbeck made no answer. He went to fetch another log for the fire.

'Why doesn't he say something about them?' she thought angrily. 'Why doesn't he say something about papa? – about his illness? – ask me any questions? He may have hated him – but it would be only decent. He is a very grand, imposing person, I suppose, with his melancholy airs, and his family – Papa was worth a hundred of him! Oh! – past a quarter to ten? Time to go, and let him have his prayers to himself. Augustina told me ten.'

She sprang up, and stiffly held out her hand.

'Good-night, Mr Helbeck. I ought to go to Augustina and settle her for the night. To-morrow I should like to tell you what the doctor said about her; she is not strong at all. What time do you breakfast?'

'Half-past eight. But, of course –'

'Oh, no! of course Augustina won't come down! I will carry her up her tray myself. Good-night.'

Helbeck touched her hand. But as she turned away, he followed her a few steps irresolutely, and then said: 'Miss Fountain' – she looked round in surprise – 'I should like you to understand that everything that can be done in this poor house for my sister's comfort – and yours – I should wish done. My resources are not great, but my will is good.'

He raised his eyelids, and she saw the eyes beneath, full, for the first time – eyes grey like her own, but far darker and profounder. She felt a momentary flutter, perhaps of compunction. Then she thanked him and went her way.

When she had made her stepmother comfortable for the night, Laura Fountain went back to her room, shielding her candle with difficulty from the gusts that seemed to tear along the dark passages of the old house. The March rawness made her shiver, and she looked shrinkingly into the gloom before her, as she paused outside her own door. There, at the end of the passage, lay the old tower; so Mrs Denton had told her. The thought of all the locked and empty rooms in it – dark, cold spaces – haunted perhaps by strange sounds and presences of the past, seemed to let loose upon her all at once a little whirlwind of fear. She hurried into her room, and was just setting down her candle before turning to lock her door, when a sound from the distant hall caught her ear.

A deep monotonous sound, rising and falling at regular intervals – Mr Helbeck reading prayers, with the two maids, who represented the only service of the house.

Laura lingered with her hand on the door. In the silence of the ancient house, there was something touching in the sound, a kind of appeal. But it was an appeal which, in the girl's mind, passed instantly into reaction. She locked the door, and turned away, breathing fast as though under some excitement.

The tears, long held down, were rising, and the room, where a large wood fire was burning – wood was the only provision of which there was a plenty at Bannisdale – seemed to her suddenly stifling. She went to the casement window and threw it open. A rush of mild wind came through, and with it the roar of the swollen river.

The girl leant forward, bathing her hot face in the wild air. There was a dark mist of trees below her, trees tossed by the wind; then, far down, a ray of moonlight on water; beyond, a fell-side, clear a moment beneath a sky of sweeping cloud; and last of all, highest of all, amid the clouds, a dim radiance, intermittent and yet steady, like the radiance of moonlit snow.

A strange nobility and freedom breathed from the wide scene; from its mere depth below her; from the spacious curve of the river, the mountains half shown, half hidden, the great race of the clouds, the fresh beating of the wind. The north spoke to her, and the mountains. It was like the rush of something passionate and straining through her girlish sense; intensifying all that was already there. What was this thirst, this yearning, this physical anguish of pity that crept back upon her in all the pauses of the day and night?

It was nine months since she had lost her father, but all the scenes of his last days were still so clear to her that it seemed to her often sheer incredibility that the room, the bed, the helpless form, the noise of the breathing, the clink of the medicine glasses, the tread of the doctor, the gasping words of the patient, were all alike fragments and phantoms of the past – that the house was empty, the bed sold, the patient gone. Oh! the clinging of the thin hand round her own, the piteousness of suffering – of failure! Poor, poor papa! – he would not say, even to comfort her, that they would meet again. He had not believed it – and so she must not.

No, and she would not! She raised her head fiercely and dried her tears. Only – why was she here – in the house of a man who had never spoken to her father – his brother-in-law – for thirteen years – who had made his sister feel that her marriage had been a disgrace – who was all the time, no doubt, cherishing such thoughts in that black, proud head of his, while she, her father's daughter, was sitting opposite to him?

'How am I ever going to bear it – all these months?' she asked herself.

CHAPTER TWO

But the causes which had brought Laura Fountain to Bannisdale were very simple. It had all come about in the most natural inevitable way.

When Laura was eight years old – nearly thirteen years before this date – her father, then a widower with one child, had fallen in with and married Alan Helbeck's sister. At the time of their first meeting with the little Catholic spinster, Stephen Fountain and his child were spending part of the Cambridge vacation at a village on the Cumberland coast where a fine air could be combined with cheap lodgings. Fountain himself was from the North Country. His grandfather had been a small Lancashire yeoman, and Stephen Fountain had an inbred liking for the fells, the farmhouses, and even the rain of his native district. Before descending to the sea, he and his child had spent a couple of days with his cousin by marriage, James Mason, in the lonely stone house among the hills, which had belonged to the family since the Revolution. He left it gladly, however, for the farm life seemed to him much harder and more squalid than he had remembered it to be, and he disliked James Mason's wife. As he and Laura walked down the long rough track connecting the farm with the main road on the day of their departure, Stephen Fountain whistled so loud and merrily that the skipping child beside him looked at him with astonishment.

It was his way no doubt of thanking Providence for the happy chance that had sent his father to a small Local Government post at Newcastle, and himself to a grammar school with openings on the University. Yet as a rule he thought himself anything but a successful man. He held a lectureship at Cambridge in an obscure scientific subject, and was in his way both learned and diligent. But he had few pupils, and had never cared to have them. They interfered with his own research, and he had the passionate scorn for popularity which grows up naturally in those who have no power with the crowd. His religious opinions, or rather the manner in which he chose to express them, divided him from many good men. He was poor, and he hated his poverty. A rather imprudent marriage had turned out neither particularly well nor particularly ill.

His wife had some beauty, however, and there was hardly time for disillusion. She died when Laura was still a tottering baby, and Stephen had missed her sorely for a while. Since her death he had grown to be a very lonely man, silently discontented with himself and sourly critical of his neighbours. Yet all the same he thanked God that he was not his cousin James.

Potter's Beach as a watering-place was neither beautiful nor amusing. Laura was happy there, but that said nothing. All her childhood through she had the most surprising gift for happiness. From morning till night she lived in a flutter of delicious nothings. Unless he watched her closely, Stephen Fountain could not tell for the life of him what she was about all day. But he saw that she was endlessly about something; her little hands and legs never rested; she dug, bathed, dabbled, raced, kissed, ate, slept, in one happy bustle, which never slackened except for the hours when she lay rosy and still in her bed. And even then the pretty mouth was still eagerly open, as though sleep had just breathed upon its chatter for a few charmed moments, and 'the joy within' was already breaking from the spell.

Stephen Fountain adored her, but his affections were never enough for him. In spite of the child's spirits he himself found Potter's Beach a desolation, all the more that he was cut off from his books for a time by doctor's orders and his own common sense. Suddenly, as he took his daily walk over the sands with Laura, he began to notice a thin lady in black, sitting alone under a bank of sea-thistles, and generally struggling with an umbrella which she had put up to shelter herself and her book from a prevailing and boisterous wind. Sometimes when he passed her in the little street, he caught a glimpse of timid eyes, or he saw and pitied the slight involuntary jerk of the head and shoulders, which seemed to tell of nervous delicacy. Presently they made friends, and he found her lonely and discontented like himself. She was a Catholic, he discovered; but her Catholicism was not that of the convert, but of an old inherited sort which sat easily enough on a light nature. Then, to his astonishment, it appeared that she lived with a brother at an old house in North Lancashire – a well-known and even, in its degree, famous house – which lay not seven miles distant from his grandfather's little property, and had been quite familiar to him by repute, and even by sight as a child. When he was a small lad staying at Browhead Farm, he had once or twice found his way to the Greet, and had strayed along its course through Bannisdale Park. Once even, when he was in the act of fishing a particular pool where the trout were rising in a manner to tempt a very archangel, he had been seized and his primitive rod broken over his shoulder by an old man whom he believed to have been the owner, Mr Helbeck, himself – a magnificent white-haired person, about whom tales ran freely in the countryside.

So this little shabby old maid was a Helbeck of Bannisdale! As he looked at her, Fountain could not help thinking with a hidden amusement of all the awesome prestige the name had once carried with it for his boyish ear. Thirty years back, what a gulf had seemed to yawn between the yeoman's grandson and the lofty owners of that stern and ancient house upon the Greet! And now, how glad was old Helbeck's daughter to sit or walk with him and his child! – and how plain it grew, as the weeks passed on, that if he, Stephen Fountain, willed it, she would make no difficulty at all about a much longer companionship! Fountain held himself to be the most convinced of democrats, a man who had a reasoned right to his Radical opinions that commoner folk must do without. Nevertheless, his pride fed on this small turn of fortune, and when he carelessly addressed his new friend, her name gave him pleasure.

It seemed that she possessed but little else, poor lady. Even in his young days, Fountain could remember that the Helbecks were reported to be straitened, to have already much difficulty in keeping up the house and the estate. But clearly things had fallen by now to a much lower depth. Miss Helbeck's dress, talk, lodgings, all spoke of poverty, great poverty. He himself had never known what it was to have a superfluous ten pounds; but the feverish strain that belongs to such a situation as the Helbecks' awoke in him a new and sharp pity. He was very sorry for the little harassed creature; that physical privation should touch a woman had always seemed to him a monstrosity.

What was the brother about? – a great strong fellow by all accounts, capable, surely, of doing something for the family fortunes. Instinctively Fountain held him responsible for the sister's fatigue and delicacy. They had just lost their mother, and Augustina had come to Potter's Beach to recover from long months of nursing. And presently Fountain discovered that what stood between her and health was not so much the past as the future.

'You don't like the idea of going home,' he said to her once abruptly, after they had grown intimate. She flushed and hesitated; then her eyes filled with tears.

Gradually he made her explain herself. The brother, it appeared, was twelve years younger than herself, and had been brought up first at Stonyhurst, and afterwards at Louvain, in constant separation from the rest of the family. He had never had much in common with his home, since, at Stonyhurst, he had come under the influence of a Jesuit teacher, who, in the language of old Helbeck, had turned him into 'a fond sort of fellow,' swarming with notions that could only serve to carry the family decadence a step farther.

'We have been Catholics for twenty generations,' said Augustina in her quavering voice. 'But our ways – father's ways – weren't good enough for Alan. We thought he was making up his mind to be a Jesuit, and father was mad about it, because of the old place. Then father died, and Alan came home. He and my mother got on best – oh! he was very good to her. But he and I weren't brought up in the same way – you'd think he was already under a rule. I don't – know – I suppose it's too high for me –'

She took up a handful of sand, and threw it, angrily, from her thin fingers, hurrying on, however, as if the unburdenment, once begun, must have its course.

'And it's hard to be always pulled up and set right by some one you've nursed in his cradle. Oh! I don't mean he says anything – he and I never had words in our lives. But it's the way he has of doing things – the changes he makes. You feel how he disapproves of you – he doesn't like my friends – our old friends – the house is like a desert since he came. And the money he gives away! The priests just suck us dry – and he hasn't got it to give. Oh! I know it's all very wicked of me – but when I think of going back to him – just us two, you know, in that old house – and all the trouble about money –'

Her voice failed her.

'Well, don't go back,' said Fountain, laying his hand on her arm.

And twenty-four hours later he was still pleased with himself and her. No doubt she was stupid, poor Augustina, and more ignorant than he had supposed a human being could be. Her only education seemed to have been supplied by two years at the 'Couvent des Dames Anglaises' at St-Omer, and all that she had retained from it was a small stock of French idioms, most of which she had forgotten how to use, though she did use them frequently, with a certain timid pretension. Of that habit Fountain, the fastidious, thought that he should break her. But for the rest, her religion, her poverty – well, she had a hundred a year, so that he and Laura would be no worse off for taking her in, and the child's prospects, of course, should not suffer by a halfpenny. And as to the Catholicism, Fountain smiled to himself. No doubt there was some inherited feeling. But even if she did keep up her little mummeries, he could not see that they would do him or Laura any harm. And for the rest she suited him. She somehow crept into his loneliness and fitted it. He was getting too old to go farther, and he might well fare worse. In spite of her love of talk, she was not a bad listener; and longer experience showed her to be in truth the soft and gentle nature that she seemed. She had a curious kind of vanity which showed itself in her feeling towards her brother. But Fountain did not find it disagreeable; it even gave him pleasure to flatter it; as one feeds or caresses some straying half-starved creature, partly for pity, partly that the human will may feel its power.

'I wonder how much fuss that young man will make,' Fountain asked himself, when at last it became necessary to write to Bannisdale.

Augustina, however, was thirty-five, in full possession of her little moneys, and had no one to consult but herself. Fountain enjoyed the writing of the letter, which was brief, if not curt.

Alan Helbeck appeared without an hour's delay at Potter's Beach. Fountain felt himself much inclined beforehand to treat the tall dark youth, sixteen years his junior, as a tutor treats an undergraduate. Oddly enough, however, when the two men stood face to face, Fountain was once more awkwardly conscious of that old sense of social distance which the sister had never recalled to him. The sting of it made him rougher than he had meant to be. Otherwise, the young man's very shabby coat, his superb good looks, and courteous reserve of manner might almost have disarmed the irritable scholar.

As it was, Helbeck soon discovered that Fountain had no intention of allowing Augustina to apply for any dispensation for the marriage, that he would make no promise of Catholic bringing-up, supposing there were children, and that his idea was to be married at a registry office.

'I am one of those people who don't trouble themselves about the affairs of another world,' said Fountain in a suave voice, as he stood in the lodging-house window, a bearded, broad-shouldered person, his hands thrust wilfully into the very baggy pockets of his ill-fitting light suit. 'I won't worry your sister – and I don't suppose there'll be any children. But if there are, I really can't promise to make Catholics of them. And as for myself, I don't take things so easy as it's the fashion to do now. I can't present myself in church, even for Augustina.'

Helbeck sat silent for a few minutes with his eyes on the ground. Then he rose.

'You ask what no Catholic should grant,' he said slowly. 'But that of course you know. I can have nothing to do with such a marriage, and my duty naturally will be to dissuade my sister from it as strongly as possible.'

Fountain bowed.

'She is expecting you,' he said. 'I of course await her decision.'

His tone was hardly serious. Nevertheless, during the time that Helbeck and Augustina were pacing the sands together, Fountain went through a good deal of uneasiness. One never knew how or where this damned poison in the blood might break out again. That young fanatic, a Jesuit already by the look of him, would of course try all their inherited Mumbo Jumbo upon her; and what woman is at bottom anything more than the prey of the last speaker?

When, however, it was all over, and he was allowed to see his Augustina in the evening, he found her helpless with crying indeed, but as obstinate as only the meek of the earth can be. She had broken wholly with her brother and with Bannisdale; and Fountain gathered that, after all Helbeck's arguments and entreaties, there had flashed a moment of storm between them, when the fierce 'Helbeck temper,' traditional through many generations, had broken down the self-control of the ascetic, and Augustina must needs have trembled. However, there she was, frightened and miserable, but still determined. And her terror was much more concerned with the possibility of any return to live with Alan and his all-exacting creed than anything else. Fountain caught himself wondering whether indeed she had imagination enough to lay much hold on those spiritual terrors with which she had no doubt been threatened. In this, however, he misjudged her, as will be seen.

Meanwhile he sent for an elderly Evangelical cousin of his wife's, who was accustomed to take a friendly interest in his child and himself. She, in Protestant jubilation over this brand snatched from the burning, came in haste, very nearly departing, indeed, in similar haste as soon as the unholy project of the secular marriage was mooted. However, under much persuasion, she remained, lamenting; Augustina sent to Bannisdale for her few possessions, and the scanty ceremony was soon over.

Meanwhile Laura had but found in the whole affair one more amusement and excitement added to the many that, according to her, Potter's Beach already possessed. The dancing elfish child – who had no memory of her own mother – had begun by taking the little old maid under her patronising wing. She graciously allowed Augustina to make a lap for all the briny treasures she might accumulate in the course of a breathless morning; she rushed to give her first information whenever that encroaching monster the sea broke down her castles. And as soon as it appeared that her papa liked Augustina, and had a use for her, Laura at the age of eight promptly accepted her as part of the family circle, without the smallest touch of either sentiment or opposition. She walked gaily hand in hand with her father to the registry office at St Bees. The jealously hidden stormy little heart knew well enough that it had nothing to fear.

Then came many quiet years at Cambridge. Augustina spoke no more of her brother, and apparently let her old creed slip. She conformed herself wholly to her husband's ways – a little colourless thread on the stream of academic life, slightly regarded, and generally silent out of doors, but at home a gentle, foolish, and often voluble person, very easily made happy by some small kindness and a few creature comforts.

Laura meanwhile grew up, and no one exactly knew how. Her education was a thing of shreds and patches, managed by herself throughout, and expressing her own strong will or caprice from the beginning. She put herself to school – a day school only; and took herself away as soon as she was tired of it. She threw herself madly into physical exercises like dancing or skating; and excelled in most of them by virtue of a certain wild grace, a tameless strength of spirits and will. And yet she grew up small and pale; and it was not till she was about eighteen that she suddenly blossomed into prettiness.

'Carrotina – why, what's happened to you?' said her father to her one day.

She turned in astonishment from her task of putting some books tidy on his study shelves. Then she coloured half angrily.

'I must put my hair up sometime, I suppose,' she said resentfully. There was something in the abruptness of her father's question, no less than in the new closeness and sharpness of eye with which he was examining her, that annoyed her.

'Well – you've made a young lady of yourself. I dare say I mustn't call you nicknames any more!'

'I don't mind,' she said indifferently, going on with her work, while he looked at the golden-red mass she had coiled round her little head, with an odd half welcome sense of change, a sudden prescience of the future.

Then she turned again.

'If – if you make any absurd changes,' she said with a frown, 'I'll – I'll cut it all off!'

'You'd better not – there'd be ructions,' he said, laughing. 'It's not yours till you're twenty-one.'

And to himself he said, 'Gracious! I didn't bargain for a pretty daughter. What am I to do with her? Augustina'll never get her married.'

And certainly during this early youth, Laura showed no signs of getting herself married. She did not apparently know when a young man was by; and her bright vehement ways, her sharp turns of speech, went on just the same; she neither quivered nor thrilled; and her chatter, when she did chatter, spent itself almost with indifference on anyone who came near her. She was generally gay, generally in spirits; and her girl companions knew well that there was no one so reserved, and that the inmost self of her, if such a thing existed, dwelt far away from any ken of theirs. Every now and then she would have vehement angers and outbreaks which contrasted with the nonchalance of her ordinary temper; but it was hard to find the clue to them.

Altogether she passed for a clever girl, even in a University town, where cleverness is weighed. But her education, except in two points, was, in truth, of the slightest. Any mechanical drudgery that her father could set her, she did without a murmur; or, rather, she claimed it jealously, with a silent passion. But, with an obstinacy equally silent, she set herself against the drudgery that would have made her his intellectual companion.

His rows of technical books – the scholarly and laborious details of his work, filled her with an invincible repugnance. And he did not attempt to persuade her. As to women and their claims, he was old-fashioned and contemptuous; he would have been much embarrassed by a learned daughter. That she should copy and tidy for him; that she should sit curled up for hours with a book or a piece of work in a corner of his room; that she should bring him his pipe, and break in upon his work at the right moment with her peremptory 'Papa, come out!' – these things were delightful, nay, necessary to him. But he had no dreams beyond; and he never thought of her, her education or her character, as a whole. It was not his way. Besides, girls took their chance. With a boy, of course, one plans and looks ahead. But Laura would have 200*l.* a year from her mother whatever happened, and something more at his own death. Why trouble oneself?

No doubt indirectly he contributed very largely to her growing up. The sight of his work and his methods; the occasional talks she overheard between him and his scientific comrades; the tones of irony and denial in the atmosphere about him; his antagonisms, his bitternesses, worked strongly upon her still plastic nature. Moreover, she felt to her heart's core that he was unsuccessful; there were appointments he should have had, but had failed to get, and it was the religious party, the 'clerical crew' in Congregation or the Senate, that had stood in the way. From her childhood it came natural to her to hate bigoted people who believed in ridiculous things. It was they stood between her father and his deserts. There loomed up, as it were, on her horizon, something dim and majestic, which was called Science. Towards this her father pressed, she clinging to him; while all about them was a black and hindering crowd, through which they clove their way – contemptuously.

In one direction, indeed, Fountain admitted her to his mind. Like Mill, he found the rest and balm of life in poetry; and here he took Laura with him. They read to each other, they spurred each other to learn by heart. He kept nothing from her. Shelley was a passion of his own; it became hers. She taught herself German, that she might read Heine and Goethe with him; and one evening, when she was little more than sixteen, he rushed her through the first part of 'Faust,' so that she lay awake the whole night afterwards in such a passion of emotion, that it seemed, for the moment, to change her whole existence. Sometimes it astonished him to see what capacity she had, not only for the feeling, but for the sensuous pleasure, of poetry. Lines – sounds – haunted her for days, the beauty of them would make her start and tremble.

She did her best, however, to hide this side of her nature even from him. And it was not difficult. She remained childishly immature and backward in many things. She was a personality; that was clear; one could hardly say that she was or had a character. She was a bundle of loves and hates; a force, not an organism; and her father was often as much puzzled by her as any one else.

Music perhaps was the only study which ever conquered her indolence. Here it happened that a famous musician who settled in Cambridge for a time came across her gift and took notice of it. And to please him she worked with industry, even with doggedness. Brahms, Chopin, Wagner – these great romantics possessed her in music as Shelley or Rossetti did in poetry. 'You little demon, Laura! How do you come to play like that?' a girl-friend – her only intimate friend – said to her once in despair. 'It's the expression. Where do you get it? And I practise, and you don't; it's not fair.'

'Expression!' said Laura, with annoyance – 'what does that matter? That's the amateur all over. Of course I play like that because I can't do it any better. If I could *play the notes*' – she clenched her little hand, with a curious, almost a fierce energy – 'if I had any technique – or was ever likely to have any, what should I want with expression? Any cat can give you expression! There was one under my window last night – you should just have heard it.'

Molly Friedland, the girl-friend, shrugged her shoulders. She was as soft, as normal, as self-controlled as Laura was wilful and irritable. But there was a very real affection between them.

Years passed. Insensibly Augustina's health began to fail; and with it the new cheerfulness of her middle life. Then Fountain himself fell suddenly and dangerously ill. All the peaceful habits and small pleasures of their common existence broke down after a few days, as it were, into a miserable confusion. Augustina stood bewildered. Then a convulsion of soul she had expected as little as any one else swept upon her. A number of obscure, inherited, half-dead instincts revived. She lived in terror; she slept, weeping; and at the back of an old drawer she found a rosary of her childhood to which her fingers clung night and day.

Meanwhile Fountain resigned himself to death. During his last days his dimmed senses did not perceive what was happening to his wife. But he troubled himself about her a good deal.

'Take care of her, Laura –' he said once – 'till she gets strong. Look after her. – But you can't sacrifice your life. – It may be Christian –' he added, in a murmur, 'but it isn't sense.'

Unconsciousness came on. Augustina seemed to lose her wits; and at last only Laura, sitting pale and fierce beside her father, prevented her stepmother from bringing a priest to his death-bed. 'You would not *dare!*' said the girl in her low, quivering voice; and Augustina could only wring her hands.

The day after her husband died Mrs Fountain returned to her Catholic duties. When she came back from confession, she slipped as noiselessly as she could into the darkened house. A door opened upstairs, and Laura came out of her father's room.

'You have done it?' she said, as her stepmother, trembling with agitation and weariness, came towards her. 'You have gone back to them?'

'Oh, Laura! I had to follow the call – my conscience – Laura! oh! your poor father!'

And with a burst of weeping the widow held out her hands.

Laura did not move, and the hands dropped.

'My father wants nothing,' she said.

The indescribable pride and passion of her accent cowed Augustina, and she moved away, crying silently. The girl went back to the dead, and sat beside him, in an anguish that had no more tears, till he was taken from her.

Mr Helbeck wrote kindly to his sister in reply to a letter from her informing him of her husband's death, and of her own reconciliation with the Church. He asked whether he should come at once to help them through the business of the funeral, and the winding up of their Cambridge life. 'Beg him, please, to stay away,' said Laura, when the letter was shown her. 'There are plenty of people here.'

And indeed Cambridge, which had taken little notice of the Fountains during Stephen's lifetime, was even fussily kind after his death to his widow and child. It was at all times difficult to be kind to Laura in distress, but there was much true pity felt for her, and a good deal of curiosity as to her relations with her Catholic step-mother. Only from the Friedlands, however, would she accept, or allow her stepmother to accept, any real help. Dr Friedland was a man of middle age, who had retired on moderate wealth to devote himself to historical work by the help of the Cambridge libraries. He had been much drawn to Stephen Fountain, and Fountain to him. It was a recent and a brief friendship, but there had been something in it on Dr Friedland's side – something respectful and cordial, something generous and understanding, for which Laura loved the infirm and grey-haired scholar, and would always love him. She shed some stormy tears after parting with the Friedlands, otherwise she left Cambridge with joy.

On the day before they left Cambridge Augustina received a parcel of books from her brother. For the most part they were kept hidden from Laura. But in the evening, when the girl was doing some packing in her stepmother's room, she came across a little volume lying open on its face. She lifted it, saw that it was called 'Outlines of Catholic Belief,' and that one page was still wet with tears. An angry curiosity made her look at what stood there: – 'A believer in one God who, without wilful fault on his part knows nothing of the Divine Mystery of the Trinity, is held capable of salvation by many Catholic theologians. And there is the "invincible ignorance" of the heathen. What else is possible to the Divine mercy let none of us presume to know. Our part in these matters is obedience, not speculation.'

In faint pencil on the margin was written: 'My Stephen *could* not believe. Mary – pray –'

The book contained the Bannisdale book-plate, and the name 'Alan Helbeck.' Laura threw it down. But her face trembled through its scorn, and she finished what she was doing in a kind of blind passion. It was as though she held her father's dying form in her arms, protecting him against the same meddling and tyrannical force that had injured him while he lived, and was still making mouths at him now that he was dead.

She and Augustina went to the sea – to Folkestone, for Augustina's health. Here Mrs Fountain began to correspond regularly with her brother, and it was soon clear that her heart was hungering for him, and for her old home at Bannisdale. But she was still painfully dependent on Laura. Laura was her maid and nurse; Laura managed all her business. At last one day she made her prayer. Would Laura go with her – for a little while – to Bannisdale? Alan wished it – Alan had invited them both. 'He would be so good to you, Laura – and I'm sure it would set me up.'

Laura gave a gulp. She dropped her little chin on her hands and thought. Well – why not? It would be all hateful to her – Mr Helbeck and his house together. She knew very well, or guessed what his relation to her father had been. But what if it made Augustina strong – if in time she could be left with her brother altogether, to live with him? – in one or two of his letters he had proposed as much. Why, that would bring Laura's responsibility, her sole responsibility, at any rate, to an end.

She thought of Molly Friedland – of their girlish plans – of travel, of music.

'All right,' she said, springing up. 'We will go, Augustina. I suppose, for a little while, Mr Helbeck and I can keep the peace. You must tell him to let me alone.'

She paused, then said with sudden vehemence, like one who takes her stand – 'And tell him, please, Augustina – make it very plain – that I shall never come in to prayers.'

CHAPTER THREE

The sun was shining into Laura's room when she awoke. She lay still for a little while, looking about her.

Her room – which formed part of an eighteenth-century addition to the Tudor house – was rudely panelled with stained deal, save on the fireplace wall, where, on either side of the hearth, the plaster had been covered with tapestry. The subject of the tapestry was Diana hunting. Diana, white and tall, with her bow and quiver, came, queenly, through a green forest. Two greyhounds ranged beside her, and in the dim distance of the wood her maidens followed. On the right an old castle, with pillars like a Greek temple, rose stately but a little crooked on the edge of a blue sea; the sea much faded, with the wooden handle of a cupboard thrust rudely through it. Two long-limbed ladies, with pulled patched faces, stood on the castle steps. In front was a ship, with a waiting warrior and a swelling sail; and under him, a blue wave worn very threadbare, shamed indeed by that intruding handle, but still blue enough, still windy enough for thoughts of love and flight.

Laura, half asleep still, with her hands under her cheek, lay staring in a vague pleasure at the castle and the forest. 'Enchanted casements' – 'perilous seas' – 'in fairy lands forlorn.'[3] The lines ran sleepily, a little jumbled, in her memory.

But gradually the morning and the freshness worked; and her spirits, emerging from their half-dream, began to dance within her. When she sprang up to throw the window wide, there below her was the sparkling river, the daffodils waving their pale heads in the delicate Westmoreland grass, the high white clouds still racing before the wind. How heavenly to find oneself in this wild clean country! – after all the ugly squalors of parade and lodging-house, after the dingy bow-windowed streets with the March dust whirling through them.

She leant across the broad window-sill, her chin on her hands, absorbed, drinking it in. The eastern sun, coming slanting-ways, bathed her tumbled masses of fair hair, her little white form, her bare feet raised tiptoe.

Suddenly she drew back. She had seen the figure of a man

crossing the park on the further side of the river, and the maidenly instinct drove her from the window; though the man in question was perhaps a quarter of a mile away, and had he been looking for her, could not possibly have made out more than a pale speck on the old wall.

'Mr Helbeck' – she thought – 'by the height of him. Where is he off to before seven o'clock in the morning? I hate a man that can't keep rational hours like other people! Fricka, come here!'

For her little dog, who had sprung from the bed after its mistress, was now stretching and blinking behind her. At Laura's voice it jumped up and tried to lick her face. Laura caught it in her arms and sat down on the bed, still hugging it.

'No, Fricka, I don't like him – I don't, I don't, I *don't!* But you and I have just got to behave. If you annoy that big dog downstairs, he'll break your neck – he will, Fricka. As for me' – she shrugged her small shoulders – 'well, Mr Helbeck can't break *my* neck, so I'm dreadfully afraid I shall annoy him – dreadfully, dreadfully afraid! But I'll try not. You see, what we've got to do, is just to get Augustina well – stand over her with a broomstick and pour the tonics down her throat. Then, Fricka, we'll go our way and have some fun. Now look at us! –'

She moved a little, so that the cracked glass on the dressing-table reflected her head and shoulders, with the dog against her neck.

'You know we're not at all bad-looking, Fricka – neither of us. I've seen much worse. (Oh! Fricka! I've told you scores of times I can wash my face – without you – thank you!) There's all sorts of nice things that might happen if we just put ourselves in the way of them. Oh! I do want some fun – I do! – at least sometimes!'

But again the voice dropped suddenly; the big greenish eyes filled in a moment with inconsistent tears, and Laura sat staring at the sunshine, while the drops fell on her white nightgown.

Meanwhile Fricka, being half throttled, made a violent effort and escaped. Laura too sprang up, wiped away her tears as though she were furious with them, and began to look about her for the means of dressing. Everything in the room was of the poorest and scantiest – the cottage washstand with its crockery, the bare dressing-table and dilapidated glass.

'A bath! – my kingdom for a bath! I don't mind starving, but one must wash. Let's ring for that rough-haired girl, Fricka, and try and get round her. Goodness! – no bells?'

After long search, however, she discovered a tattered shred of tapestry hanging in a corner, and pulled it vigorously. Many efforts, however, were needed before there was a sound of feet in the passage outside. Laura hastily donned a blue dressing-gown, and stood expectant.

The door was opened unceremoniously and a girl thrust in her head. Laura had made acquaintance with her the night before. She was the housekeeper's underling and niece.

'Mrs Denton says I'm not to stop. She's noa time for answerin bells. And you'll have some hot water when t' kettle boils.'

The door was just shutting again when Laura sprang at the speaker and caught her by the arm.

'My dear,' she said, dragging the girl in, 'that won't do at all. Now look here' – she held up her little white hand, shaking the forefinger with energy – 'I don't – want – to give – any trouble, and Mrs Denton may keep her hot water. But I must have a bath – and a big can – and somebody must show me where to go for water – and then – *then*, my dear – if you make yourself agreeable, I'll – well, I'll teach you how to do your hair on Sundays – in a way that will surprise you!'

The girl stared at her in sudden astonishment, her dark stupid eyes wavering. She had a round, peasant face, not without comeliness, and a lustreless shock of black hair. Laura laughed.

'I will,' she said, nodding; 'you'll see. And I'll give you notions for your best frock. I'll be a regular elder sister to you – if you'll just do a few things for me – and Mrs Fountain. What's your name – Ellen? – that's all right. Now, is there a bath in the house?'

The girl unwillingly replied that there was one in the big room at the end of the passage.

'Show it me,' said Laura, and marched her off there. The rough-headed one led the way along the panelled passage and opened a door.

Then it was Laura's turn to stare.

Inside she saw a vast room with finely panelled walls and a decorated ceiling. The sunlight poured in through an uncurtained window upon the only two objects in the room – a magnificent bed, carved and gilt, with hangings of tarnished brocade – and a round tin bath of a common, old-fashioned make, propped up against the wall. The oak boards were absolutely bare. The bed and the bath looked at each other.

'What's become of all the furniture?' said Laura, gazing round her in astonishment.

'The gentleman from Edinburgh had it all, lasst month,' said the girl, still sullenly. 'He's affther the bed now.'

'Oh! – Does he often come here?'

The girl hesitated.

'Well, he's had a lot o' things oot o' t' house, sen I came.'

'Has he?' said Laura. 'Now then – lend a hand.'

Between them they carried off the bath; and then Laura informed herself where water was to be had, and when breakfast would be ready.

'T' Squire's gone oot,' said Ellen, still watching the newcomer from under a pair of very black and beetling brows; 'and Mrs Denton said she supposed yo'd be wantin a tray for Mrs Fountain.'

'Does the Squire take no breakfast?'

'Noa. He's away to Mass – ivery mornin, an' he gets his breakfast wi' Father Bowles.'

The girl's look grew more hostile.

'Oh, does he?' said Laura in a tone of meditation. 'Well then, look here. Put another cup and another plate on Mrs Fountain's tray, and I'll have mine with her. Shall I come down to the kitchen for it?'

'Noa,' said the girl hastily. 'Mrs Denton doan't like foak i' t' kitchen.'

At that moment a call in Mrs Denton's angriest tones came pealing along the passage outside. Laura laughed and pushed the girl out of the room.

An hour later Miss Fountain was ministering to her stepmother in the most comfortable bedroom that the house afforded. The furniture, indeed, was a medley. It seemed to have been gathered out of many other rooms. But at any rate there was abundance of it; a carpet much worn, but still useful, covered the floor; and Ellen had lit the fire without being summoned to do it. Laura recognised that Mr Helbeck must have given a certain number of precise orders on the subject of his sister.

Poor Mrs Fountain, however, was not happy. She was sitting up in bed, wrapped in an unbecoming flannel jacket – Augustina had no taste in clothes – and looking with an odd repugnance at the very passable breakfast that Laura placed before her. Laura did not quite know what to make of her. In old days she had always regarded her stepmother as an easy-going, rather self-indulgent creature, who liked pleasant food and stuffed chairs, and could be best managed or propitiated through some attention to her taste in sofa-cushions or in teacakes.

No doubt, since Mrs Fountain's reconciliation with the Church of her fathers, she had shown sometimes an anxious disposition to practise the usual austerities of good Catholics. But neither doctor nor director had been able to indulge her in this respect, owing to the feebleness of her health. And on the whole she had acquiesced readily enough.

But Laura found her now changed and restless.

'Oh! Laura, I can't eat all that!'

'You must,' said Laura firmly. 'Really, Augustina, you *must*.'

'Alan's gone out,' said Augustina with a wistful inconsequence, straining her eyes as though to look through the diamond panes of the window opposite, at the park and the persons walking in it.

'Yes. He seems to go to Whinthorpe every morning for Mass. Ellen says he breakfasts with the priest.'

Augustina sighed and fidgeted. But when she was halfway through her meal, Laura standing over her, she suddenly laid a shaking hand on Laura's arm.

'Laura! – Alan's a saint! – he always was – long ago – when I was so blind and wicked. But now – oh! the things Mrs Denton's been telling me!'

'Has she?' said Laura coolly. 'Well, make up your mind, Augustina' – she shook her bright head – 'that you can't be the same kind of saint that he is – anyway.'

Mrs Fountain withdrew her hand in quick offence.

'I should be glad if you could talk of these things without flippancy, Laura. When I think how incapable I have been all these years, of understanding my dear brother –'

'No – you see you were living with papa,' said Laura slowly.

She had left her stepmother's side, and was standing with her back to an old cabinet, resting her elbows upon it. Her brows were drawn together, and poor Mrs Fountain, after a glance at her, looked still more miserable.

'Your poor papa!' she murmured with a gulp, and then, as though to propitiate Laura, she drew her breakfast back to her, and again tried to eat it. Small and slight as they both were, there was a very sharp contrast between her and her stepdaughter. Laura's features were all delicately clear, and nothing could have been more definite, more brilliant than the colour of the eyes and hair, or the whiteness – which was a beautiful and healthy whiteness – of her skin. Whereas everything about Mrs Fountain was indeterminate; the features with their slight twist to the left; the complexion, once fair, and now reddened by years and ill health; the hair, of a yellowish grey; the head and shoulders with their nervous infirmity. Only the eyes still possessed some purity of colour. Through all their timidity or wavering, they were still blue and sweet; perhaps they alone explained why a good many persons – including her stepdaughter – were fond of Augustina.

'What has Mrs Denton been telling you about Mr Helbeck?' Laura inquired, speaking with some abruptness, after a pause.

'You wouldn't have any sympathy, Laura,' said Mrs Fountain in some agitation. 'You see, you don't understand our Catholic principles. I wish you did! – oh! I wish you did! But you don't. And so perhaps I'd better not talk about it.'

'It might interest me to know the facts,' said Laura, in a little hard voice. 'It seems to me that I'm likely to be Mr Helbeck's guest for a good while.'

'But you won't like it, Laura!' cried Mrs Fountain – 'and you'll misunderstand Alan. Your poor dear father always misunderstood him.' (Laura made a restless movement.) 'It is not because we think we can save our souls by such things – of course not! – that's the way you Protestants put it –'

'I'm not a Protestant!' said Laura hotly. Mrs Fountain took no notice.

'But it's what the Church calls "mortification," ' she said, hurrying on. 'It's keeping the body under – as St Paul did. That's what makes saints – and it does make saints – whatever people say. Your poor father didn't agree, of course. But he didn't know – oh! dear, dear Stephen! – he didn't know. And Alan isn't cross, and it doesn't spoil his health – it doesn't, really.'

'What does he do?' asked Laura, trying for the point.

But poor Augustina, in her mixed flurry of feeling, could hardly explain.

'You see, Laura, there's a strict way of keeping Lent, and – well – just the common way – doing as little as you can. It used to be all much stricter, of course.'

'In the Dark Ages?' suggested Laura. Augustina took no notice.

'And what the books tell you now is much stricter than what anybody does. – I'm sure I don't know why. But Alan takes it strictly – he wants to go back to quite the old ways. Oh! I wish I could explain it –'

Mrs Fountain stopped bewildered. She was sure she had heard once that in the early Church people took no food at all till the evening – not even a drink. But Alan was not going to do that?

Laura had taken Fricka on her knee, and was straightening the ribbon round the dog's neck.

'Does he eat *anything?*' she asked carelessly, looking up. 'If it's *nothing* – that would be interesting.'

'Laura! if you only would try and understand! – Of course Alan doesn't settle such a thing for himself – nobody does with us. That's only in the English Church.'

Augustina straightened herself, with an unconscious arrogance. Laura looked at her, smiling.

'Who settles it, then?'

'Why, his director, of course. He must have leave. But they have given him leave. He has chosen a rule for himself' – Augustina gave a visible gulp – 'and he called Mrs Denton to him before Lent, and told her about it. Of course he'll hide it as much as he can. Catholics must never be singular – never! But if we live in the house with him he can't hide it. And all Lent, he only eats meat on Sundays, and other days – he wrote down a list –. Well, it's like the saints – that's all! – I just cried over it!'

Mrs Fountain shook with the emotion of saying such things to Laura, but her blue eyes flamed.

'What! fish and eggs? – that kind of thing?' said Laura. 'As if there was any hardship in that!'

'Laura! how can you be so unkind? – I must just keep it all to my-self. – I won't tell you anything!' cried Augustina in exasperation.

Laura walked away to the window, and stood looking out at the March buds on the sycamores shining above the river.

'Does he make the servants fast too?' she asked presently, turning her head over her shoulder.

'No, no,' said her stepmother eagerly; 'he's never hard to them – only to himself. The Church doesn't expect anything more than "abstinence," you understand – not real fasting – from people like them – people who work hard with their hands. But – I really believe – they do very much as he does. Mrs Denton seems to keep the house on nothing. Oh! and, Laura – I really can't be always having extra things!'

Mrs Fountain pushed her breakfast away from her.

'Please remember – nobody settles anything for themselves – in your Church,' said Laura. 'You know what that doctor – that Catholic doctor – said to you at Folkestone.'

Mrs Fountain sighed.

'And as to Mrs Denton, I see – that explains the manners. No improvement – till Lent's over?'

'Laura!'

But her stepdaughter, who was at the window again looking out, paid no heed, and presently Augustina said with timid softness –

'Won't you have your breakfast, Laura? You know it's here – on my tray.'

Laura turned, and Augustina to her infinite relief saw not frowns, but a face all radiance.

'I've been watching the lambs in the field across the river. Such ridiculous enchanting things! – such jumps – and affectations. And the river's heavenly – and all the general *feel* of it! I really don't know, Augustina, how you ever came to leave this country when you'd once been born in it.'

Mrs Fountain pushed away her tray, shook her head sadly, and said nothing.

'What is it? – and who is it?' cried Laura, standing amazed before a picture in the drawing-room at Bannisdale.

In front of her, on the panelled wall, hung a dazzling portrait of a girl in white, a creature light as a flower under wind; eyes upraised and eager, as though to welcome a lover; fair hair bound turban-like with a white veil; the pretty hands playing with a book. It shone from the brown wall with a kind of natural sovereignty over all below it and around it, so brilliant was the picture, so beautiful the woman.

Augustina looked up drearily. She was sitting shrunk together in a large chair, deep in some thoughts of her own.

'That's our picture – the famous picture,' she explained slowly.

'Your Romney?' said Laura, vaguely recalling some earlier talk of her stepmother's.

Augustina nodded. She stared at the picture with a curious agitation, as though she were seeing its long familiar glories for the first time. Laura was much puzzled by her.

'Well, but it's magnificent!' cried the girl. 'One needn't know much to know that. How can Mr Helbeck call himself poor while he possesses such a thing?'

Augustina started.

'It's worth thousands,' she said hastily. 'We know that. There was a man from London came once, years ago. But papa turned him out – he would never sell his things. And she was our great grandmother.'

An idea flashed through Laura's mind.

'You don't mean to say that Mr Helbeck is going to sell her?' said Laura impetuously. 'It would be a shame!'

'Alan can do what he likes with anything,' said Augustina in a quick resentment. 'And he wants money badly for one of his orphanages – some of it has to be rebuilt. Oh! those orphanages – how they must have weighed on him – poor Alan! – poor dear Alan! – all these years!'

Mrs Fountain clasped her thin hands together, with a sigh.

'Is it they that have eaten up the house bit by bit? – poor house! – poor dear house!' repeated Laura.

She was staring with an angry championship at the picture. Its sweet confiding air, – as of one cradled in love, happy for generations in the homage of her kindred and the shelter of the old house, – stood for all the natural human things that creeds and bigots were always trampling under foot.

Mrs Fountain, however, only shook her head.

'I don't think Alan's settled anything yet. Only Mrs Denton's afraid. – There was somebody came to see it a few days ago –'

'He certainly ought not to sell it,' repeated Laura with emphasis. 'He has to think of the people that come after. What will they care for orphanages? He only holds the picture in trust.'

'There will be no one to come after,' said Augustina slowly. 'For of course he will never marry.'

'Is he too great a saint for that too?' cried Laura. 'Then all I can say, Augustina, is that – it – would – do him a great deal of good.'

She beat her little foot on the ground impatiently, pointing the words.

'You don't know anything about him, Laura,' said Mrs Fountain, with an attempt at spirit. Then she added reproachfully - 'and I'm sure he wants to be kind to you.'

'He thinks me a little heretical toad, thank you!' said Laura, spinning round on the bare boards, and dropping a curtsey to the Romney. 'But never mind, Augustina – we shall get on quite properly. Now, aren't there a great many more rooms to see?'

Augustina rose uncertainly. 'There is the chapel, of course,' she said, 'and Alan's study –'

'Oh! we needn't go there,' said Laura hastily. 'But show me the chapel.'

Mr Helbeck was still absent, and they had been exploring Bannisdale. It was a melancholy progress they had been making through a house that had once – when Augustina left it – stood full of the hoardings and treasures of generations, and was now empty and despoiled.

It was evident that, for his sister's welcome, Mr Helbeck had gathered into the drawing-room, as into her bedroom upstairs, the best of what still remained to him. Chairs and tables, and straight-lined sofas, some of one date, some of another, collected from the garrets and remote corners of the old house, and covered with the oddest variety of faded stuffs, had been stiffly set out by Mrs Denton upon an old Turkey carpet, whereof the rents and patches had been concealed as much as possible. Here at least was something of a cosmos – something of order and of comfort.

The hall too, and the dining-room, in spite of their poor new furnishings, were still human and habitable. But most of the rooms on which Laura and Mrs Fountain had been making raid were like that first one Laura had visited, mere homes of lumber and desolation. Blinds drawn; dust-motes dancing in the stray shafts of light that struck across the gloom of the old walls and floors. Here and there some lingering fragment of fine furniture; but as a rule bareness, poverty, and void – nothing could be more piteous, or, to Mrs Fountain's memory, more surprising. For some years before she left Bannisdale, her father had not known where to turn for a pound of ready money. Yet when she fled from it, the house and its treasures were still intact.

The explanation of course was very simple. Alan Helbeck had been living upon his house, as upon any other capital. Or rather he had been making alms of it. The house stood gashed and bare that Catholic orphans might be put to school – was that it? Laura hardly listened to Augustina's plaintive babble as they crossed the hall. It was all about Alan, of course – Alan's virtues, Alan's charities. As for the orphans, the girl hated the thought of them. Grasping little wretches! She could see them all in a sanctimonious row, their eyes cast up, and rosaries – like the one Augustina was always trying to hide from her – in their ugly little hands.

They turned down a long stone passage leading to the chapel. As they neared the chapel door there was a sound of voices from the hall at their back.

'It's Alan,' said Augustina peering, 'and Father Bowles!'

She hurried back to meet them, skirts and cap-strings flying. Laura stood still.

But after a few words with his sister, Helbeck came up to his guest with outstretched hand.

'I hope we have not kept you waiting for dinner. May I introduce Father Bowles to you?'

Laura bowed with all the stiffness of which a young back is capable. She saw an old grey-haired priest, with a round face and a pair of chubby hands, which he constantly held crossed or clasped upon his breast. His long irregular mouth seemed to fold over at the corners above his very small and childish chin. The mouth and the light blue eyes wore an expression of rather mincing gentleness. His short figure, though bent a little with years, was still vigorous, and his gait quick and bustling.

He addressed Miss Fountain with a lisping and rather obsequious politeness, asking a great many unnecessary questions about her journey and her arrival.

Laura answered coldly. But when he passed to Mrs Fountain, Augustina was all effusion.

'When I think what has been granted to us since I was here last!' she said to the priest as they moved on, – clasping her hands, and flushing.

'The dear Bishop took such trouble about it,' he said in a little murmuring voice. 'It was not easy – but the Church loves to content her children.'

Involuntarily Laura glanced at Helbeck.

'My sister refers to the permission which has been granted to us to reserve the Blessed Sacrament in the chapel,' he said gravely. 'It is a privilege we never enjoyed till last year.'

Laura made no reply.

'Shall I slip away?' she thought, looking round her.

But at that moment Mr Helbeck lifted the heavy latch of the chapel door; and her young curiosity was too strong for her. She followed the others.

Mr Helbeck held the door open for her.

'You will perhaps care to look at the frescoes,' he said to her as she hurried past him. She nodded, and walked quickly away to the left, by herself. Then she turned and looked about her.

It was the first time that she had entered a Catholic church, and every detail was new to her. She watched the other three sign themselves with holy water and drop low on one knee before the altar. So that was the altar. She stared at it with a scornful repugnance; yet her pulse quickened as though what she saw excited her. What was that erection above it, with a veil of red silk drawn round it – and why was that lamp burning in front of it?

She recalled Mr Helbeck's words – 'permission to reserve the Blessed Sacrament.' Then, in a flash, a hundred vague memories, the deposit of a hearsay knowledge, enlightened her. She knew and remembered much less than any ordinary girl would have done. But still, in the main, she guessed at what was passing. That of course was the Sacrament, before which Mr Helbeck and the others were kneeling! – for instinctively she felt that it was to no empty shrine the adoration of those silent figures was being offered.

Fragments from Augustina's talk at Folkestone came back to her. Once she had overheard some half-whispered conversation between her stepmother and a Catholic friend, from which she had vaguely understood that the 'Blessed Sacrament' was kept in the Catholic churches, was always there, and that the faithful 'visited' it – that these 'visits' were indeed specially recommended as a means to holiness. And she recalled how, as they came home from their daily walk to the beach, Mrs Fountain would disappear from her, through the shadowy door of a Catholic church that stood in the same street as their lodgings – how she would come home half an hour afterwards, shaken with fresh ardours, fresh remorse.

But how could such a thing be allowed, be possible, in a private chapel – in a room that was really part of a private house? GOD – the Christ of Calvary – in that gilt box, upon that altar!

The young girl's arms fell by her side in a sudden rigidity. A wave of the most passionate repulsion swept through her. What a gross, what an intolerable superstition! – how was she to live with it, beside it? The next instant it was as though her hand clasped her father's – clinging to him proudly, against this alien world. Why should she feel lonely? – the little heretic, left standing there alone in her distant corner. Let her rather rejoice that she was her father's daughter!

She drew herself up, and coolly looked about her. The worshippers had risen; long as the time had seemed to Laura, they had only been two or three minutes on their knees; and she could see that Augustina was talking eagerly to her brother, pointing now to the walls, now to the altar.

It seemed as though Augustina were no less astonished than her stepdaughter by the magnificence of the chapel. Was it all new, the frescoes, the altar with its marble and its gold, the white figure of the Virgin, which gleamed above the small side-altar to the left? It had the air of newness – and of costliness – an air which struck the eye all the more sharply because of the contrast between it and the penury, the starvation of the great house that held the chapel in its breast.

But while Laura was still wondering at the general impression of rich beauty, at the Lenten purple of the altar, at the candelabra, and the perfume, certain figures and colours on the wall close to her seized her, thrusting the rest aside. On either side of the altar the walls to right and left, from the entrance up to the sanctuary, were covered with what appeared to be recent painting – painting, indeed, that was still in the act. On either hand, long rows of life-sized saints, men and women, turned their adoring faces towards the Christ looking down upon them from a crucifix above the tabernacle. On the north wall, about half the row was unfinished; faces, haloes, drapery, strongly outlined in red, still waited for the completing hand of the artist. The rest glowed and burned with colour – colour the most singular, the most daring. The carnations and rose colours, the golds and purples, the blues and lilacs and greens – in the whole concert of tone, in spite of its general simplicity of surface, there was something at once ravishing and troubling, something that spoke as it were from passion to passion.

Laura's nature felt the thrill of it at once, just as she had felt the thrill of the sunshine lighting up the tapestry of her room.

'Why isn't it crude and hideous?' she asked herself, in a marvel. 'But it isn't. One never saw such blues – except in the sea – or such greens – and rose! And the angels between! – and the flowers under their feet! – Heavens! how lovely! Who did it?'

'Do you admire the frescoes?' said a little voice behind her.

She turned hastily and saw Father Bowles, smiling upon her, his plump white hands clasped in front of him as usual. It was an attitude which seemed to make the simplest words sound intimate and possessive. Laura shrank from it in quick annoyance.

'They are very strange and – and startling,' she said stiffly, moving as far away from the grey-haired priest as possible. 'Who painted them?'

'Mr Helbeck first designed them. But they were carried out for a time by a youth of great genius.' Father Bowles dwelt softly upon the word '*ge*-nius,' as though he loved it. 'He was once a lad from these parts, but has now become a Jesuit. So the work was stopped.'

'What a pity!' said Laura impetuously. 'He ought to have been a painter.'

The priest smiled, and made her an odd little bow. Then, without saying anything more about the artist, he chattered on about the frescoes and the chapel, as though he had beside him the most sympathetic of listeners. Nothing that he said was the least interesting or striking; and Laura, in a passion of silent dislike, kept up a steady movement towards the door all the time.

In the passage outside Mrs Fountain was lingering alone. And when Laura appeared she caught hold of her stepdaughter and detained her while the priest passed on. Laura looked at her in surprise, and Mrs Fountain, in much agitation, whispered in the girl's ear:

'Oh, Laura – do remember, dear! – don't ask Alan about those pictures – those frescoes – by young Williams. I can tell you some time – and you might say something to hurt him – poor Alan!'

Laura drew herself away.

'Why should I say anything to hurt him? What's the mystery?'

'I can't tell you now' – Mrs Fountain looked anxiously towards the hall. 'People have been so hard on Alan – *so* unkind about it! It's been a regular persecution. And you wouldn't understand – wouldn't sympathise –'

'I really don't care to know about it, Augustina! And I'm so hungry – famished! Look, there's Mr Helbeck signing to us. Joy! – that's dinner.'

Laura expected the midday meal with some curiosity. But she saw no signs of austerity. Mr Helbeck pressed the roast chicken on

Father Bowles, took pains that he should enjoy a better bottle of wine than usual, and as to himself, ate and drank very moderately indeed, but like anybody else. Laura could only imagine that it was not seemly to outdo your priest.

The meal of course was served in the simplest way, and all the waiting was done by Mr Helbeck, who would allow nobody to help him in the task.

The conversation dragged. Laura and her host talked a little about the country and the weather. Father Bowles and Augustina tried to pick up the dropped threads of thirteen years; and Mrs Fountain was alternately eager for Whinthorpe gossip, or reduced to an abrupt unhappy silence by some memory of the past.

Suddenly Father Bowles got up from his chair, ran across the room to the window with his napkin in his hand, and pounced eagerly upon a fly that was buzzing on the pane. Then he carefully opened the window, and flicked the dead thing off the sill.

'I beg your pardon,' he said humbly to Mrs Fountain as he returned to his seat. 'It was a nasty fly. I can't abide 'em. I always think of Beelzebub who was the prince of the flies.'

Laura's mouth twitched with laughter. She promised herself to make a study of Father Bowles. And, indeed, he was a character in his own small way. He was a priest of an old-fashioned type, with no pretentions to knowledge or to manners. Wherever he went he was a meek and accommodating guest, for his recollection went back to days when a priest coming to a private house to say mass would as likely as not have his meals in the pantry. And he was naturally of a gentle and yielding temper – though rather sly.

But he had several tricks as curious as they were persistent. Not even the presence of his bishop could make him spare a bluebottle. And he had, on the other hand, a peculiar passion for the smell of wax. He would blow out a candle on the altar before the end of mass that he might enjoy the smell of it. He disliked Jesuits, and religious generally, if the truth were known; excepting only the Orphanage nuns, who knew his weaknesses and were kind to them. He had no love for modern innovations, or modern devotions; there was a hidden Gallican strain in him; and he firmly believed that in the old days before Catholic emancipation, and before the Oxford movement, the Church made more converts than she did now.

*

Towards the end of the lunch Laura inquired of Mr Helbeck whether any conveyance was to be got in the village.

'I wish to go to Browhead Farm this afternoon,' she said, rather shortly.

'Certainly,' said Helbeck. 'Certainly. I will see that something is found for you.'

But his voice had no cordiality, and Laura at once thought him ungracious.

'Oh, pray don't give yourself any trouble,' she said flushing, 'I can walk to the village.'

Helbeck paused.

'If you could wait till to-morrow,' he said after a moment, 'I could promise you the pony. Unfortunately he is busy this afternoon.'

'Oh, do wait, Laura!' cried Augustina. 'There is so much unpacking to do.'

'Very well,' said the girl unwillingly.

As she turned away from him Helbeck's look followed her. She was in a dress of black serge, which followed the delicate girlish frame with perfect simplicity, and was relieved at the neck and wrists with the plainest of white collars and cuffs. But there was something so brilliant in the hair, so fawnlike in the carriage of the head, that she seemed to Helbeck to be all elegance; had he been asked to describe her, he would have said she was in *grande toilette*. Little as he spoke to her, he found himself perpetually conscious of her. Her evident, – childishly evident dislike of her new surroundings half amused, half embarrassed him. He did not know what topic to start with her; soon, perhaps, he might have a difficulty in keeping the peace! It was all very absurd.

After luncheon they gathered in the hall for a while, Father Bowles talking eagerly with Helbeck and Augustina about 'orphans' and 'new buildings.' Laura stood apart awhile – then went for her hat.

When she reappeared, in walking dress – with Fricka at her heels – Helbeck opened the heavy outer door for her.

'May I have Bruno?' she said.

Helbeck turned and whistled.

'You are not afraid?' he said, smiling, and looking at Fricka.

'Oh dear no! I spent an hour this morning introducing them.'

At that moment Bruno came bounding up. He looked from his master, to Laura in her hat, and seemed to hesitate. Then, as she descended the steps, he sprang after her. Laura began to run; the two dogs leapt about her; her light voice, checking or caressing, came back to Helbeck on the spring wind. He watched her and her companions so long as they were in sight – the golden hair among the trees, the dancing steps of the girl, the answering frolic of the dogs.

Then he turned back to his sister, his grave mouth twitching.

'How thankful she is to get rid of us!'

He laughed out. The priest laughed too, more softly.

'It was the first time, I presume, that Miss Fountain had ever been within a Catholic church?' he said to Augustina.

Augustina flushed.

'Of course it is the first time. Oh! Alan, you can't think how strange it is to her.'

She looked rather piteously at her brother.

'So I perceive,' he said. 'You told me something, but I had not realised –'

'You see, Alan –' cried Augustina, watching her brother's face – 'it was with the greatest difficulty that her mother got Stephen to consent even to her being baptised. He opposed it for a long time.'

Father Bowles murmured something under his breath.

Helbeck paused for a moment, then said –

'What was her mother like?'

'Every one at Cambridge used to say she was "a sweet woman" – but – but Stephen, – well, you know, Alan, Stephen always had his way! I always wonder she managed to persuade him about the baptism.'

She coloured still more deeply as she spoke, and her nervous infirmity became more pronounced. Alas! it was not only with the first wife that Stephen had had his way! Her own marriage had begun to seem to her a mere sinful connection. Poor soul – poor Augustina!

Her brother must have divined something of what was passing in her mind, for he looked down upon her with a peculiar gentleness.

'People are perhaps more ready to talk of that responsibility than to take it,' he said kindly. 'But, Augustina –' his voice changed – 'how pretty she is! – You hardly prepared me –'

Father Bowles modestly cast down his eyes. These were not questions that concerned him. But Helbeck went on, speaking with decision, and looking at his sister –

'I confess – her great attractiveness makes me a little anxious – about the connection with the Masons. Have you ever seen any of them, Augustina?'

No – Augustina had seen none of them. She believed Stephen had particularly disliked the mother, the widow of his cousin, who now owned the farm jointly with her son.

'Well, no –' said Helbeck, dryly, 'I don't suppose he and she would have had much in common.'

'Isn't she a dreadful Protestant – Alan?'

'Oh, she's just a specimen of the ordinary English Bible-worship run mad,' he said, carelessly. 'She is a strange woman, very well known about here. And there's a foolish parson, living near them, up in the hills, who makes her worse. But it's the son I'm thinking of.'

'Why, Alan – isn't he respectable?'

'Not particularly. He's a splendid athletic fellow – doing his best to make himself a blackguard, I'm afraid. I've come across him once or twice, as it happens. He's not a desirable cousin for Miss Fountain – that I can vouch for! And unluckily –' he smiled – 'Miss Fountain won't hear any good of this house at Browhead Farm.'

Even Augustina drew herself up proudly.

'My dear Alan, what does it matter what that sort of people think?'

He shook his head.

'It's a queer business. They were mixed up with young Williams.'

Augustina started.

'Mrs Mason was a great friend of his mother, who died. They hate me like poison. However –'

The priest interposed.

'Mrs Mason is a very violent, a most unseemly woman,' he said, in his mincing voice. 'And the father – the old man – who is now dead, was concerned in the rioting, near the bridge –'

'When Alan was struck? Mrs Denton told me! How *abominable!*'

Augustina raised her hands in mingled reprobation and distress. Helbeck looked annoyed.

'That doesn't matter one brass farthing,' he said, in some haste. 'Father Bowles was much worse treated than I on that occasion. But you see the whole thing is unlucky – it makes it difficult to give Miss Fountain the hints one would like to give her.'

He threw himself down beside his sister, talking to her in low tones. Father Bowles took up the local paper.

Presently Augustina broke out – with another wringing of the hands.

'Don't put it on me, my dear Alan! I tell you – Laura has always done exactly what she liked since she was a baby.'

Mr Helbeck rose. His face and air already expressed a certain haughtiness; and at his sister's words there was a very definite tightening of the shoulders.

'I do not intend to have Hubert Mason hanging about the house,' he said quietly, as he thrust his hands into his pockets.

'Of course not! – but she wouldn't expect it,' cried Augustina in dismay. 'It's the keeping her away from them, that's the difficulty. She thinks so much of her cousins, Alan. They're her father's only relations. I know she'll want to be with them half her time!'

'For love of them – or dislike of us? Oh! I dare say it will be all right,' he added, abruptly. 'Father Bowles, shall I drive you half-way? The pony will be round directly.'

CHAPTER FOUR

It was a Sunday morning – bright and windy. Miss Fountain was driving a shabby pony through the park of Bannisdale – driving with a haste and glee that sent the little cart spinning down the road.

Six hours – she calculated – till she need see Bannisdale again. Her cousins would ask her to dinner – and to tea. Augustina and Mr Helbeck might have all their Sunday antics to themselves. There were several priests coming to luncheon – and a function in the chapel that afternoon. Laura flicked the pony sharply as she thought of it. Seven miles between her and it? Joy!

Nevertheless, she did not get rid of the old house and its suggestions quite as easily as she wished. The park and the river had many windings. Again and again the grey gabled mass thrust itself upon her attention, recalling each time, against her will, the face of its owner.

A high brow – hollows in the temples, deep hollows in the cheeks – pale blue eyes – a short and pointed beard, greyish-black like the hair – the close whiskers black too against the skin – a general impression of pallor, dark lines, strong shadows, melancholy force –

She burst out laughing.

A pose! – nothing in the world but a pose. There was a wretched picture of Charles I in the dining-room – a daub 'after' some famous thing, she supposed – all eyes and hair, long face, and lace collar. Mr Helbeck was 'made up' to that – she was sure of it. He had found out the likeness, and improved upon it. Oh! if one could only present him with the collar and blue ribbon complete!

'– Cut his head off, and have done with him!' she said aloud, whipping up the pony, and laughing at her own petulance.

Who could live in such a house – such an atmosphere?

As she drove along, her mind was all in a protesting whirl. On her return from her walk with the dogs the day before, she had found a service going on in the chapel, Father Bowles officiating, and some figures in black gowns and white-winged coifs assisting. She had fled to her own room, but when she came down again, the black-garbed 'sisters' were still there, and she had been introduced to them. Ugh! what manners! Must one always, if one was a Catholic, make that cloying, hypocritical impression? 'Three of them kissed me,' she reminded herself, in a quiver of wrath.

They were Sisters from the orphanage apparently, or one of the orphanages, and there had been endless talk of new buildings and money, while she, Laura, sat dumb in her corner looking at old photographs of the house. Helbeck, indeed, had not talked much. While the black women were chattering with Augustina and Father Bowles, he had stood, mostly silent, under the picture of his great-grandmother, only breaking through his reverie from time to time to ask or answer a question. Was he pondering the sale of the great-grandmother, or did he simply know that his silence and aloofness were picturesque, that they compelled other people's attention, and made him the centre of things more effectively than more ordinary manners could have done? In recalling him the girl had an impatient sense of something commanding; of something, moreover, that held herself under observation. 'One thinks him shy at first, or awkward – nothing of the sort! He is as proud as Lucifer. Very soon one sees that he is just looking out for his own way in everything.

'And as for temper! –'

After the sisters departed, a young architect had appeared at supper. A point of difference had arisen between him and Mr Helbeck. He was to be employed, it appeared, in the enlargement of this blessed orphanage. Mr Helbeck, no doubt with a view to his pocket – to do him justice, there seemed to be no other pocket concerned than his – was of opinion that certain existing buildings could be made use of in the new scheme. The architect – a nervous young fellow, with awkward manners, and the ambitions of an artist – thought not, and held his own, insistently. The discussion grew vehement. Suddenly Helbeck lost his temper.

'Mr Munsey! I must ask you to give more weight, if you please, to my wishes in this matter! They may be right or wrong – but it would save time, perhaps, if we assumed that they would prevail.'

The note of anger in the voice made every one look up. The Squire stood erect a moment; crumpled in his hand a half-sheet of paper on which young Munsey had been making some calculations, and flung it into the fire. Augustina sat cowering. The young man himself turned white, bowed, and said nothing. While Father Bowles, of course, like the old tabby that he was, had at once begun to purr conciliation.

'Would I have stood meek and mum if I'd been the young man!' thought Laura. 'Would I! Oh! if I'd had the chance! And he should not have made up so easily either.'

For she remembered, also, how after Father Bowles was gone, she had come in from the garden to find Mr Helbeck and the architect pacing the long hall together, on what seemed to be the friendliest of terms. For nearly an hour, while she and Augustina sat reading over the fire, the colloquy went on.

Helbeck's tones then were of the gentlest; the young man too spoke low and eagerly, pressing his plans. And once, when Laura looked up from her book, she had seen Helbeck's arm resting for a moment on the young fellow's shoulder. Oh! no doubt Mr Helbeck could make himself agreeable when he chose – and struggling architects must put up with the tempers of their employers.

All the more did Miss Fountain like to think that the Squire could compel no court from her.

She recalled that when Mr Munsey had said goodnight, and they three were alone in the firelit hall, Helbeck had come to stand beside her. He had looked down upon her with an air which was either kindness or weariness; he had been willing – even, she thought, anxious to talk with her. But she did not mean to be first trampled on, then patronised, like the young man. So Mr Helbeck had hardly begun – with that occasional timidity which sat so oddly on his dark and strong physique – to speak to her of the two Sisters of Charity who had been his guests in the afternoon, when she abruptly discovered it was time to say good-night. She winced a little as she remembered the sudden stiffening of his look, the careless touch of his hand.

The day was keen and clear. A nipping wind blew beneath the bright sun, and the opening buds had a parched and hindered look. But to Laura the air was wine, and the country all delight. She was mounting the flank of a hill towards a straggling village. Straight along the face of the hill lay her road, past the villages and woods that clothed the hill slope, till some one should show her the gate beyond which lay the rough ascent to Browhead Farm.

Above her, now, to her right, rose a craggy fell with great screes plunging sheer down into the woods that sheltered the village; below, in the valley-plain, stretched the purples and greens of the moss; the rivers shone in the sun as they came speeding from the mountains to the sea; and in the far distance the heights of Lakeland made one pageant with the sun and the clouds – peak after peak thrown blue against the white, cloud after cloud breaking to show the dappled hills below, in such a glory of silver and of purple, such a freshness of atmosphere and light, that mere looking soon became the most thrilling, the most palpable of joys. Laura's spirits began to sing and soar, with the larks and the blackcaps!

Then, when the village was gone, came a high stretch of road, looking down upon the moss and all its bounding fells, which ran out upon its purple face like capes upon a sea. And these nearer fields – what were these thick white specks upon the new-made furrows? Up rose the gulls for answer; and the girl felt the sea-breath from their dazzling wings, and turned behind her to look for that pale opening in the south-west through which the rivers passed.

And beyond the fields a wood – such a wood as made Laura's south-country eyes stand wide with wonder! Out she jumped, tied the pony's rein to a gate beside the road, and ran into the hazel brushwood with little cries of pleasure. A Westmoreland wood in daffodil time – it was nothing more and nothing less. But to this child with the young passion in her blood, it was a dream, an ecstasy. The golden flowers, the slim stalks, rose from a mist of greenish-blue, made by their speary leaf amid the en-circling browns and purples, the intricate stem and branch-work of the still winter-bound hazels. Never were daffodils in such a wealth before! They were flung on the fell-side through a score of acres, in sheets and tapestries of gold, – such an audacious, unreckoned plenty as went strangely with the frugal air and temper of the northern country, with the bare walled fields, the ruggedness of the crags above, and the melancholy of the treeless marsh below. And within this common lavishness, all possible delicacy, all possible perfection of the separate bloom and tuft – each foot of ground had its own glory. For below the daffodils there was a carpet of dark violets, so dim and close that it was their scent first bewrayed them; and as Laura lay gathering with her face among the flowers, she could see behind their gold, and between the hazel stems, the light-filled greys and azures of the mountain distance. Each detail in the happy whole struck on the girl's eager sense and made there a poem of northern spring –

spring as the fell-country sees it, pure, cold, expectant, with flashes of a blossoming beauty amid the rocks and pastures, unmatched for daintiness and joy.

Presently Laura found herself sitting – half crying! – on a mossy tuft, looking along the wood to the distance. What was it in this exquisite country that seized upon her so – that spoke to her in this intimate, this appealing voice?

Why, she was of it – she belonged to it – she felt it in her veins! Old inherited things leapt within her – or it pleased her to think so. It was as though she stretched out her arms to the mountains and fields, crying to them, 'I am not a stranger – draw me to you – my life sprang from yours!' A host of burning and tender thoughts ran through her. Their first effect was to remind her of the farm and of her cousins; and she sprang up, and went back to the cart.

On they rattled again, downhill through the wood, and up on the further side – still always on the edge of the moss. She loved the villages, and their medley of grey houses wedged among the rocks; she loved the stone farms with their wide porches, and the white splashes on their grey fronts; she loved the tufts of fern in the wall crannies, the limestone ribs and bonework of the land breaking everywhere through the pastures, the incomparable purples of the woods, and the first brave leafing of the larches and the sycamores. Never had she so given her heart to any new world, and through her delight flashed the sorest, tenderest thoughts of her father. 'Oh! papa – oh, papa!' she said to herself again and again in a little moan. Every day perhaps he had walked this road as a child, and she could still see herself as a child, in a very dim vision, trotting beside him down the Browhead Road. She turned at last into the fell-gate to which a passing boy directed her, with a long breath that was almost a sob.

She had given them no notice; but surely, surely they would be glad to see her!

They? She tried to split up the notion, to imagine the three people she was going to see. Cousin Elizabeth – the mother? Ah! she knew her, for they had never liked Cousin Elizabeth. She herself could dimly remember a hard face – an obstinate voice raised in discussion with her father. Yet it was Cousin Elizabeth who was the Fountain born, who had carried the little family property as her dowry to her husband James Mason. For the grandfather had been free to leave it as he chose, and on the death of his eldest son – who had settled at the farm after his marriage, and taken the heavy work of it off his father's shoulders – the old man had passionately preferred to leave it to the strong, capable granddaughter, who was already provided with a lover, who understood the land, moreover, and could earn and 'addle' as he did – rather than to his bookish milksop of a second son, so richly provided for already, in his father's contemptuous opinion, by the small Government post at Newcastle.

'Let us always thank God, Laura, that my grandfather was a brute to yours!' Stephen Fountain would say to his girl on the rare occasions when he could be induced to speak of his family at all. 'But for that I might be a hedger and ditcher to this day.'

Well, but Cousin Elizabeth's children? Laura herself had some vague remembrance of them. As the pony climbed the steep lane she shut her eyes and tried hard to recall them. The fair-haired boy – rather fat and masterful – who had taken her to find the eggs of a truant hen in a hedge behind the house – and had pushed her into a puddle on the way home because she had broken one? Then the girl, the older girl Polly, who had cleaned her shoes for her, and lent her a pinafore? No! Laura opened her eyes again – it was no good straining to remember. Too many years had rolled between that early visit and her present self – years during which there had been no communication of any sort between Stephen Fountain and his cousins.

Why had Augustina been so trying and tiresome about the Masons? Instead of flying to her cousins on the earliest possible opportunity, here was a whole fortnight gone since her arrival, and it was not till this Sunday morning that Laura had been able to achieve her visit. Augustina had been constantly ailing or fretful; either unwilling to be left alone, or possessed by absurd desires for useless trifles only to be satisfied by Laura's going to shop in Whinthorpe. And such melancholy looks whenever the Masons were mentioned – coupled with so formal a silence on Mr Helbeck's part! What did it all mean? No doubt her relations were vulgar, low-born folk! – but she did not ask Mr Helbeck or her stepmother to entertain them. At last there had been a passage of arms between her and her stepmother. Perhaps Mr Helbeck had overheard it, for immediately afterwards he had emerged from his study into the hall, where she and Augustina were sitting.

'Miss Fountain – may I ask – do you wish to be sent into Whin-thorpe on Sunday morning?'

She had fronted him at once.

'No, thank you, Mr Helbeck. I don't go to church – I never did with papa.'

Had she been defiant? He surely had been stiff.

'Then perhaps you would like the pony – for your visit? He is quite at your service for the day. Would that suit you?'

'Perfectly.'

So here she was – at last! – climbing up and up into the heart of the fells. The cloud-pageant round the high mountains, the valley with its flashing streams, its distant sands, and widening sea – she had risen as it seemed above them all; they lay beneath her in a map-like unity. She could have laughed and sung out of sheer physical joy in the dancing air – in the play of the cloud gleams and shadows as they swept across her, chased by the wind. All about her the little mountain sheep were feeding in the craggy 'intaks' or along the edges of the tiny tumbling streams; and at intervals amid the reds and yellows of the still wintry grass rose great wind-beaten hollies, sharp and black against the blue distance, marching beside her, like scattered soldiers, up the height.

Not a house to be seen, save on the far slopes of distant hills – not a sound, but the chink of the stone-chat, or the fall of lonely water.

Soon the road, after its long ascent, began to dip; a few trees appeared in a hollow, then a gate and some grey walls.

Laura jumped from the cart. Beyond the gate, the road turned downward a little, and a great block of barns shut the farmhouse from view till she was actually upon it.

But there it was at last – the grey roughly built house, that she still vaguely remembered, with the whitewashed porch, the stables and cowsheds opposite, the little garden to the side, the steep fell behind.

She stood with her hand on the pony, looking at the house in some perplexity. Not a soul apparently had heard her coming. Nothing moved in the farmhouse or outside it. Was everybody at church? But it was nearly one o'clock.

The door under the deep porch had no knocker, and she looked in vain for a bell. All she could do was to rap sharply with the handle of her whip.

No answer. She rapped again – louder and louder. At last in the intervals of knocking, she became conscious of a sound within – something deep and continuous, like the buzzing of a gigantic bee.

She put her ear to the door, listening. Then all her face dissolved in laughter. She raised her arm and brought the whip-handle down noisily on the old blistered door, so that it shook again.

'Hullo!'

There was a sudden sound of chairs overturned, or dragged along a flagged floor. Then staggering steps – and the door was opened.

'I say – what's all this – what are you making such a damned noise for?'

Inside stood a stalwart young man, still half asleep, and drawing his hand irritably across his blinking eyes.

'How do you do, Mr Mason?'

The young man drew himself together with a start. Suddenly he perceived that the young girl standing in the shade of the porch was not his sister, but a stranger. He looked at her with astonishment, – at the elegance of her dress, and the neatness of her small gloved hand.

'I beg your pardon, Miss, I'm sure! Did you want anything?'

The visitor laughed. 'Yes, I want a good deal! I came up to see my cousins – you're my cousin – though of course you don't remember me. I thought – perhaps – you'd ask me to dinner.'

The young man's yawns ceased. He stared with all his eyes, instinctively putting his hair and collar straight.

'Well, I'm afraid I don't know who you are, Miss,' he said at last, putting out his hand in perplexity to meet hers. 'Will you walk in?'

'Not before you know who I am!' – said Laura, still laughing – 'I'm Laura Fountain. Now do you know?'

'What – Stephen Fountain's daughter – as married Miss Helbeck?' said the young man in wonder. His face which had been at first vague and heavy with sleep, began to recover its natural expression.

Laura surveyed him. He had a square, full chin and an upper lip slightly underhung. His straight fair hair straggled loose over his brow. He carried his head and shoulders well, and was altogether a finely built, rather magnificent young fellow, marred by a general expression that was half clumsy, half insolent.

'That's it,' she said, in answer to his question – 'I'm staying at Bannisdale, and I came up to see you all. – Where's Cousin Elizabeth?'

'Mother, do you mean? – Oh! she's at church.'

'Why aren't you there, too?'

He opened his blue eyes, taken aback by the cool clearness of her voice.

'Well, I can't abide the parson – if you want to know. Shall I put up your pony?'

'But perhaps you've not had your sleep out?' said Laura, politely interrogative.

He reddened, and came forward with a slow and rather shambling gait.

'I don't know what else there is to do up here of a Sunday morning,' he said, with a boyish sulkiness, as he began to lead the pony towards the stables opposite. 'Besides, I was up half the night seeing to one of the cows.'

'You don't seem to have many neighbours,' said Laura, as she walked beside him.

'There's rooks and crows' (which he pronounced broadly – 'craws') – 'not much else, I can tell you. Shall I take the pony out?'

'Please. I'm afraid you'll have to put up with me for hours!'

She looked at him merrily, and he returned the scrutiny. She wore the same thin black dress in which Helbeck had admired her the day before, and above it a cloth jacket and cap, trimmed with brown fur. Mason was dazzled a moment by the milky whiteness of the cheek above the fur, by the brightness of the eyes and hair; then was seized with fresh shyness, and became extremely busy with the pony.

'Mother'll be back in about an hour,' he said gruffly.

'Goodness! what'll you do with me till then?'

They both laughed, he with an embarrassment that annoyed him. He was not at all accustomed to find himself at a disadvantage with a good-looking girl.

'There's a good fire in the house, any way,' he said – 'you'll want to warm yourself, I should think, after driving up here.'

'Oh! I'm not cold – I say, what jolly horses!'

For Mason had thrown open the large worm-eaten door of the stables, and inside could be seen the heads and backs of two cart-horses, huge, majestic creatures, who were peering over the doors of their stalls, as though they had been listening to the conversation.

Their owner glanced at them indifferently.

'Aye, they're not bad. We bred 'em three years ago, and they've taken more'n one prize already. I dare say old Daffady, now, as looks after them, would be sorry to part with them.'

'I dare say he would. But why should he part with them?'

The young man hesitated. He was shaking down a load of hay for the pony, and Laura was leaning against the door of the stall watching his performance.

'Well, I reckon we shan't be farmin here all our lives,' he said at last with some abruptness.

'Don't you like it then?'

'I'd get quit on it to-morrow if I could!'

His quick reply had an emphasis that astonished her.

'And your mother?'

'Oh! of course it's mother keeps me at it,' he said, relapsing into the same accent of a sulky child that he had used once before.

Then he led his new cousin back to the farmhouse. By this time he was beginning to find his tongue and use his eyes. Laura was conscious that she was being closely observed, and that by a man who was by no means indifferent to women. She said to herself that she would try to keep him shy.

As they entered the farmhouse kitchen Mason hastened to pick up the chairs he had overturned in his sudden waking.

'I say, mother would be mad if she knew you'd come into this scrow!' he said with vexation, kicking aside some sporting papers that were littered over the floors, and bringing forward a carved oak chair with a cushion to place it before the fire for her acceptance.

'Scrow? What's that?' said Laura, lifting her eyebrows. 'Oh, please don't tidy any more. I really think you make it worse. Besides, it's all right. What a dear old kitchen!'

She had seated herself in the cushioned chair, and was warming a slender foot at the fire. Mason wished she would take off her hat — it hid her hair. But he could not flatter himself that she was in the least occupied with what he wished. Her attention was all given to her surroundings — to the old raftered room with its glowing fire and deep-set windows.

Bright as the April sun was outside, it hardly penetrated here. Through the mellow dusk, as through the varnish of an old picture, one saw the different objects in a golden light and shade – the brass warming-pan hanging beside the tall eight-day clock – the table in front of the long window-seat, covered with its checked red cloth – the carved door of a cupboard in the wall bearing the date 1679 – the miscellaneous store of things packed away under the black rafters, dried herbs and tools, bundles of list and twine, the spindles of old spinning wheels, cattle-medicines and the like – the heavy oaken chairs – the settle beside the fire, with its hard cushions and scrolled back. It was a room for winter, fashioned by the needs of winter. By the help of that great peat fire, built up year by year from the spoils of the moss a thousand feet below, generations of human beings had fought with snow and storm, had maintained their little polity there on the heights, self-centred, self-supplied. Across the yard, commanded by the window of the farm-kitchen, lay the rude byres where the cattle were prisoned from October to April. The cattle made the wealth of the farm, and there must be many weeks when the animals and their masters were shut in together from the world outside by wastes of snow.

Laura shut her eyes an instant, imagining the goings to and fro – the rising on winter dawns to feed the stock – the shepherd on the fell side, wrestling with sleet and tempest – the returns at night to food and fire. Her young fancy, already played on by the breath of the mountains, warmed to the farmhouse and its primitive life. Here surely was something more human – more poetic even – than the tattered splendour of Bannisdale.

She opened her eyes wide again, as though in defiance – and saw Hubert Mason looking at her.

Instinctively she sat up straight, and drew her foot primly under the shelter of her dress.

'I was thinking of what it must be in winter,' she said hurriedly. 'I know I should like it.'

'What, this place?' He gave a rough laugh. 'I don't see what for, then. It's bad enough in summer. In winter it's fit to make you cut your throat. I say, where are you staying?'

'Why, at Bannisdale!' said Laura in surprise. 'You knew my stepmother was still living, didn't you?'

'Well, I didn't think aught about it,' he said, falling into candour, because the beauty of her grey eyes, now that they were fixed fair and full upon him, startled him out of his presence of mind.

'I wrote to you – to Cousin Elizabeth – when my father died,' she said simply, rather proudly, and the eyes were removed from him.

'Aye – of course you did,' he said in haste. 'But mother's never yan to talk aboot letters. And you haven't dropped us a line since, have you?' he added, almost with timidity.

'No. I thought I'd surprise you. We've been a fortnight at Bannisdale.'

His face flushed and darkened.

'Then you've been a fortnight in a queer place!' he said with a sudden, almost a violent change of tone. 'I wonder you can bide so long under that man's roof!'

She stared.

'Do you mean because he disliked my father?'

'Oh, I don't know nowt about that!' He paused. His young face was crimson, his eyes angry and sinister. 'He's a *snake* – is Helbeck!' he said slowly, striking his hands together as they hung over his knees.

Laura recoiled – instinctively straightening herself.

'Mr Helbeck is quite kind to me,' she said sharply. 'I don't know why you speak of him like that. I'm staying there till my stepmother gets strong.'

He stared at her, still red and obstinate.

'Helbeck an his house together stick in folk's gizzards aboot here,' he said. 'Yo'll soon find that oot. And good reason too. Did you ever hear of Teddy Williams?'

'Williams?' she said, frowning. 'Was that the man that painted the chapel?'

Mason laughed and slapped his knee.

'Man, indeed? He was just a lad – down at Marsland School. I was there myself, you understand, the year after him. He was an awful clever lad – beat every one at books – an he could draw anything. You couldn't mak much oot of his drawins, I daur say – they were queer sorts o' things. I never could make head or tail on 'em myself. But old Jackson, our master, thowt a lot of 'em, and so did the passon down at Marsland. An his father an mother – well, they thowt he was going to make all their fortunes for 'em. There was a scholarship – or soomthin o' that sort – and he was to get it an go to college, an make 'em all rich. They were just common wheelwrights, you understand – down on t' Whinthorpe road. But my word, Mr Helbeck spoilt their game for 'em!'

He lifted another sod of turf from the basket and flung it on the fire. The animus of his tone and manner struck Laura oddly. But she was at least as curious to hear as he was anxious to tell. She drew her chair a little nearer to him.

'What did Mr Helbeck do?'

Mason laughed.

'Well, he just made a Papist of Teddy – took him an done him – brown. He got hold on him in the park one evening – Teddy was drawing a picture of the bridge, you understand – 'ticed him up to his place soomhow – an Teddy was set to a job of paintin up at the chapel before you could say Jack Robinson. An in six months they'd settled it between 'em. Teddy wouldn't go to school no more. And one night he and his father had words – the owd man gie'd him a thrashing – and Teddy just cut and run. Next thing they heard he was at a Papist school, somewhere over Lancashire way, an he sent word to his mother – she was dyin then, you understan – and she's dead since – that he'd gone to be a priest, and if they didn't like it, they might just do the other thing!'

'And the mother died?' said Laura.

'Aye – double quick! My mother went down to nurse her. And they sent Teddy back, just too late to see her. He came in two-three hours after they'd screwed her down. An his father chivvyed him oot – they wouldn't have him at the funeral. But folks were a deal madder with Mr Helbeck, you understan, nor with Teddy. Teddy's father and brothers are chapel folk – Primitive Methodists they call 'em. They've got a big chapel in Whinthorpe – an they raised the whole place on Mr Helbeck, and one night, coming out of Whinthorpe, he was set on by a lot of fellows, chapel fellows, a bit fresh, you understan. Father was there – he never denied it – not he! – Helbeck just got into the old mill by the bridge in time, but they'd marked his face for him all the same.'

'Ah!' said Laura, staring into the fire. She had just remembered a dark scar on Mr Helbeck's forehead, under the strong ripples of black hair. 'Go on – do!'

'Oh, afterwards there was a lot of men bound over – father among 'em. There was a priest with Mr Helbeck who got it hot too – that old chap Bowles – I dare say you've seen him. Aye, he's a *snake*, is Helbeck!' the young man repeated. Then he reddened still more deeply and added with vindictive emphasis – 'and an interfering, – hypocritical, – canting sort of party into t' bargain. He'd like to lord it over everybody aboot here, if he was let. But he's as poor as a church rat – who minds him?'

The language was extraordinary – so was the tone. Laura had been gazing at the speaker in a growing amazement.

'Thank you!' she said impetuously, when Mason stopped. 'Thank you! – but, in spite of your story, I don't think you ought to speak like that of the gentleman I am staying with!'

Mason threw himself back in his chair. He was evidently trying to control himself.

'I didn't mean no offence,' he said at last, with a return of the sulky voice. 'Of course I understand that you're staying with the quality, and not with the likes of us.'

Laura's face lit up with laughter. 'What an extraordinary silly thing to say! But I don't mind – I'll forgive you – like I did years ago, when you pushed me into the puddle!'

'I pushed you into a puddle? But – I never did owt o' t' sort!' cried Mason, in a slow crescendo of astonishment.

'Oh yes, you did,' she nodded her little head. 'I broke an egg, and you bullied me. Of course I thought you were a horrid boy – and I loved Polly, who cleaned my shoes and put me straight. Where's Polly, is she at church?'

'Aye – I dare say,' said Mason stupidly, watching his visitor meanwhile with all his eyes. She had just put up a small hand and taken off her cap. Now, mechanically, she began to pat and arrange the little curls upon her forehead, then to take out and replace a hairpin or two, so as to fasten the golden mass behind a little more securely. The white fingers moved with an exquisite sureness and daintiness, the lifted arms showed all the young curves of the girl's form.

Suddenly Laura turned to him again. Her eyes had been staring dreamily into the fire, while her hands had been busy with her hair.

'So you don't remember our visit at all? You don't remember papa?'

He shook his head.

'Ah! well' – she sighed. Mason felt unaccountably guilty.

'I was always terr'ble bad at remembering,' he said hastily.

'But you ought to have remembered papa.' Then, in quite a different voice, 'Is this your sitting-room' – she looked round it – 'or – or your kitchen?'

The last words fell rather timidly, lest she might have hurt his feelings.

Mason jumped up.

'Why, yon's the parlour,' he said. 'I should ha' taken you there fust thing. Will you coom? I'll soon make a fire.'

And walking across the kitchen, he threw open a further door ceremoniously. Laura followed, pausing just inside the threshold to look round the little musty sitting-room, with its framed photographs, its woollen mats, its rocking-chairs, and its square of mustard-coloured carpet. Mason watched her furtively all the time, to see how the place struck her.

'Oh, this isn't as nice as the kitchen,' she said decidedly. 'What's that?' she pointed to a pewter cup standing stately and alone upon the largest possible wool mat in the centre of a table.

Mason threw back his head and chuckled. His great chest seemed to fill out; all his sulky constraint dropped away.

'Of course you doan't know anythin' about these parts,' he said to her with condescension. 'You don't know as I came near bein' champion for the County lasst year – no, I'll reckon you don't. Oh! thet cup's nowt – thet's nobbut Whinthorpe sports, lasst December. Maybe there'll be a better there, by-and-by.'

The young giant grinned, as he took up the cup and pointed with assumed indifference to its inscription.

'What – football?' said Laura, putting up her hand to hide a yawn. 'Oh! I don't care about football. But I *love* cricket. Why – you've got a piano – and a new one!'

Mason's face cleared again – in quite another fashion.

'Do you know the maker?' he said eagerly. 'I believe he's thowt a deal of by them as knows. I bought it myself out o' the sheep. The lambs had done fust-rate, – an I'd had more'n half the trooble of 'em, ony ways. So I took no heed o' mother. I went down straight to Whinthrupp, an paid the first instalment an browt it up in the cart mesel'. Mr Castle – do yo knaw 'im? – he's the organist at the parish church – he came with me to choose it.'

'And is it you that play it,' said Laura wondering, 'or your sister?'

He looked at her in silence for a moment – and she at him. His aspect seemed to change under her eyes. The handsome points of the face came out; its coarseness and loutishness receded. And his manner became suddenly quiet and manly – though full of an almost tremulous eagerness.

'You like it?' she asked him.

'What – music? I should think so!'

'Oh! I forgot – you're all musical in these northern parts, aren't you?'

He made no answer, but sat down to the piano and opened it. She leant over the back of a chair, watching him, half incredulous, half amused.

'I say – did you ever hear this? I believe it was some Cambridge fellow made it – Castle said so. He played it to me. And I can't get further than just a bit of it.'

He raised his great hands and brought them down in a burst of chords that shook the little room and the raftered ceiling. Laura stared. He played on – played like a musician, though with occasional stumbling – played with a mingled energy and delicacy, an understanding and abandonment that amazed her – then grew crimson with the effort to remember – wavered – and stopped.

'Goodness!' – cried Laura. 'Why, that's Stanford's music to the Eumenides! How on earth did you hear that? Go away. I can play it.'

She pushed him away and sat down. He hung over her, his face smiling and transformed, while her little hands struggled with the chords, found the after melody, pursued it, – with pauses now and then, in which he would strike in, prompting her, putting his hand down with hers – and finally, after modulations which she made her way through, with laughter and head-shakings, she fell into a weird dance, to which he beat time with hands and limbs, urging her with a rain of comments.

'Oh! my goody – isn't that rousing? Play that again – just that change – just once! Oh! Lord – isn't that good, that chord – and that bit afterwards – what a bass! – I say, *isn't* it a bass! Don't you like it – don't you like it *awfully*?'

Suddenly she wheeled round from the piano, and sat fronting him, her hands on her knees. He fell back into a chair.

'I say' – he said slowly – 'you are a grand 'un! If I'd only known you could play like that!'

Her laugh died away. To his amazement she began to frown.

'I haven't played – ten notes – since papa died. He liked it so.'

She turned her back to him, and began to look at the torn music at the top of the piano.

'But you will play – you'll play to me again' – he said,

beseechingly. 'Why it would be a sin if you didn't play! Wouldn't I play if I could play like you! I never had more than a lesson, now and again, from old Castle. I used to steal mother's eggs to pay him – I can play anything I hear – and I've made a song – old Castle's writing it down – he says he'll teach me to do it some day. But of course I'm no good for playing – I never shall be any good. Look at those fingers – they're like bits of stick – beastly things!'

He thrust them out indignantly for her inspection. Laura looked at them with a professional air.

'I don't call it a bad hand. I expect you've no patience.'

'Haven't I! I tell you I'd play all day, if it 'ld do any good – but it won't.'

'And how about the poor farm?' said Laura, with a lifted brow.

'Oh! the farm – the farm – dang the farm!' – said Mason, violently, slapping his knee.

Suddenly there was a sound of voices outside, a clattering on the stones of the farmyard.

Mason sprang up, all frowns.

'That's mother. Here, let's shut the piano – quick! She can't abide it.'

CHAPTER FIVE

Mason went out to meet his mother, and Laura waited. She stood where she had risen, beside the piano, looking nervously towards the door. Childish remembrances and alarms seemed to be thronging back into her mind.

There was a noise of voices in the outer room. Then a handle was roughly turned, and Laura saw before her a short stout woman, with grey hair, and the most piercing black eyes. Intimidated by the eyes, and by the sudden pause of the newcomer on the threshold, Miss Fountain could only look at her interrogatively.

'Is it Cousin Elizabeth?' she said, holding out a wavering hand.

Mrs Mason scarcely allowed her own to be touched.

'We're not used to visitors i' church-time,' she said abruptly, in a deep funeral voice. 'Mappen you'll sit down.'

And still holding the girl with her eyes, she walked across to an old rocking-chair, let herself fall into it, and with a loud sigh loosened her bonnet strings.

Laura, in her amazement, had to strangle a violent inclination to laugh. Then she flushed brightly, and sat down on the wooden stool in front of the piano. Mrs Mason, still staring at her, seemed to wait for her to speak. But Laura would say nothing.

'Soa – thoo art Stephen Fountain's dowter – art tha?'

'Yes – and you have seen me before,' was the girl's quiet reply.

She said to herself that her cousin had the eyes of a bird of prey. So black and fierce they were, in the greyish white face under the shaggy hair. But she was not afraid. Rather she felt her own temper rising.

'How long is 't sen your feyther deed?'

'Nine months. But you knew that, I think – because I wrote it you.'

Mrs Mason's heavy lids blinked a moment, then she said with slowly quickening emphasis, like one mounting to a crisis –

'Wat art tha doin' wi Bannisdale Hall? What call has thy feyther's dowter to be visitin onder Alan Helbeck's roof?'

Laura's open mouth showed first wonderment, then laughter.

'Oh! I see,' she said impatiently – 'you don't seem to understand.

But of course you remember that my father married Miss Helbeck for his second wife?'

'Aye, and she cam oot fra amang them' – exclaimed Mrs Mason – 'she put away from her the accursed thing!'

The massive face was all aglow, transformed, with a kind of sombre fire. Laura stared afresh.

'She gave up being a Catholic, if that's what you mean' – she said, after a moment's pause. 'But she couldn't keep to it. When papa fell ill and she was unhappy, she went back. And then of course she made it up with her brother.'

The triumph in Mrs Mason's face yielded first to astonishment, then to anger.

'The poor weak doited thing' – she said at last in a tone of indescribable contempt – 'The poor silly fule! But naebody need ha' luked for onything betther from a Helbeck. – And I daur say' – she lifted her voice fiercely – 'I daur say she took yo' wi' her, an it's along o' thattens as yo're coom to spy on us oop here?'

Laura sprang up.

'Me!' she said indignantly. 'You think I'm a Catholic and a spy? How kind of you! But of course you don't know anything about my father, nor how he brought me up. As for my poor little stepmother, I came here with her to get her well, and I shall stay with her till she is well. I really don't know why you talk to me like this. I suppose you have cause to dislike Mr Helbeck, but it is very odd that you should visit it on me, papa's daughter, when I come to see you!'

The girl's voice trembled, but she threw back her slender neck with a gesture that became her. The door, which had been closed, stealthily opened. Hubert Mason's face appeared in the doorway. It was gazing eagerly – admiringly – at Miss Fountain.

Mrs Mason did not see him. Nor was she daunted by Laura's anger.

'It's aw yan' – she said, stubbornly. 'Thoo ha' made a covenant wi' the Amorite an' the Amalekite. They ha' called tha, an thoo art eatin o' their sacrifices!'

There was an uneasy laugh from the door, and Laura, turning her astonished eyes in that direction, perceived Hubert standing in the doorway, and behind him another head thrust eagerly forward – the head of a young woman in a much betrimmed Sunday hat.

'I say, mother, let her be, wil tha?' said a hearty voice; and, pushing Hubert aside, the owner of the hat entered the room. She went up to Laura, and gave her a loud kiss.

'I'm Polly – Polly Mason. An I know who you are weel enough. Doan't you pay ony attention to mother. That's her way. Hubert an I take it very kind of you to come and see us.'

'Mother's rats on Amorites!' said Hubert, grinning.

'Rats? – Amorites?' – said Laura, looking piteously at Polly, whose hand she held.

Polly laughed, a bouncing good-humoured laugh. She herself was a bouncing good-humoured person, the apparent antithesis of her mother with her lively eyes, her frizzled hair, her high cheek-bones touched with a bright pink.

'Yo'll have to get oop early to understan them two,' she declared. 'Mother's allus talkin out o' t' Bible, an Hubert picks up a lot o' low words out o' Whinthrupp streets – an there 'tis. But now look here – yo'll stay an tak a bit o' dinner with us?'

'I don't want to be in your way,' said Laura formally. Really, she had some difficulty to control the quiver of her lips, though it would have been difficult to say whether laughter or tears came nearest.

At this Polly broke out in voluble protestations, investigating her cousin's dress all the time, fingering her little watch-chain, and even taking up a corner of the pretty cloth jacket that she might examine the quality of it. Laura, however, looked at Mrs Mason –

'If Cousin Elizabeth wishes me to stay,' she said proudly.

Polly burst into another loud laugh.

'Yo see, it goes agen mother to be shakin hands wi' yan that's livin wi' Papists – and Misther Helbeck by the bargain. So wheniver mother talks aboot Amorites or Jebusites, or any o' thattens, she nobbut means Papist – Romanists as our minister coes 'em. He's every bit as bad as her. He would as lief shake hands wi' Mr Helbeck as wi' the owd 'un!'

'I'll uphowd ye – Mr Bayley hasn't preached a sermon this ten year wi'oot chivvyin Papists!' said Hubert from the door. 'An yo'll not find yan o' them in his parish if yo were to hunt it wi' a lantern for a week o' Sundays. When I was a lad I thowt Romanists were a soart o' varmin. I awmost looked to see 'em nailed to t' barndoor, same as stöats!'

'But how strange!' cried Laura – 'when there are so few Catholics about here. And no one *hates* Catholics now. One may just – despise them.'

She looked from mother to son in bewilderment. Not only Hubert's speech, but his whole manner had broadened and coarsened since his mother's arrival.

'Well, if there isn't mony, they make a deal o' talk,' said Polly – 'onyways sence Mr Helbeck came to t' Hall. – Mother, I'll take Miss Fountain oopstairs, to get her hat off.'

During all the banter of her son and daughter Mrs Mason had sat in a disdainful silence, turning her strange eyes – the eyes of a fanatic, in a singularly shrewd and capable face – now on Laura, now on her children. Laura looked at her again, irresolute whether to go or stay. Then an impulse seized her which astonished herself. For it was an impulse of liking, an impulse of kinship; and as she quickly crossed the room to Mrs Mason's side, she said in a pretty pleading voice –

'But you see, Cousin Elizabeth, I'm not a Catholic – and papa wasn't a Catholic. And I couldn't help Mrs Fountain's going back to her old religion – you shouldn't visit it on me!'

Mrs Mason looked up.

'Why art tha not at church on t' Lord's day?'

The answer came stern and quick.

Laura wavered, then drew herself up.

'Because I'm not your sort either. I don't believe in your church, or your ministers. Father didn't, and I'm like him.'

Her voice had grown thick, and she was quite pale. The old woman stared at her.

'Then yo're nobbut yan o' the heathen!' – she said with slow precision.

'I dare say!' cried Laura, half laughing, half crying – 'That's my affair. But I declare I think I hate Catholics as much as you – there, Cousin Elizabeth! I don't hate my stepmother, of course. I promised father to take care of her. But that's another matter.'

'Dost tha hate Alan Helbeck?' said Mrs Mason suddenly, her black eyes opening in a flash.

The girl hesitated, caught her breath – then was seized with the strangest, most abject desire to propitiate this grim woman with the passionate look.

'Yes!' she said wildly. 'No, no! – that's silly. I haven't had time to hate him. But I don't like him, any way. I'm nearly sure I *shall* hate him!'

There was no mistaking the truth in her tone.

Mrs Mason slowly rose. Her chest heaved with one long breath, then subsided; her brow tightened. She turned to her son.

'Art tha goin to let Daffady do all thy work for tha?' she said sharply. 'Has t' roan calf bin looked to?'

'Aye – I'm going,' said Hubert evasively, and sheepishly straightening himself he made for the front door, throwing back more than one look as he departed at his new cousin.

'And you really want me to stay?' – repeated Laura insistently, addressing Mrs Mason.

'Yo're welcome,' was the stiff reply. 'Nobbut yo'd been mair welcome if yo hadna brokken t' Sabbath to coom here. Mappen yo'll goa wi' Polly, an tak your bonnet off.'

Laura hesitated a moment longer, bit her lip, and went.

Polly Mason was a great talker. In the few minutes she spent with Laura upstairs, before she hurried down again to help her mother with the Sunday dinner, she asked her new cousin innumerable questions, showing an intense curiosity as to Bannisdale and the Helbecks, a burning desire to know whether Laura had any money of her own, or was still dependent upon her stepmother, and a joyous, appropriative pride in Miss Fountain's gentility and good looks.

The frankness of Polly's flatteries, and the exuberance of her whole personality, ended by producing a certain stiffness in Laura. Every now and then, in the intervals of Polly's questions, when she ceased to be inquisitive and became confidential, Laura would wonder to herself. She would half shut her eyes, trying to recall the mental image of her cousins and of the farm, with which she had started that morning from Bannisdale; or she would think of her father, his modes of life and speech – was he really connected, and how, with this place and its inmates? She had expected something simple and patriarchal. She had found a family of peasants, living in a struggling, penurious way – a grim mother speaking broad dialect, a son with no pretensions to refinement or education, except perhaps through his music – and a daughter –

Laura turned an attentive eye on Polly – on her high and red cheek-bones, the extravagant fringe that vulgarised all her honest face, the Sunday dress of stone-coloured alpaca, profusely trimmed with magenta ribbons.

'I will – I *will* like her!' she said to herself – 'I am a horrid, snobbish, fastidious little wretch.'

But her spirits had sunk. When Polly left her she leant for a moment upon the sill of the open window, and looked out. Across the dirty, uneven yard, where the manure lay in heaps outside the byre doors, she saw the rude farm buildings huddled against each other in a mean, unsightly group. Down below, from the houseporch apparently, a cracked bell began to ring, and from some doors opposite three labourers, the 'hired men,' who lived and boarded on the farm, came out. The first two were elderly men, gnarled and bent like tough trees that have fought the winter; the third was a youth. They were tidily dressed in Sunday clothes, for their work was done, and they were ready for the afternoon's holiday.

They walked across to the farmhouse in silence, one behind the other. Not even the young fellow raised his eyes to the window and the girl framed within it. Behind them came a gust of piercing easterly wind. A cloud had covered the sun. The squalid farmyard, the bare fell-side beyond it, the distant levels of the marsh, had taken to themselves a cold forbidding air. Laura again imagined it in December – a waste of snow, with the farm making an ugly spot upon the white, and the little black-bearded sheep she could see feeding on the fell, crowding under the rocks for shelter. But this time she shivered. All the spell was broken. To live up here with this madwoman, this strange youth – and Polly! Yet it seemed to her that something drew her to Cousin Elizabeth – if she were not so mad. How strange to find this abhorrence of Mr Helbeck among these people – so different, so remote! She remembered her own words – 'I am sure I *shall* hate him!' – not without a stab of conscience. What had she been doing – perhaps – but adding her own injustice to theirs?

She stood lost in a young puzzle and heat of feeling – half angry, half repentant.

But only for a second. Then certain phrases of Augustina's rang through her mind – she saw herself standing in the corner of the chapel while the others prayed. Every pulse tightened – her whole nature leapt again in defiance. She seemed to be holding something at bay – a tyrannous power that threatened humiliation and hypocrisy, that seemed at the same time to be prying into secret things – things it should never, never know – and never rule!

Yes, she did understand Cousin Elizabeth – she *did!*

The dinner went sadly. The viands were heavy: so were the faces of the labourers, and the air of the low-raftered kitchen, heated as it was by a huge fire, and pervaded by the smell from the farmyard. Laura felt it all very strange, the presence of the farm-servants at the same table with the Masons and herself – the long silences that no one made an effort to break – the relations between Hubert and his mother.

As for the labourers, Mason addressed them now and then in a bullying voice, and they spoke to him as little as they could. It seemed to Laura that there was an alliance between them and the mother against a lazy and incompetent master; and that the lad's vanity was perpetually alive to it. Again and again he would pull himself together, attempt the gentleman, and devote himself to his young lady guest. But in the midst of their conversation he would hear something at the other end of the table, and suddenly there would come a burst of fierce unintelligible speech between him and the mistress of the house, while the labourers sat silent and sly, and Polly's loud laugh would break in, trying to make peace.

Laura's cool grey eyes followed the youth with a constant critical wonder. In any other circumstances she would not have thought him worth an instant's attention. She had all the supercilious impatience of the pretty girl accustomed to choose her company. But this odd fact of kinship held and harassed her. She wanted to understand these Masons – her father's folk.

'Now he is really talking quite nicely,' she said to herself on one occasion, when Hubert had found in the gifts and accomplishments of his friend Castle, the organist, a subject that untied his tongue and made him almost agreeable. Suddenly a question caught his ear.

'Daffady, did tha turn the coo?' said his mother in a loud voice. Even in the homeliest question, it had the same penetrating, passionate quality that belonged to her gaze – to her whole personality indeed.

Hubert dropped his phrase – and his knife and fork – and stared angrily at Daffady, the old cowman and carter.

Daffady threw his master a furtive look, then munched through a mouthful of bread and cheese without replying.

He was a grey and taciturn person, with a provocative look of patience.

'What tha bin doin wi' th' coo?' said Hubert sharply. 'I left l mysel nobbut half an hour sen.'

Daffady turned his head again in Hubert's direction for a moment, then deliberately addressed the mistress –

'Aye, aye, missus' – he spoke in a high small voice – 'A turned her reet enoof, an a gied her soom fresh straa for her yed. She doin verra middlin.'

'If she'd been turned yesterday in a proper fashion, she'd ha' bin on her feet by now,' said Mrs Mason with a glance at her son.

'Nowt o' t' soart, mother,' cried Hubert. He leant forward, flushed with wrath, or beer – his potations had begun to fill Laura with dismay – and spoke with a hectoring violence. 'I tell tha when t' farrier cam oop last night, he said she'd been managed first-rate! If yo an Daffady had yor way wi' yor fallals an yor non-sense, yo'd never leave a poor sick creetur alone for five minutes – I towd Daffady to let her be, an I'll let him knaa who's mëaster here!'

He glared at the carter, quite regardless of Laura's presence. Polly coughed loudly and tried to make a diversion by getting up to clear away the plates. The three combatants took no notice.

Daffady slowly ran his tongue round his lips; then he said, again looking at the mistress –

'If a hadna turned her I dew believe she'd ha' gien oos t' slip – she was terr'ble swollen as 'twos.'

'I tell tha to let her be!' thundered Hubert. 'If she deas, that's ma consarn – I'll ha' noa meddlin wi' my orders – dost tha hear?'

'Aye, it wor thirrty poond thraan awa lasst month, an it'll be thirrty poond this' – said his mother slowly – 'thoo art fine at shoutin. Bit thy fadther had need ha' addlet his brass – to gie thee summat to thraw oot o' winder.'

Hubert rose from the table with an oath, – stood for an instant looking down at Laura – glowering and pulling fiercely at his moustache – then, noisily opening the front door, he strode across the yard to the byres.

There was an instant's silence. Then Mrs Mason rose with her hands clasped before her, her eyes half closed.

'___ ___at we ha' received the Lord mak us truly thankful' – she
___ ___ voice – 'Amen.'

___ ___ut on an apron of Polly's, and helped her
___ Mrs Mason had gruffly bade her sit still, but
she herself – flushed with dinner and combat

– took her seat on the settle, opposite to old Daffady, and deliberately made holiday – watching Stephen's daughter all the time from the black eyes that roved and shone so strangely under the shaggy brows and the white hair.

The old cowman sat hunched over the fire, smoking his pipe for a time in beatific silence.

But presently Laura, as she went to and fro, caught snatches of conversation.

'Did tha go ta Laysgill last Sunday?' said Mrs Mason abruptly. Daffady removed his pipe.

'Aye – a went – an a preeched. It wor a varra stirrin meetin. Sum o' yor paid preests sud ha bin theer. A gien it 'em strang. A tried ta hit 'em all – baith gert an lile.'

There was a pause, then he added, placidly –

'A likely suden't suit them varra weel. Theer was a mon beside me, as pooed me down afoor a'd hofe doon.'

'Tha sudna taak o' "paid preests," Daffady,' said Mrs Mason severely. 'Tha doosna understand nowt o' thattens.'

Daffady glanced slyly at his mistress – at the 'Church-pride' implied in the attitude of her capacious form, in the shining of the Sunday alpaca and black silk apron.

'Mebbe not,' he said mildly, 'mebbe not.' And he resumed his pipe.

On another occasion, as Laura went flitting across the kitchen, drawing to herself the looks of both its inmates, she heard what seemed to be a fragment of talk about a funeral.

'Aye – poor Jenny!' said Mrs Mason. 'They didna mak' mich account on her whan t' breath wor yanst oot on her.'

'Nay –' Daffady shook his head for sympathy – 'It wor a varra poor set-oot, wor Jenny's buryin. Nowt but tay, an sic-like.'

Mrs Mason raised two gaunt hands and let them drop again on her knee.

'I shud ha' thowt they'd ha' bin ashamed,' she said. 'Jenny's brass ull do 'em noa gude. She wor a fule to leave it to un.'

Daffady withdrew his pipe again. His lantern-jawed face, furrowed with slow thought, hung over the blaze.

'Aye –' he said – 'aye. Wal, I've buried three childer – an I'm nobbut a labrin mon – but a thank the Lord I ha buried them aw – wi' ham.'

The last words came out with solemnity. Laura, at the other end of the kitchen, turned open-mouthed to look at the pair. Not a feature moved in either face. She sped back into the dairy, and Polly looked up in astonishment.

'What ails tha?' she said.

'Oh, nothing!' said Laura, dashing the merry tears from her eyes. She proceeded to roll up her sleeves, and plunge her hands and arms into the bowl of warm water that Polly had set before her. Meanwhile, Polly, very big and square, much reddened also by the fuss of household work, stood just behind her cousin's shoulder, looking down, half in envy, half in admiration, at the slimness of the white wrists and pretty fingers.

A little later the two girls, all traces of their housework removed, came back into the kitchen. Daffady and Mrs Mason had disappeared.

'Where is Cousin Elizabeth?' said Laura rather sharply, as she looked round her.

Polly explained that her mother was probably shut up in her bedroom reading her Bible. That was her custom on a Sunday afternoon.

'Why, I haven't spoken to her at all!' cried Laura. Her cheek had flushed.

Polly showed embarrassment.

'Next time yo coom, mother'll tak mair noatice. She was takkin stock o' you t' whole time, I'll uphowd yo.'

'That isn't what I wanted,' said Laura.

She walked to the window and leaned her head against the frame. Polly watched her with compunction, seeing quite plainly the sudden drop of the lip. All she could do was to propose to show her cousin the house.

Laura languidly consented.

So they wandered again through the dark stone-slabbed dairy, with its milk pans on the one side and its bacon-curing troughs on the other; and into the little stuffy bedrooms upstairs, each with its small oak fourposter and patchwork counterpane. They looked at the home-made quilt of goosedown – Polly's handiwork – that lay on Hubert's bed; at the clusters of faded photographs and coloured prints that hung on the old uneven walls; at the vast meal-ark in Polly's room that held the family store of meal and oatcake for the year.

'When we wor little uns, fadther used to give me an Hubert a

silver saxpence the day he browt home t' fresh melder fro' t' mill' –
said Polly – 'theer was parlish little nobbut paritch an oatcake to
eat when we wor small. An now I'll uphold yo there isn't a farm
servant but wants his white bread yanst a day whativver happens.'

The house was neat and clean, but there were few comforts in it,
and no luxuries. It showed, too, a number of small dilapidations
that a very little money and care would soon have set to rights.
Polly pointed to them sadly. There was no money, and Hubert
didn't trouble himself. 'Fadther was allus workin. He'd be up at
half-past four this time o' year, an he didna go to bed soa early
noather. But Hubert 'ull do nowt he can help. Yo can hardly get
him to tak t' peäts i' ter Whinthorpe when t' peät-cote's brastin wi'
em. An' as fer doin a job o' cartin fer t' neebors, t' horses may be
eatin their heads off, Hubert woan't stir hissel. "Let 'em lead their
aan muck for theirsels" – that's what he'll say. Iver sen fadther
deed it's bin janglin atwixt mother an Hubert. It makes her mad to
see iverything goin downhill. An he's that masterful he woan't be
towd. Yo saw how he went on wi' Daffady at dinner. But if it
weren't for Daffady an us, there'd be no stock left.'

And poor Polly, sitting on the edge of the meal-ark and dangling
her large feet, went into a number of plaintive details, that were
mostly unintelligible, sometimes repulsive, in Laura's ears.

It seemed that Hubert was always threatening to leave the farm.
'Give me a bit of money, and you'll soon be quit of me. I'll go to
Froswick, and make my fortune' – that was what he'd say to his
mother. But who was going to give him money to throw about?
And he couldn't sell the farm while Mrs Mason lived, by the
father's will.

As to her mother, Polly admitted that she was 'gey ill to live
wi'.' There was no one like her for 'addlin a bit here and addlin a
bit there.' She was the best maker and seller of butter in the countryside; but she had been queer about religion ever since an illness
that attacked her as a young woman.

And now it was Mr Bayley, the minister, who excited her, and
made her worse. Polly, for her part, hated him. 'My worrd, he do
taak!' said she. And every Sunday he preached against Catholics,
and the Pope, and such like. And as there were no Catholics any-
where near but Mr Helbeck at Bannisdale, and a certain number
at Whinthorpe, people didn't know what to make of him. And they
laughed at him, and left off going – except occasionally for curiosity,

because he preached in a black gown, which, so Polly heard tell, was very uncommon nowadays. But mother would listen to him by the hour. And it was all along of Teddy Williams. It was that had set her mad.

Here, however, Polly broke off to ask an eager question. What had Mr Helbeck said when Laura told him of her wish to go and see her cousins?

'I'll warrant he wasn't best pleased! Feyther couldn't abide him – because of Teddy. He didn't thraw no stones that neet i' Whinthrupp Lane – feyther was a strict man an read his Bible reg'lar – but he stood wi' t' lads and looked on – he didn't say owt to stop 'em. Mr Helbeck called to him – he had a priest with him – "Mr Mason!" he ses, "this is an old man – speak to those fellows!" But feyther wouldn't. "Let 'em trounce tha!" he ses – "aye, an him too! It'ull do tha noa harm." – Well, an what did he say, Mr Helbeck? – I'd like to know.'

'Say? Nothing – except that it was a long way, and I might have the pony carriage.'

Laura's tone was rather dry. She was sitting on the edge of Polly's bed, with her arm round one of its oaken posts. Her cheek was laid against the post, and her eyes had been wandering about a good deal while Polly talked. Till the mention of Helbeck. Then her attention came back. And during Polly's account of the incident in Whinthorpe Lane she began to frown. What bigotry, after all! As to the story of young Williams – it was very perplexing – she would get the truth of it out of Augustina. But it was extraordinary that it should be so well known in this upland farm – that it should make a kind of link – a link of hatred – between Mr Helbeck and the Masons. After her movement of wild sympathy with Mrs Mason, she realised now, as Polly's chatter slipped on, that she understood her cousins almost as little as she did Helbeck.

Nay, more. The picture of Helbeck stoned and abused by these rough, uneducated folk had begun to rouse in her a curious sympathy. Unwillingly her mind invested him with a new dignity.

So that when Polly told a rambling story of how Mr Bayley, after the street fight, had met Mr Helbeck at a workhouse meeting and had placed his hands behind his back when Mr Helbeck offered his own, Laura tossed her head.

'What a ridiculous man!' she said disdainfully – 'what can it matter to Mr Helbeck whether Mr Bayley shakes hands with him or not?'

Polly looked at her in some astonishment, and dropped the subject. The elder woman, conscious of plainness and inferiority, was humbly anxious to please her new cousin. The girl's delicate and characteristic physique, her clear eyes and decided ways, and a certain look she had in conversation – half absent, half critical – which was inherited from her father, – all of them combined to intimidate the homely Polly, and she felt perhaps less at ease with her visitor as she saw more of her.

Presently they stood before some old photographs on Polly's mantelpiece; Polly looked timidly at her cousin.

'Doan't yo think as Hubert's varra handsome?' she said.

And taking up one of the portraits, she brushed it with her sleeve and handed it to Laura.

Laura held it up for scrutiny.

'No – o,' she said coolly – 'not really handsome.'

Polly looked disappointed.

'There's not a many gells aboot here as doan't coe Hubert handsome,' she said with emphasis.

'It's Hubert's business to call the girls handsome,' said Laura, laughing, and handing back the picture.

Polly grinned – then suddenly looked grave.

'I wish he'd leave t' gells alone!' she said with an accent of some energy – 'he'll mappen get into trooble yan o' these days!'

'They don't keep him in his place, I suppose,' said Laura, flushing, she hardly knew why. She got up and walked across the room to the window. What did she want to know about Hubert and 't'gells'? She hated vulgar and lazy young men! – though they might have a musical gift that, so to speak, did not belong to them.

Nevertheless she turned round again to ask, with some imperiousness –

'Where is your brother? – what is he doing all this time?'

'Sittin alongside the coo, I dare say – lest Daffady should be gettin the credit of her,' said Polly, laughing. 'The poor creetur fell three days sen – summat like a stroke, t' farrier said – an Hubert's bin that jealous o' Daffady iver sen. He's actually poo'ed hissel oot o' bed mornin's to luke after her! – Lord bless us – I mun goa and feed t' calves!'

And hastily throwing an apron over her Sunday gown, Polly clattered down the stairs in a whirlwind.

*

Laura followed her more leisurely, passed through the empty kitchen and opened the front door.

As she stood under the porch, looking out, she put up a small hand to hide a yawn. When she set out that morning she had meant to spend the whole day at the farm. Now it was not yet tea-time, and she was more than ready to go. In truth her heart was hot, and rather bitter. Cousin Elizabeth, certainly, had treated her with a strange coolness. And as for Hubert – after that burst of friendship, beside the piano! – She drew herself together sharply – she would go at once and ask him for her pony-cart.

Lifting her skirt daintily, she picked her way across the dirty yard, and fumbled at a door opposite – the door whence she had seen old Daffady come out at dinnertime.

'Who's there?' shouted a threatening voice from within.

Laura succeeded in lifting the clumsy latch. Hubert Mason, from inside, saw a small golden head appear in the doorway.

'Would you kindly help me get the pony-cart?' said the light, half-sarcastic voice of Miss Fountain. 'I must be going, and Polly's feeding the calves.'

Her eyes at first distinguished nothing but a row of dim animal forms, in crowded stalls under a low roof. Then she saw a cow lying on the ground, and Hubert Mason beside her, amid the wreaths of smoke that he was puffing from a clay pipe. The place was dark, close, and fetid. She withdrew her head hastily. There was a mut-tering and movement inside, and Mason came to the door, thrusting his pipe into his pocket.

'What do you want to go for, just yet?' he said abruptly.

'I ought to get home.'

'No! – you don't care for us, nor our ways. That's it – an I don't wonder.'

She made polite protestations, but he would not listen to them. He strode on beside her in a stormy silence, till the impulse to prick him overmastered her.

'Do you generally sit with the cows?' she asked him sweetly. She shot her grey eyes towards him, all mockery and cool examination. He was not accustomed to such looks from the young women whom he chose to notice.

'I was not going to stay and be treated like that before strangers!' he said, with a sulky fierceness. 'Mother thinks she and Daffady can just have their own way with me, as they'd used to do when I was nobbut a lad. But I'll let her know – aye, and the men too!'

'But if you hate farming, why don't you let Daffady do the work?'

Her sly voice stung him afresh.

'Because I'll be mëaster!' he said, bringing his hand violently down on the shaft of the pony-cart. 'If I'm to stay on in this beastly hole I'll make every one knaw their place. Let mother give me some money – an I'll soon take myself off, an leave her an Daffady to draw their own water their own way. But if I'm here I'm *mëaster!*' – he struck the cart again.

'Is it true you don't work nearly as hard as your father?'

He looked at her – amazed. If Susie Flinders down at the mill had spoken to him like that, he would have known how to shut her mouth for her.

'An I daur say it is!' he said hotly. 'I'm not goin' to lead the dog's life my father did – all for the sake of diddlin another sixpence or two oot o' the neighbours. Let mother give me my money oot o' the farm – I'd go to Froswick fast enough. That's the place to get on. I've got friends – I'd work up in no time.'

Laura glanced at him. She said nothing.

'You doan't think I would?' he asked her angrily, pausing in his handling of the harness to throw back the challenge of her manner. His wrath seemed to have made him handsomer, better-braced, more alive. Physically she admired him for the first time, as he stood confronting her.

But she only lifted her eyebrows a little.

'I thought one had to have a particular kind of brains for business – and begin early, too?'

'I could learn,' he said gruffly, after which they were both silent till the harnessing was done.

Then he looked up.

'I'd like to drive you to the bridge – if you're agreeable?'

'Oh, don't trouble yourself, pray!' she said in polite haste.

His brows knit again.

'I know how 'tis – you won't come here again.'

Her little face changed.

'I'd like to,' she said, her voice wavering, 'because papa used to stay here.'

He stared at her.

'I do remember Cousin Stephen,' he said at last, 'though I towd you I didn't. I can see him standing at the door there – wi' a big hat – an a beard – like straw – an a check coat wi' great bulgin pockets.'

He stopped in amazement, seeing the sudden beauty of her eyes and cheeks.

'That's it,' she said, leaning towards him. 'Oh, that's it!' She closed her eyes a moment, her small lips trembling. Then she opened them with a long breath:

'Yes, you may drive me to the bridge if you like.'

And on the drive she was another being. She talked to him about music, so softly and kindly that the young man's head swam with pleasure. All her own musical enthusiasms and experiences – the music in the college chapels, the music at the Greek plays, the few London concerts and operas she had heard, her teachers and her hero-worships – she drew upon it all in her round light voice, he joining in from time to time with a rough passion and yearning that seemed to transfigure him. In half an hour, as it were, they were friends; their relations changed wholly. He looked at her with all his eyes; hung upon her with all his ears. And she – she forgot that he was vulgar and a clown; such breathless pleasure, such a humble absorption in superior wisdom, would have blunted the sternest standard.

As for him, the minutes flew. When at last the bridge over the Bannisdale River came in sight, he began to check the pony.

'Let's drive on a bit,' he said entreatingly.

'No, no – I must get back to Mrs Fountain.' And she took the reins from his hands.

'I say, when will you come again?'

'Oh, I don't know.' She had put on once more the stand-off town-bred manner that puzzled his countryman's sense.

'I say, mother sha'n't talk that stuff to you next time. I'll tell her –' he said imploringly. – 'Halloa! let me out, will you?'

And to her amazement, before she could draw in the pony, he had jumped out of the cart.

'There's Mr Helbeck!' he said to her with a crimson face. 'I'm off. Good-bye!'

He shook her hand hastily, turned his back, and strode away.

She looked towards the gate in some bewilderment, and saw that Helbeck was holding it open for her. Beside him stood a tall priest –

not Father Bowles. It was evident that both of them had seen her parting from her cousin.

Well, what then? What was there in that, or in Mr Helbeck's ceremonious greeting to make her cheeks hot all in a moment? She could have beaten herself for a silly lack of self-possession. Still more could she have beaten Hubert for his clownish and hurried departure. What was he afraid of? Did he think that she would have shown the smallest shame of her peasant relations?

CHAPTER SIX

'Is that Mrs Fountain's stepdaughter?' said Helbeck's companion, as Laura and her cart disappeared round a corner of the winding road on which the two men were walking.

Helbeck made a sign of assent.

'You may very possibly have known her father?' He named the Cambridge college of which Stephen Fountain had been a Fellow.

The Jesuit, who was a convert, and had been a distinguished Cambridge man, considered for a moment.

'Oh! Yes – I remember the man! A strange being, who was only heard of, if I recollect right, in times of war. If there was any dispute going – especially on a religious point – Stephen Fountain would rush into it with broad-sheets. Oh yes, I remember him perfectly – a great untidy, fair-haired, truculent fellow, to whom anybody that took any thought for his soul was either fool or knave. How much of him does the daughter inherit?'

Helbeck returned the other's smile. 'A large slice, I think. She comes here in the curious position of having never lived in a Christian household before, and she seems already to have great difficulty in putting up with us.'

Father Leadham laughed, then looked reflective.

'How often have I known that the best of all possible beginnings! Is she attached to her stepmother?'

'Yes. But Mrs Fountain has no influence over her.'

'It is a striking colouring – that white skin and reddish hair. And it is a face of some power too.'

'Power?' Helbeck demurred. 'I think she is clever,' he said, dryly. 'And, of course, coming from a university town, she has heard of things that other girls know nothing of. But she has had no training, moral or intellectual.'

'And no Christian education?'

Helbeck shrugged his shoulders.

'She was only baptised with difficulty. When she was eleven or twelve she was allowed to go to church two or three times, I understand, on the helot principle – was soon disgusted – her father of course supplying a running comment at home – and she has stood absolutely outside religion of all kinds since.'

'Poor child!' said the priest with heartiness. The parental note in the words was more than official. He was a widower, and had lost his wife and infant daughter two years before his entrance into the Church of Rome.

Helbeck smiled. 'I assure you Miss Fountain spends none of her pity upon herself!'

'I dare say more than you think. The position of the unbeliever in a house like yours is always a painful one. You see, she is alone. There must be a sense of exile – of something touching and profound going on beside her, from which she is excluded. She comes into a house with a chapel, where the Blessed Sacrament is reserved, where everybody is keeping a strict Lent. She has not a single thought in common with you all. No; I am very sorry for Miss Fountain.'

Helbeck was silent a moment. His dark face showed a shade of disturbance.

'She has some relations near here,' he said at last, 'but unfortunately I can't do much to promote her seeing them. You remember Williams's story?'

'Of course. You had some local row, didn't you? Ah! I remember.'

And the two men walked on, discussing a case which had been and was still of great interest to them as Catholics. The hero, moreover – the Jesuit novice himself – was well known to them both.

'So Miss Fountain's relations belong to that peasant class?' said the Jesuit, musing. 'How curious that she should find herself in such a double relation to you and Bannisdale!'

'Consider me a little, if you please,' said Helbeck, with his slight, rare smile. 'While that young lady is under my roof – you see how attractive she is – I cannot get rid, you will admit, of a certain responsibility. Augustina has neither the will nor the authority of a mother, and there is literally no one else. Now there happens to be a young man in this Mason family –'

'Ah!' said the priest; 'the young gentleman who jumped out at the bridge, with such a very light pair of heels?'

Helbeck nodded. 'The old people were peasants and fanatics. They thought ill of me in the Williams affair, and the mother, who is still alive, would gladly hang and quarter me to-morrow if she could. But that is another point. The old people had their own dignity, their own manners and virtues – or, rather, the manners and virtues of their class. The old man was coarse and boorish, but he was hard-working and honourable, and a Christian after his own sort. But the old man is dead, and the son, who now works the farm jointly with his mother, is of no class and no character. He has just education enough to despise his father and his father's hard work. He talks the dialect with his inferiors, or his kindred, and drops it with you and me. The old traditions have no hold upon him, and he is just a vulgar and rather vicious hybrid who drinks more than is good for him, and has a natural affinity for any sort of low love-affair. I came across him at our last hunt ball. I never go to such things, but last year I went.'

'Good!' ejaculated the Jesuit, turning a friendly face upon the speaker.

Helbeck paused. The word, still more the emphasis with which it was thrown out, challenged him. He was about to defend himself against an implied charge, but thought better of it, and resumed:

'And unfortunately, considering the way in which all the clan felt towards me already, I found this youth in the supper-room, misbehaving himself with a girl of his own sort, and very drunk. I fetched a steward, and he was told to go. After which, you may imagine that it is scarcely agreeable to me to see my guest – a very young lady, very pretty, very distinguished – driving about the country in cousinly relations with this creature!'

The last words were spoken with considerable vivacity. The aristocrat and the ascetic, the man of high family and the man of scrupulous and fastidious character, were alike expressed in them.

The Jesuit pondered a little.

'No; you will have to keep watch. Why not distract her? You must have plenty of other neighbours to show her.'

Helbeck shook his head.

'I live like a hermit. My sister is in the first year of her widowhood and very delicate.'

'I see.' The Jesuit hesitated, then said, smiling, in the tone of one who makes a venture: 'The Bishop and I allowed ourselves to discuss these cloistered ways of yours the other day. We thought you would forgive us as a pair of old friends.'

'I know,' was the somewhat quick interruption, 'the Bishop is of Manning's[4] temper in these things. He believes in acting on and with the Protestant world – in our claiming prominence as citizens.

It was to please him that I joined one or two committees last year –
that I went to the hunt ball –'

Then, suddenly, in a very characteristic way, Helbeck checked
his own flow of speech, and resumed more quietly: 'Well, all
that –'

'Leaves you of the same opinion still?' said the Jesuit, smiling.

'Precisely. I don't belong to my neighbours, nor they to me. We
don't speak the same language, and I can't bring myself to speak
theirs. The old conditions are gone, I know. But my feeling remains
pretty much what that of my forefathers was. I recognise that it is
not common nowadays – but I have the old maxim in my blood:
"Extra ecclesiam nulla salus." '[5]

'There is none which has done us more deadly harm in England,'
cried the Jesuit. 'We forget that England is a baptised nation, and
is therefore in the supernatural state.'

'I remind myself of it very often,' said Helbeck, with a kind of proud
submission; 'and I judge no man. But my powers, my time, are all
limited. I prefer to devote them to the "household of faith." '

The two men walked on in silence for a time. Presently Father
Leadham's face showed amusement, and he said:

'Certainly we modern converts have a better time of it than our
predecessors! The Bishop tells me the most incredible things about
the old feeling towards them in this Vicariate. And wherever I go I
seem to hear the tale of the old priest who thanked God that he had
never received anyone into the Church. Everybody has met some
one who knew that old fellow! He may be a myth – but there is
clearly history at the back of him!'

'I understand him perfectly,' said Helbeck, smiling; and he added
immediately, with a curious intensity, 'I too, have never influenced,
never tried to influence, anyone in my life.'

The priest looked at him, wondering.

'Not Williams?'

'Williams! But Williams was born for the faith. Directly he saw
what I wanted to do in the chapel, he prayed to come and help me.
It was his summer holiday – he neglected no duty; it was wonderful
to see his happiness in the work – as I thought, an artistic happiness
only. He used to ask me questions about the different saints; once or
twice he borrowed a book – it was necessary to get the emblems
correct. But I never said a single controversial word to him. I never
debated religious subjects with him at all, till the night when he

took refuge with me after his father had thrashed him so cruelly that he could not stand. Grace taught him, not I.'

'Grace taught him, but through you,' said the priest with quiet emphasis. 'Perhaps I know more about that than you do.'

Helbeck flushed.

'I think you are mistaken. At any rate, I should prefer that you were mistaken.'

The priest raised his eyebrows.

'A man who holds "no salvation outside the Church," ' he said slowly, 'and rejoices in the thought that he has never influenced anybody?'

'I should hope little from the work achieved by such an instrument. Some men have enough to do with their own souls,' was the low but vehement answer.

The priest threw a wondering glance at his companion, at the signs of feeling – profound and morbid feeling – on the harsh face beside him.

'Perhaps you have never cared enough for anyone outside to wish passionately to bring them within,' he said. 'But if that ever happens to you, you will be ready – I think you will be ready – to use any tool, even yourself.'

The priest's voice changed a little. Helbeck, somewhat startled, recalled the facts of Father Leadham's personal history, and thought he understood. The subject was instantly dropped, and the two men walked on to the house, discussing a great canonisation service at St Peter's, and the Pope's personal part of it.

The old Hall, as Helbeck and Father Leadham approached it, looked down upon a scene of animation to which in these latter days it was but little accustomed. The green spaces and gravelled walks in front of it were sprinkled with groups of children in a blue-and-white uniform. Three or four Sisters of Mercy in their winged white caps moved about among them, and some of the children hung clustered like bees about the Sisters' skirts, while others ran here and there, gleefully picking the scattered daffodils that starred the grass.

The invaders came from the Orphanage of St Ursula, a house founded by Mr Helbeck's exertions, which lay halfway between Bannisdale and Whinthorpe. They had not long arrived, and were now waiting for Rosary and Benediction in the chapel before they were admitted to the tea which Mrs Denton and Augustina had already spread for them in the big hall.

At sight of the children Helbeck's face lit up and his step quickened. They on their side ran to him from all parts; and he had hardly time to greet the Sisters in charge of them, before the eager creatures were pulling him into the walled garden behind the Hall, one small girl hanging on his hand, another perched upon his shoulder. Father Leadham went into the house to prepare for the service.

The garden was old and dark like the Tudor house that stood between it and the sun. Rows of fantastic shapes carved in living yew and box stood ranged along the straight walks. A bowling green enclosed in high beech hedges was placed in the exact centre of the whole formal place, while the walks and alleys from three sides, west, north, and south, converged upon it, according to a plan unaltered since it was first laid down in the days of James II. At this time of the year there were no flowers in the stiff flowerbeds; for Mr Helbeck had long ceased to spend any but the most necessary moneys upon his garden. Only upon the high stone walls that begirt this strange and melancholy pleasure-ground, and in the 'wilderness' that lay on the eastern side, between the garden and the fell, were Nature and the spring allowed to show themselves. Their joint magic had covered the old walls with fruit blossom and spread the 'wilderness' with daffodils. Otherwise all was dark, tortured, fantastic, a monument of old-world caprice that the heart could not love, though piety might not destroy it.

The children, however, brought life and brightness. They chased each other up and down the paths, and in and out of the bowlinggreen. Helbeck set them to games, and played with them himself. Only for the orphans now did he ever thus recall his youth.

Two Sisters, one comparatively young, the other a woman of fifty, stood in an opening of the bowling green looking at the games.

The younger one said to her companion, who was the Superior of the Orphanage, 'I do like to see Mr Helbeck with the children! It seems to change him altogether.'

She spoke with eager sympathy, while her eyes, the visionary eyes of the typically religious, sunk in a face that was at once sweet and peevish, followed the children and their host.

The other – shrewd-faced and large – had a movement of impatience.

'I should like to see Mr Helbeck with some children of his own. For five years now I have prayed our Blessed Mother to give him a good wife. That's what he wants. Ah! Mrs Fountain –'

And as Augustina advanced with her little languid air, accompanied by her stepdaughter, the Sisters gathered round her, chattering and cooing, showing her a hundred attentions, enveloping her in a homage that was partly addressed to the sister of their benefactor, and partly – as she well understood – to the sheep that had been lost and was found. To the stepdaughter they showed a courteous reserve. One or two of them had already made acquaintance with her, and had not found her amiable.

And, indeed, Laura held herself aloof, as before. But she shot a glance of curiosity at the elderly woman who had wished Mr Helbeck a good wife. The girl had caught the remark as she and her stepmother turned the corner of the dense beechen hedge that, with openings to each point of the compass, enclosed the bowling-green.

Presently Helbeck, stopping to take breath in a game of which he had been the life, caught sight of the slim figure against the red-brown of the hedge. The next moment he perceived that Miss Fountain was watching him with an expression of astonishment.

His first instinct was to let her be. Her manner towards him since her arrival, with hardly a break, had been such as to chill the most sociable temper. And Helbeck's temper was far from sociable.

But something in her attitude – perhaps its solitariness – made him uncomfortable. He went up to her, dragging with him a crowd of small children, who tugged at his coat and hands.

'Miss Fountain, will you take pity on us? My breath is gone.'

He saw her hesitate. Then her sudden smile broke out.

'What'll you have?' she said, catching hold of the nearest child. 'Mother Bunch?'

And off she flew, running, twisting, turning with the merriest of them, her loosened hair gleaming in the sun, her small feet twinkling. Now it was Helbeck's turn to stand and watch. What a curious grace and purpose there was in all her movements! Even in her play Miss Fountain was a personality.

At last a little girl who was running with her began to drag and turn pale. Laura stopped to look at her.

'I can't run any more,' said the child, piteously. 'I had a bone took out of my leg last year.'

She was a sickly-looking creature: rickety and consumptive, a waif from a Liverpool slum. Laura picked her up and carried her to a seat in a yew arbour away from the games. Then the child studied her with shy-looking eyes, and suddenly slipped an arm like a bit of stick round the pretty lady's neck.

'Tell me a story, please, teacher,' she said, imploringly.

Laura was taken aback, for she had forgotten the tales of her own childhood, and had never possessed any younger brothers or sisters, or paid much attention to children in general. But with some difficulty she stumbled through Cinderella.

'Oh, yes, I know that; but it's lovely,' said the child, at the end, with a sigh of content. 'Now, I'll tell you one.'

And in a high nasal voice, like one repeating a lesson in class, she began upon something which Laura soon discovered to be the life of a saint. She followed the phrases of it with a growing repugnance, till at last the speaker said, with the unction of one sure of her audience:

'And once the good Father went to a hospital to visit some sick people. And as he was hearing a poor sailor's confession, he found out that it was his own brother, whom he had not seen for a long, long time. Now the sailor was very ill, and going to die, and he had been a bad man, and done a great many wicked things. But the good Father did not let the poor man know who he was. He went home and told his Superior that he had found his brother. And the Superior forbade him to go and see his brother again, because, he said, God would take care of him. And the Father was very sad, and the devil tempted him sorely. But he prayed to God, and God helped him to be obedient.

'And a great many years afterwards a poor woman came to see the good Father. And she told him she had seen our Blessed Lady in a vision. And our Blessed Lady had sent her to tell the Father that because he had been so obedient, and had not been to see his brother again, our Lady had prayed our Lord for his brother. And his brother had made a good death, and was saved, all because the good Father had obeyed what his Superior told him.'

Laura sprang up. The child, who had expected a kiss and a pious phrase, looked up, startled.

'Wasn't that a pretty story?' she said, timidly.

'No; I don't like it at all,' said Miss Fountain, decidedly. 'I wonder they tell you such tales!'

The child stared at her for a moment. Then a sudden veil fell across the clearness of her eyes which had the preternatural size and brilliance of disease. Her expression changed. It became the slyness of the watching animal, that feels the enemy. She said not another word.

Laura felt a pang of shame, even though she was still vibrating with the repulsion the child's story had excited in her.

'Look!' she said, raising the little one in her arms; 'the others are all going into the house. Shall we go too?'

But the child struggled resolutely.

'Let me get down. I can walk.' Laura set her down, and the child walked as fast as her lame leg would let her to join the others. Once or twice she looked round furtively at her companion; but she would not take the hand Laura offered her, and she seemed to have wholly lost her tongue.

'Little bigot!' thought Laura, half angry, half amused; 'do they catch it from their cradle?'

Presently they found themselves in the tail of a crowd of children and Sisters who were ascending the stairs of a doorway opening on the garden. The doorway led, as Laura knew, to the corridor of the chapel. She let herself be carried along, irresolute, and presently she found herself within the curtained doorway, mechanically helping the Sisters and Augustina to put the children in their places.

One or two of the older children noticed that the young lady with Mrs Fountain did not sign herself with holy water, and did not genuflect in passing the altar, and they looked at her with a stealthy surprise. A gentle-looking young Sister came up to her as she was lifting a very small child to a seat.

'Thank you,' murmured the Sister. 'It is very good of you.' But the voice, though soft, was cold, and Laura at once felt herself the intruder, and withdrew to the back of the crowd.

Yet again, as at her first visit to the chapel, so now, she was too curious, for all her soreness, to go. She must see what they would be at.

'Rosary' passed, and she hardly understood a word. The voice of the Jesuit intoning suggested nothing intelligible to her, and it was some time before she could even make out what the children were saying in their loud-voiced responses. 'Holy Mary, Mother of God, pray for us sinners, now and at the hour of our death' – was that it?

And occasionally an 'Our Father' thrown in – all of it gabbled as fast as possible, as though the one object of both priest and people were to get through and make an end. Over and over again, without an inflection, or a change – with just the one monotonous repetition and the equally monotonous variation. What a barbarous and foolish business!

Very soon she gave up listening. Her eyes wandered to the frescoes, to the bare altar with its purple covering, to the tall candles sparkling before the tabernacle; and the coloured and scented gloom, pierced with the distant lights, gave her a vague pleasure.

Presently there was a pause. The children settled themselves in their seats with a little clatter. Father Leadham retired, while the Sisters knelt, each bowed profoundly on herself, eyes closed under her coif, hands clasped in front of her.

What were they waiting for? Ah! there was the priest again, but in a changed dress – a white cope of some splendour. The organ, played by one of the Sisters, broke out upon the silence, and the voices of the rest rose suddenly, small and sweet, in a Latin hymn. The priest went to the tabernacle, and set it open. There was a swinging of incense, and the waves of fragrant smoke flowed out upon the chapel, dimming the altar and the figure before it. Laura caught sight for a moment of the young Sister who had spoken to her. She was kneeling, and singing with sweet, shut eyes; it was clear that she was possessed by a fervour of feeling. Miss Fountain thought to herself, with wonder, 'She cannot be much older than I am!'

After the hymn it was the children's turn. What were they singing so lustily to so dancing a tune? Laura bent over to look at the book of a Sister in front of her.

'Virgo prudentissima, Virgo veneranda, Virgo praedicanda –'[6]

With difficulty she found the place in another book that lay upon a chair beside her. Then for a few minutes she lost herself in a first amazement over that string of epithets and adjectives with which the Catholic Church throughout the world celebrates day by day and Sunday after Sunday the glories of Mary. The gay music, the harsh and eager voices of the children, flowed on, the waves of incense spread throughout the chapel. When she raised her eyes they fell upon Helbeck's dark head in the far distance, above his server's cotta. A quick change crossed her face, transforming it to a passionate contempt.

*

But of her no one thought – save once. The beautiful 'moment' of the ceremony had come. Father Leadham had raised the monstrance, containing the Host, to give the Benediction. Every Sister, every child, except a few small and tired ones, was bowed in humblest adoration.

Mr Helbeck, too, was kneeling in the little choir. But his attention wandered. With the exception of his walk with Father Leadham, he had been in church since early morning, and even for him response was temporarily exhausted. His look strayed over the chapel.

It was suddenly arrested. Above the kneeling congregation, a distant face showed plainly in the April dusk amid the dimness of incense and painting – a girl's face, delicately white and set – a face of revolt.

'Why is she here?' was his first thought. It came with a rush of annoyance, even resentment. But immediately other thoughts met it: 'She is lonely; she is here under my roof; she has lost her father; poor child!'

The last mental phrase was not so much his own as an echo from Father Leadham. In Helbeck's mind it was spoken very much as the priest had spoken it – with that strange tenderness, at once so intimate and so impersonal, which belongs to the spiritual relations of Catholicism. The girl's soul – lonely, hostile, uncared for – appealed to the charity of the believer. At the same time there was something in her defiance, her crude disapproval of his house and his faith, that stimulated and challenged the man. Conscious for the first time of a new conflict of feeling within himself, he looked steadily towards her across the darkness.

It was as though he had sought and found a way to lift himself above her young pride, her ignorant enmity. For a moment there was a curious exaltation and tyranny in his thought. He dropped his head and prayed for her, the words falling slow and deliberate within his consciousness. And she could not resent it or stop it. It was an aggression before which she was helpless; it struck down the protest of her pale look.

At supper, when the Sisters and their charges had departed, Father Bowles appeared, and never before had Helbeck been so lamentably aware of the absurdities and inferiorities of his parish priest.

The Jesuit, too, was sharply conscious of them, and even Augustina felt that something was amiss. Was it that they were all — except Father Bowles — affected by the presence of the young lady on Helbeck's right — by the cool detachment of her manner, the self-possession that appealed to no one and claimed none of the prerogatives of sex and charm, while every now and then it made itself felt in tacit and resolute opposition to her environment?

'He might leave those things alone!' thought the Jesuit, angrily, as he heard Father Bowles giving Mrs Fountain a gently complacent account of a geological lecture lately delivered in Whinthorpe.

'What I always say, you know, my dear lady, is this: you must show me the evidence! After all, you geologists have done much — you have dug here and there, it is true. But dig all over the world — dig everywhere — lay it all bare. Then you may ask me to listen to you!'

The little round-faced priest looked round the table for support. Laura bit her lip and bent over her plate. Father Leadham turned hastily to Helbeck, and began to discuss with him a recent monograph on the Roman Wall, showing a plentiful and scholarly knowledge of the subject. And presently he drew in the girl opposite, addressing her with a man-of-the-world ease and urbanity which disarmed her. It appeared that he had just come back from mission-work in British Guiana, that he had been in India, and was in all respects a travelled and accomplished person. But the girl did not yield herself, though she listened quite civilly and attentively while he talked.

But again through the Jesuit's easy or polished phrases there broke the purring inanity of Father Bowles.

'Lourdes, my dear lady? Lourdes? How can there be the smallest doubt of the miracles of Lourdes? Why! they keep two doctors on the spot to verify everything!'

The Jesuit's sense of humour was uncomfortably touched. He glanced at Miss Fountain, but could only see that she was gazing steadily out of the window.

As for himself, convert and ex-Fellow of a well-known college, he gave a strong inward assent to the judgment of some of his own leaders, that the older Catholic priests of this country are as a rule lamentably unfit for their work. 'Our chance in England is broadening every year,' he said to himself. 'How are we to seize it with such tools? But all round we want *men*. Oh! for a few more of those who were "out in forty-five"!'

In the drawing-room after dinner, Laura, as usual, entrenched herself in one of the deep oriel windows, behind a heavy table. Augustina showed an anxious curiosity as to the expedition of the morning – as to the Masons and their farm. But Laura would say very little about them.

When the gentlemen came in, Helbeck sent a searching look round the drawing-room. He had the air of one who enters with a purpose.

The beautiful old room lay in a half-light. A lamp at either end could do but little against the shadows that seemed to radiate from the panelled walls and from the deep red hangings of the windows. But the wood fire on the hearth sent out a soft glow, which fastened on the few points of brilliance in the darkness – on the ivory of the fretted ceiling, on the dazzling dress of the Romney, on the gold of Miss Fountain's hair.

Laura looked up with some surprise as Helbeck approached her; then, seeing that he apparently wished to talk, she made a place for him among the old 'Books of Beauty' with which she had been bestrewing the seat that ran round the window.

'I trust the pony behaved himself this morning?' he said, as he sat down.

Laura answered politely.

'And you found your way without difficulty?'

'Oh, yes! Your directions were exact.'

Inwardly she said to herself, 'Does he want to cross-examine me about the Masons?' Then, suddenly, she noticed the scar under his hair – a jagged mark, testifying to a wound of some severity – and it made her uncomfortable. Nay, it seemed in some curious way to put her in the wrong, to shake her self-reliance.

But Helbeck had not come with the intention of talking about the Masons. His avoidance of their name was indeed a pointed one. He drew out her admiration of the daffodils and of the view from Browhead Lane.

'After Easter we must show you something of the high mountains. Augustina tells me you admire the country. The head of Windermere will delight you.'

His manner of offering her these civilities was somewhat stiff and conventional – the manner of one who had been brought up among country gentry of the old school apart from London and the *beau monde*. But it struck Laura that, for the first time, he was speaking to her as a man of his breeding might be expected to speak to a lady visiting his house. There was consideration, and an apparent desire to please. It was as though she had grown all at once into something more in his eyes than Mrs Fountain's little stepdaughter, who was, no doubt, useful as a nurse and a companion, but radically unwelcome and insignificant none the less.

Inevitably the girl's vanity was soothed. She began to answer more naturally; her smile became more frequent. And gradually an unwonted ease and enjoyment stole over Helbeck also. He talked with so much animation at last as to draw the attention of another person in the room. Father Leadham, who had been leaning with some languor against the high, carved mantle, while Father Bowles and Augustina babbled beneath him, began to take increasing notice of Miss Fountain, and of her relation to the Bannisdale household. For a girl who had 'no training, moral or intellectual,' she was showing herself, he thought, possessed of more attraction than might have been expected, for the strict master of the house.

Presently Helbeck came to a pause in what he was saying. He had been describing the country of Wordsworth, and had been dwelling on Grasmere and Rydal Mount, in the tone, indeed, of one who had no vital concern whatever with the Lake poets or their poetry, but still with an evident desire to interest his companion. And following closely on this first effort to make friends with her something further suggested itself.

He hesitated, looked at Laura, and at last said, in a lower voice than he had been using, 'I believe your father, Miss Fountain, was a great lover of Wordsworth, Augustina has told me so. You and he were accustomed, were you not, to read much together? Your loss must be very great. You will not wonder, perhaps, that for me there are painful thoughts connected with your father. But I have not been insensible – I have not been without feeling – for my sister – and for you.'

He spoke with embarrassment, and a kind of appeal. Laura had been startled by his first words, and while he spoke she sat very pale and upright, staring at him. The hand on her lap shook.

When he ceased she did not answer. She turned her head, and he saw her pretty throat tremble. Then she hastily raised her handkerchief; a struggle passed over the face; she wiped away her tears, and threw back her head, with a sobbing breath and a little shake of the bright hair, like one who reproves herself. But she said nothing; and it was evident that she could say nothing without breaking down.

Deeply touched, Helbeck unconsciously drew a little nearer to her. Changing the subject at once, he began to talk to her of the children and the little festival of the afternoon. An hour before he would have instinctively avoided doing anything of the kind. Now, at last, he ventured to be himself, or something near it. Laura regained her composure, and bent her attention upon him, with a slightly frowning brow. Her mind was divided between the most contradictory impulses and attractions. How had it come about, she asked herself, after a while, that *she* was listening like this to his schemes for his children and his new orphanage? – she, and not his natural audience, the two priests and Augustina.

She actually heard him describe the efforts made by himself and one or two other Catholics in the county to provide shelter and education for the county's Catholic orphans. He dwelt on the death and disappearance of some of his earlier colleagues, on the urgent need for a new building in the neighbourhood of the county town, and for the enlargement of the 'home' he himself had put up some ten years before, on the Whinthorpe Road.

'But, unfortunately, large plans want large means,' he added, with a smile, 'and I fear it will come to it – Has Augustina said anything to you about it? – I fear there is nothing for it, but that our beauteous lady there must provide them.'

He nodded towards the picture that gleamed from the opposite wall. Then he added gravely, and with a perfect simplicity:

'It is my last possession of any value.'

Several times during the fortnight that she had known him, Laura had heard him speak with a similar simplicity about his personal and pecuniary affairs. That anyone so stately should treat himself and his own worldly concerns with so much *naïveté* had been a source of frequent surprise to her. To what, then, did his dignity, his reserve apply?

Nevertheless, because, childishly, she had already taken a side, as it were, about the picture, his manner, with its apparent indifference, annoyed her. She drew back.

'Yes, Augustina told me. But isn't it cruel? isn't it unkind? A picture like that is alive — It has been here so long — one could hardly feel it belonged only to oneself. It is part of the house, isn't it? — part of the family? Won't other people — people who come after — reproach you?'

Helbeck lifted his shoulders, his dark face half amused, half sad.

'She died a hundred years ago, pretty creature! She has had her turn; so have we — in the pleasure of looking at her.'

'But she belongs to you,' said the girl, insistently. 'She is your own kith and kin.'

He hesitated, then said, with a new emphasis that answered her own:

'Perhaps there are two sorts of kindred —'

The girl's cheek flushed.

'And the one you mean may always push out the other? I know, because one of your children told me a story to-day — such a frightful story! — of a saint who would not go to see his dying brother, for obedience' sake. She asked me if I liked it. How could I say I liked it. I told her it was horrible! I wondered how people could tell her such tales.'

Her bearing was again all hostility — a young defiance. She was delighted to confess herself. Her crime, untold, had been pressing upon her conscience, hurting her natural frankness.

Helbeck's face changed. He looked at her attentively, the fine dark eye, under the commanding brow, straight and sparkling.

'You said that to the child?'

'Yes.'

Her breast fluttered. She trembled, he saw, with an excitement she could hardly repress.

He, too, felt an over excitement — the excitement of a strong will provoked. It was clear to him that she meant to provoke him — that her young personality threw itself wantonly across his own. He spoke with a harsh directness:

'You did wrong, I think — quite wrong. Excuse the word, but you have brought me to close quarters. You sowed the seeds of doubt, of revolt, in a child's mind.'

'Perhaps,' said Laura quickly. 'What then?'

She wore her half-wild, half-mocking look. Everything soft and touching had disappeared. The eyes shone under the golden mass of hair; the small mouth was close and scornful. Helbeck looked at her in amazement, his own pulse hurrying.

'What then?' he echoed, with a sternness that astonished himself. 'Ask your own feeling. What has a child – a little child under orders – to do with doubt, or revolt? For her – for all of us – doubt is misery.'

Laura rose. She forced down her agitation – made herself speak plainly.

'Papa taught me – it was life – and I believed him.'

The old clock in the farther corner of the room struck a quarter to ten – the hour of prayers. The two priests on the farther side of the room stood up, and Augustina sheathed her knitting-needles.

Laura turned towards Helbeck and coldly held out her little hand. He touched it, and she crossed the room. 'Good-night, Augustina.'

She kissed her stepmother, and bowed to the two priests. Father Leadham ceremonious, opened the door for her. Then he and Helbeck, Father Bowles and Augustina followed across the dark hall on their way to the chapel. Laura took her candle, and her light figure could be seen ascending the Jacobean staircase, a slim and charming vision against the shadows of the old house.

Father Leadham followed it with eyes and thoughts. Then he glanced towards Helbeck. An idea – and one that was singularly unwelcome – was forcing its way into the priest's mind.

BOOK TWO

CHAPTER ONE

From that night onwards the relations between Helbeck and his sister's stepdaughter took another tone. He no longer went his own way, with no more than a vague consciousness that a curious and difficult girl was in the house; he watched her with increasing interest; he began to taste, as it were, the thorny charm that was her peculiar possession.

Not that he was allowed to see much of the charm. After the conversation of Passion Sunday her manner to him was no less cold and distant than before. Their final collision, on the subject of the child, had, he supposed, undone the effects of his conciliatory words about her father. It must be so, no doubt, since her hostile observation of him and of his friends seemed to be in no whit softened.

That he should be so often conscious of her at this particular time annoyed and troubled him. It was the most sacred moment of the Catholic year. Father Leadham, his old Stonyhurst friend, had come to spend Passion Week and Holy Week at Bannisdale, as a special favour to one whom the Church justly numbered among the most faithful of her sons; while the Society of Jesus had many links of mutual service and affection, both with the Helbeck family in the past and with the present owner of the Hall. Helbeck, indeed, was of real importance to Catholicism in this particular district of England. It had once abounded in Catholic families, but now hardly one of them remained, and upon Helbeck, with his small resources and dwindling estate, devolved a number of labours which should have been portioned out among a large circle. Only enthusiasm such as his could have sufficed for the task. But, for the Church's sake, he had now remained unmarried some fifteen years. He lived like an ascetic in the great house, with a couple of women-servants; he spent all his income – except a fraction – on the good works of a wide district; when larger sums were necessary he was ready, nay, eager, to sell the land necessary to provide them; and whenever he journeyed to other parts of England, or to the Continent, it was generally assumed that he had gone, not as other men go, for pleasure and recreation, but simply that he might pursue some Catholic end, either of money or administration, among the rich and powerful of the faith elsewhere. Meanwhile, it was believed that he had bequeathed the house and park of Bannisdale to a distant cousin, also a strict Catholic, with the warning that not much else would remain to his heir from the ancient and splendid inheritance of the family.

It was not wonderful, then, that the Jesuits should be glad to do such a man a service; and no service could have been greater in Helbeck's eyes than a visit from a priest of their order during these weeks of emotion and of penance. Every day Mass was said in the little chapel; every evening a small flock gathered to Litany or Benediction. Ordinary life went on as it could in the intervals of prayer and meditation. The house swarmed with priests – with old and infirm priests, many of them from a Jesuit house of retreat on the western coast, not far away, who found in a visit to Bannisdale one of the chief pleasures of their suffering or monotonous lives; while the Superiors of Helbeck's own orphanages were always ready to help the Bannisdale chapel, on days of special sanctity, by sending a party of Sisters and children to provide the singing.

Meanwhile all else was forgotten. As to food, Helbeck and Father Leadham – according to the letters describing her experiences which Laura wrote during these weeks to a Cambridge girl-friend – lived upon 'a cup of coffee and a banana' per day, and she had endless difficulty in restraining her charge, Augustina, from doing likewise. For Augustina, indeed – Stephen Fountain's little black-robed widow – her husband was daily receding further and further into a dim and dreadful distance, where she feared and yet wept to think of him. She passed her time in the intoxication of her recovered faith, excited by the people around her, by the services in the chapel, and by her very terrors over her own unholy union, lapse, and restoration. The sound of intoning, the scent of incense, seemed to pervade the house; and at the centre of all brooded that mysterious Presence upon the altar, which drew the passion of Catholic hearts to itself in ever deeper measure as the great days of Holy Week and Easter approached.

Through all this drama of an inventive and exacting faith Laura Fountain passed like a being from another world, an alien and a mocking spirit. She said nothing, but her eyes were satires. The effect of her presence in the house was felt probably by all its inmates, and by many of its visitors. She did not again express herself – except rarely to Augustina – with the vehemence she had shown to the little lame orphan; she was quite ready to chat and laugh upon occasion with Father Leadham, who had a pleasant wit, and now and then deliberately sought her society; and, owing to the feebleness of Augustina, she, quite unconsciously, established certain household ways which spoke the woman, and were new to Bannisdale. She filled the drawing-room with daffodils; she made the tea-table by the hall-fire a cheerful place for any who might visit it; she flitted about the house in the prettiest and neatest of spring dresses; her hair, her face, her white hands and neck shone amid the shadows of the panelling like jewels in a casket. Everyone was conscious of her – uneasily conscious. She yielded herself to no one, was touched by no one. She stood apart, and through her cold, light ways spoke the world and the spirit that deny – the world at which the Catholic shudders.

At the same time, like everybody else in the house – even the sulky housekeeper – she grew pale and thin from Lenten fare. Mr Helbeck had of course given orders to Mrs Denton that his sister and Miss Fountain were to be well provided. But Mrs Denton was grudging or forgetful; and it amused Laura to see that Augustina was made to eat, while she herself fared with the rest. The viands of whatever sort were generally scanty and ill-cooked; and neither the Squire nor Father Leadham cared anything about the pleasures of the table, in Lent or out of it. Mr Helbeck hardly noticed what was set before him. Once or twice indeed he woke up to the fact that there was not enough for the ladies and would say an angry word to Mrs Denton. But on the whole Laura was able to follow her whim and to try for herself what this Catholic austerity might be like.

'My dear,' she wrote to her friend, 'one thing you learn from a Catholic Lent is that food matters "nowt at aw," as they would say in these parts. You can do just as well without it as with it. Why you should think yourself a saint for not eating it puzzles me. Otherwise – *vive la faim!* And as we are none of us likely to starve ourselves half so much as the poor people of the world, the soldiers, and sailors, and explorers are always doing, to please themselves or their country, I don't suppose that anybody will come to harm.

'You are to understand, nevertheless, that our austerities are rather unusual. And when anyone comes in from the outside they are concealed as much as possible . . . The old Helbecks, as far as I can hear, must have been very different people from their modern descendant. They were quite good Catholics, understand. What the Church prescribed they did – but not a fraction beyond. They were like the jolly lazy sort of schoolboy, who *just* does his lesson, but would think himself a fool if he did a word more. Whereas the man who lives here now can never do enough!

'And in general these old Catholic houses – from Augustina's tales – must have been full of fun and feasting. Well, I can vouch for it, there is no fun in Bannisdale now! It is Mr Helbeck's personality, I suppose. It makes its own atmosphere. He *can* laugh – I have seen it myself! – but it is an event.'

As Lent went on, the mingling of curiosity and cool criticism with which Miss Fountain regarded her surroundings became perhaps more apparent. Father Leadham, in particular, detected the young lady's fasting experiments. He spoke of them to Helbeck as showing a lack of delicacy and good taste. But the Squire, it seemed, was rather inclined to regard them as the whims of a spoilt and wilful child.

This difference of shade in the judgment of the two men may rank as one of the first signs of all that was to come.

Certainly Helbeck had never before felt himself so uncomfortable in his own house as he had done since the arrival of this girl of twenty-one. Nevertheless, as the weeks went on, the half-amused, half-contemptuous embarrassment, which had been the first natural effect of her presence upon the mind of a man so little used to women and their ways, had passed imperceptibly into something else. His reserved and formal manner remained the same. But Miss Fountain's goings and comings had ceased to be indifferent to him. A silent relation – still unknown to her – had arisen between them.

When he first noticed the fact in himself, it produced a strong, temporary reaction. He reproached himself for a light and unworthy temper. Had his solitary life so weakened him that any new face and personality about him could distract and disturb him, even amid the great thoughts of these solemn days? His heart, his life were in his faith. For more than twenty years by prayer and meditation, by all the ingenious means, that the Catholic Church provides, he had developed the sensibilities of faith; and for the Catholic these sensibilities are centred upon and sustained by the Passion. Now, hour by hour, his Lord was moving to the Cross. He stood perpetually beside the sacred form in the streets of Jerusalem, in Gethsemane, on the steps of the Prætorium. A varied and dramatic ceremonial was always at hand to stimulate the imagination, the penitence, and the devotion of the believer. That anything whatever should break in upon the sacred absorption of these days would have seemed to him beforehand a calamity to be shrunk from – nay, a sin to be repented. He had put aside all business that could be put aside with one object, and one only – to make 'a good Easter.'

And yet, no sooner did he come back from service in the chapel, or from talk of Church matters with Catholic friends, than he found himself suddenly full of expectation. Was Miss Fountain in the hall, in the garden? or was she gone to those people at Browhead? If she was not in the house – above all, if she was with the Masons – he would find it hard to absorb himself again in the thoughts that had held him before. If she was there, if he found her sitting reading or working by the hall fire, with the dogs at her feet, he seldom indeed went to speak to her. He would go into his library, and force himself to do his business, while Father Leadham talked to her and Augustina. But the library opened on the hall, and he could still hear that voice in the distance. Often, when she caressed the dogs, her tones had the note in them which had startled him on her very first evening under his roof. It was the emergence of something hidden and passionate; and it awoke in himself a strange and troubling echo – the passing surge of an old memory long since thrust down and buried. How fast his youth was going from him! It was fifteen years since a woman's voice, a woman's presence, had mattered anything at all to him.

So it came about that, in some way or other, he knew, broadly, all that Miss Fountain did, little as he saw of her. It appeared that she had discovered a pony-carriage for hire in the little village near the bridge, and once or twice during this fortnight, he learned from Augustina that she had spent the afternoon at Browhead Farm, while the Bannisdale household had been absorbed in some function of the season.

Augustina disliked the news as much as he did, and would throw up her hands in annoyance.

'What *can* she be doing there? They seem the roughest kind of people. But she says the son plays so wonderfully. I believe she plays duets with him. She goes out with the cart full of music.'

'Music!' said Helbeck, in frank amazement. 'That lout!'

'Well, she says so,' said Augustina crossly, as though it were a personal affront. 'And what do you think, Alan? She talks of going to a dance up there after Easter – next Thursday, I think.'

'At the Farm?' Helbeck's tone was incredulous.

'No; at the mill – or somewhere. She says the schoolmaster is giving it, or something of that sort. Of course it's most unsuitable. But what am I to do, Alan? They *are* her relations!'

'At the same time they are not her class,' said Helbeck decidedly. 'She has been brought up in a different way, and she cannot behave as though she belonged to them. And a dance, with that young man to look after her! You ought to stop it.'

Augustina said dismally that she would try, but her head shook with more feebleness than usual as she went back to her knitting.

Next day Helbeck made a point of finding his sister alone. But she only threw him a deprecatory look.

'I tried, Alan – indeed I did. She says that she wants some amusement – that it will do her good – and that of course her father would have let her go to a dance with his relations. And when I say anything to her about not being quite like them, she fires up. She says she would be ashamed to be thought any better than they, and that Hubert has a great deal more good in him than some people think.'

'Hubert!' exclaimed Mr Helbeck, raising his shoulders in disgust. After a little silence he turned round as he was leaving the room, and said abruptly: 'Is she to stay the night at the Farm?'

'No! oh no! She wants to come home. She says she won't be late; she promises not to be late.'

'And that young fellow will drive her home, of course?'

'Well, she couldn't drive home alone, Alan, at that time of night. It wouldn't be proper.'

Mr Helbeck smiled rather sourly. 'One may doubt where the propriety comes in. Well, she seems determined. We must just arrange it. There is the tower door. Kindly tell her, Augustina, that I will let her have the key of it. And kindly tell her also – as from yourself, of course – that she will be treating us all with courtesy if she does come home at a reasonable hour. We have been a very quiet, prim household all these years, and Mrs Denton, for all her virtues, has a tongue.'

'So she has,' said Augustina, sighing. 'And she doesn't like Laura – not at all.'

Helbeck raised his head quickly. 'She does nothing to make Miss Fountain uncomfortable, I trust?'

'Oh – no,' said Augustina, undecidedly. 'Besides, it doesn't matter. Laura has got Ellen under her thumb.'

Helbeck's grave countenance showed a gleam of amusement.

'How does Mrs Denton take that?'

'Oh! she has to bear it. Haven't you seen, Alan, how the girl has brightened up? Laura has shown her how to do her hair; she helped her to make a new frock for Easter; the girl would do anything in the world for her. It's like Bruno. Do you notice, Alan – I really thought you would be angry – that the dog will hardly go with you when Laura's there?'

'Oh! Miss Fountain is a very attractive young lady – to those she likes,' said Helbeck dryly.

And on that he went away.

On Good Friday afternoon Laura, in a renewed passion of revolt against all that was going on in the house, went to her room and wrote to her friend. Litanies were being said in the chapel. The distant melancholy sounds mounted to her now and then. Otherwise the house was wrapped in a mourning silence; and outside, trailing clouds hung round the old walls, making a penitential barrier all about it.

'After this week,' wrote Laura to her friend, 'I shall always feel kindly towards "sin" – and the "world"! How they have been scouted and scourged! And what, I ask you, would any of us do without them? The "world," indeed! I seem to hear it go rumbling on, the poor, patient, toiling thing, while these people are praying. It works, and makes it possible for them to pray – while they abuse and revile it.

'And as to "sin," and the gloom in which we all live because of it – what on earth does it really mean to any decently taught and brought-up creature? You are greedy, or selfish, or idle, or ill-behaved. Very well, then – nature, or your next-door neighbour, knocks you down for it, and serve you right. Next time you won't do it again, or not so badly, and by degrees you don't even like to think of doing it – you would be "ashamed," as people say. It's the process that everybody has to go through, I suppose – being sent into the world the sort of beings we are, and without any leave of ours, altogether. But why make such a wailing and woe and hullabaloo about it! Oh – such a waste of time! Why doesn't Mr Helbeck go and learn geology? I vow he hasn't an idea what the rocks of his own valley are made of!

'Of course there are the *very* great villains – I don't like to think about them. And the people who are born wrong and sick. But by-and-by we shall have weeded them out, or improved the breed. And why not spend your energies on doing that, instead of singing litanies, and taking ridiculous pains not to eat the things you like?

'. . . I shall soon be in disgrace with Augustina and Mr Helbeck, about the Masons – worse disgrace, that is to say. For now that I have found a pony of my own, I go up there two or three times a week. And really – in spite of all those first experiences I told you of – I like it! Cousin Elizabeth has begun to talk to me; and when I come home, I read the Bible to see what it was all about. And I don't let her say too bad things about Mr Helbeck – it wouldn't be quite gentlemanly on my part. And I know most of the Williams story now, both from her and Augustina.

'Imagine, my dear! – a son not allowed to come and see his mother before she died, though she cried for him night and day. He was at a Jesuit school in Wales. They shilly-shallied, and wrote endless letters – and at last they sent him off – the day she died. He arrived three hours too late, and his father shut the door in his face. "Noa, yo shan't see her," said the grim old fellow – "an if there's a God above, yo shan't see her in heaven nayder!" Augustina of course calls it "holy obedience."

'The painting in the chapel is really extraordinary. Mr Helbeck seems to have taught the young man, to begin with. He himself used to paint long ago – not very well, I should think, to judge from the bits of his work still left in the chapel. But at any rate the youth learnt the rudiments from him, and then of course went far beyond his teacher. He was almost two years here, working in the house – tabooed by his family all the time. Then there seems to have been a year in London, when he gave Mr Helbeck some trouble. I don't know – Augustina is vague. How it was that he joined the Jesuits I can't make out. No doubt Mr Helbeck induced them to take him. But *why* – I ask you – with such a gift? They say he will be here in the summer, and one will have to set one's teeth and shake hands with him.

'Oh! that droning in the chapel – there it is again! I will open the window and let the howl of the rain in to get rid of it. And yet I can't always keep myself away from it. It is all so new – so horribly intimate. Every now and then the music or a prayer or something sends a stab right down to my heart of hearts. – A voice of suffering, of torture – oh! so ghastly, so *real*. Then I come and read Papa's note-books for an hour to forget it. I wish he had ever taught me anything – strictly! But *of course* it was my fault.

'. . . As to this dance, why shouldn't I go? – just tell me! It is being given by the new schoolmaster, and two or three young farmers, in the big room at the old mill. The schoolmaster is the most tiresomely virtuous young man, and the whole thing is so respectable, it makes me yawn to think of it. Polly implores me to go, and I like Polly. (Very soon she'll let me halve her fringe!) I gave Hubert a preliminary snub, and now he doesn't dare implore me to go. But that is all the more engaging. I *don't* flirt with him! – heavens! – unless you call bear-taming flirtation. But one can't see his music running to waste in such a bog of tantrums and tempers. I must try my hand. And as he is my cousin I can put up with him.'

After High Mass on Easter Sunday Helbeck walked home from Whinthorpe alone, as his companion Father Leadham had an engagement in the town.

Through the greater part of Holy Week the skies had been as grey and penitential as the season. The fells and the river flats had been scourged at night with torrents of rain and wind, and in the pale mornings any passing promise of sun had been drowned again before the day was high. The roofs and eaves, the small panes of the old house, trickled and shone with rain; and at night the wind tore through the gorge of the river with great boomings and onslaughts from the west. But with Easter eve there had come appeasement – a quiet dying of the long storm. And as Helbeck made his way along the river on Easter morning, mountain and flood, grass and tree, were in a glory of recovered sun. The distant fells were drawn upon the sky in the heavenliest brushings of blue and purple; the river thundered over its falls and weirs in a foamy splendour; and the deer were feeding with a new zest amid the fast-greening grass.

He stopped a moment to rest upon his stick and look about him. Something in his own movement reminded him of another solitary walk some five weeks before. And at the same instant he perceived a small figure sitting on a stone seat in front of him. It was Miss Fountain. She had a book on her knee, and the two dogs were beside her. Her white dress and hat seemed to make the centre of a whole landscape. The river bent inward in a great sweep at her feet, the crag rose behind her, and the great prospect beyond the river of dale and wood, of scar and cloud, seemed spread there for her eyes alone. A strange fancy seized on Helbeck. This was his world – his world by inheritance and by love. Five weeks before he had walked about it as solitary. And now this figure sat enthroned, as it were, at the heart of it. He roughly shook the fancy off and walked on.

Miss Fountain greeted him with her usual detachment. He stood a minute or two irresolute, then threw himself on the slope in front of her.

'Bruno will hardly look at his master now,' he said to her pleasantly, pointing to the dog's attitude as it lay with its nose upon the hem of her dress.

Laura closed her book in some annoyance. He usually returned by the other side of the river, and she was not grateful to him for his breach of habit. Why had he been meddling in her affairs? She perfectly understood why Augustina had been making herself so difficult about the dance, and about the Masons in general. Let him keep his proprieties to himself. She, Laura, had nothing to do with them. She was hardly his guest – still less his ward. She had come to Bannisdale against her will, simply and solely as Augustina's nurse. In return, let Mr Helbeck leave her alone to enjoy her plebeian relations as she pleased.

Nevertheless, of course she must be civil; and civil she intermittently tried to be. She answered his remark about Bruno by a caress to the dog that brought him to lay his muzzle against her knee.

'Do you mind? Some people do mind. I can easily drive him away.'

'Oh no! I reckon on recovering him – some day,' he said with a frank smile.

Laura flushed.

'Very soon, I should think. Have you noticed, Mr Helbeck, how much better Augustina is already? I believe that by the end of the summer, at least, she will be able to do without me. And she tells me that the Superior at the Orphanage has a girl to recommend her as a companion when I go.'

'Rather officious of the Reverend Mother, I think,' said Helbeck sharply. He paused a moment, then added with some emphasis – 'Don't imagine, Miss Fountain, that anybody else can do for my sister what you do.'

'Ah! but – well – one must live one's life – mustn't one, Fricka?' –

Fricka was by this time jealously pawing her dress. 'I want to work at my music – hard – this winter.'

'And I fear that Bannisdale is not a very gay place for a young lady visitor?'

He smiled. And so did she; though his tone, with its shade of proud humility, embarrassed her.

'It is as beautiful as a dream!' she said, with sudden energy, throwing up her little hand. And he turned to look, as she was looking, at the river and the woods.

'You feel the beauty of it so much?' he asked her, wondering. His own strong feeling for his native place was all a matter of old habit and association. The flash of wild pleasure in her face astounded him. There was in it that fiery, tameless something that was the girl's distinguishing mark, her very soul and self. Was it beginning to speak from her blood to his?

She nodded, then laughed.

'But, of course, it isn't my business to live here. I have a great friend – a Cambridge girl – and we have arranged it all. We are to live together, and travel a great deal, and work at music.'

'That is what young ladies do nowadays, I understand.'

'And why not?'

He lifted his shoulders, as though to decline the answer, and was silent – so silent that she was forced at last to take the field.

'Don't you approve of "new women," Mr Helbeck? Oh! I wish I was a new woman,' she threw out defiantly. 'But I'm not good enough – I don't know anything.'

'I wasn't thinking of them,' he said simply. 'I was thinking of the life that women used to live here, in this place, in the past – of my mother and my grandmother.'

She could not help a stir of interest. What might the Catholic women of Bannisdale have been like? She looked along the path that led downward to the house, and seemed to see their figures upon it – not short and sickly like Augustina, but with the morning in their eyes and on their white brows, like the Romney lady. Helbeck's thoughts meanwhile were peopled by the more solid forms of memory.

'You remember the picture?' he said at last, breaking the silence. 'The husband of that lady was a boor and a gambler. He soon broke her heart. But her children consoled her to some extent, especially the daughters, several of whom became nuns. The poor wife came from a large Lancashire family, but she hardly saw her relations after her marriage; she was ashamed of her husband's failings, and of their growing poverty. She became very shy and solitary, and very devout. These rock seats along the river were placed by her. It is said that she used in summer to spend long hours on that very seat where you are sitting, doing needlework, or reading the Little Office of the Virgin, at the hours when her daughters in their French convent would be saying their office in chapel. She died before her husband, a very meek, broken creature. I have a little book of her meditations, that she wrote out by the wish of her confessor.

'Then my grandmother – ah! well, that is too long a story. She was a Frenchwoman – we have some of her books in my study. She never got on with England and English people – and at last, after her husband's death, she never went outside the house and park. My father owed much of his shyness and oddity to her bringing up. When she felt herself dying she went over to her family to die at Nantes. She is buried there; and my father was sent to the Jesuit school at Nantes for a long time. Then my mother – But I mustn't bore you with these family tales.'

He turned to look at his listener. Laura was by this time half embarrassed, half touched.

'I should like to hear about your mother,' she said, rather stiffly.

'You may talk to me if you like, but don't, pray, presume upon it!' – that was what her manner said.

Helbeck smiled a little, unseen, under his black moustache.

'My mother was a great lover of books – the only Helbeck, I think, that ever read anything. She was a friend and correspondent of Cardinal Wiseman's – and she tried to make a family history out of the papers here. But in her later years she was twisted and crippled by rheumatic gout – her poor fingers could not turn the pages. I used to help her sometimes; but we none of us shared her tastes. She was a very happy person, however.'

Happy! Why? Laura felt a fresh prick of irritation as he paused. Was she never to escape – not even here, in the April sun, beside the river bank! For, of course, what all this meant was that the really virtuous and admirable woman does not roam the world in search of art and friendship; she makes herself happy at home with religion and rheumatic gout.

But Helbeck resumed. And instantly it struck her that he had dropped a sentence, and was taking up the thread further on.

'But there was no priest in the house then, for the Society could not spare us one; and very few services in the chapel. Through all her young days nothing could be poorer or raggeder than English Catholicism. There was no church at Whinthorpe. Sunday after Sunday my father used to read the prayers in the chapel, which was half a lumber-room. I often think no Dissent could have been barer; but we heard Mass when we could, and that was enough for us. One of the priests from Stonyhurst came when she died. This is her little missal.'

He raised it from the grass – a small volume bound in faded morocco – but he did not offer to show it to Miss Fountain, and she felt no inclination to ask for it.

'Why did they live so much alone?' she asked him, with a little frown. 'I suppose there were always neighbours?'

He shook his head.

'A difference that has law and education besides religion behind it, goes deep. Times are changed, but it goes deep still.'

There was a pause. Then she looked at him with a whimsical lifting of her brows.

'Bannisdale was not amusing?' she said.

He laughed good-humouredly. 'Not for a woman, certainly. For a man, yes. There was plenty of rough sport and card-playing, and a good deal of drinking. The men were full of character, often full of ability. But there was no outlet – and a wretched education. My great-grandfather might have been saved by a commission in the army. But the law forbade it him. So they lived to themselves and by themselves; they didn't choose to live with their Protestant neighbours – who had made them outlaws and inferiors! And, of course, they sank in manners and refinement. You may see the results in all the minor Catholic families to this day – that is, the old families. The few great houses that remained faithful escaped many of the drawbacks of the position. The smaller ones suffered, and succumbed. But they had their compensations!'

As he spoke he rose from the grass, and the dogs, springing up, barked joyously about him.

'Augustina will be waiting dinner for us, I think.'

Laura, who had meant to stay behind, saw that she was expected to walk home with him. She rose unwillingly, and moved on beside him.

'Their compensations?' That meant the Mass and all the rest of this tyrannous clinging religion. What did it honestly mean to Mr Helbeck – to anybody? She remembered her father's rough laugh. 'There are twelve hundred men, my dear, belonging to the Athenæum Club. I give you the bishops. After them, what do you suppose religion has to say to the rest of the twelve hundred? How many of them ever give a thought to it?'

She raised her eyes, furtively, to Helbeck's face. In spite of its melancholy lines, she had lately begun to see that its fundamental expression was a contented one. That, no doubt, came from the 'compensations.' But to-day there was more. She was positively startled by his look of happiness as he strode silently along beside her. It was all the more striking because of the plain traces left upon him by Lenten fatigue and 'mortification.'

It was Easter day, and she supposed he had come from Communion.

A little shiver passed through her, caused by the recollection of words she had heard, acts of which she had been a witness, in the chapel during the foregoing week – words and acts of emotion, of abandonment – love crying to love. A momentary thirst seized her – an instant's sense of privation, of longing, gone almost as soon as it had come.

Helbeck turned to her.

'So this dance you are going to is on Thursday?' he said pleasantly.

She came to herself in a moment.

'Yes, on Thursday, at eight. I shall go early. I have engaged a fly to take me to the farm – thank you! – and my cousins will see me home. I am obliged to you for the key. It will save my giving any trouble.'

'If you did we should not grudge it,' he said quietly.

She was silent for a few more steps, then she said:

'I quite understand, Mr Helbeck, that you do not approve of my going. But I must judge for myself. The Masons are my own people. I am sorry they should have – Well – I don't understand – but it seems you have reason to think badly of them.'

'Not of *them*,' he said with emphasis.

'Of my cousin Hubert, then?'

He made no answer. She coloured angrily, then broke out, her words tumbling childishly over one another:

'There are a great many things said of Hubert that I don't believe he deserves! He has a great many good tastes – his music is wonderful. At any rate, he is my cousin; they are papa's only relations in the world. He would have been kind to Hubert; and he would have despised me if I turned my back on them because I was staying in a grand house with grand people!'

'Grand people!' said Helbeck, raising his eyebrows. 'But I am sorry I led you to say these things, Miss Fountain. Excuse me – may I open this gate for you?'

She reached her own room as quickly as possible, and dropped upon the chair beside her dressing-table in a whirl of angry feeling. A small and heated face looked out upon her from the glass. But after the first instinctive moment she took no notice of it. With the mind's eye she still saw the figure she had just parted from, the noble poise of the head, thrown back on the broad shoulders, the black and greys of the hair, the clear penetrating glance – all the slight signs of age and austerity that had begun to filch away the Squire's youth. It was at least ten minutes before she could free herself enough from the unwelcome memories of her walk to find a vindictive pleasure in running hastily to look at her one white dress – all she had to wear at the Browhead dance.

On Thursday afternoon Helbeck was fishing in the park. The sea-trout were coming up, the day was soft, and he had done well. But just as the evening rise was beginning he put up his rod and went home. Father Leadham had taken his departure. Augustina, Miss Fountain, and he were again alone in the house.

He went into his study, and left the door open, while he busied himself with some writing.

Presently Augustina put her head in. She looked dishevelled, and rather pinker than usual, as always happened when there was the smallest disturbance of her routine.

'Laura has just gone up to dress, Alan. Is it fine?'

'There is no rain,' he said, without turning his head. 'Don't shut the door, please. This fire is oppressive.'

She went away, and he wrote on a little while – then listened. He heard hurrying feet and movements overhead, and presently a door opened hastily, and a voice exclaimed, 'Just two or three, you know, Ellen – from that corner under the kitchen-window! Run, there's a good girl!'

And there was a clattering noise as Ellen ran down the front stairs, and then flew along the corridor to the garden-door.

In a minute she was back again, and as she passed his room Helbeck saw that she was carrying a bunch of white narcissus.

Then more sounds of laughter and chatter overhead. At last Augustina hurried down and looked in upon him again, flurried and smiling.

'Alan, you really must see her. She looks so pretty.'

'I am afraid I'm busy,' he said, still writing. And she retired disappointed, careful, however, to follow his wishes about the door.

'Augustina, hold Bruno!' cried a light voice suddenly. 'If he jumps on me I'm done for!'

A swish of soft skirts and she was there – in the hall. Helbeck could see her quite plainly as she stood by the oak table in her white dress. There was just room at the throat of it for a pearl necklace, and at the wrists for some thin gold bracelets. The narcissus were in her hair, which she had coiled and looped in a wonderful way, so that Helbeck's eyes were dazzled by its colour and abundance, and by the whiteness of the slender neck below it. She meanwhile was quite unconscious of his neighbourhood, and he saw that she was all in a happy flutter, hastily putting on her gloves, and chattering alternately to Augustina and to the transformed Ellen, who stood in speechless admiration behind her, holding a cloak.

'There, Ellen, that'll do. You're a darling – and the flowers are perfect. Run now, and tell Mrs Denton that I didn't keep you more than twenty minutes. Oh yes, Augustina, I'm quite warm. I can't choke, dear, even to please you. There now – here goes! If you do lock me out, there's a corner under the bridge, quite snug. My dress will mind – I sha'n't. Good-night. My compliments to Mr Helbeck.'

Then a hasty kiss to Augustina and she was gone.

Helbeck went out into the hall. Augustina was standing on the steps, watching the departing fly. At the sight of her brother she turned back to him, her poor little face aglow.

'She did look so nice, Alan! I wish she had gone to a proper dance, and not to these odd farmers and people. Why, they'll all go in their high dresses, and think her stuck-up.'

'I assure you I never saw anything so smart as Miss Mason at the hunt ball,' said Helbeck. 'Did you give her the key, Augustina? But

I shall probably sit up. There are some Easter accounts that must be done.'

The old clock in the hall struck one. Helbeck was sitting in his familiar chair before the log fire, which he had just replenished. In one hand was a life of St Philip Neri,[7] the other played absently with Bruno's ears. In truth he was not reading, but listening.

Suddenly there was a sound. He turned his head, and saw that the door leading from the hall to the tower staircase, and thence to the kitchen regions, had been opened.

'Who's there?' he said in astonishment.

Mrs Denton appeared.

'You, Denton! What are you up for at this time?'

'I came to see if the yoong lady had coom back,' she said in a low voice, and with her most forbidding manner. 'It's late, and I heard nowt.'

'Late? Not at all! Go to bed, Denton, at once; Miss Fountain will be here directly.'

'I'm not sleepy; I can wait for her,' said the housekeeper, advancing a step or two into the hall. 'You mun be tired, sir, and should take your rest.'

'I'm not the least tired, thank you. Good-night. Let me recommend you to go to bed as quickly as possible.'

Mrs Denton lingered for a moment, as though in hesitation, then went with a sulky unwillingness that was very evident to her master.

Helbeck laid down his book on his knee with a little laugh.

'She would have liked to get in a scolding, but we won't give her the chance.'

The reverie that followed was not a very pleasant one. He seemed to see Miss Fountain in the large rustic room, with a bevy of young men about her – young fellows in Sunday coats, with shiny hair and limbs bursting out of their ill-fitting clothes. There would be loud talking and laughter, rough jokes that would make her wince, compliments that would disgust her – they not knowing how to take her, nor she them. She would be wholly out of her place – a butt for impertinence – perhaps worse. And there would be a certain sense of dragging a lady from her sphere – of making free with the old house and the old family.

He thought of it with disgust. He was an aristocrat to his fingers' ends.

But how could it have been helped? And when he remembered her as she had stood there in the hall, so young and pretty, so eager for her pleasure, he said to himself with sudden heartiness:

'Nonsense! I hope the child has enjoyed herself.' It was the first time that, even in his least formal thoughts, he had applied such a word to her.

Silence again. The wind breathed gently round the house. He could hear the river rushing.

Once he thought there was a sound of wheels, and he went to the outer door, but there was nothing. Overhead the stars shone, and along the track of the river lay a white mist.

As he was turning back to the hall, however, he heard voices from the mist – a loud man's voice, then a little cry as of someone in fright or anger, then a song. The rollicking tune of it shouted into the night, into the stately stillness that surrounded the old house, had the abruptest, unseemliest effect.

Helbeck ran down the steps. A dog-cart with lights approached the gateway in the low stone enclosure before the house. It shot through so fast and so awkwardly as to graze the inner post. There was another little cry. Then, with various lurches and lunges, the cart drove round the gravel, and brought up somewhere near the steps.

Hubert Mason jumped down.

'Who's that? Mr Helbeck? O Lord! glad to see yer, I'm sure! There's that little silly – she's been making such a fuss all the way – thought I was going to upset her into the river, I do believe. She would try and get at the reins, though I told her it was the worst thing to do, whatever – to be interfering with the driver. Lord! I thought she'd have used the whip to me!'

And Mason stood beside the shafts, with his arms on the side, laughing loudly and looking at Laura.

'Stand out of the way, sir!' said Helbeck sternly, 'and let me help Miss Fountain.'

'Oh! I say! – Come now, I'm not going to stand you coming it over me twice in the same sort – not I,' cried the young man with a violent change of tone. '*You* get out of the way – d—mn you! I brought Miss Fountain home, and she's my cousin – so there – not yours.'

'Hubert, go away at once!' said Laura's shaking but imperious voice. 'I prefer that Mr Helbeck should help me.'

She had risen and was clinging to the rail of the dogcart, while her face drooped so that Helbeck could not see it.

Mason stepped back with another oath, caught his foot in the reins, which he had carelessly left hanging, and fell on his knees on the gravel.

'No matter,' said Helbeck, seeing that Laura paused in terror. 'Give me your hand, Miss Fountain.'

She slipped on the step in the darkness, and Helbeck caught her and set her on her feet.

'Go in, please. I will look after him.'

She ran up the steps, then turned to look.

Mason, still swearing and muttering, had some difficulty in getting up. Helbeck stood by till he had risen and disentangled the reins.

'If you don't drive carefully down the park in the fog you'll come to harm,' he said, shortly, as Mason mounted to his seat.

'That's none of your business,' said Mason, sulkily. 'I brought my cousin all right – I suppose I can take myself. Now, come up, will you!'

He struck the pony savagely on the back with the reins. The tired animal started forward; the cart swayed again from side to side. Helbeck held his breath as it passed the gate-posts; but it shaved through, and soon nothing but the gallop of retreating hoofs could be heard through the night.

He mounted the steps, and shut and barred the outer door. When he entered the hall, Laura was sitting by the oak table, one hand supporting and hiding her face, the other hanging listlessly beside her.

She struggled to her feet as he came in. The hood of her blue cloak had fallen backwards, and her hair was in confusion round her face and neck. Her cheeks were very white, and there were tears in her eyes. She had never seemed to him so small, so childish, or so lovely.

He took no notice of her agitation or of her efforts to speak. He went to a tray of wine and biscuits that had been left by his orders on a side-table, and poured out some wine.

'No, I don't want it,' she said, waving it away. 'I don't know what to say –'

'You would do best to take it,' he said, interrupting her.

His quiet insistence overcame her, and she drank it. It gave her back her voice and a little colour. She bit her lip, and looked after Helbeck as he walked away to the farther end of the hall to light a candle for her.

'Mr Helbeck,' she began, as he came near. Then she gathered force. 'You must – you ought to let me apologise.'

'For what? I am afraid you had a disagreeable and dangerous drive home. Would you like me to wake one of the servants – Ellen, perhaps – and tell her to come to you?'

'Oh! you won't let me say what I ought to say,' she exclaimed in despair. 'That my cousin should have behaved like this – should have insulted you –'

'No! no!' he said, with some peremptoriness. 'Your cousin insulted you by daring to drive with you in such a state. That is all that matters to me – or should, I think, matter to you. Will you have your candle, and shall I call anyone?'

She shook her head and moved towards the staircase, he accompanying her. When he saw how feebly she walked, he was on the point of asking her to take his arm and let him help her to her room; but he refrained.

At the foot of the stairs she paused. Her 'Good-night' died in her throat as she offered her hand. Her dejection, her girlish shame, made her inexpressibly attractive to him; it was the first time he had ever seen her with all her arms thrown down. But he said nothing. He bade her good-night with a cheerful courtesy, and, returning to the hall fire, he stood beside it till he heard the distant shutting of her door.

Then he sank back into his chair and sat motionless, with knitted brows for nearly an hour, staring into the caverns of the fire.

CHAPTER TWO

Laura awoke very early the following morning, but though the sun was bright outside, it brought no gaiety to her. The night before she had hurried her undressing, that she might bury herself in her pillow as quickly as possible, and force sleep to come to her. It was her natural instinct in the face of pain or humiliation. To escape from it by any summary method was always her first thought. 'I will, I must go to sleep!' she had said to herself, in a miserable fury with herself and fate; and by the help of an intense exhaustion sleep came.

But in the morning she could do herself no more violence. Memory took its course, and a very disquieting course it was. She sat up in bed, with her hands round her knees, thinking not only of all the wretched and untoward incidents connected with the ball, but of the whole three weeks that had gone before it. What had she been doing, how had she been behaving, that this odious youth should have dared to treat her in such a way?

Fricka jumped up beside her, and Laura held the dog's nose against her cheek for comfort, while she confessed herself. Oh! what a fool she had been. Why, pray, had she been paying all these visits to the Farm, and spending all these hours in this young fellow's company? Her quick intelligence unravelled all the doubtful skein. Yearning towards her kindred? – yes, there had been something of that. Recoil from the Bannisdale ways, an angry eagerness to scout them and fly them? – yes, that there had always been in plenty. But she dived deeper into her self-disgust, and brought up the real bottom truth, disagreeable and hateful as it was: mere excitement about a young man, as a young man – mere love of power over a great hulking fellow whom other people found unmanageable! Aye, there it was, in spite of all the glosses she had put upon it in her letters to Molly Friedland. All through, she had known perfectly well that Hubert Mason was not her equal; that on a number of subjects he had vulgar habits and vulgar ideas; that he often expressed his admiration for her in a way she ought to have resented. There were whole sides of him, indeed, that she shrank from exploring – that she wanted, nay, was determined, to know nothing about.

On the other hand, her young daring, for want of any better prey, had taken pleasure from the beginning in bringing him under her yoke. With her second visit to the Farm she saw that she could make him her slave – that she had only to show him a little flattery, a little encouragement, and he would be as submissive and obedient to her as he was truculent and ill-tempered towards the rest of the world. And her vanity had actually plumed itself on so poor a prey! One excuse – yes, there was the one excuse! With her he had shown the side that she alone of his kindred could appreciate. But for the fear of Cousin Elizabeth she could have kept him hanging over the piano hour after hour while she played, in a passion of delight. Here was common ground. Nay, in native power he was her superior, though she, with her better musical training, could help and correct him in a thousand ways. She had the woman's passion for influence; and he seemed like wax in her hands. Why not help him to education and refinement, to the cultivation of the best that was in him? She would persuade Cousin Elizabeth – alter and amend his life for him – and Mr Helbeck should see that there were better ways of dealing with people than by looking down upon them and despising them.

And now the very thought of these vain and silly dreams set her face aflame. Power over him? Let her only remember the humiliations through which she had been dragged! All the dance came back upon her – the strange people, the strange young men, the strange, raftered room, with the noise of the mill-stream and the weir vibrating through it, and mingling with the chatter of the fiddles. But she had been determined to enjoy it, to give herself no airs, to forget with all her might that she was any way different from these dale-folk, whose blood was hers. And with the older people all had been easy. With the elderly women especially, in their dark gowns and large Sunday collars, she had felt herself at home; again and again she had put herself under their wing, while in their silent way they turned their shrewd motherly eyes upon her, and took stock of her and every detail of her dress. And the old men, with their patriarchal manners and their broad speech – it had been all sweet and pleasant to her. 'Noo, miss, they tell ma as yo are Stephen Fountain's dowter. An I mut meäk bold ter cum an speak to thee, for a knew 'un when he was a lile lad.' Or 'Yo'll gee ma your hand, Miss Fountain, for we're pleased an proud to git yo here. Yer fadther an mea gaed to skule togedther. My worrd,

but he was parlish cliver! An I daursay as you teäk afther him.'
Kind folk! with all the signs of their hard and simple life about
them.

But the young men – how she had hated them! – whether they
were shy, or whether they were bold; whether they romped with
their sweethearts, and laughed at their own jokes like bulls of
Bashan, or whether they wore their best clothes as though the
garments burnt them, and danced the polka in a perspiring and
anguished silence! No; she was not of *their* class, thank Heaven! She
never wished to be. One man had asked her to put a pin in his
collar; another had spilt a cup of coffee over her white dress; a third
had confided to her that his young lady was 'that luvin' to him in
public, he had been fair obliged to bid her 'keep hersel to hersel
afore foak.' The only partner with whom it had given her the
smallest pleasure to dance had been the schoolmaster and principal
host of the evening, a tall, sickly young man, who wore spectacles
and talked through his nose. But he talked of things she understood,
and he danced tolerably. Alas! there had come the rub. Hubert
Mason had stood sentinel beside her during the early part of the
evening. He had assumed the proudest and most exclusive airs with
regard to her, and his chief aim seemed to be to impress upon her
the prestige he enjoyed among his fellows as a football-player and
an athlete. In the end his patronage and his boasting had become
insupportable to a girl of any spirit. And his dancing! It seemed to
her that he held her before him like a shield, and then charged the
room with her. She had found herself the centre of all eyes, her
pretty dress torn, her hair about her ears. So that she had shaken
him off – with too much impatience, no doubt, and too little consideration for the touchiness of his temper. And then, what stormy
looks, what mutterings, what disappearances into the refreshment-
room – and, finally, what fierce jealousy of the schoolmaster! Laura
awoke at last to the disagreeable fact that she had to drive home
with him – and he had already made her ridiculous. Even Polly –
the bedizened Polly – looked grave, and there had been angry
conferences between her and her brother.

Then came the departure, Laura by this time full of terrors, but
not knowing what to do, nor how else she was to get home. And,
oh! that grinning band of youths round the door – Mason's triumphant leap into the cart and boisterous farewells to his friends –
and that first perilous moment, when the pony had almost backed

into the mill-stream, and was only set right again by half a dozen stalwart arms, amid the laughter of the street!

As for the wild drive through the dark, she shivered again, half with anger, half with terror, as she thought of it. How had they ever got home? She could not tell. He was drunk, of course. He seemed to her to have driven into everything and over everything, abusing the schoolmaster and Mr Helbeck and his mother all the time, and turning upon her when she answered him, or showed any terror of what might happen to them, now with fury, and now with attempts at love-making which it had taken all her power over him to quell.

Their rush up the park had been like the ride of the wild horseman. Every moment she had expected to be in the river. And with the approach of the house he had grown wilder and more unmanageable than before. 'Dang it! let's wake up the old Papist!' he had said to her when she had tried to stop his singing. 'What harm'll it do?'

As for the shame of their arrival, the very thought of Mr Helbeck standing silent on the steps as they approached, of Hubert's behaviour, of her host's manner to her in the hall, made her shut her eyes and hide her red face against Fricka for sympathy. How was she ever to meet Mr Helbeck again, to hold her own against him any more!

An hour later Laura, very carefully dressed, and holding herself very erect, entered Augustina's room.

'Oh, Laura!' cried Mrs Fountain as the door opened. She was very flushed, and she stared from her bed at her stepdaughter in an agitated silence.

Laura stopped short.

'Well, what is it, Augustina? What have you heard?'

'Laura! how *can* you do such things!'

And Augustina, who already had her breakfast beside her, raised her handkerchief to her eyes and began to cry. Laura threw up her head and walked away to a far window, where she turned and confronted Mrs Fountain.

'Well, he has been quick in telling you,' she said, in a low but fierce voice.

'He? What do you mean? My brother? As if he had said a word! I don't believe he ever would. But Mrs Denton heard it all.'

'Mrs Denton?' said Laura. '*Mrs Denton?* What on earth had she to do with it?'

'She heard you drive up. You know her room looks on the front.'

'And she listened? sly old creature!' said Laura, recovering herself. 'Well, it can't be helped. If she heard, she heard, and whatever I may feel, I'm not going to apologise to Mrs Denton.'

'But, Laura – Laura – was he –'

Augustina could not finish the odious question.

'I suppose he was,' said Laura, bitterly. 'It seems to be the natural thing for young men of that sort.'

'Laura, do come here.'

Laura came unwillingly, and Augustina took her hands and looked up at her.

'And, Laura, he was abominably rude to Alan!'

'Yes, he was, and I'm very sorry,' said the girl slowly. 'But it can't be helped, and it's no good making yourself miserable, Augustina.'

'Miserable? I? It's you, Laura, who look miserable. I never saw you so white and dragged. You must never, never see him again.'

The girl's obstinacy awoke in a moment.

'I don't know that I shall promise that, Augustina.'

'Oh, Laura! as if you could wish to,' said Augustina, in tears.

'I can't give up my father's people,' said the girl, stiffly. 'But he shall never annoy Mr Helbeck again, I promise you that, Augustina.'

'Oh! you did look so nice, Laura, and your dress was so pretty!'

Laura laughed, rather grimly.

'There's not much of it left this morning,' she said. 'However, as one of the gentlemen who kindly helped to ruin it said last night, "Lor, bless yer, it'll wesh!" '

After breakfast Laura found herself in the drawing-room, looking through an open window at the spring green in a very strained and irritable mood.

'I would not begin if I could not go on,' she said to herself with disdain. But her lip trembled.

So Mr Helbeck had taken offence, after all. Hardly a word at breakfast, except such as the briefest, barest civility required. And he was going away, it appeared, for three days, perhaps a week, on business. If he had given her the slightest opening, she had meant to master her pride sufficiently to renew her apologies and ask his advice, subject, of course, to her own final judgment as to what kindred and kindness might require of her. But he had given her no opening, and the subject was not, apparently, to be renewed between them.

She might have asked him, too, to curb Mrs Denton's tongue. But no, it was not to be. Very well. The girl drew her small frame together and prepared, as no one thought for or befriended her, to think for and befriend herself.

She passed the next few days in some depression. Mr Helbeck was absent. Augustina was very ailing and querulous, and Laura was made to feel that it was her fault. Not a word of regret or apology came from Browhead Farm.

Meanwhile Mrs Denton had apparently made her niece understand that there was to be no more dallying with Miss Fountain. Whenever she and Laura met, Ellen lowered her head and ran. Laura found that the girl was not allowed to wait upon her personally any more. Meanwhile the housekeeper herself passed Miss Fountain with a manner and a silence which were in themselves an insult.

And two days after Helbeck's departure, Laura was crossing the hall towards tea-time, when she saw Mrs Denton admitting one of the Sisters from the Orphanage. It was the Reverend Mother herself, the portly shrewd-faced woman who had wished Mr Helbeck a good wife. Laura passed her, and the nun saluted her coldly. 'Dear me! – you shall have Augustina to yourself, my good friend,' thought Miss Fountain. 'Don't be afraid.' And she turned into the garden.

An hour later she came back. As she opened the door in the old wall she saw the Sister on the steps, talking with Mrs Denton. At sight of her they parted. The nun drew her long black cloak about her, ran down the steps, and hurried away.

And indoors, Laura could not imagine what had happened to her stepmother. Augustina was clearly excited, yet she would say nothing. Her restlessness was incessant, and at intervals there were furtive tears. Once or twice she looked at Laura with the most tragic eyes, but as soon as Laura approached her she would hastily bury herself in her newspaper, or begin counting the stitches of her knitting.

At last, after luncheon, Mrs Fountain suddenly threw down her work with a sigh that shook her small person from top to toe.

'I wish I knew what was wrong with you,' said Laura, coming up behind her, and dropping a pair of soft hands on her shoulders. 'Shall I get you your new tonic?'

'No!' said Augustina, pettishly; then, with a rush of words that she could not repress:

'Laura, you must – you positively must give up that young man.'

Laura came round and seated herself on the fender-stool in front of her stepmother.

'Oh! so that's it. Has anybody else been gossiping?'

'I do wish you wouldn't – you wouldn't take things so coolly!' cried Augustina. 'I tell you, the least trifle is enough to do a young girl of your age harm. Your father would have been so annoyed.'

'I don't think so,' said Laura, quietly. 'But who is it now? The Reverend Mother?'

Augustina hesitated. She had been recommended to keep things to herself. But she had no will to set against Laura's, and she was, in fact, bursting with suppressed remonstrance.

'It doesn't matter, my dear. One never knows where a story of that kind will go to. That's just what girls don't remember.'

'Who told a story, and what? I didn't see the Reverend Mother at the dance.'

'Laura! But you never thought, my dear – you never knew – that there was a cousin of Father Bowles' there – the man who keeps that little Catholic shop in Market Street. That's what comes, you see, of going to parties with people beneath you.'

'Oh! a cousin of Father Bowles was there?' said Laura slowly. 'Well, did he make a pretty tale?'

'Laura! you are the most provoking – You don't the least understand what people think. How could you go with him when everybody remonstrated?'

'Nobody remonstrated,' said the girl sharply.

'His sister begged you not to go.'

'His sister did nothing of the kind. She was staying the night in the village, and there was literally nothing for me to do but come home with Hubert or to throw myself on some stranger.'

'And such stories as one hears about this dreadful young man!' cried Augustina.

'I dare say. There are always stories.'

'I couldn't even tell you what they are about!' said Augustina. 'Your father would *certainly* have forbidden it altogether.'

There was a silence. Laura held her head as high as ever. She was, in fact, in a fever of contradiction and resentment, and the interference of people like Mrs Denton and the Sisters was fast bringing about Mason's forgiveness. Naturally, she was likely to hear the worst of him in that house. What Helbeck, or what dependent on a Helbeck, would give him the benefit of any doubt?

Augustina knitted with all her might for a few minutes, and then looked up.

'Don't you think,' she said, with a timid change of tone – 'don't you think, dear, you might go to Cambridge for a few weeks? I am sure the Friedlands would take you in. You would come in for all the parties, and – and you needn't trouble about me. Sister Angela's niece could come and stay here for a few weeks. The Reverend Mother told me so.'

Laura rose.

'Sister Angela suggested that? Thank you, I won't have my plans settled for me by Sister Angela. If you and Mr Helbeck want to turn me out, why, of course I shall go.'

Augustina held out her hands in terror at the girl's attitude and voice.

'Laura, don't say such things! As if you weren't an angel to me! As if I could bear the thought of anybody else!'

A quiver ran through Laura's features. 'Well, then, don't bear it,' she said, kneeling down again beside her stepmother. 'You look quite ill and excited, Augustina. I think we'll keep the Reverend Mother out in future. Won't you lie down and let me cover you up?'

So it ended for the time – with physical weakness on Augustina's part, and caresses on Laura's.

But when she was alone, Miss Fountain sat down and tried to think things out.

'What are the Sisters meddling for? Do they find me in their way? I'm flattered! I wish I was. Well! – is drunkenness the worst thing in the world?' she asked herself deliberately. 'Of course, if it goes beyond a certain point it is like madness – you must keep out of its way, for your own sake. But papa used to say there were many things a great deal worse. So there are! – meanness, and shuffling with truth for the sake of your soul. As for the other tales, I don't believe them. But if I did, I am not going to marry him!'

She felt herself very wise. In truth, as Stephen Fountain had realised with some anxiety before his death, among Laura's many ignorances, none was so complete or so dangerous as her ignorance of all the ugly ground facts that are strewn round us, for the stumbling of mankind. She was as determined not to know them, as he was invincibly shy of telling them.

For the rest, her reflections represented, no doubt, many dicta that in the course of her young life she had heard from her father. To Stephen Fountain the whole Christian doctrine of sin was 'the enemy'; and the mystical hatred of certain actions and habits, as such was the fount of half the world's unreason.

The following day it was Father Bowles's turn. He came over in what seemed to be his softest and most catlike mood, rubbing his hands over his chest in a constant glee at his own jokes. He was amiability itself to Laura. But he, too, had his twenty minutes alone with Augustina; and afterwards Mrs Fountain ventured once more to speak to Laura of change and amusement. Miss Fountain smiled, and replied as before – that, in the first place, she had no invitations, and in the next, she had no dresses. But again, as before – if Mr Helbeck should express a wish that her visit to Bannisdale should come to an end, that would be another matter.

Next morning Laura was taking a walk in the park, when a letter was brought to her by old Wilson, the groom, cowman, and general factotum.

She took it to a sheltered nook by the riverside and read it. It was from Hubert Mason, in his best commercial hand, and it ran as follows:

'Dear Miss Fountain, – You would not allow me, I know, to call you cousin Laura any more, so I don't attempt it. And of course I don't deserve it – nor that you should ever shake hands with me again. I can't get over thinking of what I've done. Mother and Polly will tell you that I have hardly slept at nights – for of course you won't believe me. How I can have been such a blackguard I don't understand. I must have taken too much. All I know is it didn't seem much, and but for the agitation of my mind, I don't believe anything would ever have gone wrong. But I couldn't bear to see you dancing with that man and despising me. And there it is – I can never get over it, and you will never forgive me. I feel I can't stay here any more, and mother has consented at last to let me have some money on the Farm. If I could just see you before I go, to say good-bye, and ask your pardon, there would be a better chance for me. I can't come to Mr

Helbeck's house, of course, and I don't suppose you would come here. I shall be coming home from Kirby Whardale fair to-morrow night, and shall be crossing the little bridge in the park – upper end – some time between eight and nine. But I know you won't be there. I can't expect it, and I feel it pretty badly, I can tell you. I did hope I might have become something better through knowing you. Whatever you may think of me, I am always

'Your respectful and humble cousin,

'HUBERT MASON.'

'Well – upon my word!' said Laura. She threw the letter on to the grass beside her, and sat, with her hands round her knees, staring at the river, in a sparkle of anger and amazement.

What audacity! – to expect her to steal out at night – in the dusk, any way – to meet him – *him!* She fed her wrath on the imagination of all the details that would belong to such an escapade. It would be after supper, of course, in the fast lengthening twilight. Helbeck and his sister would be in the drawing-room – for Mr Helbeck was expected home on the following day – and she might perfectly well leave them, as she often did, to talk their little Catholic gossip by themselves, and then slip out by the chapel passage and door, through the old garden, to the gate in the wall above the river bank, and so to the road that led along the Greet through the upper end of the park. Nothing, of course, could be easier – nothing!

Merely to think of it, for a girl of Laura's temperament, was already bit by bit to incline to it. She began to turn it over, to taste the adventure of it – to talk very fast to Fricka, under her breath, with little gusts of laughter. And no doubt there was something mollifying in the boy's humble expressions. As for his sleepless nights – how salutary! how very salutary! Only the nail must be driven in deeper – must be turned in the wound.

It would need a vast amount of severity, perhaps, to undo the effects of her mere obedience to his call – supposing she made up her mind to obey it. Well! she would be quite equal to severity. She would speak very plain things to him – very plain things indeed. It was her first serious adventure with any of these big, foolish, troublesome creatures of the male sex, and she rose to it much as Helbeck might have risen to the playing of a salmon in the Greet. Yes! he should say good-bye to her, let priests and nuns talk what scandal they pleased. Yes! – he should go on his way forgiven and admonished – if he wished it – for kindred's sake.

Her cheek burned, her heart beat fast. He and she were of one blood – both of them ill-regarded by aristocrats and holy Romans. As for him, he was going to ruin at home; and there was in him this strange, artistic gift to be thought for and rescued. He had all the faults of the young cub. Was he to be wholly disowned for that? Was she to cast him off for ever at the mere bidding of the Helbecks and their friends?

He would never, of course, be allowed to enter the Bannisdale drawing-room, and she had no intention at present of going to Browhead Farm. Well, then, under the skies and the clouds! A gracious pardon, an appropriate lecture – and a short farewell.

All that day and the next Laura gave herself to her whim. She was perfectly conscious meanwhile that it was a reckless and a wilful thing that she was planning. She liked it none the less for that. In fact, the scheme was the final crystallisation of all that bitterness of mood that had poisoned and tormented her ever since her first coming to Bannisdale. And it gave her for the moment the morbid pleasure that all angry people get from letting loose the angry word or act.

Meanwhile she became more and more conscious of a certain network of blame and discussion that seemed to be closing about her and her actions. It showed itself by a number of small signs. When she went into Whinthorpe to shop for Augustina she fancied that the assistants in the shop, and even the portly draper himself, looked at her with a sly curiosity. The girl's sore pride grew more unmanageable hour by hour. If there was some ill-natured gossip about her, going the round in the town and neighbourhood, had she – till now – given the least shadow of excuse for it? Not the least shade of a shadow!

Mr Helbeck, his sister, and Laura were in the drawing-room after supper. Laura had been observing Mrs Fountain closely.

'She is longing to have her talk with him,' thought the girl; 'and she shall have it – as much as she likes.'

The shutters were not yet closed, and the room, with its crackling logs, was filled with a gentle mingled light. The sun, indeed, was gone, but the west still glowed, and the tall larches in the front enclosure stood black against a golden dome of sky. Laura rose and left the room. As she opened the door she caught Augustina's quick look of relief and the drop of the knitting-needles.

Fricka was safely prisoned upstairs. Laura slipped on a hat and a dark cloak that were hanging in the hall, and ran down the passage leading to the chapel. The heavy seventeenth-century door at the end of it took her some trouble to open without noise, but it was done at last, and she was in the old garden.

Her little figure in its cloak, among the dark yews, was hardly to be seen in the dusk. The garden was silence itself, and the gate in the wall was open. Once on the road beside the river she could hardly restrain herself from running, so keen was the air, so free and wide the evening solitude. All things were at peace; nothing moved but a few birds and the tiniest intermittent breeze. Overhead, great thunderclouds kept the sunset; beneath, the blues of the evening were all interwoven with rose; so, too, were the wood and sky reflections in the gently moving water. In some of the pools the trout were still lazily rising; pigeons and homing rooks were slowly passing through the clear space that lay between the tree-tops and the just emerging stars; and once Laura stopped, holding her breath, thinking that she saw through the dusk the blue flash of a kingfisher making for a nest she knew. Even in this dimmed light the trees had the May magnificence – all but the oaks, which still dreamed of a best to come. Here and there a few tufts of primroses, on the bosom of the crag above the river, lonely and self-sufficing, like all loveliest things, starred the dimness of the rock.

Laura's feet danced beneath her; the evening beauty and her passionate response flowed as it were into each other, made one beating pulse; never, in spite of qualms and angers, had she been more physically happy, more alive. She passed the seat where she and Helbeck had lingered on Easter Sunday; then she struck into a path high above the river, under spreading oaks; and presently a little bridge came in sight, with some steps in the crag leading down to it.

At the near end of the bridge, thrown out into the river a little way, for the convenience of fishermen, was a small wooden platform, with a railing, which held a seat. The seat was well hidden under the trees and bank, and Laura settled herself there.

She had hardly waited five minutes, absorbed in the sheer pleasure of the rippling river and the soft air, when she heard steps approaching the bank. Looking up, she saw Mason's figure against the sky. He paused at the top of the rocky staircase, to scan the bridge and its approaches. Not seeing her, he threw up his hand, with some exclamation that she could not hear.

She smiled and rose.

As her small form became visible, between the paleness of the wooden platform and a luminous patch in the river, she heard a cry, then a hurrying down the rock steps.

He stopped about a yard from her. She did not offer her hand, and after an instant's pause, during which his eyes tried to search her face in the darkness, he took off his hat and drew his hand across his brow with a deep breath.

'I never thought you'd come,' he said, huskily.

'Well, certainly you had no business to ask me! And I can only stay a very few minutes. Suppose you sit down there.'

She pointed to one of the rock steps, while she settled herself again on the seat, some little distance away from him.

Then there was an awkward silence, which Laura took no trouble to break. Mason broke it at last in desperation.

'You know that I'm an awful hand at saying anything, Miss – Miss Fountain. I can't – so it's no good. But I've got my lesson. I've had a pretty rough time of it, I can tell you, since last week.'

'You behaved about as badly as you could – didn't you?' said Laura's soft yet cutting voice out of the dark.

Mason fidgeted.

'I can't make it no better,' he said at last. 'There's no saying I can, for I can't. And if I did give you excuses, you'd not believe em. There was a devil got hold of me that evening – that's the truth on't. And it was only a glass or two I took. Well, there! – I'd have cut my hand off sooner.'

His tone of miserable humility began to affect her rather strangely. It was not so easy to drive in the nail.

'You needn't be so repentant,' she said, with a little shrinking laugh. 'One has to forget – everything – in good time. You've given Whinthorpe people something to talk about at my expense – for which I am not at all obliged to you. You nearly killed me, which doesn't matter. And you behaved disgracefully to Mr Helbeck. But it's done – and now you've got to make up – somehow.'

'Has he made you pay for it – since?' said Mason, eagerly.

'He? Mr Helbeck?' She laughed. Then she added, with all the severity she could muster, 'He treated me in a most kind and gentlemanly way – if you want to know. The great pity is that you – and Cousin Elizabeth – understand nothing at all about him.'

He groaned. She could hear his feet restlessly moving.

'Well – and now you are going to Froswick,' she resumed. 'What are you going to do there?'

'There's an uncle of mine in one of the shipbuilding yards there. He's got leave to take me into the fitting department. If I suit he'll get me into the office. It's what I've wanted this two years.'

'Well, now you've got it,' she said impatiently, 'don't be dismal. You have your chance.'

'Yes, and I don't care a haporth about it,' he said, with sudden energy, throwing his head up and bringing his fist down on his knee.

She felt her power, and liked it. But she hurried to answer:

'Oh! yes you do! If you're a man, you *must*. You'll learn a lot of new things – you'll keep straight, because you'll have plenty to do. Why, it will "hatch you over again, and hatch you different," as somebody said. You'll see.'

He looked at her, trying hard to catch her expression in the dusk.

'And if I do come back different, perhaps – perhaps – soom day you'll not be ashamed to be seen wi' me? Look here, Miss Laura. From the first time I set eyes on you – from that day you came up – that Sunday – I haven't been able to settle to a thing. I felt, right enough, I wasn't fit to speak to you. And yet I'm your – well, your kith and kin, don't you see? There can't be no such tremendous gap atween us as all that. If I can just manage myself a bit, and find the work that suits me, and get away from these fellows here, and this beastly farm –'

'Ah! – have you been quarrelling with Daffady all day?'

She looked for him to fly out. But he only stared, and then turned away.

'O Lord! what's the good of talking?' he said, with an accent that startled her.

She rose from her seat.

'Are you sorry I came to talk to you? You didn't deserve it – did you?'

Her voice was the pearliest, most musical, and yet most distant of things. He rose, too – held by it.

'And now you must just go and make a man of yourself. That's what you have to do – you see? I wish papa was alive. He'd tell you how – I can't. But if you forget your music, it'll be a sin – and if you send me your song to write out for you, I'll do it. And tell Polly I'll come and see her again some day. Now good-night! They'll be locking up if I don't hurry home.'

But he stood on the step, barring the way.

'I say, give me something to take with me,' he said, hoarsely. 'What's that in your hat?'

'In my hat?' she said, laughing – (but if there had been light he would have seen that her lips had paled). 'Why, a bunch of buttercups. I bought them at Whinthorpe yesterday.'

'Give me one,' he said.

'Give you a sham buttercup? What nonsense!'

'It's better than nothing,' he said doggedly, and he held out his hand.

She hesitated; then she took off her hat and quietly loosened one of the flowers. Her golden hair shone in the dimness. Mason never took his eyes off her little head. He was keeping a grip on himself that was taxing a whole new set of powers – straining the lad's unripe nature in wholly new ways.

She put the flower in his hand.

'There; now we're friends again, aren't we? Let me pass, please – and good-night!'

He moved to one side, blindly fighting with the impulse to throw his powerful arms round her and keep her there, or carry her across the bridge – at his pleasure.

But her light fearlessness mastered him. He let her go; he watched her figure on the steps, against the moonlight between the oaks overhead.

'Good-night!' she dropped again, already far away – far above him. The young man felt a sob in his throat.

'My God! I sha'n't ever see her again,' he said to himself in a sudden terror. 'She is going to that house – to that man!'

For the first time a wild jealousy of Helbeck awoke in him. He rushed across the bridge, dropped on a stone halfway up the further bank, then strained his eyes across the river.

... Yes, there she passed, a swift moving whiteness, among the great trees that stood like watchmen along the high edge of the water. Below him flowed the stream, a gulf of darkness, rent here and there by sheets and jags of silver. And she, that pale wraith – across it – far away – was flitting from his ken.

All the fountains of the youth's nature surged up in one great outcry and confusion. He thought of his boyish loves and sensualities — of the girls who had provoked them — of some of the ugly facts connected with them. A great astonishment, a great sickening, came upon him. He felt the burden of the flesh, the struggle of the spirit. And through it all, the maddest and most covetous yearning! — welling up through schemes and hopes, that like the moonlit ripples on the Greet, dissolved as fast as they took shape.

Meanwhile Laura went quickly home. A new tenderness, a new remorse towards the 'cub' was in the girl's mind. Ought she to have gone? Had she been kind? Oh! she would be his friend and good angel — without any nonsense, of course.

She hurried through the trees and along the dimly gleaming path. Suddenly she perceived in the distance the sparkle of a lantern.

How vexatious! Was there no escape for her? She looked in some trouble at the climbing woods above, at the steep bank below.

Ah! well, her hat was large, and hid her face. And her dress was all covered by her cloak. She hastened on.

It was a man — an old man — carrying a bundle and a lantern. He seemed to waver and stop as she approached him, and at the actual moment of her passing him, to her amazement, he suddenly threw himself against one of the trees on the mountain side of the path, and his lantern showed her his face for an instant — a white face, stricken with — fear, was it? or what?

Fright gained upon herself. She ran on, and as she ran it seemed to her that she heard something fall with a clang, and, afterwards, a cry. She looked back. The old man was still there, erect, but his light was gone.

Well, no doubt he had dropped his lantern. Let him light it again. It was no concern of hers.

Here was the door in the wall. It opened to her touch. She glided in — across the garden — found the chapel door ajar, and in a few more seconds was safe in her own room.

CHAPTER THREE

Laura was standing before her looking-glass, straightening the curls that her rapid walk had disarranged, when her attention was caught by certain unusual sounds in the house. There was a hurrying of distant feet – calls, as though from the kitchen region – and lastly, the deep voice of Mr Helbeck. Miss Fountain paused, brush in hand, wondering what had happened.

A noise of fluttering skirts, and a cry for 'Laura!' – Miss Fountain opened her door, and saw Augustina, who never ran, hurrying as fast as her feebleness would let her, towards her stepdaughter.

'Laura! – where is my sal volatile? You gave me some yesterday, you remember, for my headache. There's somebody ill, downstairs.'

She paused for breath.

'Here it is,' said Laura, finding the bottle, and bringing it. 'What's wrong?'

'Oh, my dear, such an adventure! There's an old man fainted in the kitchen. He came to the back-door to ask for a light for his lantern. Mrs Denton says he was shaking all over when she first saw him, and as white as her apron. He told her he'd seen the ghost! "I've often heard tell of the Bannisdale Lady," he said, "and now I've seen her!" She asked him to sit down a minute to rest himself, and he fainted straight away. He's that old Scarsbrook, you know, whose wife does our washing. They live in that cottage by the weir, the other end of the park. – I must go! – Mrs Denton's giving him some brandy – and Alan's gone down. Isn't it an extraordinary thing?'

'Very,' said Laura, accompanying her stepmother along the passage. 'What did he see?'

She paused, laying a restraining hand on Augustina's arm – cudgelling her brains the while. Yes! she could remember now a few contemptuous remarks of Mr Helbeck to Father Leadham on the subject of a ghost story that had sprung up during the Squire's memory in connection with the park and the house – a quite modern story, according to Helbeck, turning on the common motive of a gipsy woman and her curse, started some forty years before this date, with a local success not a little offensive, apparently, to the owner of Bannisdale.

'What did he see?' repeated the girl. 'Don't hurry, Augustina; you know the doctor told you not. Shall I take the sal volatile?'

'Oh, no! – they want me.' In any matter of doctoring small or great, Augustina had the happiest sense of her own importance. 'I don't know what he saw exactly. It was a lady, he says – he knew it was, by the hat and the walk. She was all in black – with "a Dolly Varden hat" – fancy the old fellow! – that hid her face – and a little white hand that shot out sparks as he came up to her! Did you ever hear such a tale? Now, Laura, I'm all right. Let me go. Come when you like.'

Augustina hurried off; Laura was left standing pensive in the passage.

'H'm, that's unlucky,' she said to herself.

Then she looked down at her right hand. An old-fashioned diamond ring with a large centre stone, which had been her mother's, shone on the third finger. With an involuntary smile she drew off the ring and went back to her room.

'What's to be done now?' she thought, as she put the ring in a drawer. 'Shall I go down and explain – say I was out for a stroll?' – She shook her head. – 'Won't do now – I should have had more presence of mind a minute ago. Augustina would suspect a hundred things. It's really dramatic. Shall I go down? He didn't see my face – no, that I'll answer for! Here's for it!'

She pulled out the golden mass of her hair till it made a denser frame than usual round her brow, looked at her white dress – shook her head dubiously – laughed at her own flushed face in the glass, and calmly went downstairs.

She found an anxious group in the great bare servants' hall. The old man, supported by pillows, was stretched on a wooden settle, with Helbeck, Augustina, and Mrs Denton standing by. The first things she saw were the old peasant's closed eyes and pallid face – then Helbeck's grave and puzzled countenance above him. The squire turned at Miss Fountain's step. Did she imagine it – or was there a peculiar sharpness in his swift glance?

Mrs Denton had just been administering a second dose of brandy, and was apparently in the midst of her own report to her master of Scarsbrook's story.

' "I wor just aboot to pass her," he said, "when I nawticed 'at her feet made noa noise. She keäm glidin – an glidin – an my hair stood reet oop – it lifted t' whole top o' my yed. An she gaed passt me like a puff o' wind – as cauld as ice – an I wor mair deed nor alive. An I luked afther her, an she vanisht i' th' varra middle o' t' path. An my leet went oot – an I durstn't ha gane on, if it wor iver so – so I just crawled back tet hoose –" '

'The door in the wall!' thought Laura. 'He didn't know it was there.'

She had remained in the background while Mrs Denton was speaking, but now she approached the settle. Mrs Denton threw a sour look at her and flounced out of her way. Helbeck silently made room for her. As she passed him, she felt instinctively that his distant politeness had become something more pronounced. He left her questions to Augustina to answer, and himself thrust his hands into his pockets and moved away.

'Have you sent for any one?' said Laura to Mrs Fountain.

'Yes. Wilson's gone in the pony-cart for the wife. And if he doesn't come round by the time she gets here – some one will have to go for the doctor, Alan?'

She looked round vaguely.

'Of course. Wilson must go on,' said Helbeck from the distance. 'Or I'll go myself.'

'But he is coming round,' said Laura, pointing.

'If yo'll nobbut move oot o' t' way, miss, we'll be able to get at im,' said Mrs Denton sharply. Laura hastily obeyed her. The housekeeper brought more brandy; then signs of returning force grew stronger, and by the time the wife appeared the old fellow was feebly beginning to move and look about him.

Amid the torrent of lamentations, questions, and hypotheses that the wife poured forth, Laura withdrew into the background. But she could not prevail on herself to go. Daring or excitement held her there, till the old man should be quite himself again.

He struggled to his feet at last, and said, with a long sigh that was still half a shudder, 'Aye – noo I'll goa home – Lisbeth.'

He was a piteous spectacle as he stood there, still trembling through all his stunned frame, his wrinkled face drawn and bloodless, his grey hair in a tragic confusion. Suddenly, as he looked at his wife, he said with a clear solemnity, 'Lisbeth – I ha got my death warrant!'

'Don't say any such thing, Scarsbrook,' said Helbeck, coming forward to support him. 'You know I don't believe in this ghost business – and never did. You saw some stranger in the park – and she passed you too quickly for you to see where she went to. You may be sure that'll turn out to be the truth. You remember – it's a public path – anybody might be there. Just try and take that view of it – and don't fret, for your wife's sake. We'll make inquiries, and I'll come and see you to-morrow. And as for death warrants, we're all in God's care, you know – don't forget that.'

He smiled with a kindly concern and pity on the old man. But Scarsbrook shook his head.

'It wur t' Bannisdale Lady,' he repeated; 'I've often heerd on her – often – and noo I've seen her.'

'Well, to-morrow you'll be quite proud of it,' said Helbeck cheerfully. 'Come, and let me put you into the cart. I think, if we make a comfortable seat for you, you'll be fit to drive home now.'

Supported by the squire's strong arm on one side, and his wife on the other, Scarsbrook managed to hobble down the long passage leading to the door in the inner courtyard, where the pony-cart was standing. It was evident that his perceptions were still wholly dazed. He had not recognised or spoken to any one in the room but the squire – not even to his old crony, Mrs Denton.

Laura drew a long breath.

'Augustina, do go to bed,' she said, going up to her stepmother – 'or you'll be ill next.'

Augustina allowed herself to be led upstairs. But it was long before she would let her stepdaughter leave her. She was full of supernatural terrors and excitements, and must talk about all the former appearances of the ghost – the stories that used to be told in her childhood – the new or startling details in the old man's version, and so forth. 'What could he have meant by the light on the hand?' she said, wondering. 'I never heard of that before. And she used always to be in grey; and now he says that she had a black dress from top to toe.'

'Their wardrobes are so limited – poor, damp, sloppy things!' said Laura flippantly, as she brushed her stepmother's hair. 'Do you suppose this nonsense will be all over the country side to-morrow, Augustina?'

'What do you *really* think he saw, Laura?' cried Mrs Fountain, wavering between doubt and belief.

'Goodness! – don't ask me.' Miss Fountain shrugged her small shoulders. 'I don't keep a family ghost.'

When at last Augustina had been settled in bed, and persuaded to take some of her sleeping medicine, Laura was bidding her good-night, when Mrs Fountain said, 'Oh! I forgot, Laura – there was a letter brought in for you from the post-office, by Wilson this afternoon – he gave it to Mrs Denton, and she forgot it till after dinner – '

'Of course – because it was mine,' said Laura vindictively. 'Where is it?'

'On the drawing-room chimney-piece.'

'All right. I'll go for it. But I shall be disturbing Mr Helbeck.'

'Oh! no – it's much too late. Alan will have gone to his study.'

Miss Fountain stood a moment outside her stepmother's door, consulting her watch.

For she was anxious to get her letter, and not at all anxious to fall in with Mr Helbeck. At least, so she would have explained herself had any one questioned her. In fact, her wishes and intentions were in tumultuous confusion. All the time that she was waiting on Augustina her brain, her pulse was racing. In the added touch of stiffness which she had observed in Helbeck's manner, she easily divined the result of that conversation he had no doubt held with Augustina after dinner, while she was by the river. Did he think even worse of her than he had before? Well! – if he and Augustina could do without her, let them send her away – by all manner of means! She had her own friends, her own money, was in all respects her own mistress, and only asked to be allowed to lead her life as she pleased.

Nevertheless – as she crossed the darkness of the hall, with her candle in her hand – Laura Fountain was very near indeed to a fit of wild weeping. During the months following her father's death, these agonies of crying had come upon her night after night – unseen by any human being. She felt now the approach of an old enemy, and struggled with it. 'One mustn't have this excitement every night!' she said to herself, half mocking. 'No nerves would stand it.'

A light under the library door. Well and good. How – she wondered – did he occupy himself there, through so many solitary hours? Once or twice she had heard him come upstairs to bed, and never before one or two o'clock.

Suddenly she stood abashed. She had thrown open the drawing-room door, and the room lay before her, almost in darkness. One dim lamp still burnt at the further end, and in the middle of the room stood Mr Helbeck, arrested in his walk to and fro, and the picture of astonishment.

Laura drew back in real discomfiture. 'Oh, I beg your pardon, Mr Helbeck! I had no notion that any one was still here.'

'Is there anything I can do for you?' he said, advancing.

'Augustina told me there was a letter for me this evening.'

'Of course. It is here on the mantelpiece. I ought to have remembered it.'

He took up the letter and held it towards her. Then suddenly he paused – and sharply withdrawing it, he placed it on a table beside him, and laid his hand upon it. She saw a flash of quick resolution in his face, and her own pulses gave a throb.

'Miss Fountain – will you excuse my detaining you for a moment? I have been thinking much about this old man's story, and the possible explanation of it. It struck me in a very singular way. As you know, I have never paid much attention to the ghost story here – we have never before had a testimony so direct. Is it possible – that you might throw some light upon it? You left us, you remember, after dinner. Did you by chance go into the garden? – the evening was tempting, I think. If so, your memory might possibly recall to you some – slight thing.'

'Yes,' she said, after a moment's hesitation, 'I did go into the garden.'

His eye gleamed. He came a step nearer.

'Did you see or hear anything – to explain what happened?'

She did not answer for a moment. She made a vague movement, as though to recover her letter – looked curiously into a glass case that stood beside her, containing a few Stuart relics and autographs. Then, with absolute self-possession, she turned and confronted him, one hand resting on the glass case.

'Yes – I can explain it all. I was the ghost!'

There was a moment's silence. A smile – a smile that she winced under, showed itself on Helbeck's lip.

'I imagined as much,' he said quietly.

She stood there, torn by different impulses. Then a passion of annoyance with herself, and anger with him, descended on her.

'Now perhaps you would like to know why I concealed it?' she said, with all the dignity she could command. 'Simply – because I had gone out to meet and say good-bye to a person – who is my relation – whom I cannot meet in this house, and against whom there is here an unreasonable' – She hesitated; then resumed, leaning obstinately on the words – 'Yes! take it all in all, it *is* an unreasonable prejudice!'

'You mean Mr Hubert Mason?'

She nodded.

'You think it an unreasonable prejudice after what happened the other night?'

She wavered.

'I don't want to defend what happened the other night,' she said, while her voice shook.

Helbeck observed her carefully. There was a great decision in his manner, and at the same time a fine courtesy.

'You knew, then, that he was to be in the park? Forgive my questions. They are not mere curiosity.'

'Perhaps not,' she said indifferently. 'But I think I have told you all that needs to be told. May I have my letter?'

She stepped forward.

'One moment. I wonder, Miss Fountain,' – he chose his words slowly – 'if I could make you understand my position. It is this. My sister brings a young lady, her stepdaughter, to stay under my roof. That young lady happens to be connected with a family in this neighbourhood, which is already well known to me. For some of its members I have nothing but respect – about one I happen to have a strong opinion. I have reason for my opinion. I imagine that very few people of any way of thinking would hold me either unreasonable or prejudiced in the matter. Naturally, it gives me some concern that a young lady towards whom I feel a certain responsibility should be much seen with this young man. He is not her equal socially, and – pardon me – she knows nothing at all about the type to which he belongs. Indirectly I try to warn her. I speak to my sister as gently as I can. But from the first she rejects all I have to say – she gives me credit for no good intention – and she will have none of my advice. At last a disagreeable incident happens – and unfortunately the knowledge of it is not confined to ourselves –'

Laura threw him a flashing look.

'No! – there are people who have taken care of that!' she said.

Helbeck took no notice.

'It is known not only to ourselves,' he repeated steadily. 'It starts gossip. My sister is troubled. She asks you to put an end to this state of things, and she consults me, feeling that indeed we are all in some way concerned.'

'Oh, say at once that I have brought scandal on you all!' cried Laura. 'That of course is what Sister Angela and Father Bowles have been saying to Augustina. They are pleased to show the greatest anxiety about me – so much so, that they most kindly wish to relieve me of the charge of Augustina. So I understand! But I fear I am neither docile nor grateful! – that I never shall be grateful –'

Helbeck interrupted.

'Let us come to that presently. I should like to finish my story. While my sister and I are consulting, trying to think of all that can be done to stop a foolish talk and undo an unlucky incident, this same young lady' – his voice took a cold clearness – 'steals out by night to keep an appointment with this man, who has already done her so great a disservice. Now I should like to ask her, if all this is kind – is reasonable – is generous towards the persons with whom she is at present living – if such conduct is not' – he paused – 'unwise towards herself – unjust towards others.'

His words came out with a strong and vibrating emphasis. Laura confronted him with crimson cheeks.

'I think that will do, Mr Helbeck!' she cried. 'You have had your say. – Now just let me say this – These people were my relations – I have no other kith and kin in the world.'

He made a quick step forward as though in distress. But she put up her hand.

'I want very much to say this, please. I knew perfectly well when I came here that you couldn't like the Masons – for many reasons.' Her voice broke again. 'You never liked Augustina's marriage – you weren't likely to want to see anything of papa's people. I didn't ask you to see them. All my standards and theirs are different from yours. But I prefer theirs – not yours! I have nothing to do with yours. I was brought up – well, to *hate* yours – if one must tell the truth.'

She paused, half suffocated, her chest heaving. Helbeck's glance enveloped her – took in the contrast between her violent words and the shrinking delicacy of her small form. A great melting stole over the man's dark face. But he spoke dryly enough.

'I imagine the standards of Protestants and Catholics are pretty much alike in matters of this kind. But don't let us waste time any more over what has already happened. I should like, I confess, to plead with you as to the future.'

He looked at her kindly, even entreatingly. All through this scene she had been unwillingly, angrily conscious of his personal dignity and charm – a dignity that seemed to emerge in moments of heightened action or feeling, and to slip out of sight again under the absent hermit-manner of his ordinary life. She was smarting under his words – ready to concentrate a double passion of resentment upon them, as soon as she should be alone and free to recall them. And yet –

'As to the future,' she said coldly. 'That is simple enough as far as one person is concerned. Hubert Mason is going to Froswick immediately, into business.'

'I am glad to hear it – it will be very much for his good.'

He stopped a moment, searching for the word of persuasion and conciliation.

'Miss Fountain! – if you imagine that certain incidents which happened here long before you came into this neighbourhood had anything to do with what I have been saying now, let me assure you – most earnestly – that it is not so! I recognise fully that with regard to a certain case – of which you may have heard – the Masons and their friends honestly believed that wrong and injustice had been done. They attempted personal violence. I can hardly be expected to think it argument! But I bear them no malice. I say this because you may have heard of something that happened three of four years ago – a row in the streets, when Father Bowles and I were set upon. It has never weighed with me in the slightest, and I could have shaken hands with old Mason – who was in the crowd, and refused to stop the stone-throwing – the day after. As for Mrs Mason' – he looked up with a smile – 'if she could possibly have persuaded herself to come with her daughter and see you here, my welcome would not have been wanting. But, you know, she would as soon visit Gehenna! Nobody could be more conscious than I, Miss Fountain, that this is a dreary house for a young lady to live in – and –'

The colour mounted into his face, but he did not shrink from what he meant to say.

'And you have made us all feel that you regard the practices and observances by which we try to fill and inspire our lives, as mere hateful folly and superstition!' He checked himself. 'Is that too strong?' he added, with a sudden eagerness. 'If so, I apologise for and withdraw it!'

Laura, for a moment, was speechless. Then she gathered her forces, and said, with a voice she in vain tried to compose:

'I think you exaggerate, Mr Helbeck; at any rate, I hope you do. But the fact is, I – I ought not to have tried to bear it. Considering all that had happened at home – it was more than I had strength for! And perhaps – no good will come of going on with it – and it had better cease. Mr Helbeck! – if your Superior can really find a good nurse and companion at once, will you kindly communicate with her? I will go to Cambridge immediately, as soon as I can arrange with my friends. Augustina, no doubt, will come and stay with me somewhere at the sea, later on in the year.'

Helbeck had been listening to her – to the sharp determination of her voice – in total silence. He was leaning against the high mantel-piece, and his face was hidden from her. As she ceased to speak, he turned, and his mere aspect beat down the girl's anger in a moment. He shook his head sadly.

'Dr MacBride stopped me on the bridge yesterday, as he was coming away from the house.'

Laura drew back. Her eyes fastened upon him.

'He thinks her in a serious state. We are not to alarm her, or interfere with her daily habits. There is valvular disease – as I think you know – and it has advanced. Neither he nor any one can forecast.'

The girl's head fell. She recognised that the contest was over. She could not go; she could not leave Augustina; and the inference was clear. There had not been a word of menace, but she understood Mr Helbeck's will must prevail. She had brought this humiliating half-hour on herself – and she would have to bear the consequences of it. She moved towards Helbeck.

'Well, then, I must stay,' she said huskily, 'and I must try to – to remember where I am in future. I ought to be able to hide every-thing I feel – of course! But that unfortunately is what I never learnt. And – there are some ways of life – that – that are too far apart. However!' – she raised her hand to her brow, frowned, and thought a little – 'I can't make any promise about my cousins, Mr Helbeck. *I* know perfectly well – whatever may be said – that I have done nothing whatever to be ashamed of. I have wanted to –

to help my cousin. He is worth helping – in spite of everything –
and I *will* help him, if I can! But if I am to remain your guest, I see
that I must consult your wishes –'

Helbeck tried again to stop her with a gesture, but she hurried
on.

'As far as this house and neighbourhood are concerned, no one
shall have any reason – to talk.'

Then she threw her head back with a sudden flush.

'Of course, if people are born to say and think ill-natured things!
– like Mrs Denton –'

Helbeck exclaimed.

'I will see to that,' he said. 'You shall have no reason to complain
there.'

Laura shrugged her shoulders.

'Will you kindly give me my letter?'

As he handed it to her, she made him a little bow, walked to the
door before he could open it for her, and was gone.

Helbeck turned back, with a smothered exclamation. He put the
lamps out, and went slowly to his study.

As the master of Bannisdale closed the door of his library behind
him, the familiar room produced upon him a sharp and singular
impression. The most sacred and the most critical hours of his life
had been passed within its walls. As he entered it now, it seemed to
repulse him, to be no longer his.

The room was not large. It was the old library of the house, and
the Helbecks in their palmiest days had never been a literary race.
There was a little seventeenth century theology; and a few English
classics. There were the French books of Helbeck's grandmother –
'Madame,' as she was always known at Bannisdale; and amongst
them the worn brown volumes of St François de Sales, with the
yellowish paper slips that Madame had put in to mark her favourite
passages, somewhere in the days of the First Empire. Near by were
some stray military volumes, treatises on tactics and fortification,
that had belonged to a dashing young officer in the Dillon Regi-
ment, close to some 'Epîtres Amoureuses,' a translation of 'Daphnis
and Chloe,' and the like – all now sunk together into the same
dusty neglect.

On the wall above Helbeck's writing-table were ranged the books
that had been his mother's, together with those that he himself

habitually used. Here every volume was an old friend, a familiar tool. Alan Helbeck was neither a student nor a man of letters; but he had certain passionate prejudices, instincts, emotions, of which some books were the source and sustenance.

For the rest – during some years he had been a member of the Third Order of St Francis, and in its other features the room was almost the room of a religious. A priedieu stood against the inner wall, and a crucifix hung above it. A little further on was a small altar of St Joseph with its pictures, its statuette, and its candles; and a poor lithograph of Pio Nono looked down from the mantelpiece. The floor was almost bare, save for a few pieces of old matting here and there. The worn Turkey carpet that had formerly covered it had been removed to make the drawing-room comfortable for Augustina; so had most of the chairs. Those left were of the straightest and hardest.

In that dingy room, however, Helbeck had known the most blessed, the most intimate moments of the spiritual life. To-night he entered it with a strange sense of wrench – of mortal discouragement. Mechanically he went to his writing-table, and, sitting down before it, he took a key from his watch-chain and opened a large locked note-book that lay upon it.

The book contained a number of written meditations, a collection of passages and thoughts, together with some faded photographs of his mother, and of his earliest Jesuit teachers at Stonyhurst.

On the last page was a paragraph that only the night before he had copied from one of his habitual books of devotion – copying it as a spiritual exercise – making himself dwell upon every word of it.

'When shall I desire Thee alone – feed on Thee alone – O my Delight, my only good! O my loving and almighty Lord! free now this wretched heart from every attachment, from every earthly affection; adorn it with Thy holy virtues, and with a pure intention of doing all things to please Thee, that so I may open it to Thee, and with gentle violence compel Thee to come in, that Thou, O Lord, mayest work therein without resistance all those effects which from all Eternity Thou has desired to produce in me.'

He lingered a little on the words, his face buried in his hands. Then slowly he turned back to an earlier page –

'Man must use creatures as being in themselves indifferent. He must not be under their power, but use them for his own purpose, his own first and chiefest purpose, the salvation of his soul.'

A shudder passed through him. He rose hastily from his seat, and began to pace the room. He had already passed through a wrestle of the same kind, and had gone away to fight down temptation. To-night the struggle was harder. The waves of rising passion broke through him.

'Little pale, angry face! I gave her a scolding like a child – what joy to have forgiven her like a child! – to have asked her pardon in return – to have felt the soft head against my breast. She was very fierce with me – she hates me, I suppose. And yet – she is not indifferent to me! – she knows when I am there. Downstairs she was conscious of me all through – I knew it. Her secret was in her face. I guessed it – foolish child – from the first moment. Strange, stormy nature! – I see it all – her passion for her father, and for these peasants as belonging to him – her hatred of me and of our faith, because her father hated us – her feeling for Augustina – that rigid sense of obligation she has, just on the two or three points – points of natural affection. It is this sense, perhaps, that makes the soul of her struggle with this house – with me. How she loathes all that we love – humility, patience, obedience! She would sooner die than obey. Unless she loved! Then what an art, what an enchantment to command her! It would tax a lover's power, a lover's heart, to the utmost. Ah!'

He stood still, and with an effort of iron resolution put from him the fancies that were thronging on the brain. If it were possible for him to conquer her, conceivable that he might win her – such a dream was forbidden to him, Alan Helbeck, a thousandfold! Such a marriage would be the destruction of innumerable schemes for the good of the Church, for the perfecting of his own life. It would be the betrayal of great trusts, the abandonment of great opportunities. 'My life would centre in her. She would come first – the Church second. Her nature would work on mine – not mine on hers. Could I ever speak to her even of what I believe? – the very alphabet of it is unknown to her. I shrink from proselytism. God forgive me! – it is her wild pagan self that I love – that I desire –'

The blast of human longing, human pain, was hard to meet – hard to subdue. But the Catholic fought – and conquered.

'I am not my own – I have taken tasks upon me that no honest man could betray. There are vows on me also, that bind me specially to our Lord – to his Church. The Church frowns on such a love – such marriages. She does not forbid them – but they pain her heart. I have accepted her judgment till now, without difficulty, without conflict. Now to obey is hard. But I can obey – we are not asked impossibilities.'

He walked to the crucifix, and threw himself down before it. A midnight stillness brooded over the house.

But far away, in an upper room, Laura Fountain had cried herself to sleep – only to wake again and again, with the tears flooding her cheeks. Was it merely a disagreeable and exciting scene she had gone through? What was this new invasion of her life? – this new presence to the inward eye of a form and look that at once drew her and repulsed her. A hundred alien forces were threatening and pressing upon her – and out from the very heart of them came this strange drawing – this magnetism – this troubling misery.

To be prisoned in Bannisdale – under Mr Helbeck's roof – for months and months longer – this thought was maddening to her.

But when she imagined herself free to go – and far away once more from this old and melancholy house – among congenial friends and scenes – she was no happier than before. A little moan of anger and pain came, that she stifled against her pillow, calling passionately on the sleep that would, that must chase all these phantoms of fatigue or excitement – and give her back her old free self.

BOOK THREE

CHAPTER ONE

'We shall get there in capital time – that's nice!' said Polly Mason, putting down the little railway guide she had just purchased at Marsland Station, with a general rustle of satisfaction.

Polly indeed shone with good temper and new clothes. Her fringe – even halved – was prodigious. Her cheap, lemon-coloured gloves were cracking on her large hands; and round her beflowered hat she had tied clouds on clouds of white tulle, which to some extent softened the tans and crimsons of her complexion. Her dress was of a stiff white cotton stuff, that fell into the most startling folds and angles; and at every movement of it, the starch rattled.

On the opposite seat of the railway carriage was Laura Fountain – an open book upon her knee, that she was not reading. She made no answer, however, to Polly's remark; the impression left by her attitude was that she took no interest in it. Miss Fountain herself hardly seemed to have profited much by that Westmoreland air whereof the qualities were to do so much for Augustina. It was now June, the end of June, and Laura was certainly paler, less blooming than she had been in March. She seemed more conscious; she was certainly less radiant. Whether her prettiness had gained by the slight change, might be debated. Polly's eyes, indeed, as they sped along, paid her cousin one long covetous tribute. The difficulty that she always had in putting on her own clothes, and softening her own physical points, made her the more conscious of Laura's delicate ease, of all the yielding and graceful lines into which the little black and white muslin frock fell so readily, of all that natural kinship between Laura and her hats, Laura and her gloves, which poor Polly fully perceived, knowing well and sadly that she herself could never attain to it.

Nevertheless – pretty, Miss Fountain might be; elegant she certainly was; but Polly did not find her the best of companions for a festal day. They were going to Froswick – the big town on the coast – to meet Hubert and another young man, one Mr Seaton, foreman in a large engineering concern, whose name Polly had not been able to mention without bridling for some time past.

It was more than a fortnight since the sister, driven by Hubert's

incessant letters, had proposed to Laura that they two should spend
a summer day at Froswick and see the great steel works on which
the fame of that place depended, escorted and entertained by the
two young men. Laura at first had turned a deaf ear. Then all at
once – a very flare of eagerness and acceptance! – a sudden choosing
of day and train. And now that they were actually on their way,
with everything arranged, and a glorious June sun above their
heads, Laura was so silent, so reluctant, so irritable – you might
have thought –

Well! – Polly really did not know what to think. She was not
quite happy herself. From time to time, as her look dwelt on
Laura, she was conscious of certain guilty reserves and conceal-
ments in her own breast. She wished Hubert had more sense –
she hoped to goodness it would all go off nicely! But of course it
would. Polly was an optimist and took all things simply. Her
anxieties for Laura did not long resist the mere pleasure of the
journey and the trip, the flatteries of expectation. What a very
respectable and, on the whole, good-looking young man was Mr
Seaton! Polly had met him first at the Browhead dance; so that
what was a mere black and ugly spot in Laura's memory shone
rosy-red in her cousin's.

Meanwhile Laura, mainly to avoid Polly's conversation, was
looking hard out of window. They were running along the southern
shore of a great estuary. Behind the loitering train rose the hills
they had just left, the hills that sheltered the stream and the woods
of Bannisdale. That rich, dark patch beneath the further brow was
the wood in which the house stood. To the north, across the bay,
ran the line of high mountains, a dim paradise of sunny slopes and
steeps, under the keenest and brightest of skies – blue ramparts
from which the gently opening valleys flowed downwards, one
beside the other, to the estuary and the sea.

Not that the great plunging sea itself was much to be seen as yet.
Immediately beyond the railway line stretched leagues of firm reddish sand, pierced by the innumerable channels of the Greet. The
sun lay hot and dazzling on the wide flat surfaces, on the flocks of
gulls, on the pools of clear water. The window was open, and
through the June heat swept a sharp, salt breath. Laura, however,
felt none of the physical exhilaration that as a rule overflowed in
her so readily. Was it because the Bannisdale Woods were still
visible? What made the significance of that dark patch to the girl's

restless eye? She came back to it again and again. It was like a flag, round which a hundred warring thoughts had come to gather.

Why?

Were not she and Mr Helbeck on the best of terms? Was not Augustina quite pleased – quite content? 'I always knew, my dear Laura, that you and Alan would get on, in time. Why, anyone could get on with Alan – he's so kind!' When these things were said, Laura generally laughed. She did not remind Mrs Fountain that she, at one time of her existence, had not found it particularly easy and simple to get on with 'Alan'; but the girl did once allow herself the retort – 'It's not so easy to quarrel, is it, when you don't see a person from week's end to week's end?' 'Week's end to week's end?' Mrs Fountain repeated vaguely. 'Yes – Alan is away a great deal – people trust him so much – he has so much business.'

Laura was of opinion that his first business might very well have been to see a little more of his widowed sister! She and Augustina spent days and days alone; while Mr Helbeck pursued the affairs of the Church. One precious attempt indeed had been made to break the dulness of Bannisdale. Miss Fountain's cheeks burned when she thought of it. There had been an afternoon party! though Augustina's widowhood was barely a year old! Miss Fountain had been sent about the country delivering notes and cards. And the result: – oh, such a party! – such an interminable afternoon! Where had the people come from? – who were they? If Polly, full of curiosity, asked for some details, Laura would toss her head and reply that she knew nothing at all about it; that Mrs Denton had provided bad tea and worse cakes, and the guests had 'filled their chairs,' and there was nothing else to say. Mr Helbeck's shyness and efforts; the glances of appeal he threw every now and then towards his sister; his evident depression when the thing was done – these things were not told to Polly. There was a place for them in the girl's sore mind; but they did not come to speech. Anyway she believed – nay, was quite sure – that Bannisdale would not be so tried a second time. For whose benefit was it done? – whose!

One evening –

As the train crossed the bridge of the estuary, from one stretch of hot sand to another, Laura, staring at the view, saw really nothing but an image of the mind, felt nothing except what came through the magic of memory.

The hall of Bannisdale, with the lingering daylight of the north still coming in at ten o'clock through the uncurtained oriel windows – herself at the piano, Augustina on the settle – a scent of night and flowers spreading through the dim place from the open windows of the drawing-room beyond. One candle is beside her – and there are strange glints of moonlight here and there on the panelling. A tall figure enters from the chapel passage. Augustina makes room on the settle – the Squire leans back and listens. And the girl at the piano plays; the stillness and the night seem to lay releasing hands upon her; bonds that have been stifling and cramping the soul break down; she plays with all her self as she might have talked or wept to a friend – to her father . . . And at last, in a pause, the Squire puts a new candle beside her, and his deep shy voice commends her, asks her to go on playing. Afterwards, there is a pleasant and gentle talk for half an hour – Augustina can hardly be made to go to bed – and when at last she rises, the girl's small hand slips into the man's, is lost there, feels a new lingering touch, from which both withdraw in almost equal haste. And the night, for the girl, is broken with restlessness, with wild efforts to draw the old fetters tight again, to clamp and prison something that flutters – that struggles.

Then next morning there is an empty chair at the breakfast table. 'The Squire left early on business.' Without any warning – any courteous message? One evening at home, after a long absence, and then – off again! A good Catholic, it seems, lives in the train, and makes himself the catspaw of all who wish to use him for their own ends!

. . . As to that old peasant, Scarsbrook, what could be more arbitrary, more absurd than Mr Helbeck's behaviour? The matter turns out to be serious. Fright blanches the old fellow's beard and hair; he takes to his bed, and the doctor talks of severe nervous 'shock' – very serious, often deadly, at the patient's age. Why not confess everything at once, set things straight, free the poor shaken mind from its oppression? Who's afraid? – what harm is there in an after-dinner stroll?

But there! – truth apparently is what no one wants, what no one will have – least of all, Mr Helbeck. She sees a meeting in the park, under the oaks – the same tall man and the girl – the girl bound impetuously for confession, and the soothing of old Scarsbrook's terrors once for all – the man standing in the way, as tough and prickly as one of his own hawthorns. Courtesy, of course! there is no one can make courtesy so galling; and then such a shooting out of will and personality, so sudden, so volcanic a heat of remonstrance! And a woman is such a poor ill-strung creature, even the boldest of them! She yields when she should have pressed forward – goes home to rage, when she should have stayed to wrestle.

Afterwards, another absence – the old house silent as the grave – and Augustina so fretful, so wearisome! But she is better, much better. How unscrupulous are doctors, and those other persons who make them say exactly what suits the moment!

The dulness seems to grow with the June heat. Soon it becomes intolerable. Nobody comes; nobody speaks; no mind offers itself to yours for confidence and sympathy. Well, but change and excitement of some sort, one *must* have! – who is to blame, if you get it where you can?

A day in Froswick with Hubert Mason? Yes – why not? Polly proposes it – has proposed it once or twice before to no purpose. For two months now the young man has been in training. Polly writes to him often; Laura sometimes wonders whether the cross-examinations through which Polly puts her may not partly be for Hubert's benefit. She herself has written twice to him in answer to some half-dozen letters, has corrected his song for him – has played altogether a very moral and sisterly part. Is the youth really in love? Perhaps. Will it do him any harm?

Augustina of course dislikes the prospect of the Froswick day. But, really, Augustina must put up with it! The Reverend Mother will come for the afternoon, and keep her company. Such civility of late on the part of all the Catholic friends of Bannisdale towards Miss Fountain! – a civility always on the watch, week by week, day by day – that never yields itself for an instant, has never a human impulse, an unguarded tone. Father Leadham is there one day – he makes a point of talking with Miss Fountain. He leads the conversation to Cambridge, to her father – his keen glance upon her all the time, the hidden life of the convert and the mystic leaping every now and then to the surface, and driven down again by a will that makes itself felt – even by so cool a listener – as a living tyrannous thing, developed out of all proportion to, nay at the cruel expense of the rest of the personality. Yet it is no will of the man's own – it is the will of his order, of his faith. And why these repeated stray references to Bannisdale – to its owner – to the owner's goings and comings? They are hardly questions, but they might easily have done the work of questions had the person addressed been willing. Laura laughs to think of it.

Ah! well – but discretion to-day, discretion to-morrow, discretion always, is not the most amusing of diets. How dumb, how tame has she become! There is no one to fight with, nothing whereon to let loose the sharp-edged words and sayings that lie so close behind the girl's shut lips. How amazing that one should positively miss those fuller activities in the chapel that depend on the Squire's presence! Father Bowles says Mass there twice a week; the light still burns before the altar; several times a day Augustina disappears within the heavy doors. But when Mr Helbeck is at home, the place becomes, as it were, the strong heart of the house. It beats through the whole organism; so that no one can ignore or forget it.

What is it that makes the difference when he returns? Unwillingly, the mind shapes its reply. A sense of unity and law comes back into the house – a hidden dignity and poetry. The Squire's black head carries with it stern reminders, reminders that challenge or provoke; but 'he nothing common does nor mean,'[8] and smaller mortals, as the weeks go by, begin to feel their hot angers and criticisms driven back upon themselves, to realise the strange persistency and force of the religious life.

Inhuman force! But force of any kind tends to draw, to conquer. More than once Laura sees herself at night almost on the steps of the chapel, in the dark shadows of the passage – following Augustina. But she has never yet mounted the steps – never passed the door. Once or twice she has angrily snatched herself from listening to the distant voice.

. . . Mr Helbeck makes very little comment on the Froswick plan. One swift involuntary look at breakfast, as who might say – 'Our compact?' But there was no compact. And go she will.

And at last all opposition clears away. It must be Mr Helbeck who has silenced Augustina – for even she complains no more. Trains are looked out; arrangements are made to fetch Polly from a halfway village; a fly is ordered to meet the 9.10 train at night. Why does one feel a culprit all through? Absurdity! Is one to be mewed up all one's life, to throw over all fun and frolic at Mr Helbeck's bidding – Mr Helbeck, who now scarcely sets foot in Bannisdale, who seems to have turned his back upon his own house, since that precise moment when his sister and her stepdaughter came to inhabit it? Never till this year was he restless in this way

– so says Mrs Denton, whose temper grows shorter and shorter.

Oh – as to fun and frolic! The girl yawns as she looks out of window. What a long hot day it is going to be – and how foolish are all expeditions, all formal pleasures! 9.10 at Marsland – about seven, she supposes, at Froswick? Already her thoughts are busy, hungrily busy with the evening, and the return.

The train sped along. They passed a little watering-place under the steep wooded hills – a furnace of sun on this hot June day, in winter a soft and sheltered refuge from the north. Further on rose the ruins of a great Cistercian Abbey, great ribs and arches of red sandstone, that still, in ruin, made the soul and beauty of a quiet valley; then a few busy towns with mills and factories, the fringe of that industrial district which lies on the southern and western border of the Lake Country; more wide valleys sweeping back into blue mountains; a wealth of June leaf and blossoming tree; and at last docks and buildings, warehouses and 'works,' a network of spreading railway lines, and all the other signs of an important and growing town. The train stopped amid a crowd, and Polly hurried to the door.

'Why, Hubert! – Mr Seaton! – Here we are!'

She beckoned wildly, and not a few passers-by turned to look at the nodding clouds of tulle.

'We shall find them, Polly – don't shout,' said Laura behind her, in some disgust.

Shout and beckon, however, Polly did and would, till the two young men were finally secured.

'Why, Hubert, you never towd me what a big place 'twas,' said Polly joyously. 'Lor, Mr Seaton, doant fash yoursel. This is Miss Fountain – my cousin. You'll remember her, I knaw.'

Mr Seaton began a polite and stilted speech while possessing himself of Polly's shawl and bag. He was a very superior young man of the clerk or foreman type, somewhat ill put together at the waist, with a flat back to his head, and a cadaverous countenance. Laura gave him a rapid look. But her chief curiosity was for Hubert. And at her first glance she saw the signs of that strong and silent process perpetually going on amongst us that tames the countryman to the life and habits of the town. It was only a couple of months since the young athlete from the fells had been brought within its sway, and already the marks of it were evident in dress, speech, and manner. The dialect was almost gone; the black Sunday coat was of the most fashionable cut that Froswick could provide; and as they walked along, Laura detected more than once in the downcast eyes of her companion a stealthy anxiety as to the knees of his new grey trousers. So far the change was not an embellishment. The first loss of freedom and rough strength is never that. But it roused the girl's notice, and a sort of secret sympathy. She too had felt the curb of an alien life! – she could almost have held out her hand to him, as to a comrade in captivity.

Outside the station, to Laura's surprise – considering the object of the expedition – Hubert made a sign to his sister, and the two dropped behind a little.

'What's the matter with her?' said Hubert abruptly, as soon as he judged that they were out of hearing of the couple in front.

'Who do you mean? Laura? Why, she's well enoof!'

'Then she don't look it. She's fretting. What's wrong with her?'

As Hubert looked down upon his sister, Polly was startled by the impatient annoyance of look and manner. And how red-rimmed and weary were the lad's eyes! You might have thought he had not slept for a week. Polly's mind ran through a series of conjectures; and she broke out with Westmoreland plainness –

'Hubert, I do wish tha wouldn't be sich a fool! I've towd tha so times and times.'

'Aye, and you may tell me so till kingdom come – I sha'n't mind you,' he said doggedly. 'There's something between her and the Squire. I know there is. I know it by the look of her.'

Polly laughed.

'How you jump! I tell tha she never says a word aboot him.'

Hubert looked moodily at Laura's little figure in front.

'All the more reason!' he said between his teeth. 'She'd talk about him when she first came. But I'll find out – never fear.'

'For goodness' sake, Hubert, let her be!' said Polly, entreating. 'Sich wild stuff as thoo's been writin me. Yan might ha thowt yo'd be fer cuttin yor thröat, if yo didn't get her doon here. – What art tha thinkin of, lad? She'll never marry tha! She doan't belong to us – and there's noa undoin it.'

Hubert made no reply, but unconsciously his muscular frame took a passionate rigidity; his face became set and obstinate.

'Well, you keep watch,' he said. 'You'll see – I'll make it worth your while.'

Polly looked up – half laughing. She understood his reference to herself and her new sweetheart. Hubert would play her game if she would play his. Well – she had no objection whatever to help him to the sight of Laura when she could. Polly's moral sense was not over-delicate, and as to the upshot and issues of things, her imagination moved but slowly. She did not like to let herself think of what might have been Hubert's relations to women – to one or two wild girls about Whinthorpe for instance. But Laura – Laura who was so much their social better, whose manners and self-possession awed them both, what smallest harm could ever come to her from any act or word of Hubert's? For this rustic Westmoreland girl, Laura Fountain stood on a pedestal robed and sceptred like a little queen. Hubert was a fool to fret himself – a fool to go courting some one too high for him. What else was there to say or think about it?

At the next street corner Laura made a resolute stop. Polly should not any longer be defrauded of her Mr Seaton. Besides she, Laura, wished to talk to Hubert. Mr Seaton's long words, and way of mouthing his highly correct phrases, had already seemed to take the savour out of the morning.

When the exchange was made – Mr Seaton, alas! showing less eagerness than might have been expected – Laura quietly examined her companion. It seemed to her that he was taller than ever; surely she was not much higher than his elbow! Hubert, conscious that he was being scrutinised, turned red, looked away, coughed, and apparently could find nothing to say.

'Well – how are you getting on?' said the light voice, sending its vibration through all the man's strong frame.

'I suppose I'm getting on all right,' he said, switching at the railings beside the road with his stick.

'What sort of work do you do?'

He gave her a stumbling account, from which she gathered that he was for the time being the factotum of an office, sent on everybody's errands, and made responsible for everybody's shortcomings.

She threw him a glance of pity. This young Hercules, with his open-air traditions, and his athlete's triumphs behind him, turned into the butt and underling of half a dozen clerks in a stuffy office!

'I don't mind,' he said hastily. 'All the others paid for their places; I didn't pay for mine. I'll be even with them all some day. It was the chance I wanted, and my uncle gives me a lift now and then. It was to please him they gave me the berth; he's worth thousands and thousands a year to them!'

And he launched into a boasting account of the importance and abilities of his uncle, Daniel Mason, who was now managing director of the great shipbuilding yard into which Hubert had been taken, as a favour to his kinsman.

'He began at the bottom, same as me – only he was younger than me,' said Hubert, 'so he had the pull. But you'll see, I'll work up. I've learnt a lot since I've been here. The classes at the Institute – well, they're fine!'

Laura showed an astonished glance. New sides of the lad seemed to be revealing themselves.

She inquired after his music. But he declared he was too busy to think of it. By and by in the winter he would have lessons. There was a violin class at the Institute – perhaps he'd join that. Then abruptly, staring down upon her with his wide blue eyes –

'And how have you been getting on with the Squire?'

He thought she started, but couldn't be quite sure.

'Getting on with the Squire? Why, capitally! Whenever he's there to get on with.'

'What – he's been away?' he said eagerly.

She raised her shoulders.

'He's always away –'

'Why, I thought they'd have made a Papist of you by now,' he said.

His laugh was rough, but his eyes held her with a curious insistence.

'Think something more reasonable, please, next time! Now, where are we going to lunch?'

'We've got it all ready. But we must see the yard first . . . Miss Fountain – Laura – I've got that flower you gave me.'

His voice was suddenly hoarse.

She glanced at him, lifting her eyebrows.

'Very foolish of you, I'm sure . . . Now do tell me, how did you get off so early?'

He sulkily explained to her that work was unusually slack in his own yard; that, moreover, he had worked special overtime during the week in order to get an hour or two off this Saturday, and that Seaton was on night-duty at a large engineering 'works,' and lord therefore of his days. But she paid small attention. She was occupied

in looking at the new buildings and streets, the brand new squares
and statues of Froswick.

'How can people build and live in such ugly places?' she said at
last, standing still that she might stare about her – 'when there are
such lovely things in the world; Cambridge, for instance – or –
Bannisdale.'

The last word slipped out, dreamily, unaware.

The lad's face flushed furiously.

'I don't know what there is to see in Bannisdale,' he said hotly.
'It's a damp, dark, beastly hole of a place.'

'I prefer Bannisdale to this, thank you,' said Laura, making a
little face at the very ample bronze gentleman in a frock coat who
was standing in the centre of a great new-built empty square,
haranguing a phantom crowd. 'Oh! how ugly it is to succeed – to
have money!'

Mason looked at her with a half-puzzled frown – a frown that of
late had begun to tease his handsome forehead habitually.

'What's the harm of having a bit of brass?' he said angrily. 'And
what's the beauty o' livin in an old ramshackle place, without a
sixpence in your pocket, and a pride fit to bring you to the workhouse!'

Laura's little mouth showed amusement, an amusement that
stung. She lifted a little fan that hung at her girdle.

'Is there any shade in Froswick?' she said, looking round her.

Mason was silenced, and as Polly and Mr Seaton joined them, he
recovered his temper with a mighty effort and once more set himself
to do the honours – the slighted honours – of his new home.

. . . But oh! the heat of the shipbuilding yard. Laura was already
tired and faint, and could hardly drag her feet up and down the sides
of the great skeleton ships that lay building in the docks, or through
the interminable 'fitting' sheds with their piles of mahogany and
teak, their whirring lathes and saws, their heaps of shavings, their
resinous wood-smell. And yet the managing director appeared in
person for twenty minutes, a thin, small, hawk-eyed man, not at all
unwilling to give a brief patronage to the young lady who might be
said to link the houses of Mason and Helbeck in a flattering equal-
ity.

'He wad never ha doon it for *us!*' Polly whispered in her awe to
Miss Fountain. 'It's you he's affther!'

Laura, however, was not grateful. She took her industrial lesson
ill, with much haste and inattention, so that once when the director

and his nephew fell behind, the great man, whose speech to his kinsman in private was often little less broad than Mrs Mason's own – said scornfully,

'An I doan't think much o' your fine cousin, mon! she's nobbut a flighty miss.'

The young man said nothing. He was still slavishly ill at ease with his uncle, on whose benevolence all his future depended.

'Is there something more to see?' said Laura languidly.

'Only the steel works,' said Mr Seaton, with a patronising smile. 'You young ladies, I presume, would hardly wish to go away without seeing our chief establishment. Froswick Steel and Hematite Works employ three thousand workmen.'

'Do they? – and does it matter?' said Laura, playing with the salt.

She wore a little plaintive, tired air, which suited her soft paleness, and made her extraordinarily engaging in the eyes of both the young men. Mason watched her perpetually, anticipating her slightest movement, waiting on her least want. And Mr Seaton, usually so certain of his own emotions and so wholly in command of them, began to feel himself confused. It was with a distinct slackening of ardour that he looked from Miss Fountain to Polly – his Polly, as he had almost come to think of her, honest managing Polly, who would have a bit of 'brass,' and was in all respects a tidy and suitable wife for such a man as he. But why had she wrapped all that silly white stuff round her head? And her hands? – Mr Seaton slyly withdrew his eyes from Polly's reddened members to fix them on the thin white wrist that Laura was holding poised in the air, and the pretty fingers twirling the salt spoon.

Polly meantime sat up very straight, and was no longer talkative. Lunch had not improved her complexion, as the mirror hanging opposite showed her. Every now and then she too threw little restless glances across at Laura.

'Why, we needn't go to the works at all if we don't like,' said Polly. 'Can't we get a fly, Hubert, and take a jaunt soomwhere?'

Hubert bent forward with alacrity. Of course they could. If they went four miles up the river or so, they would come to real nice country and a farmhouse where they could have tea.

'Well, I'm game,' said Mr Seaton, magnanimously slapping his pocket. 'Anything to please these ladies.'

'I don't know about that seven o'clock train?' said Mason doubtfully.

'Well, if we can't get that, there's a later one.'

'No, that's the last.'

'You may trust me,' said Seaton pompously. 'I know my way about a railway guide. There's one a little after eight.'

Hubert shook his head. He thought Seaton was mistaken. But Laura settled the matter.

'Thank you – we'll not miss our train,' she said, rising to put her hat straight before the glass – 'so it's the works, please. What is it – furnaces and red-hot things?'

In another minute or two they were in the street again. Mr Seaton settled the bill with a magnificent 'Damn the expense' air, which annoyed Mason – who was of course a partner in all the charges of the day – and made Laura bite her lip. Outside he showed a strong desire to walk with Miss Fountain that he might instruct her in the details of the Bessemer process and the manufacture of steel rails. But the ease with which the little nonchalant creature disposed of him, the rapidity with which he found himself transferred to Polly, and left to stare at the backs of Laura and Hubert hurrying along in front, amazed him.

'Isn't she nice-looking?' said poor Polly, as she too stared helplessly at the distant pair.

Her shawl weighed upon her arm, Mr Seaton had forgotten to ask for it. But there was a little sudden balm in the irritable vexation of his reply –

'Some people may be of that opinion, Miss Mason. I own I prefer a greater degree of balance in the fair sex.'

'Oh! does he mean me?' thought Polly.

And her spirits revived a little.

Meanwhile, as Laura and Hubert walked along to the desolate road that led to the great steel works, Hubert knew a kind of jealous and tormented bliss. She was there, fluttering beside him, her delicate face often turned to him, her feet keeping step with his. And at the same time what strong intangible barriers between them! She had put away her mocking tone – was clearly determined to be kind and cousinly. Yet every word only set the tides of love and misery swelling more strongly in the lad's breast. 'She doan't belong to us, an there's noa undoin it.' Polly's phrase haunted his ear. Yet he dared ask her no more questions about Helbeck; small and frail as she was, she could wrap herself in an unapproachable dignity; nobody had ever yet solved the mystery of Laura's inmost feeling against her will; and Hubert knew despairingly that his clumsy methods had small chance with her. But he felt a kind of rage that there were signs of suffering about her; he divined something to know, at the same time that he realised with all plainness it was not for his knowing. Ah! that man – that ugly starched hypocrite – after all had he got hold of her? Who could live near her without feeling this pain – this pang? . . . Was she to be surrendered to him without a struggle – to that canting droning fellow, with his jail of a house? Why, he would crush the life out of her in six months!

There was a rush and whirl in the lad's senses. A cry of animal jealousy – of violence – rose in his being.

'How wonderful! – how enchanting!' cried Laura, her glance sparkling, her whole frame quivering with pleasure.

They had just entered the great main shed of the steel works. The foreman, who had been induced by the young men to take them through, was in the act of placing Laura in the shelter of a brick screen, so as to protect her from a glowing shower of sparks that would otherwise have swept over her; and the girl had thrown a few startled looks around her.

A vast shed, much of it in darkness, and crowded with dim forms of iron and brick – at one end, and one side, openings, where the June day came through. Within – a grandiose mingling of fire and shadow – a vast glare of white or bluish flame from a huge furnace roaring against the inner wall of the shed – sparks, like star-showers, whirling through dark spaces – ingots of glowing steel, pillars of pure fire passing and repassing, so that the heat of them scorched the girl's shrinking cheek – and everywhere, dark against flame, the human movement answering to the elemental leap and rush of the fire, black forms of men in a constant activity, masters and ministers at once of this crackling terror round about them.

'Aye!' said their guide, answering the girl's questions as well as he could in the roar – 'that's the great furnace where they boil the steel. Now you watch – when the flame – look! it's white now – turns blue – that means the process is done – the steel's cooked.

Then they'll bring the vat beneath – turn the furnace over – you'll see the steel pour out.'

'Is that a railway?'

She pointed to a raised platform in front of the furnace. A truck bearing a high metal tub was running along it.

'Yes – it's from there they feed the furnace – in a minute you'll see the tub tip over.'

There was a signal bell – a rattle of machinery. The tub tilted – a great jet of white flame shot upwards from the furnace – the great mouth had swallowed down its prey.

'And those men with their wheelbarrows? Why do they let them go so close?'

She shuddered and put her hand over her eyes.

The foreman laughed.

'Why, it's quite safe! – the tub's moved out of the way. You see the furnace has to be fed with different stuffs – the tub brings one sort and the barrows another. Now look – they're going to turn it over. Stand back!'

He held up his hand to bid Mason come under shelter.

Laura looked round her.

'Where are the other two?' she asked.

'Oh! they've gone to see the bar-testing – they'll be here soon. Seaton knows the man in charge of the testing workshop.'

Laura ceased to think of them. She was absorbed in the act before her. The great lip of the furnace began to swing downwards; fresh showers of sparks fled in wild curves and spirals through the shed; out flowed the stream of liquid steel into the vat placed beneath. Then slowly the fire-cup righted itself; the flame roared once more against the wall; the swarming figures to either side began once more to feed the monster – men, and trucks, and wheelbarrows, the little railway line, and the iron pillars supporting it, all black against the glare –

Laura stood breathless – her wild nature wrapt by what she saw. But while she hung on the spectacle before her, Mason never spared it a glance. He was conscious of scarcely anything but her – her childish form, in the little clinging dress, her white face, every soft feature clear in the glow, her dancing eyes, her cloud of reddish hair, from which her wide black hat had slipped away in the excitement of her upward gaze. The lad took the image into his heart – it burnt there as though it too were fire.

'Now let's look at something else!' said Laura at last, turning away with a long breath.

And they took her to see the vat that had been filled from the furnace, pouring itself into the ingot moulds – then the four moulds travelling slowly onwards till they paused under a sort of iron hand that descended and lifted them majestically from the white-hot steel beneath, uncovering the four fiery pillars that reddened to a blood colour as they moved across the shed – till, on the other side, one ingot after another was lowered from the truck, and no sooner felt the ground than it became the prey of some unseen force, which drove it swiftly onwards from beneath, to where it leapt with a hiss and crunch into the jaws of the mill. Then out again on the further side, lengthened, and pared, the demon in it already half tamed! – flying as it were from the first mill, only to be caught again in the squeeze of the second, and the third – until at last the quivering rail emerged at the further end, a twisting fire-serpent, still soft under the controlling rods of the workmen. On it glided, on, and out of the shed, into the open air, till it reached a sort of platform over a pit, where iron claws caught at it from beneath, and brought it to a final rest, in its own place, beside its innumerable fellows, waiting for the market and its buyers.

'Mayn't we go back once more to the furnace?' said Miss Fountain eagerly to her guide – 'just for a minute!'

He smiled at her, unable to say no.

And they walked back across the shed, to the brick shelter. The great furnace was roaring as before, the white sheet of flame was nearing its last change of colour, tub after tub, barrow after barrow poured its contents into the vast flaring throat. Behind the shelter was an elderly woman with a shawl over her head. She had brought a jar of tea for some workmen, and was standing like any stranger, watching the furnace and hiding from the sparks.

Now there is only one man more – and after that, one more tub to be lowered – and the hell-broth is cooked once again, and will come streaming forth.

The man advances with his barrow. Laura sees his blackened face in the intolerable light, as he turns to give a signal to those behind him. An electric bell rings.

Then –

What was that?

God! – what was that?

A hideous cry rang through the works. Laura drew her hand in bewilderment across her eyes. The foreman beside her shouted and ran forward.

'Where's the man?' she said helplessly to Mason.

But Mason made no answer. He was clinging to the brick wall, his eyes staring out of his head. A great clamour rose from the little railway – from beneath it – from all sides of it. The shed began to swarm with running men, all hurrying towards the furnace. The air was full of their cries. It was like the loosing of a maddened hive.

Laura tottered, fell back against the wall. The old woman who had come to bring the tea rushed up to her.

'Oh Lord, save us! – Lord, save us!' she cried, with a wail to rend the heart.

And the two women fell into each other's arms, shuddering, with wild broken words, which neither of them heard or knew.

CHAPTER TWO

'Look out there! For God's sake, go to your places!'

The cry of the foreman reached the ears of the clinging women. They fell apart – each peering into the crowd and the tumult.

Mounted on a block of wood about a dozen yards from them – waving his arm and shouting to the stream of panic-stricken workmen – they saw the man who had been their guide through the works. Four white-hot ingots, just uncovered, blazed deserted on their truck close to him, and a multitude of men and boys were pushing past them, tumbling over each other in their eagerness to reach the neighbourhood of the furnace. The space between the ingots and some machinery near them was perilously narrow. At any moment, those rushing past might have been pushed against the death-bearing truck. Ah! another cry. A man's coat-sleeve has caught fire. He is pulled back – another coat is flung about him – the line of white faces turns towards him an instant – wavers – then the crowd flows on as before.

Another man in authority comes up also shouting. The man on the block dismounts, and the two hold rapid colloquy. 'Have they sent for Mr Martin?' 'Aye.' 'Where's Mr Barlow?' 'He's no good!' 'Have they stopped the mills?' 'Aye – there's not a man'll touch a thing – you'd think they'd gone clean out of their minds. There'll be accidents all over the place if somebody can't quiet 'em.'

Suddenly the buzzing groups behind the foreman parted, and a young broad-shouldered workman, grimed from head to foot, his blue eyes rolling in his black face, came staggering through.

'Give ma a drink,' he said, clutching at the old woman; 'an let ma sit down!'

He almost fell upon an iron barrow that lay face downwards on the path. Laura, sitting crouched and sick upon the ground, raised her head to look at him. Another man, evidently a comrade, followed him, took the mug of cold tea from the old woman's shaking hand, lifted his head and helped him drink it.

'Blast yer! – why ain't it spirits?' said the youth, throwing himself back against his companion. His eyes closed on his smeared cheeks; his jaw fell; his whole frame seemed to sink into collapse; those gazing at him saw, as it were, the dislocation and undoing of a man.

'Cheer up, Ned – cheer up,' said the older man, kneeling down behind him – 'you'll get over it, my boy – it worn't none o' your fault. Stand back there, you fellows, an gie im air.'

'Oh, damn yer! let ma be,' gasped the young fellow, stretching himself against the other's support, like one who feels the whole inner being of him sick to death, and cannot be still for an instant under the anguish.

The woman with the tea began to cry loudly and ask questions. Laura rose to her feet, and touched her.

'Don't cry – can't you get some brandy?' Then in her turn she felt herself caught by the arm.

'Miss Fountain – Miss Laura – I can get you out of this! – there's a way out here by the back.'

Mason's white countenance showed over her shoulder as she turned.

'Not yet – can't any one find some brandy? Ah!'

For their guide came up at the moment with a bottle in his hand. It was Laura who handed him the mug, and it was she who, stooping down, put the spirit to the lips of the fainting workman. Her mind seemed to float in a mist of horror, but her will asserted itself; she recovered her power of action sooner than the men around her. They stared at the young lady for a moment but no more. The one hideous fact that possessed them robbed all else of meaning.

'Did he see it?' said Laura to the man's friend. Her voice reached no ear but his. For they were surrounded by two uproars – the noise of the crowd of workmen, a couple of thousand men aimlessly surging and shouting to each other, and the distant thunder of the furnace.

'Aye, Miss. He wor drivin the tub, an he saw Overton in front – it wor the wheel of his barrer slipped, an soomthin must ha took him – if he'd ha let goa straight theer ud bin noa harm doon – bit he mut ha tried to draw it back – an the barrer pulled him right in.'

'He didn't suffer?' said Laura eagerly, her face close under his.

'Thank the Lord, he can ha known nowt aboot it! – nowt at aw. The gas ud throttle him, Miss, afore he felt the fire.'

'Is there a wife?'

'Noa – he coom here a widower three weeks sen – there's a little gell –'

'Aye! they be gone for her an t' passon boath,' said another voice; 'what's passon to do whan he cooms?'

'Salve the masters' consciences!' cried a third in fury. 'They'll burn us to hell first, and then quieten us with praying.'

Many faces turned to the speaker, a thin wiry man, one of the 'agitators' of the town, and a dull groan went round.

'Make way there!' cried an imperious voice, and the crowd between them and the entrance side of the shed began to part. A gentleman came through, leading a clergyman, who walked hurriedly, with eyes downcast, holding his book against his breast.

There was a flutter of caps through the vast shed. Every head stood bared and bent. On went the parson towards the little platform with the railway. The furnace had sunk somewhat – its roar was less acute – Laura looking at it thought of the gorged beast that falls to rest.

But another parting of the throng – one sob! – the common sob of hundreds.

Laura looked.

'It's t' little gell, Ned! t' little gell!' said the elder workman to the youth he was supporting.

And there in the midst of the blackened crowd of men was a child, frightened and weeping, led tenderly forward by a grey-haired workman, who looked down upon her, quite unconscious of the tears that furrowed his own cheeks.

'Oh let me – let me go!' cried Laura. The men about her fell back. They made a way for her to the child. The old woman had disappeared. In an instant Laura, as of right, took the place of her sex. Half an hour before she had been the merest passing stranger in that vast company; now she was part of them, organically necessary to the act passing in their midst. The men yielded her the child instinctively, at once; she caught the little one in her sheltering arm.

'Ought she to be here?' she asked sharply of the grey-haired man.

'They're goin to read the Burial Service, Miss,' he said, as he dashed away the mist from his eyes. 'An we thowt that the little un would like soom day to think she'd been here. So I found her – she wor in school.'

The child looked round her in terror. The platform in front of the furnace had been hurriedly cleared. It was now crowded with men – masters and managers in black coats mingled with workmen, to the front the parson in his white. He turned to the throng below and opened his book.

'*I am the Resurrection and the Life.*'

A great pulsation passed through the mob of workmen. On all sides strong men broke down and wept.

The child stared at the platform, then at these faces round her that were turned upon her.

'Daddy – where's Daddy?' she said trembling, her piteous eyes travelling up and down the pretty lady beside her.

Laura sat down on the edge of a truck and drew the little shaking creature to her breast. Such a power of tenderness went out from her, so soft was the breast, so lulling the scent of the roses pinned into the lady's belt, that the child was stilled. Every now and then, as she looked at the men pressing round her, a passion of fear seemed to run through her; she shuddered and struggled in Laura's hold. Otherwise she made not a sound. And the great words swept on.

How the scene penetrated! – leaving great stabbing lines never to be effaced in the quivering tissues of the girl's nature. Once before she had heard the English burial service. Her father – groaning and fretting under the penalties of friendship – had taken her, when she was fifteen, to the funeral of an old Cambridge colleague. She remembered still the cold cemetery chapel, the gowned mourners, the academic decorum, or the mild regret amid which the function passed. Then her father's sharp impatience as they walked home – that reasonable men in a reasonable age should be asked to sit and listen to Paul's logic, and the absurdities of Paul's cosmical speculations!

And now – from what movements, what obscurities of change within herself, had come this new sense, half loathing, half attraction, that could not withdraw itself from the stroke, from the attack of this Christian poetry – these cries of the soul, now from the Psalms, now from Paul, now from the unknown voices of the Church?

Was it merely the setting that made the difference – the horror of what had passed, the infinite relief to eye and heart of this sudden calm that had fallen on the terror and distraction of the workmen – the strangeness of this vast shed for church, with its fierce perpetual drama of assaulting flame and flying shadow, and the gaunt tangled forms of its machinery – the dull glare of that distant furnace that had made so little – hardly an added throb, hardly a leaping flame! of the living man thrown to it half an hour before, and seemed to be still murmuring and growling there, behind this great act of human pity, in a dying discontent?

Whence was it – this stilling, pacifying power?

All round her men were sobbing and groaning, but as the wave dies after the storm. They seemed to feel themselves in some grasp that sustained, some hold that made life tolerable again. 'Amens' came thick and fast. The convulsion of the faces was abating; a natural human courage was flowing back into contracted hearts.

'*Blessed are the dead – for they rest from their labours –*' '*as our hope is this our brother doth.*'

Laura shivered. The constant agony of the world, in its constant search for all that consoles, all that eases, laid its compelling hand upon her. By a natural instinct she wrapped her arms closer, more passionately, round the child upon her knee.

'Won't she come?' said Mason.

He and Seaton were standing in the downstairs parlour of a small house in a row of workmen's cottages, about half a mile from the steel works.

Mason still showed traces, in look and bearing, of the horror he had witnessed. But he had sufficiently recovered from it to be conscious into the bargain of his own personal grievance, of their spoilt day, and his lost chances. Seaton, too, showed annoyance and impatience; and as Polly entered the room he echoed Mason's question.

Polly shook her head.

'She says she won't leave the child till the last moment. We must go and have our tea, and come back for her.'

'Come along then!' said Mason gloomily, as he led the way to the door.

The little garden outside, as they passed through it, was crowded with women discussing the accident, and every now and then a crowd would gather on the pavement and disperse again. To each and all the speakers, the one intolerable thing was the total disappearance of the poor lost one. No body – no clothes – no tangible relic of the dead: it was a sore trial to customary beliefs. Heaven and hell seemed alike inconceivable when there was no phantom grave-body to make trial of them. One woman after another declared that it would send her mad if it ever happened to any belonging of hers. 'But it's a mercy there's no one to fret – nobbut t' little gell – an she's too sma'.' There was much talk about the young lady that had come home with her – 'a nesh pretty lukin yoong creetur' – to whom little Nelly clung strangely – no doubt because she and her father had been so few weeks in Froswick that there had been scarcely time for them to make friends of their own. The child held the lady's gown in her clutch perpetually, Mr Dixon reported – would not lose sight of her for a moment. But the lady herself was only a visitor to Froswick, was being just taken through the works, when the accident happened, and was to leave the town by an evening train – so it was said. However there would be those left behind who would look after the poor lamb – Mrs Starr, who had taken the tea to the works, and Mrs Dixon, the Overtons' landlady. They were in the house now; but the lady had begged every one else to keep outside.

The summer evening crept on.

At half past six Polly with Hubert behind her climbed the stairs of the little house. Polly pushed open the door of the back room, and Hubert peered over her shoulder.

Inside was a small workman's room, with a fire burning, and the window wide open. There were tea-things on the table; a canary bird singing loudly in a cage beside the window; and a suit of man's clothes with a clean shirt hanging over a chair near the fire.

In a rocking-chair by the window lay the little girl – a child of about nine years old. She was quite colourless, but she was not crying. Her eyes still had the look of terror that the sight of the works had called up in them, and she started at every sound. Laura was kneeling beside her, trying to make her drink some tea. The child kept pushing the tea away, but her other hand held fast to Laura's arm. On the further side of the table sat two elderly women.

'Laura, there's only just time!' said Polly softly, putting her head through the door.

The child started painfully, and the cup Laura held was with difficulty saved from falling.

Laura stooped and kissed the little one's cheek.

'Dear, will you let me go now? Mrs Dixon will take care of you – and I'll come and see you again soon.'

Nelly began to breathe fast. She caught Laura's sleeve with both hands.

'Don't you go, Miss – I'll not stay with her.' She nodded towards her landlady.

'Now, Nelly, you must be a good girl,' said Mrs Dixon, rising and coming forward – she was a strange, ugly woman, with an almost bald head – 'you must do what your poor papa wud ha wished you to do. Let the lady go, an I'll take care on you same as one o' my own, till they can come and take you to the House.'

'Oh! don't say that!' cried Laura.

But it was too late. The child had heard the word – had understood it.

She looked wildly from one to the other, then she threw herself against the side of the chair, in a very madness of crying. Now, she pushed even Laura away. It seemed as though at the sound of that one word she had felt herself indeed forsaken, she had become acquainted with her grief.

Laura's eyes filled with tears.

Polly, standing at the door, spoke to her in vain.

'There's another train – Mr Seaton said so!' Laura threw the words over her shoulder as though in anger. Hubert Mason stood behind her. In her excitement it seemed to her that he was dragging her by force from this sobbing and shrieking misery before her.

'I don't believe he's right. I never heard of any train later than the 7.10,' said Mason in perplexity.

'Go and ask him.'

Mason went away and returned.

'Of course he swears there is. You won't get Seaton to say he's mistaken in a hurry. All I know is I never heard of it.'

'He must be right,' said Laura obstinately. 'Don't trouble about me – send a cab. Oh!'

She put her hands to her ears for an instant, as they stood by the door, as though to shut out the child's cries. Hubert looked down upon her, hesitating, his face flushed, his eyes drawn and sombre.

'Now – you'll let me take you home, Miss Laura? It'll be very late for you. I can get back to-morrow.'

She looked up suddenly.

'No, *no!*' she said, almost stamping. 'I can get home alone quite well. I want no one.'

Then she caught the lad's expression – and put her hand to her brow a moment.

'Come back for me now at any rate – in an hour,' she said, in another voice. 'Please take me to the train – of course. I must go then.'

'Oh, Laura, I *can't* wait!' cried Polly from the stairs – 'I wish I could. But mother's sending Daffady with the cart – and she'd be that cross.'

Laura came out to the stairway.

'Don't wait. Just tell the carriage – mind' – she hung over the banisters enforcing the words – 'tell them that I'm coming by the later train. They're not to send down for me again – I can get a cab at the inn. Mind, Polly – did you hear?'

She bent forward, caught Polly's assent, and ran back to the child.

An hour later Mason found Laura with little Nelly lying heavily asleep in her arms. At sight of him she put finger on lip, and, rising, carried the child to her bed. Tenderly she put her down – tenderly kissed the little hand. The child's utter sleep seemed to soothe her, for she turned away with a smile on her blanched lips. She gave money to Mrs Starr, who was to nurse the little one for a week, and then, it seemed to Mason, she was all alacrity, all eagerness to go.

'Oh! but we're late!' she said, looking at her watch in the street. And she hastily put her head out of the window and implored the cabman to hurry.

Mason said nothing.

The station, when they reached it, was in a Saturday night ferment. Trains were starting and arriving, the platforms were packed with passengers.

Mason said a word to a porter as they rushed in. The porter answered; then, while they fled on, the man stopped a moment and looked back as though about to run after them. But a dozen passengers with luggage laid hands upon him at once, and he was left with no time for more than the muttered remark:

'Marsland? Why, there's no train beyond Braeside to-night.'

'No. 4 platform,' said Hubert to his companion. 'Train just going.' Laura threw off her exhaustion and ran.

The guard was just putting his whistle to his lips. Hubert lifted her into her carriage.

'Good-bye,' she said, waving to him, and disappeared at once into a crowd of fellow-passengers.

'Right for Marsland?' cried Hubert to the guard.

The guard, who had already whistled, waved his flag as he replied:

'Marsland? No train beyond the junction to-night.'

Hubert paused for a moment, then, as the train was moving briskly out, sprang upon the footboard. A porter rushed up, the door was opened, and he was shoved in amid remonstrances from front and rear.

The heavily laden train stopped at every station – was already nearly an hour late. Holiday crowds got in and out; the platforms were gay with talk and laughter.

Mason saw nothing and heard nothing. He sat leaning forward, his hat slouched over his eyes. The man opposite thought he had fallen asleep.

Whose fault was it? Not his! He might have made sure? Why, wasn't Seaton's word good enough? *She* thought so.

Why hadn't he made sure? – in that interval before he came back for her! She might have stayed at Froswick for the night. Plenty of decent people would have put her up. He remembered how he had delayed to call the cab till the last moment.

. . . Good God! how could a man know what he had thought! He was fair moidered – bedazzled – by that awful thing – and all the change of plans. And there was Seaton's word for it. Seaton was a practical man, and always on the railway.

What would she say – when the train stopped? In anticipation he already heard the cry of the porters – 'Braeside! All change!' The perspiration started on his brow. Why, there was sure to be a decent inn at Braeside, and he would do everything for her. She would be glad – of course she would be glad to see him – as soon as she discovered her dilemma. After all he was her cousin – her blood relation.

And Mr Helbeck? The lad's hand clenched. A clock-face came slowly into view at a wayside station. 8.45. He was now waiting for her at Marsland. For the Squire himself would bring the trap; there was no coachman at Bannisdale. A glow of fierce joy passed through the lad's mind, as he thought of the Squire waiting, the train's arrival, the empty platform, the returning carriage. What would the Squire think? Damn him! – let him think what he liked.

Meanwhile, in another carriage, Laura leant back with shut eyes, pursued by one waking dream after another. Shadow and flame – the whirling sparks – the cry! – that awful wrenching of the heart in her breast – the parting crowd, and the white-faced child, phantom-like, in its midst. She sat up, shaken anew by the horror of it, trying to put it from her.

The carriage was now empty. All the other travellers had dis-mounted, and she seemed to be rushing through the summer night alone. For the long daylight was nearly done. The purple of the June evening was passing into the more mysterious purple of the starlight; a clear and jewelled sky hung softly over valleys with 'seaward parted lips,' over woods with the wild rose bushes shining dimly at their edge; over knolls of rocky ground, crowned with white spreading farms; over those distant forms to the far north where the mountains melted into the night.

Her heart was still wrung for the orphaned child – prized yester-day, no doubt – they said he was a good father! – desolate to-day – like herself. 'Daddy! – where's Daddy?' She laid her brow against the window sill and let the tears come again, as she thought of that trembling cry. For it was her own – the voice of her own hunger – orphan to orphan.

And yet, after this awful day – this never to be forgotten shock and horror – she was not unhappy. Rather, a kind of secret joy possessed her as the train sped onward. Her nature seemed to be sinking wearily into soft gulfs of reconciliation and repose. Froswick, with its struggle and death, its newness and restlessness, was behind her – she was going home, to the old house, with its austerity and peace.

Home? Bannisdale, home? How strange! But she was too tired to fight herself to-night – she let the word pass. In her submission to it there was a secret pleasure.

. . . The first train had come in by now. Eagerly, she saw Polly on the platform – Polly looking for the pony-cart. Was it old Wilson – or Mr Helbeck? Wilson, of course! And yet – yet – she knew that Wilson had been away in Whinthorpe on farm business all day. And Mr Helbeck was careful of the old man. Ah well! – there would be something – and some one – to meet her when she arrived. Her heart knew that.

Now they were crossing the estuary. The moon was rising over the sands, and those far hills, the hills of Bannisdale. There on the further bank were the lights of Braeside. She had forgotten to ask whether they changed at the junction – probably the Marsland train would be waiting.

The Greet! – its voice was in her ears, its many channels shone in the flooding light. How near the hills seemed! – just a moonlight walk along the sands, and one was there, under the old tower and the woods. The sands were dangerous, people said. There were quicksands among them, and one must know the paths. Ah! well – she smiled. Humdrum trains and cabs were good enough for her to-night.

She hung at the open window, looking down into the silver water. How strange, after these ghastly hours, to feel yourself floating in beauty and peace – a tremulous peace – like this? The world going your way – the soul yielding itself to fate – taking no more painful thought for the morrow –

'Braeside! All change!'

Laura sprang from the carriage. The station clock opposite told her to her dismay that it was nearly half-past eleven.

'Where's the Marsland train?' she said to the porter who had come forward to help her. 'And how dreadfully late we are!'

'Marsland train, Miss! Last one left an hour ago – no other till 6.12 to-morrow morning.'

'What do you mean? Oh! you didn't hear! – it's the train for *Marsland* I want.'

'Afraid you won't get it, then, Miss, till to-morrow. Didn't they warn you at Froswick? – they'd ought to. This train only makes the main-line connection – for Crewe and Rugby – no connection Whinthorpe way after 8.20.'

Laura's limbs seemed to waver beneath her. A step on the platform. She turned and saw Hubert Mason.

'You!'

Mason thought she would faint. He caught her arm to support her. The porter looked at them curiously, then moved away, smiling to himself.

Laura tottered to the railing at the back of the platform and supported herself against it.

'What are you here for?' she said to him in a voice – a voice of hatred – a voice that stung.

He glanced down upon her, pulling his fair moustache. His handsome face was deeply flushed.

'I only heard there was no train on, from the guard, just as you were starting – so I jumped into the next carriage that I might be of some use to you here if I could. You needn't look at me like that,' he broke out violently – 'I couldn't help it!'

'You might have found out,' she said hoarsely.

'Say you believe I did it on purpose! – to get you into trouble! – you may as well. You'd believe anything bad about me, I know.'

Already there was a new note in his voice, a hoarse, tyrannous note, as though he felt her in his power. In her terror the girl recalled that wild drive from the Browhead dance, with its disgusts and miseries. Was he sober now? What was she to do? – how was she to protect herself? She felt a passionate conviction that she was trapped, that he had planned the whole catastrophe, knowing well what would be thought of her at Bannisdale – in the neighbourhood.

She looked round her, making a desperate effort to keep down exhaustion and excitement. The main-line train had just gone, and the station-master, with a lantern in his hand, was coming up the platform.

Laura went to meet him.

'I've made a mistake and missed the last train to Marsland. Can I sit here in the station till the morning?'

The station-master looked at her sharply – then at the man standing a yard or two behind her. The young lady had to his eye a wild dishevelled appearance. Her fair hair had escaped its bonds in all directions, and was hanging loose upon her neck behind. Her hat had been crumpled and bent by the child's embracing arms; the little muslin dress showed great smears of coaldust here and there, and the light gloves were black.

'No, Miss,' he said, with rough decision. 'You can't sit in the station. There'll be one more train down directly – the express – and then we shut the station for the night.'

'How long will that be?' she asked faintly. He looked at his watch.

'Thirty-five minutes. You can go to the hotel, Miss. It's quite respectable.'

He gave her another sharp glance. He was a Dissenter, a man of northern piety, strict as to his own morals and other people's. What on earth was she doing here, in that untidy state, with a young man, at an hour going on for midnight? Missed train? The young man said nothing about missed trains.

But just as he was turning away the girl detained him.

'How far is it across the sands to Marsland station?'

'Eight miles, about – shortest way.'

'And the road?'

'Best part of fifteen.'

He walked off, throwing a parting word behind him.

'Now understand, please – I can't have anybody here when we lock up for the night.'

Laura hardly heard him. She was looking first to one side of the station, then to the other. The platform and line stood raised under the hill. Just outside the station to the north, the sands of the estuary stretched bare and wide under the moon. In the other direction, on her right hand, the hills rose steeply, and close above the line a limestone quarry made a huge gash in the fell-side. She stood and stared at the wall of glistening rock that caught the moon – at the little railing at the top, sharp against the sky – at the engine-house and empty trucks.

Suddenly she turned back towards Mason. He stood a few yards away on the platform, watching her, and possessed by a dumb rage of jealousy that entirely prevented him from playing any rational or plausible part. Her bitter tone – her evident misery – her refusal an hour or two before to let him be her escort home – all that he had feared and suspected that morning – during the past few weeks – these things made a dark tumult about him, in which nothing else was audible than the alternate cries of anger and passion.

But she walked up to him boldly. She tried to laugh.

'Well! it is very unlucky and very disagreeable. But the station-master says there is a respectable inn. Will you go and see – while I wait? If it won't do – if it isn't a place I can go to – I'll rest here while you ask, and then I shall walk on over the sands to Marsland. It's eight miles – I can do it.'

He exclaimed:

'No, you can't.' – His voice had a note of which he was unconscious, a note that increased the girl's fear of him. – 'Not unless you let me take you. And I suppose you'd sooner die than put up with another hour of me! – The sands are dangerous. You can ask them.'

He nodded towards the men in the distance.

She put a force on herself, and smiled. 'Why shouldn't you take me? But go and look at the inn first – please! – I'm very tired. Then come and report.'

She settled herself on a seat, and drew a little white shawl about her. From its folds her small face looked up softened and beseeching.

He lingered – his mind half doubt, half violence. He meant to force her to listen to him – either now, or in the morning. For all her scorn, she should know, before they parted, something of this misery that burnt in him. And he would say, too, all that it pleased him to say of that priest-ridden fool at Bannisdale.

She seemed so tiny, so fragile a thing, as he looked down upon her. An ugly sense of power came to consciousness in him. Coupled with despair, indeed! For it was her very delicacy, her gentlewoman's grace – maddeningly plain to *him* through all the stains of the steel works – that made hope impossible, that thrust him down as her inferior for ever.

'Promise you won't attempt anything by yourself – promise you'll sit here till I come back,' he said, in a tone that sounded like a threat.

'Of course.'

He still hesitated. Then a glance at the sands decided him. How, on their bare openness, could she escape him? – if she did give him the slip. Here and there streaks of mist lay thin and filmy in the moonlight. But as a rule the sands were clear, the night without a stain.

'All right. I'll be back in ten minutes – less!'

She nodded. He hurried along the platform, asked a question or two of the station-master, and disappeared.

She turned eagerly to watch. She saw him run down the road outside the station – past a grove of trees – out into the moonlight again. Then the road bent and she saw him no more. Just beyond the bend appeared the first houses of the little town.

She rose. Her heart beat so, it seemed to her to be a hostile thing hindering her. A panic terror drove her on, but exhaustion and physical weakness caught at her will, and shod her feet with lead.

She walked down the platform, however, to the station-master. 'The gentleman has gone to inquire at the inn. Will you kindly tell him when he comes back that I had made up my mind after all to walk to Marsland? He can catch me up on the sands.'

'Very good, Miss. But the sands aren't very safe for those that don't know 'em. If you're a stranger you'd better not risk it.'

'I'm not a stranger, and my cousin knows the way perfectly. You can send him after me.'

She left the station. In her preoccupation she never gave another thought to the station-master.

But there was something in the whole matter that roused that person's curiosity. He walked along the raised platform to a point where he could see what became of the young lady.

There was only one exit from the station. But just outside, the road from the town passed in a tunnel under the line. To get at the sands one must double back on the line after leaving the station, walk through the tunnel, and then leave the road to your right. The stony edge of the sands came up to the road, which shot away eastwards along the edge of the estuary, a straight white line that gradually lost itself in the night.

The man watching saw the small figure emerge. But the girl never once turned to the tunnel. She walked straight towards the town, and he lost sight of her in a dense patch of shadow made by some overhanging trees about a hundred yards from the station.

'Upon my word, she's a deep 'un!' he said, turning away – 'it beats me – fair.'

'Hi!' shouted the porter from the end of the platform. 'There's a message just come in, sir.'

The station-master turned to the telegraph office in some astonishment. It was not the ordinary signal message, or the down signal would have dropped.

He read off. 'If a lady arrives by 10.20, too late for Marsland train, kindly help her make arrangements for night. Direct her to White Hart Inn, tell her will meet her Marsland first train. Reply. Helbeck, Bannisdale.'

The station-master stared at the message. It was, of course, long after hours, and Mr Helbeck – whose name he knew – must have had considerable difficulty in sending the message from Marsland, where the station would have been shut before ten o'clock, after the arrival of the last train.

Another click – and the rattle of the signal outside. The express was at hand. He was not a man capable of much reasoning at short

notice, and he had already drawn a number of unfavourable in-
ferences from the conduct of the two people who had just been
hanging about the station. So he hastily replied:

'Lady left station, said intended to walk by sands, but has gone
towards town. Gentleman with her.'

Then he rushed out to attend to the express.

But Laura had not gone to the town. From the platform she had
clearly seen a path on the fell-side, leading over some broken ground
to the great quarry above the station. The grove of trees had hidden
the starting of the path from her, but some outlet into the road
there must be; she had left the station in quest of it.

And as soon as she reached the trees a gate appeared in the wall
to the left. She passed through it, and hurried up the steep path
beyond it. Again and again she hid herself behind the boulders
with which the fell was strewn, lest her moving figure should be
seen from below – often she stopped in terror, haunted by the
sound of steps, imagining a breath, a voice, behind her.

She ran and stumbled – ran again – tore her light dress – gulped
down the sob in her throat – fearing at every step to faint, and so be
taken by the pursuer; or to slip into some dark hole – the ground
seemed full of them – and be lost there – still worse, found there! –
wounded, defenceless.

But at last the slope is climbed. She sees before her a small
platform, on a black network of supporting posts – an engine-house
– and beyond, truck lines with half a dozen empty trucks upon
them, lines that run away in front of her along the descending edge
of the first low hill she has been climbing.

Further on, a dark gulf – then the dazzling wall of the quarry. A
patch of deepest, blackest shadow, at the seaward end of the engine-
house, caught her eye. She gained it, sank down within it, strength-
less and gasping.

Surely no one could see her here! Yet presently she perceived
beside her a low pile of planks within the shadow, and for greater
protection crept behind them. Her eyes topped them. The whole
lower world, the roofs of the station, the railway line, the sands
beyond, lay clear before her in the moon.

Then her nerve gave way. She laid her head against the stones of
the engine-house and sobbed. All her self-command, her cool clearness was gone. The shock of disappointment, the terrors of this

sudden loneliness, the nightmare of her stumbling flight coming upon a nature already shaken, and powers already lowered, had worked with miserable effect. She felt degraded by her own fears. But the one fear at the root of all, that included and generated the rest, held her in so crippling, so torturing a vice, that do what she would, she could not fight herself – could only weep – and weep.

And yet supposing she had walked over the sands with her cousin, would anybody have thought so ill of her – would Hubert himself have dared to offer her any disrespect?

Then again, why not go to the inn? Could she not easily have found a woman on whom to throw herself, who would have befriended her?

Or why not have tried to get a carriage? Fifteen miles to Marsland – eighteen to Bannisdale. Even in this small place, and at midnight, the promise of money enough would probably have found her a fly and a driver.

But these thoughts only rose to be shuddered away. All her rational being was for the moment clouded. The presence of her cousin had suddenly aroused in her so strong a disgust, so hot a misery, that flight from him was all she thought of. On the sands, at the inn, in a carriage, he would still have been there, within reach of her, or beside her. The very dream of it made her crouch more closely behind the pile of planks.

The moon is at her height; across the bay, mountains and lower hills rise towards her, 'ambitious' for that silver hallowing she sheds upon shore and bay. The night is one sigh of softness. The rivers glide glistening to the sea. Even the shining roofs of the little station and the white line of the road have beauty, mingle in the common spell. But on Laura it does not work. She is in the hall at Bannisdale – on the Marsland platform – in the woodland roads through which Mr Helbeck has driven home.

No! – by now he is in his study. She sees the crucifix, the books, the little altar. There he sits – he is thinking, perhaps, of the girl who is out in the night with her drunken cousin, the girl whom he has warned, protected, thought for in a hundred ways – who had planned this day out of mere wilfulness – who cannot possibly have made any honest mistake as to times and trains.

She wrings her hands. Oh! but Polly must have explained, must have convinced him that owing to a prig's self-confidence they were all equally foolish, equally misled. Unless Hubert – ? But then, how is she at fault? In imagination she says it all through Polly's lips. The words glow hot and piteous, carrying her soul with them. But that face in the oak chair does not change.

Yet in flashes the mind works clearly; it rises and rebukes this surging pain that breaks upon it like waves upon a reef. Folly! If a girl's name were indeed at the mercy of such chances, why should one care – take any trouble? Would such a ravening world be worth respecting, worth the fearing?

It is her very innocence and ignorance that rack her. Why should there be these mysterious suspicions and penalties in the world? Her mind holds nothing that can answer. But she trembles none the less.

How strange that she should tremble! Two months before, would the same adventure have affected her at all? Why, she would have laughed it down; would have walked, singing perhaps, across the sands with Hubert.

Some secret cause has weakened the will – paralysed all the old daring. Will he never even scold or argue with her again? Nothing but a cold tolerance – bare civility and protection for Augustina's sake? But never the old rare kindness – never! He has been much away, and she has been secretly bitter, ready to revenge herself by some caprice, like a crossed child! But the days of return – the hours of expectation, of recollection!

Her heart opens to her own reading – like some great flower that bursts its sheath. But such pain – oh, such pain! She presses her little fingers on her breast, trying to drive back this humiliating truth that is escaping her, tearing its way to the light.

How is it that contempt and war can change like this? She seems to have been fighting against something that all the time had majesty, had charm – that bore within itself the forces that tame a woman. In all ages the woman falls before the ascetic – before the man who can do without her. The intellect may rebel; but beneath its revolt the heart yields. Oh! to be guided, loved, crushed if need be, by the mystic, whose first thought can never be for you – who puts his own soul, and a hundred torturing claims upon it, before your lips, your eyes! Strange passion of it! – it rushes through the girl's nature in one blending storm of longing and despair . . .

. . . What sound was that?

She raised her head. A call came from the sands – a distant call floating through the night. Another – and another! She stood up –

she sprang on the heap of planks, straining her eyes. Yes – surely she saw a figure on that wide expanse of sand, moving quickly, moving away? And one after another the cries rose, waking dim echoes from the shore.

It was Hubert, no doubt – Hubert in pursuit, and calling to her, lest she should come unawares upon the danger spots that marked the sands.

She stood and watched the moving speck till it was lost in a band of shadow. Then she saw it no more and the cries ceased.

Would he be at Bannisdale before she was? She dashed away her tears, and smiled. Ah! Let him seek her there! – let him herald her. Light broke upon her; she began to rise from her misery.

But she must sleep a little, or she would never have the strength to begin her walk with the dawn. For walk she would, instead of waiting for tardy trains. She saw herself climbing the fell – she would never trust herself to the road, the open road, where cousins might be hiding after all – finding her way through back lanes into sleeping villages, waking some one, getting a carriage to a point above the park, then slipping down to the door in the garden and so entering by the chapel, when entrance was possible. She would go straight to Augustina. Poor Augustina! there would be little sleep for her to-night. The tears rose again in the girl's eyes.

She drew her thin shawl round her, and crept again into the shadow of the engine-house. Not three hours, and the day would have returned. But already the dawn-breath seemed to be blowing through the night. For it had grown cold and her limbs shivered.

... She woke often in terror, pursued by sheets of flame, or falling through unfathomed space; haunted all through by a sense of doom, an awful expectancy – like one approaching some grisly Atreus-threshold [9] and conscious of the death behind it. But sleep seized her again, a cold tormented sleep, and the hours passed.

Meanwhile the light that had hardly gone came welling gently back. The stars paled; the high mountains wrapped themselves in clouds; a clear yellow mounted from the east, flooding the dusk with cheerfulness. Then the birds woke. The diminished sands, on which the tide was creeping, sparkled with sea-birds; the air was soon alive with their white curves.

With a start Laura awoke. Above the eastern fells scarlet feather-clouds were hovering; the sun rushed upon them as she looked; and in that blue dimness to the north lay Bannisdale.

She sprang up, stared half aghast at the black depths of the quarry, beside which she had been sleeping, then searched the fell with her eyes. Yes, there was the upward path. She struck into it, praying that friend and houses might meet her soon.

Meanwhile it seemed that nothing moved in the world but she.

CHAPTER THREE

It was on the stroke of midnight when the message from Braeside was handed to Mr Helbeck by the sleepy station-master, who had been dragged by that gentleman's urgency from his first slumbers in the neat cottage beside the line.

The master of Bannisdale thrust the slip of paper into his pocket, and stood an instant with bent head, as though reflecting.

'Thank you, Mr Brough,' he said at last. 'I will not ask you to do anything more. Good-night.'

Rightful reward passed, and Mr Helbeck left the station. Outside, his pony-cart stood tied to the station railing.

Before entering it he debated with himself whether he should drive on to the town of Marsland, get horses there and then, and make for Braeside at once.

He could get there in about a couple of hours. And then?

To search a sleeping town for Miss Fountain – would that mend matters?

A carriage arriving at two o'clock in the morning – the inn awakened – no lady there, perhaps – for what was to prevent her having found decent shelter in some quite other quarter? Was he to make a house-to-house visitation at that hour? How wise! How quenching to the gossip that must in any case get abroad!

He turned the pony homewards

Augustina, all shawls and twitching, opened the door to him. A message had been sent on to her an hour before to the effect that Miss Fountain had missed her train, and was not likely to arrive that night.

'Oh, *Alan!* – where is she?'

'I got a telegram through to the station-master. Don't be anxious, Augustina. I asked him to direct her to the inn. The old White Hart, they say, has passed into new management and is quite comfortable. She may arrive by the first train – 7.20. Anyway I shall meet it.'

Augustina pursued him with fretful inquiries and surmises. Helbeck, pale and gloomy, threw himself down on the settle, and produced the story of the accident, so far as the garrulous and incoherent Polly had enabled him to understand it. Fresh wails on Augustina's part. What a horrible, horrible thing! Why, of course the child was terribly upset – hurt perhaps – or she would never have been so foolish about the trains. And now one could not even be sure that she had found a place to sleep in! She would come home a wreck – a simple wreck. Helbeck moved uneasily.

'She was not hurt, according to Miss Mason.'

'I suppose young Mason saw her off?'

'I suppose so.'

'What were they all about, to make such a blunder?'

Helbeck shrugged his shoulders, and at last he succeeded in quieting his sister, by dint of a resolute suppression of all but the most ordinary and comforting suggestions.

'Well, after all, thank goodness, Laura has a great deal of common sense – she always had,' said Mrs Fountain, with a clearing countenance.

'Of course. She will be here, I have little doubt, before you are ready for your breakfast. It is unlucky, but it should not disturb your night's rest. Please go to bed.' With some difficulty he drove her there.

Augustina retired, but it was to spend a broken and often tearful night. Alan might say what he liked – it was all most disagreeable. Why! – would the inn take her in? Mrs Fountain had often been told that an inn, a respectable inn, required a trunk as well as a person. And Laura had not even a bag – positively not a handbag. A reflection which was the starting-point of a hundred new alarms, under which poor Mrs Fountain tossed till the morning.

Meanwhile Helbeck went to his study. It was nearly one o'clock when he entered it, but the thought of sleep never occurred to him. He took out of his pocket the telegram from Braeside, re-read it, and destroyed it.

So Mason was with her – for of course it was Mason. Not one word of such a conjunction was to be gathered from the sister. She had clearly supposed that Laura would start alone and arrive alone. Or was she in the plot? Had Mason simply arranged the whole 'mistake,' jumped into the same train with her, and confronted her at the junction?

Helbeck moved blindly up and down the room, traversed by one of those storms of excitement to which the men of his stock were liable. The thought of those two figures leaving the Braeside station together at midnight roused in him a madness half jealousy, half pride. He saw the dainty head, the cloud of gold under the hat, the pretty gait, the girlish waist, all the points of delicacy or charm he had worshipped through his pain these many weeks. To think of them in the mere neighbourhood of that coarse and sensual lad had always been profanation. And now who would not be free to talk, to spatter her girlish name? The sheer unseemliness of such a kinship! – such a juxtaposition.

If he could only know the true reason of that persistency she had shown about the expedition, in the face of Augustina's wailings, and his own silence? She had been dull – heaven knows she had been dull at Bannisdale, for these two months. On every occasion of his return from those intermediate absences to which he had forced himself, he had perceived that she drooped, that she was dumbly at war with the barriers that shut her youth away from change and laughter, and the natural amusements, flatteries and courtings that wait, or should wait, on sweet-and-twenty. More than once he had realised the fever pulsing through the girl's unrest. Of course she was dissatisfied and starved. She was not of the sort that accepts the *rôle* of companion or sick nurse without a murmur. What could he do – he, into whose being she had crept with torturing power – he who could not marry her even if she should cease to hate him – who could only helplessly put land and distance between them? And then, who knows what a girl plans, to what she will stoop, out of the mere ebullience and rush of her youth – with what haloes she will surround even the meanest heads? Her blood calls her – not this man or that! She takes her decisions – behind that veil of mystery that masks the woman at her will. And who knows – who can know? A mother, perhaps. Not Augustina – not he – nor another.

Groans broke from him. In vain he scourged himself and the vileness of his own thoughts. In vain he said to himself, 'All her instincts, her preferences, are pure, guileless, delicate – I could swear it, I who have watched her every look and motion.' Temper? – yes. Caprice? – yes. A hundred immaturities and rawnesses? – yes! but at the root of all, the most dazzling, the most convincing maidenliness. Not the down-dropt eyes, the shrinking modesties of your old Christian or Catholic types – far from it. But something that, as you dwelt upon it, seemed to make doubt a mere folly.

And yet his very self-assurances, his very protests, left him in torment. There is something in the Catholic discipline on points of sex-relation that perhaps weakens a man's instinctive confidence in women. Evil and its varieties, in this field, are pressed upon his thoughts perpetually with a scholastic fulness so complete, a deductive frankness so compelling, that nothing stands against the process. He sees corruption everywhere – dreads it everywhere. There is no part of its empire, or its action, that his imagination is allowed to leave in shadow. It is the confessional that works. The devout Catholic sees all the world *sub specie peccati*.[10] The flesh seems to him always ready to fall – the devil always at hand.

– Little restless proud creature! What a riddle she has been to him all the time – flitting about the house so pale and inaccessible, so silent, too, in general, since that night when he had wrestled with her in the drawing-room. One moment of fresh battle between them there has been – in the park – on the subject of old Scarsbrook. Preposterous! – that she should think for one moment she could be allowed to confess herself – and so bring all the low talk of the neighbourhood about her ears. He could hear the old man's plaintive cogitations over the strange experience which had blanched his hair and beard and brought him a visible step nearer to his end. 'Soombody towd my owd woman tudther day, Misther Helbeck at yoong Mason o' t' Browhead had been i' th' park that neet. Mappen tha'll tell me it was soom gell body he'd been coortin. Noa! – he doan't gaa about wi' the likes o' thattens! Theer was never a soun' ov her feet, Misther Helbeck! She gaed ower t' grass like a bit cloud i' summer, an she wor sma' an nesh as a wagtail on t' steëans. I ha seen aw maks o' gells, but this one bet 'em aw.' And after that, to think of her pouring herself out in impetuous explanation to the old peasant and his wife! It had needed a strong will to stop her. 'Mr Helbeck, I wish to tell the truth, and I ought to tell it! And your arguments have no weight with me whatever.'

But he had made them prevail. And she had not punished him too severely. A little more pallor, a little more silence for a time – that was all!

A score of poignant recollections laid hold upon him as he paced the night away. That music in the summer dusk – the softness of her little face – the friendliness – first, incredible friendliness! – of her lingering hand. Next morning he had banished himself to Paris, on a Catholic mission devised for the purpose. He had gone, torn with passion – gone, in the spirit that drives the mystic through all the forms of self-torture that religious history records – *ad majorem Dei gloriam*.[11] He had returned to find her frozen and hostile as before – all wilfulness with Augustina – all contradiction with himself. The Froswick plan was already on foot – and he had furthered it – out of a piteous wish to propitiate her, to make her happy. What harm could happen to her? The sister would go with her and bring her back. Why must he always play the disobliging and tyrannical host? Could he undo the blood-relationship between her and the Masons? If for mere difficulty and opposition's sake there were really any fancy in her mind for this vulgar lad, perhaps after all it were the best thing to let her see enough of him for disenchantment! There are instincts that can be trusted.

Such had been the thoughts of the morning. They do not help him through these night hours, when, in spite of all the arguments of common sense, he recurs again and again to the image of her as alone, possibly defenceless, in Mason's company.

Suddenly he perceived that the light was changing. He put his lamp out and threw back the curtain. A pale gold was already creeping up the east. The strange yew forms in the garden began to emerge from the night. A huge green lion showed his jaw, his crown, his straight tail quivering in the morning breeze; a peacock nodded stiffly on its pedestal; a great H that had been reared upon its post-supports before Dryden's death stood black against the morning sky, and everywhere between the clumsy crowding forms were roses, straggling and dew-drenched, or wallflowers in a June wealth of bloom, or peonies that made a crimson flush amid the yews. The old garden, so stiff and sad through all the rest of the year, was in its moment of glory.

Helbeck opened one of the lattices of the oriel and stood there gazing. Six months before there had been a passionate oneness between him and his inheritance, between his nature and the spirit of his race. Their privations and persecutions, their faults, their dumb or stupid fidelities, their very vices even, had been the source in him of a constant and secret affection. For their vices came from their long martyrdom, and their martyrdom from their faith. New influences had worked upon himself, influences linking him with a more European and militant Catholicism, as compared with that starved and local type from which he sprang. But through it all his family pride, his sense of ancestry with all its stimulus and obligations, had but grown. He was proud of calamity, impoverishment, isolation;

they were the scars on pilgrims' feet – honour-marks left by the oppressor. His bare and ruined house, his melancholy garden, where not a bed or path had suffered change since the man who planned them had refused to comply with the Test Act,[12] and so forfeited his seat in Parliament; his dwindling resources, his hermit's life and fare – were they not all joy to him? For years he had desired to be a Jesuit; the obligations of his place and name had stood in the way. And short of being a son of St Ignatius, he exulted in being a Helbeck – the more stripped and despised, the more happy – with those maimed generations behind him, and the triumph of his faith, his faith and theirs, gilding the mind's horizon.

And now after just four months of temptation he stands there, racked with desire for this little pagan creature, this girl without a single Christian sentiment or tradition, the child of an infidel father, herself steeped in denial and cradled in doubt, with nothing meekly feminine about her on which to press new stamps – and knowing well why she denies, if not personally and consciously, at least by a kind of inheritance.

The tangled garden, slowly yielding its splendours to the morning light, the walls of the old house, springing sheer from the grass like the native rock itself – for the first time he feels a gulf between himself and them. His ideals waver in the soul's darkened air; the breath of passion drives them to and fro.

With an anguished 'Domine, exaudi!'[13] he snatched himself from the window, and leaving the room he crossed the hall, where the Tudor badges on the ceiling, the arms of 'Elizabetha Regina' above the great hearth were already clear in the cold dawn, and made his way as noiselessly as possible to the chapel.

Those strange figures on the wall had already shaken the darkness from them. Wing rose on wing, halo on halo, each face turning in a mystic passion to the altar and its steadfast light.

Domine Deus, Agnus Dei, Filius Patris, qui tollis peccata mundi, suscipe deprecationem nostram. Qui sedes ad dexteram Patris, miserere nobis.[14]

In prayer and passionate meditation he passed through much of the time that had still to be endured. But meanwhile he knew well, in his sinful and shrinking mind, that, for that night at least, he was only praying because he could do nothing else – nothing that would give him Laura, or deliver him from the fears that shook his inmost being.

*

A little before six Helbeck left the chapel. He must bathe and dress – then to the farm for the pony-cart. If she did not arrive by the first train he would get a horse at Marsland and drive on to Braeside. But first he must take care to leave a message for Mrs Denton, whose venomous face, as she stood listening the night before to his story of Miss Fountain's mishaps, recurred to him disagreeably.

The housekeeper would not be stirring yet, perhaps, for an hour. He went back to his study to write her some short directions covering the hours of his possible absence.

The room, as he entered it, struck him as musty and airless, in spite of the open lattice. Instinctively, before writing, he went to throw another window wide. In rushed a fresh rose-scented air, and he leant forward an instant, letting its cool current flow through him.

Something white caught his eye beneath the window.

Laura slowly raised her head.

Had she fallen asleep in her fatigue?

Helbeck, bending over her, saw her eyes unclose. She looked at him as she had never looked before – with a sad and spiritual simplicity as though she had waked in a world where all may tell the truth, and there are no veils left between man and woman.

Her light hat fell back from her brow; her delicate pinched features, with the stamp of suffering upon them, met his look so sweetly – so frankly!

'I was *very* tired,' she said, in a new voice, a voice of appealing trust. 'And there was no door open.'

She raised her small hand, and he took it in his, trembling through all his man's strength.

'I was just starting to see if the train had brought you.'

'No – I walked – a great part of the way, at least. Will you help me up? It's very foolish, but I can't stand.'

She rose, tottering, and leaning heavily upon his hand. She drew her own across her forehead.

'It's only hunger. And I had some milk. Was Augustina in a great way?'

'She was anxious, of course. We both were.'

'Yes! it was stupid. But look –' she clung to him. 'Will you take me into the drawing-room, and get me some wine – before I see Augustina?'

'Lean on me.'

She obeyed, and he led her in. The drawing-room door was open, and she sank into the nearest chair. As she looked up she saw the Romney lady shining from the wall in the morning sunlight. The blue-eyed beauty looked down, as though with a careless condescension, upon the pale and tattered Laura. But Laura was neither envious nor ashamed. As Helbeck left her to get wine, she lay still and white; but in the solitude of the room while he was gone, a little smile, ghostly as the dawn itself, fluttered suddenly beneath her closed lids and was gone again.

When he returned, she did her best to drink and eat what she was told. But her exhaustion became painfully apparent, and he hung over her, torn between anxiety, remorse, and the pulsations of a frantic joy, hardly to be concealed, even by him.

'Let me wake Augustina, and bring her down!'

'No – wait a little. I have been in a quarry all night, you see! – That isn't – resting!'

'I tried to direct you – I managed to telegraph to the station-master – but it must have missed. I asked him to direct you to the inn.'

'Oh, the inn!' She shuddered suddenly. 'No, I couldn't go to the inn.'

'Why – what frightened you?'

He sat down by her, speaking very gently, as one does to a child.

She was silent. His heart beat – his ear hungered for the next word.

She lifted her tired lids.

'My cousin was there – at the junction. I did not want him. I did not wish to be with him; he had no right whatever to follow me. So I sent him to the inn, to ask – and I –'

'You –?'

'I hid myself in the quarry while he was gone. When he came back, he went on over the sands, calling for me – perhaps he thought I was lost in one of the bad places.'

She gave a little whimsical sigh, as though it pleased her to think of the lad's possible frights and wanderings.

Helbeck bent towards her.

'And so – to avoid him –?'

She followed his eye like a child.

'I had noticed a quarry beside the line. I climbed up there – under the engine-house – and sat there till it was light. You see' – her breath fluttered – 'I couldn't – I couldn't be sure – he was sober. I dare say it was ridiculous – but I was so startled – and he had no business –'

'He had given you no hint – that he wished to accompany you?' Something drove, persecuted the man to ask it in that hoarse, shaking tone.

She did not answer. She simply looked at him, while the tears rose softly in her clear eyes. The question seemed to hurt her. Yet there was neither petulance nor evasion. She was Laura, and not Laura – the pale sprite of herself. One might have fancied her clothed already in the heavenly supersensual body, with the pure heart pulsing visibly through the spirit frame.

Helbeck rose, closed the door softly, came back and stood before her, struggling to speak. But she intercepted him. There was a look of suffering, a frown.

'I saw a man die yesterday,' she said abruptly. 'Did Polly tell you?'

'I heard of the accident, and that you had stayed to comfort the child.'

'It seems very heartless – but somehow as we were in the train I had almost forgotten it. I was so glad to get away from Froswick – to be coming back. And I was very tired, of course – and never dreamt of anything going wrong. – Oh *no!* – I haven't forgotten really – I never shall forget.'

She pressed her hands together shuddering. Helbeck was still silent.

But it was a silence that pierced. Suddenly she flushed deeply. The spell that held her – that strange transparency of soul – broke up.

'Naturally I was afraid lest Augustina should be anxious,' she said hastily, 'and lest it should be bad for her.'

Helbeck knelt down beside her. She sank back in her chair, staring at him.

'You were glad to be coming back – to be coming here?' he said in his deep voice. 'Is that true? Do you know that I have sat here all night – in misery?'

The struggling breath checked the answer, cheeks and lips lost every vestige of their returning red. Only her eyes spoke. Helbeck came closer. Suddenly he snatched the little form to his breast. She made one small effort to free herself, then yielded. Soul and body were too weak – the ecstasy of his touch too great.

'You can't love me – you can't.'

She had torn herself away. They were sitting side by side; but now she would not even give him her hand. That one trembling kiss had changed their lives. But in both natures passion was proud and fastidious from its birth; it could live without much caressing.

As she spoke he met her gaze with a smiling emotion. The long stern face in its grizzled setting of hair and beard had suffered a transformation that made it almost strange to her. He was like a man loosed from many bonds, and dazzled by the effects of his own will. The last few minutes had made him young again. But she looked at him wistfully once or twice, as though her fancy nursed something which had grown dear to it.

'You can't love me,' she repeated; 'when did you begin? You didn't love me yesterday, you know – nor the day before.'

'Why do you suppose I went away the day after the ghost?' he asked her slowly.

'Because you had business – or you were tired of my very undesirable company.'

'Put it as you like! Do you explain my recent absences in the same way?'

'Oh! I can't explain you!' She raised her shoulders, but her face trembled. 'I never tried.'

'Let me show you how. I went because you were here.'

'And you were afraid – that you might love me? Was it – such a hard fate?' She turned her head away.

'What have I to offer you?' he said passionately; 'poverty – an elderly lover – a life uncongenial to you.'

She slipped a hand nearer to him, but her face clouded a little.

'It's the very strangest thing in the world,' she said deliberately, 'that we should love each other. What can it mean? I hated you when I came, and meant to hate you. And' – she sat up and spoke with an emphasis that brought the colour back into her face – 'I can never, never be a Catholic.'

He looked at her gravely.

'That I understand.'

'You know that I was brought up apart from religion, altogether?'

His eye saddened. Then he raised her hand and kissed it. The pitying tenderness of the action almost made her break down. But she tried to snatch her hand away.

'It was papa's doing, and I shall never blame him – never!'

'I have been in Belgium lately,' he said, holding the hand close, 'at a great Catholic town – Louvain – where I was educated. I went to an old priest I know, and to a Reverend Mother who has sent me Sisters once or twice, and I begged of them both – prayers for your father's soul.'

She stared. The painful tears rushed into her eyes.

'I thought that – for you – that was all sure and settled long ago.'

'I don't think you know much about us, little heretic! I have prayed for your father's soul at every mass since – you remember that Rosary service in April?'

She nodded.

'And what you said to me afterwards, about the child – and doubt? I stayed long in the chapel that night. It was borne in upon me, with a certainty I shall never lose, that all was well with your poor father. Our Blessed Lord has revealed to him in that other life what an invincible ignorance hid from him here.'

He spoke with a beautiful simplicity, like a man dealing with all that was most familiarly and yet sacredly real to his daily mind and thought.

She trembled. Words and ideas of the kind were still all strange and double-edged to her – suggesting on the one side the old feelings of contempt and resistance, on the other a new troubling of the waters of the heart.

She leant her brow against the back of the old sofa on which they were sitting. 'And – and no prayers for me?' she said huskily.

'Dear love! – at all times – in all places – at my down-sitting and mine uprising,' he answered – every word an adoration.

She was silent for a moment, then she dashed the tears from her eyes.

'All the same, I shall never be a Catholic,' she repeated resolutely; 'and how can you marry an unbeliever?'

'My Church allows it – under certain conditions.'

Her mind flew over the conditions. She had heard them named on one or two occasions during the preceding months. Then she turned away, dreading his eye.

'Suppose I am jealous of your Church and hate her?'

'No! – you will love her for my sake.'

'I can't promise. There are two selves in me. All your Catholic friends – Father Leadham – the Reverend Mother – will be in despair.'

She saw him wince. But he spoke firmly. 'I ask only what is lawful. I am free in such a matter to choose my own path – under my conscience.'

She said nothing for a little. But she pondered on all that he might be facing and sacrificing for such a marriage. Once a cloud of sudden misgiving descended upon her, as though a bird had brushed her with its black wing. But she shook it away. Her little hand crept back to him – while her face was still hidden from him.

'I ought not to marry you – but – but I will. There – take me! – will you guide me?'

'With all my strength.'

'Will you fight me?'

He laughed. 'To the best of my ability – when I must. Did I do it well – that night – about the ghost?'

She shrugged her shoulders – half laughing, half crying.

'No! – you were violent – impossible. Will you never, never let me get the upper hand?'

'How would you do it? – little atom!' He bent over her, trying to see her face, but she pressed him away from her.

'Make me afraid to mock at your beliefs!' she said passionately; 'make me afraid! – there is no other way.'

'Laura!'

At last she let his arms have their will. And it was time. The exhaustion which had been driven back for the moment by food and excitement returned upon her with paralysing force. Helbeck woke to a new and stronger alarm. He half led, half carried her through the hall, on the way to Augustina.

At the foot of the stairs, as Laura was making a tottering effort to climb them with Helbeck's arm round her, Mrs Denton came out of the dining-room straight upon them. She carried a pan and brush, and had evidently just begun her morning work.

At sight of her Laura started; but Helbeck gave her no chance to withdraw herself. He turned quietly to his housekeeper, who stood transfixed.

'Good morning, Denton. Miss Fountain has just returned, having walked most of the way from Braeside. She is very tired, as you see – let some breakfast be got ready for her at once. And let me tell you now – what I should any way have told you a few hours later – that Miss Fountain has promised to be my wife.'

He spoke with a cold dignity, scanning the woman closely. Mrs Denton grew very white. But she dropped a curtsey in old Westmoreland fashion.

'I wish you joy, sir – and Miss Fountain too.'

Her voice was low and mumbling, but Helbeck gave her a cheerful nod.

'Thank you. I shall be downstairs again as soon as I have taken Miss Fountain to my sister – and I, too, should be glad of some breakfast.'

'He's been agate all night,' said the housekeeper to herself, as she entered the study and looked at the chairs, the lamp which its master had forgotten to extinguish, the open window. 'An where's she been? Who knows? I saw it from the first. It's a bewitchment – an it'll coom to noa good.'

She went about her dusting with a shaking hand.

Augustina was not told till later in the day. When her brother, who was alone with her, had at last succeeded in making her understand that he proposed to make Laura Fountain his wife, the surprise and shock of the news was such that Mrs Fountain was only saved from faintness by her very strongest smelling-salts.

'Alan – my dear brother! Oh! Alan – you can't have thought it out. She's her father's child, Alan, all through. How can you be happy? Why, Alan, the things she says – poor Laura!'

'She *has* said them,' he replied.

'She can't help saying them – thinking them – it's in her. No one will ever change her. Oh! it's all so strange –'

And Augustina began to cry, silently, piteously.

Helbeck bent over her.

'Augustina!' He spoke with emotion. 'If she loved, wouldn't that change her? Don't all women live by their affections? I am not worth her loving – but –'

His face shone, and spoke the rest for him.

Augustina looked at him in bewilderment. Why, it was only yesterday that Laura disliked and despised him, and that Alan hardly ever spoke when her stepdaughter was there. It was utterly incomprehensible to her. Was it another punishment from Heaven for her own wilful and sacrilegious marriage? As she thought of the new conditions and relations that were coming upon them all – the disapproval of friends, the danger to her brother's Catholic life, the transformation of her own ties to Laura, her feeble soul lost itself in fear. Secretly, she said to herself, with the natural weariness of coming age:

'Perhaps I shall die – before it happens.'

BOOK FOUR

CHAPTER ONE

Augustina was sitting in the garden with Father Bowles. Their chairs were placed under a small Scotch fir, which spread its umbrella top between them and the sun. All around, the old garden was still full and flowery. For it was mid-September, and fine weather.

Mrs Fountain was lying on a sort of deck-chair, and had as usual a number of little invalid appliances about her. But in truth, as Father Bowles was just reflecting, she looked remarkably well. The influences of her native air seemed so far to have brought Dr Mac-Bride's warnings to naught. Or was it the stimulating effect of her brother's engagement? At any rate she talked more, and with more vigour; she was more liable to opinions of her own; and in these days there was that going on at Bannisdale which provoked opinion in great plenty.

'Miss Fountain is not at home?' remarked the old priest. An afternoon gossip with Mrs Fountain had become a very common feature of his recent life.

'Laura has gone, I believe, to meet my brother at the lodge. He has been over to Braeside on business.'

'He is selling some land there?'

'I hope so!' said Augustina, with fervour.

'It is time indeed that our poor orphans were housed,' said Father Bowles naïvely. 'For the last three months some of our dear nuns have been sleeping in the passages.'

Augustina sighed.

'It seems a little hard that there is nobody but Alan to do anything! And how long is it to go on?'

The priest bent forward.

'You mean –'

'How long will my stepdaughter let it go on?' said Augustina impatiently. 'She will be mistress here directly.'

The eyes of her companion flinched, as though something had struck him. But he hastened to say:

'Do not let us doubt, my dear lady, that the soul of Miss Fountain will sooner or later be granted to our prayers.'

'But there is not the smallest sign of it,' cried Augustina. And she in her turn bent towards her companion, unable to resist the temptation of these priestly ears so patiently inclined to her. 'And yet, Father, she isn't happy! – though Alan gives way to her in everything. It's not a bit like a girl in love – you'd expect her to be thinking about her clothes, and the man, and her housekeeping at least – if she won't think about – well! those other things that we should all wish her to think about. While we were at the sea, and Alan used to come down every now and then to stay near us in lodgings, it was all right. They never argued or disputed; they were out all day; and really I thought my brother began to look ten years younger. But now – since we have come back – of course my brother has all his affairs, and all his Church business to look after, and Laura doesn't seem so contented – nearly. It would be different if she cared for any of his interests – but I often think she hates the orphans! She is really naughty about them. And then the Sisters – oh dear!' – Augustina gave a worried sigh – 'I don't think the Reverend Mother can have managed it at all well.'

Father Bowles said that he understood both from the Reverend Mother and Sister Angela that they had made very great efforts to secure Miss Fountain's friendly opinion.

'Well, it didn't succeed, that's all I can say,' replied Augustina fretfully. 'And I don't know what they'll do after November.'

November had been fixed for the marriage, which was to take place at Cambridge.

Father Bowles hung his hands between his knees and looked down upon them in gentle meditation.

'Your brother seems still very much attached –'

'Attached!'

Augustina was silent. In reality she spent half her days in secretly marvelling how such a good man as Alan could allow himself to be so much in love.

'If only some one had ever warned me that this might happen – when I was coming back to live here,' she said, in her most melancholy voice; and clasping her thin hands she looked sadly down the garden paths, while her poor head shook and jerked under the influence of the thoughts – so far from agreeable! – with which it was filled.

There was a little silence. Then Father Bowles broke it.

'And our dear Squire does nothing to try and change Miss Fountain's mind towards the Church?' he asked, looking vaguely round the corner all the time.

Nothing – so Augustina declared.

'I say to him – "Alan, give her some books." Why, they always give people books to read! "Or get Father Leadham to talk to her." What's the good of a man like Father Leadham – so learned, and such manners! – if he can't talk to a girl like Laura? But no, Alan won't. He says we must let her alone – and wait God's time! – And there's no altering him, as you know.'

Father Bowles pondered a little, then said with a mild perplexity:

'I find, in my books, that a great many instances are recorded of holy wives – or even betrothed – who were instrumental under God in procuring the conversion of their unbelieving husbands – or – or lovers, if I may use such a word to a lady. But I cannot discover any of an opposite nature. There was the pious Nonna, for instance, the mother of the great St Gregory Nazianzen, who converted her husband so effectually that he became bishop, and died at the age of ninety.'

'What became of her?' inquired Augustina hastily.

The priest hesitated.

'It is a very curious case – and, I understand, much disputed. Some people suppose that St Gregory was born after his father became a bishop, and many infidel writers have made use of the story for their own malicious purposes. But if it was so, the Church may have allowed such a departure from her law, at a time of great emergency and in a scarcity of pastors. But the most probable thing is that nothing of the kind happened –' he drew himself up with decision – 'that the father of St Gregory had separated from his wife before he became a bishop – and that those writers who record the birth of St Gregory during the episcopate of his father were altogether mistaken.'

'At any rate, I really don't see how it helps us!' said Augustina.

Father Bowles looked a little crestfallen.

'There is one other case that occurs to me,' he said timidly. 'It is that of St Amator, Bishop of Auxerre. He was desired by his parents to marry Martha, a rich young lady of his neighbourhood. But he took her aside, and pressed upon her the claims of the ascetic life with such fervour that she instantly consented to renounce the world with him. She therefore went into a convent; and he received the tonsure, and was in due time made Bishop of Auxerre.'

'Well, I assure you, I should be satisfied with a good deal less than that in Laura's case!' said Augustina, half angry, half laughing.

Father Bowles said no more. His mind was a curious medley of scraps from many quarters – from a small shelf of books that held a humble place in his little parlour, from the newspapers, and from the few recollections still left to him of his seminary training. He was one of the most complacently ignorant of men; and it had ceased to trouble him that even with Augustina he was no longer of importance.

Mrs Fountain made him welcome, indeed, not only because he was one of the chief gossips of the neighbourhood, but because she was able to assume towards him certain little airs of superiority that no other human being allowed her. With him, she was the widow of a Cambridge scholar, who had herself breathed the forbidden atmosphere of an English University; she prattled familiarly of things and persons wherewith the poor priest, in his provincial poverty and isolation, could have no acquaintance; she let him understand that by marriage she had passed into hell-flame regions of pure intellect, that little parish priests might denounce but could never appreciate. He bore it all very meekly; he liked her tea and talk; and at bottom the sacerdotal pride, however hidden and silent, is more than a match for any other.

Augustina lay for a while in a frowning and flushed silence, with a host of thoughts, of the most disagreeable and heterogeneous sort, scampering through her mind. Suddenly she said:

'I don't think Sister Angela should talk as she does! She told me when she heard of the engagement that she could not help thinking of St Philip Neri, who was attacked by three devils near the Colosseum, because they were enraged by the success of his holy work among the young men of Rome. I asked her whether she meant to call Laura a devil! And she coloured, and got very confused, and said it was so sad that Mr Helbeck, of all people, should marry an unbelieving wife – and we were taught to believe that all temptations came from evil spirits.'

'Sister Angela means well, but she expresses herself very unwarrantably,' said the priest sharply. 'Now the Reverend Mother tells me that she expected something of the kind, almost from the first.'

'Why didn't she tell me?' cried Augustina. 'But I don't really think she did, Father. She makes a mistake. How *could* she? But the dear Reverend Mother – well! you know – though she is so wonderfully humble, she doesn't like anybody to be wiser than she. And I can hardly bear it – I *know* she puts it all down to some secret sin on Alan's part. She spends a great part of the night – that she told me – in praying for him in the chapel.'

Father Bowles sighed.

'I believe that our dear Reverend Mother has often and often prayed for a good wife for Mr Helbeck. Miss Fountain, no doubt, is a very attractive and accomplished young lady, but –'

'Oh, don't, please, go through the "buts,"' said Mrs Fountain with a shrug of despair. 'I don't know what's to become of us all – I don't, indeed. It isn't as though Laura could hold her tongue. Since we came back I can see her father in her all day long. I had a talk with the Bishop yesterday,' she said in a lower voice, looking plaintively at her companion.

He bent forward.

'Oh! he's just broken-hearted. He can hardly bring himself to speak to Alan about it at all. Of course, Alan will get his dispensation for the marriage. They can't refuse it to him when they give it to so many others. But!' – she threw up her hands – 'the Bishop asked me if Laura had been really baptised. I told him there was no doubt at all about it – though it was a very near thing. But her mother did insist that once. And it appears that if she hadn't –'

She looked interrogatively at the priest.

'The marriage could not have taken place,' he said slowly. 'No Catholic priest could have celebrated it, at least. There would have been a diriment impediment.'

'I thought so,' said Augustina, excitedly, 'though I wasn't sure. There are so many dispensations nowadays.'

'Ah, but not in such cases as that,' said the priest, with an unconscious sigh that rather startled his companion.

Then with a sudden movement he pounced upon something on the further side of the table, nearly upsetting the tea-tray. Augustina exclaimed.

'I beg your pardon,' he said humbly; 'it was only a nasty fly.' And he dropped the flattened creature on the grass.

Both relapsed into a melancholy silence. But several times during the course of it Mrs Fountain looked towards her companion as though on the point of saying something – then rebuked herself and refrained.

But when the priest had taken his leave, and Mrs Fountain was left alone in the garden with the flowers and the autumn wind, her thoughts were painfully concerned with quite another part of the episcopal conversation from that which she had reported to Father Bowles. What right had the Bishop or any one else to speak of 'stories' about Laura. Of course, the dear Bishop had been very kind and cautious. He had said emphatically that he did not believe the stories – nor that other report that Mr Helbeck's sudden proposal of marriage to Miss Fountain had been brought about by his chivalrous wish to protect the endangered name of a young girl, his guest, to whom he had become unwisely attached.

But why should there be 'stories,' and what did it all mean?

That unlucky Froswick business – and young Mason? But what had Mason to do with it – on that occasion? As Augustina understood, he had seen the child off from Froswick by the 8.20 train – and there was an end of him in the matter. As for the rest of that adventure, no doubt it was foolish of Laura to sit in the quarry till daylight, instead of going to the inn; but all the world might know that she took a carriage at Wryneck, halfway home, about four o'clock in the morning, and left it at the top gate of the park. Why, she was in her room by six, or a little after!

What on earth did the Bishop mean? Augustina fell into a maze of rather miserable cogitation. She recalled her brother's manner and words after his return from the station on the night of the expedition – and then next day, the news! – and Laura's abrupt admission: 'I met him in the garden, Augustina, and – well! we soon understood each other. It had to come, I suppose – it might as well come then. But I don't wonder it's all very surprising to you –' And then such a wild burst of tears – such a sudden gathering of the stepmother in the girl's young arms – such a wrestle with feelings to which the bewildered Augustina had no clue.

Was Alan up all that night? Mrs Denton had said something of the sort. Was he really making up his mind to propose – because people might talk? But why? – how ridiculous! Certainly it must have been very sudden. Mrs Denton met them coming upstairs a little after six; and Alan told her then.

'Oh, if I only *could* understand it,' thought Augustina with a little moan. 'And now Alan just lives and breathes for her. And she will be here, in my mother's place – Stephen's daughter.'

Mrs Fountain felt the burning of a strange jealousy. Her vanity and her heart were alike sore. She remembered how she had trembled before Alan in his strict youth – how she had apostatised even, merely to escape the demands which the intensity of Alan's faith made on all about him. And now this little chit of twenty, her own stepdaughter, might do and say what she pleased. She would be mistress of Alan, and of the old house. Alan's sister might creep into a corner, and pray! – that was enough for her.

And yet she loved Laura, and clung to her! She felt the humiliation of her secret troubles and envies. Her only comfort lay in her recovered faith; in the rosary to which her hands turned perpetually; in her fortnightly confession; in her visits to the sacrament. The great Catholic tradition beat through her meagre life, as the whole Atlantic may run pulsing through a drifting weed.

Meanwhile, near the entrance gate of the park, on a wooded knoll that overlooked the park wall and commanded the road beyond, Laura Fountain was sitting with the dogs – waiting for Helbeck.

He had been at Whinthorpe all day, on some business in which she was specially interested. The Romney lady was not yet sold. During May and June, Laura had often wondered why she still lingered on the wall. An offer had actually been made – so Augustina said. And there was pressing need for the money that it represented – that, every sojourner in Bannisdale must know. And yet, there still she hung.

Then, with the first day of her engagement, Laura knew why. 'You saved her,' said Helbeck. 'Since that evening when you denounced me for selling her – little termagant! – I have racked my brains to keep her.'

And now for some time there had been negotiations going on between Helbeck and a land-agent in Whinthorpe for the sale of an outlying piece of Bannisdale land, to which the growth of a little watering-place on the estuary had given of late a new value. Helbeck, in general a singularly absent and ineffective man of business, had thrown himself into the matter with an astonishing energy, had pressed his price, hurried his solicitors, and begged the patience of the nuns – who were still sleeping in doorways and praying for new buildings – till all should be complete.

That afternoon he had ridden over to Whinthorpe in the hopes of signing the contract. He did not yet know – so Laura gathered –

with whom he was really treating. The Whinthorpe agent had talked vaguely of 'a Manchester gentleman,' and Helbeck had not troubled himself to inquire further.

When they were married, would he still sell all that he had, and give to the poor – in the shape of orphanages and reformatories? Laura was almost as unpractical, and cared quite as little about money, as he. But her heart yearned towards the old house; and she already dreamt of making it beautiful and habitable again. As a woman, too, she was more alive to the habitual discomforts of the household than Helbeck himself. Mrs Denton at least should go! So much he had already promised her. The girl thought with joy of that dismissal, tightening her small lips. Oh! the tyranny of those perpetual grumblings and parsimonies, of those sour unfriendly looks! Economy – yes! But it should be a seemly economy in future – one still compatible with a little elegance, a little dignity.

Laura liked to think of her own three hundred a year; liked to feel it of importance in the narrow lot of this impoverished estate. To a rich bridegroom it would have been a trifle for contempt. To Helbeck and herself – though she scarcely believed that he had realised as yet that she possessed a farthing! – it would mean just escape from penury; a few more fires and servants and travellings; enough to ease his life from that hard strain that had tugged at it so long. For *her* money should not go to nuns or Jesuits! – she would protect it zealously, and not for her own sake.

. . . Oh! those days by the sea! Those were days for remembering. That tall form always beside her – those eyes so grey and kind – so fiery-kind, often! – revealing to her day by day more of the man, learning a new language for her alone, in all the world, a language that could set her trembling, that could draw her to him, in a humility that was strange and difficult, yet pure joy! – her hand slipping into his, her look sinking beneath his, almost with an appeal to love to let her be. Then – nothing but the sparkling sands and the white-edged waves for company! A little pleasant chat with Augustina; duty-walks with her bath-chair along the sea-wall; strolls in the summer dusk, while Mrs Fountain, wrapped in her many shawls, watched them from the balcony: their day had known no other events, no other disturbance than these.

As far as things external were concerned. – Else, each word, each look made history. And though he had not talked much to her of his religion, his Catholic friends and schemes, all that he had said on these things she had been ready to take into a softened heart. His mystic's practice and belief wore still their grand air for her — that aspect of power and mystery which had in fact borne so large a part in the winning of her imagination, the subduing of her will. She did not want then to know too much. She wished the mystery still kept up. And he, on his side, had made it plain to her that he would not attempt to disturb her inherited ideas — so long as she herself did not ask for the teaching and initiation that could only, according to his own deepest conviction, bear fruit in the willing and prepared mind.

But now — They were at Bannisdale again, and he was once more Helbeck of Bannisdale, a man sixteen years older than she, wound round with the habits and friendship and ideals which had been the slow and firm deposit of those years — habits and ideals which were not hers, which were at the opposite pole from hers, of which she still only dimly guessed the motives and foundations.

'Helbeck of Bannisdale.' Her new relation to him, brought back into the old conditions, revealed to her day by day fresh meanings and connotations of the name. And the old revolts, under different, perhaps more poignant forms, were already strong.

What *time* this religion took! Apart from the daily Mass which drew him always to Whinthorpe before breakfast, there were the morning and evening prayers, the visits to the Sacrament, the two Masses on Sunday morning, Rosary and Benediction in the evening, and the many occasional services for the marking of Saints'-days or other festivals. Not to speak of all the business that fell upon him as the chief Catholic layman of a large district.

And it seemed to her that since their return home he was more strict, more rigorous than ever in points of observance. She noticed that not only Friday was a fast-day, but Wednesday also was an 'abstinence' day; that he looked with disquiet upon the books and magazines that were often sent her by the Friedlands, and would sometimes gently beg her — for the Sisters' sake — to put them out of sight; that on the subject of balls and theatres he spoke sometimes with a severity no member of the Metropolitan Tabernacle could have out-done. What was that phrase he had dropped once as to being 'under a rule'? What was 'The Third Order of St Francis'? She had seen a book of 'Constitutions' in his study; and a printed card of devout recommendations to 'Tertiaries of the Northern Province' hung beside his table. She half thirsted, half dreaded, to know precisely what these things meant to him. But he was silent, and she shrank from asking.

Was he all the more rigid with himself on the religious side of late, because of that inevitable scandal which his engagement had given to his Catholic friends – perhaps because of his own knowledge of the weakening effects of passion on the will? For Laura's imagination was singularly free and cool where the important matters of her own life were concerned. She often guessed that but for the sudden emotion of that miserable night, and their strange meeting in the dawn, he might have succeeded in driving down and subduing his love for her – might have proved himself in that, as in all other matters, a good Catholic to the end. That she should have brought him to her feet in spite of all trammels was food for a natural and secret exultation. But now that the first exquisite days of love were over, the trammels, the forgotten trammels, were all there again – for the fretting of her patience. That his mind was often disturbed, his cheerfulness overcast, that his letters gave him frequently more pain than pleasure, and that a certain inward unrest made his dealings with himself more stern, and his manner to those around him less attractive than before – these things were constantly plain to Laura. As she dwelt upon them, they carried flame and poison through the girl's secret mind. For they were the evidences of forces and influences not hers – forces that warred with hers, and must always war with hers. Passion on her side began to put forward a hundred new and jealous claims; and at the touch of resistance in him, her own will steeled.

As to the Catholic friends, surely she had done her best! She had called with Augustina on the Reverend Mother and Sister Angela – a cold, embarrassed visit. She had tried to be civil whenever they came to the house. She had borne with the dubious congratulations of Father Bowles. She had never once asked to see any portion of that correspondence which Helbeck had been carrying on for weeks with Father Leadham, persuaded though she was, from its effects on Helbeck's moods and actions, that it was wholly concerned with their engagement, and with the problems and difficulties it presented from the Catholic point of view.

She was preparing even to welcome with politeness that young Jesuit who had neglected his dying mother, against whom – on the stories she had heard – her whole inner nature cried out . . .

*

The sound of a horse approaching. Up sprang the dogs, and she with them.

Helbeck waved his hand to her as he came over the bridge. Then at the gate he dismounted, seeing Wilson in the drive, and gave his horse to the old bailiff.

'Cross the bridge with me,' he said, as he joined her, 'and let us walk home the other side of the river. Is it too far?'

His eyes searched her face – with the eagerness of one who has found absence a burden. She shook her head and smiled. The little frown that had been marring the youth of her pretty brow smoothed itself away. She tripped beside him, feeling the contagion of his joy – inwardly repentant – and very happy.

But he was tired and disappointed by the day's result. The contract was not signed. His solicitor had been summoned in haste to make the will of a neighbouring magnate; some of the last formalities of his own business had been left uncompleted; and in short the matter was postponed for at least a day or two.

'I wish it was done,' he said, sighing – and Laura could only feel that the responsibilities and anxieties weighing upon him seemed to press with unusual strength.

A rosy evening stole upon them as they walked along the Greet. The glow caught the grey walls of the house on the further bank – lit up the reaches of the stream – and the bare branch-work of a great ruined tree in front of them. Long lines of heavy wood closed the horizon on either land; shutting in the house, the river, and their two figures.

'How solitary we are here!' he said, suddenly looking round him. 'Oh! Laura, can you be happy – with poverty – and me?'

'Well, I sha'n't read my prayer book along the river! – and I sha'n't embroider curtains for the best bedroom – alack! Perhaps a new piano might keep me quiet – I don't know!'

He looked at her, then quickly withdrew his eyes, as though they offended. Through his mind had run the sacred thought, 'Her children will fill her life – and mine!'

'When am I to teach you Latin?' he said, laughing.

She raised her shoulders.

'I wouldn't learn it if I could do without it! But you Catholics are bred upon it.'

'We are the children of the Church,' he said gently. 'And it is her tongue.'

She made no answer, and he talked of something else immediately. As they crossed the little foot-bridge he drew her attention to the deep pool on the further side, above which was built the wooden platform, where Laura had held her May tryst with Mason.

'Did I ever tell you the story of my great-grandfather drowning in that pool?'

'What, the drinking and gambling gentleman?'

'Yes, poor wretch! He had half-killed his wife, and ruined the property – so it was time. He was otter-hunting – there is an otter-hole still, halfway down that bank. Somehow or other he came to the top of the crag alone, probably not sober. The river was in flood; and his poor wife, sitting on one of those rock seats, with her needlework and her books, heard the shouts of the huntsmen – helped to draw him out, and to carry him home. Do you see that little beach?' – he pointed to a break in the rocky bank. 'It was there – so tradition says – that he lay upon her knee, she wailing over him. And in three months she too was gone.'

Laura turned away.

'I won't think of it,' she said obstinately. 'I will only think of her as she is in the picture.'

On the little platform she paused, with her hand on the railing, the dark water eddying below her, the crag above her.

'I could – tell *you* something about this place,' she said slowly. 'Do you want to hear?'

She bent over the water. He stood beside her. The solitude of the spot, the deep shadow of the crag, gave love freedom.

He drew her to him.

'Dear! – confess!'

She too whispered.

'It was here – I saw Hubert Mason – that night.'

'Culprit! Repeat every word – and I will determine the penance.'

'As if there had not been already too much! Oh! what a lecture you read me – and you have never apologised yet! Begin – *begin* – at once!'

He raised her hand and kissed it.

'So? Now – courage!'

And with some difficulty – half-laughing – she described the scene with Hubert, her rush home, her meeting with old Scarsbrook.

'I tell you,' she insisted at the end, 'there is good in that boy somewhere – there *is!* '

Helbeck said nothing.

'But you always saw the worst,' she added, looking up.

'I am afraid I only saw what there was,' he said drily. 'Dear, it gets cold, and that white frock is very thin.'

They walked on. In truth, he could hardly bear that she should take Mason's name upon her lips at all. The thoughts and comments of ill-natured persons, of some of his own friends – the sort of misgiving that had found expression in the Bishop's talk with his sister – he was perfectly aware of them all, impossible as it would have been for Augustina or any one else to say a word to him on the subject. The dignity no less than the passion of a strong man were deeply concerned. He repented and humbled himself every day for his own passing doubts; but his resolution only stiffened the more. There was no room, there should never be any room in Laura's future life, for any further contact with the Mason family.

And, indeed, the Mason family itself seemed to have arrived at very similar conclusions! All that Helbeck knew of them since the Froswick day might have been summed up in a few sentences. On the Sunday morning Mason, in a wild state, with wet clothes and bloodshot eyes, had presented himself at the Wilsons' cottage, asking for news of Miss Fountain. They told him that she was safely at home, and he departed. As far as Helbeck knew, he had spent the rest of the Sunday drinking heavily at Marsland. Since then Laura had received one insolent letter from him, reiterating his own passion for her, attacking Helbeck in the fiercest terms, and prophesying that she would soon be tired of her lover and her bargain. Laura had placed the letter in Helbeck's hands, and Helbeck had replied by a curt note through his solicitor, to the effect that if any further annoyance were offered to Miss Fountain he would know how to protect her.

Mrs Mason also had written. Madwoman! She forbade her cousin to visit the farm again or to hold any communication with Polly or herself. A girl, born of a decent stock, who was capable of such an act as marrying a Papist and idolater was not fit to cross the threshold of Christian people. Mrs Mason left her to the mercy of her offended God.

And in this matter of her cousins Laura was not unwilling

to be governed. It was as though she liked to feel the curb.

And to-night as they strolled homewards, hand locked in hand, all her secret reserves and suspicions dropped away – silenced or soothed. Her charming head drooped a little; her whole small self seemed to shrink towards him as though she felt the spell of that mere physical maturity and strength that moved beside her youth. Their walk was all sweetness; and both would have prolonged it but that Augustina had been left too long alone.

She was no longer in the garden, however, and they went in by the chapel entrance seeking for her.

'Let me just get my letters,' said Helbeck, and Laura followed him to his study.

The afternoon post lay upon his writing-table. He opened the first, read it, and handed it with a look of hesitation to Laura.

'Dear, Mr Williams comes to-morrow. They have given him a fortnight's holiday. He has had a sharp attack of illness and depression, and wants change. Will you feel it too long?'

Involuntarily her look darkened. She put down the letter without reading it.

'Why – I want to see him! I – I shall make a study of him,' she said with some constraint.

But by this time Helbeck was half through the contents of his next envelope. She heard an exclamation of disgust, and he threw down what he held with vehemence.

'One can trust nobody!' he said – *'nobody!'*

He began to pace the floor with angry energy, his hands thrust into his pockets. She – in astonishment – threw him questions which he hardly seemed to hear. Suddenly he paused.

'Dear Laura! – will you forgive me? – but after all I must sell that picture!'

'Why?'

'I hear to-day, for the first time, who is to be the real purchaser of that land, and why it is wanted. It is to be the site of a new Anglican church and vicarage. I have been tricked throughout – tricked – and deceived! But thank God it is not too late! The circumstances of this afternoon were providential. There is still time for me to write to Whinthorpe.' He glanced at the clock. 'And my lawyers may tear up the contract when they please!'

'And – that means – you will sell the Romney?' said Laura slowly.

'I must! Dear little one!' – he came to stoop over her – 'I am most truly grieved. But I am bound to my orphans by all possible engagements – both of honour and conscience.'

'Why is it so horrible that an Anglican church should be built on your land?' she said, slightly holding him away from her.

'Because I am responsible for the use of my land, as for any other talent. It shall not be used for the spread of heresy.'

'Are there any Catholics near it?'

'Not that I know of. But it has been a fixed principle with me throughout my life' – he spoke with a firm and, as she thought, a haughty decision – 'to give no help, direct or indirect, to a schismatical and rebellious church. I see now why there has been so much secrecy! My land is of vital importance to them. They apparently feel that the whole Anglican development of this new town may depend upon it. Let them feel it. They shall not have a foot – not an inch of what belongs to me!'

'Then they are to have no church,' said Laura. She had grown quite pale.

'Not on my land,' he said, with a violence that first amazed and then offended her. 'Let them find sympathisers of their own. They have filched enough from us Catholics in the past.'

And he resumed his rapid walk, his face darkened with an anger he vainly tried to curb. Never had she seen him so roused.

She too rose, trembling a little.

'But I love that picture!' she said. 'I beg you not to sell it.'

He stopped, in distress.

'Unfortunately, dear, I have promised the money. It must be found within six weeks – and I see no other way.'

She thought that he spoke stiffly, and she resented the small effect of her appeal.

'And you won't bend a single prejudice to – to save such a family possession – though I care for it so much?'

He came up to her with outstretched hands.

'I have been trying to save it all these weeks! Nothing but such a cause as this could have stood in the way. It is not a prejudice, darling – believe me! – it belongs, for me at any rate, to Catholic obligation.'

She took no notice of the hands. With her own she clung to the table behind her.

'Why do you give so much to the Sisters? It is not right! They give a very bad education!'

He stared at her. How pale she had grown – and this half-stifled voice! –

'I think we must be the judges of that,' he said, dropping his hands. 'We teach what we hold most important.'

'Nobody like Sister Angela ought to teach!' she cried – 'you give money to bring pupils to Sister Angela. And she is not well trained. I never heard any one talk so ignorantly as she does to Augustina. And the children learn nothing, of course – every one says so.'

'And you are so eager to listen to them?' he said with sparkling eyes. Then he controlled himself.

'But that is not the point. I humbly admit our teaching is not nearly so good as it might be if we had larger funds to spend upon it. But the point is that I have promised the money, and that a number of arrangements – fresh teachers among them – are already dependent on it. Dearest, won't you recognise my difficulties, and – and help me through them?'

'You make them yourself,' she said, drawing back. 'There would be none if you did not – hate – your fellow-citizens.'

'I hate no one – but I cannot aid and abet the English Church. That is impossible to me. Laura!' He observed her carefully. 'I don't understand. Why do you say these things? – why does it hurt you so much?'

'Oh! let me go,' she cried, flinging his hand away from her. 'Let me go!'

And before he could stop her, she had fled to the door, and disappeared.

Helbeck and Augustina ate a lonely dinner.

'You must have taken Laura too far this afternoon, Alan,' said Mrs Fountain fretfully. 'She says she is too tired to come down again to-night – so very unlike her!'

'She did not complain – but it may have been a long round,' said her companion.

After dinner, Helbeck took his pipe into the garden, and walked for long up and down the bowling-green, torn with solitary thought. He had put up his pipe, and was beginning drearily to feel the necessity of going back to his study, and applying himself – if he could force his will so far – to some official business that lay waiting for him there, when a light noise on the gravel caught his ear.

His heart leapt.

'Laura!'

She stopped – a white wraith in the light mist that filled the garden. He went up to her, overwhelmed with the joy of her coming – accusing himself of a hundred faults.

She was too miserable to resist him. The storm of feeling through which she had passed had exhausted her wholly; and the pining for his step and voice had become an anguish driving her to him.

'I told you to make me afraid!' she said mournfully, as she found herself once more upon his breast – 'but you can't! There is something in me that fears nothing – not even the breaking of both our hearts.'

CHAPTER TWO

A week later the Jesuit scholastic Edward Williams arrived at Bannisdale.

In Laura his coming roused a curiosity half angry, half feminine, by which Helbeck was alternately harassed and amused. She never tired of asking questions about the Jesuits – their training, their rules, their occupations. She could not remember that she had ever seen one till she made acquaintance with Father Leadham. They were alternately a mystery, and a repulsion to her.

Helbeck smilingly told her that she was no worse than the mass of English people. 'They have set up their bogey and they like it.' She would be surprised to find how simple was the Jesuit secret.

'What is it? – in two words?' she asked him.

'Obedience – training. So little?' he laughed at her, and took her hand tenderly.

She inquired if Mr Williams were yet 'a full Jesuit.'

'Oh dear no! He has taken his first vows. Now he has three years' philosophy, then four years' theology. After that they will make him teach somewhere. Then he will take orders – go through a third year's noviceship – get a doctor's degree, if he can – and after that, perhaps, he will be a professed "Father." It isn't done just by wishing for it, you see.'

The spirit of opposition reared its head. She coloured, laughed – and half without intending it repeated some of the caustic things she had heard occasionally from her father or his friends as to the learning of Jesuits. Helbeck, under his lover's sweetness, showed a certain restlessness. He hardly let himself think the thought that Stephen Fountain had been quoted to him very often of late; but it was there.

'I am no judge,' he said at last. 'I am not learned. I dare say you will find Williams ignorant enough. But he was a clever boy – besides his art.'

'And they have made him give up his art?'

'For a time – yes – perhaps altogether. Of course it has been his great renunciation. His superiors thought it necessary to cut him off from it entirely. And no doubt during the novitiate he

258

suffered a great deal. It has been like any other starved faculty.'

The girl's instincts rose in revolt. She cried out against such waste, such mutilation. The Catholic tried to appease her; but in another language. He bade her remember the Jesuit motto. 'A Jesuit is like any other soldier – he puts himself under orders for a purpose.'

'And God is to be glorified by the crushing out of all He took the trouble to give you!'

'You must take the means to the end,' said Helbeck steadily. 'The Jesuit must yield his will – otherwise the Society need not exist. In Williams's case, so long as he had a fascinating and absorbing pursuit, how could he give himself up to his superiors? Besides' – his grave face stiffened – 'in his case there were peculiar difficulties. His art had become a temptation. He wished to protect himself from it.'

Laura's curiosity was roused; but Helbeck gently put her questions aside, and at last she said in a flash of something like passion that she wondered which the young man had felt most – the trampling on his art, or the forsaking his mother.

Helbeck looked at her with sudden animation.

'I knew you had heard that story. Dear – he did not forsake his mother! He meant to go – the Fathers had given him leave. But there was a mistake, a miscalculation – and he arrived too late.'

Laura's beautiful eyes threw lightnings.

'A *miscalculation!*' she cried scornfully, her quick breath beating – 'That puts it in a nutshell.'

Helbeck looked at her sadly.

'So you are going to be very unkind to him?'

'No. I shall watch him.'

'Look into him rather! Try and make out his spring. I will help you.'

She protested that there was nothing she less desired. She had been reading some Jesuit biographies from Augustina's room, and they had made her feel that the only thing to be done with such people was to keep them at a distance.

Helbeck sighed and gave up the conversation. Then in a moment, compunctions and softenings began to creep over the girl's face. A small hand made its way to his.

'There is Wilson in the garden – shall we go and talk to him?'

They were in Helbeck's study – where Augustina had left them alone for a little after luncheon.

Helbeck put down his pipe with alacrity. Laura ran for her hat and cape, and they went out together.

A number of small improvements both inside and outside the house had been recently inaugurated to please the coming bride. Already Helbeck realised – and not without a secret chafing – the restraints that would soon be laid upon the almsgiving of Bannisdale. A man who marries, who may have children, can no longer deal with his money as he pleases. Meanwhile he found his reward in Laura's half-reluctant pleasure. She was at once full of eagerness and full of a proud shyness. No bride less grasping or more sensitive could have been imagined. She loved the old house and would fain repair its hurts. But her wild nature, at the moment, asked, in this at least, to be commanded, not to command. To be the managing wife of an obedient husband was the last thing that her imagination coveted. So that when any change in the garden, any repair in the house, was in progress, she would hover round Helbeck, half cold, half eager, now only showing a fraction of her mind, and now flashing out into a word or look that for Helbeck turned the whole business into pure joy. Day by day, indeed, amid all jars and misgivings, the once solitary master of Bannisdale was becoming better acquainted with that mere pleasantness of a woman's company which is not passion, but its best friend. In the case of those women whom nature marks for love, it is a company full of incident, full of surprise. Certainly Helbeck found it so.

A week or more had now passed since the quarrel over the picture. Not a word upon the subject had passed between them since. As for Laura, she took pains not to look at the picture – to forget its existence. It was as though she felt some hidden link between herself and it – as though some superstitious feeling attached to it in her mind.

Meanwhile a number of new understandings were developing in Helbeck. His own nature was simple and concentrated, with little introspective power of the modern kind – even through all the passions and subtleties of his religion. Nevertheless his lover's sense revealed to him a good deal of what was going on in the semi-darkness of Laura's feelings and ideas. He divined this jealousy of his religious life that had taken possession of her since their return from the sea. He felt by sympathy that obscure pain of separation that tormented her. What was he to do? – what could he do?

The change astonished him, for while they were at the sea, it seemed to him that she had accepted the situation with a remarkable resolution. But it also set him on new trains of thought; it roused in him a secret excitement, a vague hope. If her earlier mood had persisted; if amid the joys of their love she had continued to put the whole religious matter away from her, as many a girl with her training might and would have done – then indeed he must have resigned himself to a life-long difference and silence between them on these vital things.

But, since she suffered – since she felt the need of that more intimate, more exquisite link? – Since she could not let it alone, but must needs wound herself and him? –

Instinctively he felt the weakness of her intellectual defence. Once or twice he let himself imagine the capture of her little struggling soul, the break down of her childish resistance, and felt the flooding of a joy, at once mystical and very human.

But that natural chivalry and deep self-distrust he had once expressed to Father Leadham kept him in check; made him very slow and scrupulous. Towards his Catholic friends indeed he stood all along in defence of Laura, an attitude which only made him more sensitive and more vulnerable in other directions.

Meanwhile his own struggles and discomforts were not few. No strong man of Helbeck's type, endures so complete an overthrow at the hands of impulse and circumstance as he had done, without going afterwards through a period of painful readjustment. The new image of himself that he saw reflected in the astonished eyes of his Catholic companions worked in him a number of fresh forms of self-torment. His loyalty to Laura, indeed, and to his own passion was complete. Secretly, he had come to believe, with all the obstinate ardour of the religious mind, that the train of events which had first brought Laura into his life, and had then overcome his own resistance to her spell, represented, not temptation, but a Divine volition concerning him. No one so impoverished and forlorn as she in the matters of the soul! But not of her own doing. Was she responsible for her father? In the mere fact that she had so incredibly come to love him – he being what he was – there was surely a significance which the Catholic was free to interpret in the Catholic sense. So that, where others saw defection from a high ideal and danger to his own Catholic position, he, with hidden passion, and very few words of explanation even to his director, Father Leadham, felt the drawing of a heavenly force, the promise of an ultimate and joyful issue.

At the same time, the sadness of his Catholic friends should find no other pretext. Upon his fidelity now and here, not only his own eternal fate, but Laura's, might depend. Devotion to the crucified Lord and His Mother, obedience to His Church, imitation of His saints, charity to His poor – these are the means by which the Catholic draws down the grace, the condescension that he seeks. He felt his own life offered for hers. So that the more he loved her, the more set, the more rigid became all the habits and purposes of religion. Again and again he was tempted to soften them – to spend time with her that he had been accustomed to give to Catholic practice – to slacken or modify the harshness of that life of self-renouncement, solitude, unpopularity to which he had vowed himself for years – to conceal from her the more startling and difficult of his convictions. But he crushed the temptation, guided, inflamed by that profound idea of a substituted life and a vicarious obedience which has been among the root forces of Christianity.

One evening, as she was dressing for the very simple meal that only Mrs Denton dignified by the name of 'dinner,' Laura reminded herself that Mr Williams must have arrived, and that she would probably find him in the hall on her descent.

It happened to be the moment for donning a new dress, which she had ordered from a local artist. She had no mind to exhibit it to the Jesuit. On the other hand the temptation to show it to Helbeck was irresistible. She put it on.

When she entered the hall, her feelings of dislike to Mr Williams, and her pride in her new dress, had both combined to give her colour and radiance. Helbeck saw her come in with a start of pleasure. Augustina fidgeted uncomfortably. She thought that Laura might have dressed in something more quiet and retiring to meet a guest who was a religious, almost a priest.

Helbeck introduced the newcomer. Laura's quick eyes travelled over the young man who bowed to her with a cold awkwardness. She turned aside and seated herself in a corner of the settle, whither Helbeck came to bend over her.

'What have you been doing to yourself?' he asked her in a low voice. At the moment of her entrance she had thought him pale and fatigued. He had been half over the country that day on Catholic business. But now his deep-set eyes shone again. He had thrown off the load.

'Experimenting with a Whinthorpe dressmaker,' she said; 'do you approve?'

Her smile, her brilliance in her pretty dress, intoxicated him. He murmured some lover's words under his breath. She flushed a little deeper, then exerted herself to keep him by her. Till supper was announced they had not a word or look for anyone but each other. The young 'scholastic' talked ceremoniously to Augustina.

'Who talks of Jesuit tyranny now?' said Helbeck laughing, as he and Laura led the way to the dining-room. 'If it is not too much for him, Williams has leave to finish some of his work in the chapel while he is there. But he looks very ill – don't you think so?'

She understood the implied appeal to her sympathy.

'He is extraordinarily handsome,' she said, with decision.

At table, however, she came to terms more exactly with her impression. The face of the young Jesuit was indeed, in some ways, singularly handsome. The round, dark eyes, the features delicate without weakness, the high brow narrowed by the thick and curly hair that overhung it, the small chin and curving mouth, kept still something of the look and the bloom of the child – a look that was only intensified by the strange force of expression that was added to the face whenever the lids so constantly dropped over the eyes were raised. For one saw in it a mingling at once of sharp observation and of distrust; it seemed to spring from some fiery source of personality, which at the very moment it revealed itself, yet warned the spectator back, and stood, half proudly, half sullenly, on the defensive. Such a look one may often see in the eyes of a poetic and morbid child.

But the whole aspect was neither delicate nor poetic. For the beauty of the head was curiously and unexpectedly contradicted by the clumsiness of the frame below it. 'Brother' Williams might have the head of the poet; he had the form and movements, the large feet and shambling gait of the peasant. And Laura, scanning him with some closeness, noticed with distaste a good many signs of personal slovenliness and ill-breeding. His hands were not as clean as they might have been; his clerical coat badly wanted a brushing.

His talk to Augustina could hardly have been more formal. In speaking to ladies he seldom raised his eyes; and as far as she herself was concerned Laura was certain, before half an hour was over, that he meant to address her and to be addressed by her as little as possible.

Towards Helbeck the visitor's manner was more natural and more attractive. It was a manner of affection, and great deference; but even here the occasional bursts of conversation into which the Squire drew his guest were constantly interrupted by fits of silence or absence on the part of the scholastic.

Perhaps the subject on which they talked most easily was that of Jesuit Missions – especially of certain West African stations. Helbeck had some old friends there; and Laura thought she detected that the young scholastic had himself missionary ambitions.

Augustina too joined in with eagerness; Laura fell silent.

But she watched Helbeck, she listened to Helbeck throughout. How full his mind and heart were of matters, persons, causes, that must for ever represent a sealed world to her! The eagerness, the knowledge with which he discussed them, roused in her that jealous, half-desolate sense that was becoming an habitual tone of mind.

And some things offended her taste. Helbeck showed most animation, and the young Jesuit most response whenever it was a question not so much of Catholic triumphs, as of Protestant rebuffs. The follies, mistakes and defeats of Anglican missions in particular – Helbeck's memory was stored with them. By his own confession he had made a Jesuit friend departing for the mission, promise to tell him any funny or discreditable tales that could be gathered as to their Anglican rivals in the same region. And while he repeated them for Williams's amusement, he laughed immoderately – he who laughed so seldom. The Jesuit too was convulsed – threw off all restraint for the first time.

The girl flushed brightly, and began to play with Bruno. Years ago she remembered hearing her father say approvingly of Helbeck's manner and bearing that they were those 'of a man of rank, though not of a man of fashion;' and it was hardly possible to say how much of Helbeck's first effect on her imagination had been produced by that proud unworldliness, that gently cold courtesy in which he was commonly wrapped. These silly pointless stories that he had been telling with such relish disturbed and repelled her. They revealed a new element in his character, something small and ugly, that was like the speck in a fine fruit, or, rather, like the disclosure of an angry sore beneath an outward health and strength.

She recalled the incident of the land, and that cold isolation in which Helbeck held himself towards his Protestant neighbours – the passionate animosity with which he would sometimes speak of their charities or their pietisms, the contempt he had for almost all their ideals, national or social. Again and again, in the early days at Bannisdale it had ruffled or provoked her.

Helbeck soon perceived that she was jarred. When she called to Bruno he checked his flow of anecdote, and said to her in a lower voice:

'You think us uncharitable?'

She looked up – but rather at the Jesuit than at Helbeck.

'No – only it is not amusing! If Augustina or I could speak for the other side – that would be more fun!'

'Laura!' cried Augustina, scandalised.

'Oh, I know you wouldn't if you could,' said the girl gaily. 'And I can't. So there it is. One can't stop you, I suppose!'

She threw back her bright head and turned to Helbeck. The action was pretty and coquettish; but there was a touch of fever in it, nevertheless, which did not escape the stranger sitting opposite to her. Brother Williams raised his down-dropped lids an instant. Those brilliant eyes of his took in the girl's beauty and the change in Helbeck's countenance.

'You shall stop what you like,' said Helbeck. A mute conversation seemed to pass between him and Miss Fountain; then the Squire turned to his sister, and asked her cheerfully as to the merits of a new pony that she and Laura had been trying that afternoon.

After dinner, Helbeck much troubled by the pinched features and pale cheeks of his guest, descended himself to the cellar in search of a particular Burgundy laid down by his father and reputed to possess a rare medicinal force.

Mr Williams was left standing before the hearth, and the famous carved mantelpiece put up by the martyr of 1596. As soon as Helbeck was gone he looked carefully – furtively – round the room. It was the look of the peasant appraising a world not his.

A noise made by the wind at one of the old windows disturbed him. He looked up, and was caught by a photograph that had been propped against one of the vases of the mantelpiece. It was a picture – recently taken – of Miss Fountain sitting on the settle in the Hall with the dogs beside her. And it rendered the half-mocking animation of her small face with a peculiar fidelity.

The young man was conscious of a strong movement of repulsion. Mr Helbeck's engagement had sent a thrill of pain through a large section of the Catholic world; and the Jesuit had already divined a hostile force in the small and brilliant creature whose eyes had scanned him so coldly as she sat beside the Squire. He fell into a reverie, and took one or two turns up and down the room.

'Shall I?' he said to himself in an excitement that was half vanity, half religion.

Half an hour later Laura was in the oriel window of the drawing-room, looking out through the open casement at the rising of a golden moon above the fell. Her mind was full of confusion.

'Is he never to be free to say what he thinks and feels in his own house?' she asked herself passionately. 'Or am I to sit by and see him sink to the level of these bigots?'

Augustina was upstairs, and Laura, absorbed in her own thoughts and the night-loveliness of the garden, did not hear Helbeck and Mr Williams enter the room, which was as usual but dimly lighted. Suddenly she caught the words:

'So you still keep her? That's good! One could not imagine this room without her.'

The voice was the voice of the Jesuit, but in a new tone – more eager, more sincere. What were they talking of? – the picture? And she, Laura, of course was hidden from them by the heavy curtain half-drawn across the oriel. She could not help waiting for Helbeck's reply.

'Ah! – you remember how she was threatened even when you first began to come here! I have clung to her, of course – there has always been a strong feeling about her in the family. Last week I thought again that she must go. But – well! it is too soon to speak – I still have some hopes – I have been straining every nerve. You know, however, that we must begin our new buildings at the orphanage in six weeks – and that I must have the money?'

He spoke with his usual simplicity. Laura dropped her head upon the window-sill, and the tears rushed into her eyes.

'I know – we all know – what you have done and sacrificed for the faith,' said the younger man with emotion.

'*You* will not venture to make a merit of it,' said Helbeck gravely.

'For we serve the same ends – only you perceive them more clearly and follow them more persistently than I.'

'I have stronger aids – and shall have to answer for more!' said Williams, in a low voice. 'And I owe it all to you – my friend and rescuer.'

'You use a great deal too strong language,' said Helbeck smiling.

Williams threw him an uncertain look. The colour mounted in the young man's sickly cheek. He approached the Squire.

'Mr Helbeck – I know from something a common friend told me – that you think – that you have said to others – that my conversion was not your doing. You are mistaken. I should like to tell you the truth. May I?'

Helbeck looked uncomfortable, but was not ready enough to stave off the impending confidence. Williams fixed him with eyes now fully lifted, and piercingly bright.

'You said little – that is quite true. But it was what you did, what I saw as I worked here beside you week after week that conquered me. Do you remember once rebuking me in anger because I had made some mistake in the chapel work? You were very angry – and I was cut to the heart. That very night you came to me, as I was still working, and asked my pardon – you! Mr Helbeck of Bannisdale, and I, a boy of sixteen, the son of the wheelwright who mended your farm carts. You made me kneel down beside you on the steps of the sanctuary – and we said the Confiteor together. Don't say you forget it!'

Helbeck hesitated, then spoke with evident unwillingness.

'You make a great deal of nothing, my dear Edward. I had treated you to one of the Helbeck rages, I suppose – and had the grace to be ashamed of myself.'

'It made me a Catholic,' said the other emphatically, 'so I naturally dwell upon it. Next day I stole a "Garden of the Soul" and a book of meditations from your study. Then, on the pretext of the work, I used to make you tell me or read me the stories of the saints – later, I often used to follow you in the morning when you went to Mass. I watched you day by day, till the sense of something supernatural possessed me. Then you noticed my coming to Mass – you asked Father Bowles to speak to me – you seemed to shrink – or I thought so – from speaking yourself. But it was not Father Bowles – it was not my first teachers at St Aloysius – it was you – who brought me to the faith!'

'Well, if so, I thank God. But I think your humility –'

'One moment,' said the Jesuit hurriedly. 'There is something on my mind to say to you – if I might be allowed to say it – if the gratitude, the strong and filial gratitude, which I feel towards you – for that, and much, much else' – his voice shook – 'might be my excuse –'

Helbeck was silent. Laura to her dismay heard the sound of steps. Mr Williams had walked to the open door of the drawing-room and closed it. What was she to do? Indecision – a wilful passion of curiosity – held her where she was.

It was some moments, however, before the conversation was resumed. At last the young man said in a tone of strong agitation –

'You may blame me – my superiors may blame me. I have no leave – no commission whatever. The impulse to speak came to me when I was waiting for you in the dining-room just now. I can only plead your own goodness to me – and – the fact that I have remembered you before the Blessed Sacrament for these eight years . . . It was an impression at meditation that I want to tell you of – an impression so strong that I have never since been able to escape from it – it haunts me perpetually. I was in our chapel at St Aloysius. The subject of meditation was St John vii. 36. "Every man went unto his own house" – followed immediately by the first words of the eighth chapter – "and Jesus went unto Mount Olivet." . . . I endeavoured strictly to obey the advice of St Ignatius. I placed myself at the feet of our Lord. I went through the Preludes. Then I began on the meditation. I saw the multitude returning to their homes and their amusements – while our Lord went alone to the Mount of Olives. It was evening. The path seemed to me steep and weary – and He was bent with fatigue. At first He was all alone – darkness hung over the hill and the olive gardens. Then, suddenly, I became aware of forms that followed Him, at a long distance – saints, virgins, martyrs, confessors. They swept along in silence. I could just see them as a dim majestic crowd. Presently, a form detached itself from the crowd – to my amazement, I saw *you* distinctly – there seemed to be a special light upon your face. And the rest appeared to fall back. Soon I saw only the Form toiling in front – and you following. Then at the brow of the hill the Lord turned – and you, who were halfway up the last steep, paused also. The Lord beckoned to you. His Divine face was full of sweetness and encouragement – and you made a spring towards Him. Then something happened – something horrible – but I could hardly see what. But a figure seemed to snatch at you from behind – you stumbled – then you fell headlong. A black cloud fell from the sky – and covered you. I heard a wailing cry – I saw the Lord's face darkened – and immediately afterwards the train of saints swept past me once more, with bent heads, beating their breasts. I cannot describe the extraordinary vividness of it! The succession of thoughts and images never paused – and when I woke, or seemed to wake, I found myself bathed in sweat and nearly fainting.'

There was a dead silence.

The scholastic began again, in still more rapid and troubled tones, to excuse himself. Mr Helbeck might well think it presumption on his part to have repeated such a thing. He could only plead a strange pressure on his conscience – a sense of obligation. The fact was probably nothing – meant nothing. But if calamity came – if it meant calamity – and he had not delivered his message – would there not have been a burden on his soul?

Suddenly there was a sound. The handle of the drawing-room turned.

'Why, you are dark in here!' said Augustina. 'What a wretched light that lamp gives!'

At the same moment the heavy curtain over the oriel window was drawn to one side, and a light figure entered the room.

The Jesuit made a step backwards. 'Laura!' cried Helbeck in bewilderment. 'Where have you come from?'

'I was in the window watching the moon rise. Didn't you know?'

She walked up to him, and without hesitation she did what she had never yet done before a spectator: she slipped her little hand into his. He looked down upon her, rather pale, his lips moving. Then withdrawing his hand, he quietly and proudly put his arm round her. She accepted the movement with equal pride, and without a word.

Augustina looked at them with discomfort – coughed, fumbled with her spectacles, and began to hunt for her knitting. The Jesuit, whiter and sicklier than before, murmured that he would go and rest after his journey, and with eyes steadily cast down he walked away.

'I don't wonder!' thought Augustina, in an inward heat; 'they really are too demonstrative!'

That night for the first time since her arrival at Bannisdale,

Laura, instead of saying good-night as soon as the clock reached a quarter to ten, quietly walked beside Augustina to the chapel.

She knelt at some distance from Helbeck. But when the prayers, which were read by Mr Williams, were over, and the tiny congregation was leaving the chapel, she felt herself drawn back. Helbeck did not speak, but in the darkness of the corridor he raised her hands and held them long against his lips. She quickly escaped from him, and without another word to anyone she was gone.

But an hour or two later, as she lay wakeful in her room above the study, she still heard the sound of continuous voices from below.

Helbeck and the scholastic! – plunged once more in that common stock of recollections and interests in which she had no part, linked and reconciled through all difference by that Catholic freemasonry of which she knew nothing. The impertinent zeal of the evening – the young man's ill manners and hypocrisies – would be soon forgiven. In some ways Mr Helbeck was more Jesuit than the Jesuits. He would not only excuse the audacity – was she quite sure that in his inmost heart he would not shrink before the warning?

'What chance have I?' she cried, in a sudden despair; and she wept long and miserably, oppressed by new terrors, new glimpses, as it were, of some hard or chilling reality that lay waiting for her in the dim corridors of life.

Next morning after breakfast, Helbeck and Mr Williams disappeared. A light scaffolding had been placed in the chapel. Work was to begin.

Laura put on her hat, took a basket, and went into the garden to gather fresh flowers for the house. Along the edges of the bowling green stood rows of sunflowers, a golden show against the deep bronze of the thick beech hedges that enclosed the ground. Laura was trying, without much success, to reach some of the top blossoms of a tall plant, when Helbeck came upon her.

'Be as independent as you please!' – he said, laughing – 'but you will never be able to gather sunflowers without me!'

In a moment her basket was filled. He looked down upon her.

'You should live here – in the bowling green. It frames you – your white hat – your grey dress. Laura!' – his voice leapt – 'do I do enough to make you happy?'

She flushed – turned her little face, and smiled at him – but rather sadly, rather pensively. Then she examined him in her turn.

He looked jaded and tired. From want of sleep? – or merely from the daily fatigue of that long walk, foodless, to Whinthorpe, for early Mass? That morning, as usual, by seven o'clock she had seen him crossing the Park. A cheerless rain was falling from a grey sky. But she had never yet known him stopped by weather.

There was a quick association of ideas – and she said abruptly: 'Why did Mr Williams say all that to you last night, do you suppose?'

Helbeck's countenance changed. He sauntered on beside her, his hands in his pockets, frowning. But he did not reply, and she became impatient.

'I have been reading a French story this morning,' she said quickly. 'There is a character in it – a priest. The author says of him that he had "une imagination fausse et troublée." ' – She paused, then added with great vivacity – 'I thought it applied to some one else – don't you?'

The fold in Helbeck's forehead deepened a little.

'Have you judged him already? I don't know – I can't take Williams, you see, quite as you take him! To me he is still the strange gifted boy I taught to draw – whom I had to protect from his brutal father. He has chosen the higher life, and will soon be a priest. He is therefore my superior. But at the same time I think I understand him and his character. I understand the kind of impulse – the impetuosity – that made him do and say what he did last night.'

'It was our engagement, of course, that he meant – by your fall – the black cloud that covered you?'

The impetuous directness was all Laura; so was the sensitive change in eye and lip. But Helbeck neither wavered, nor caressed her. He had a better instinct. He looked at her with a penetrating glance.

'I don't think he quite knew what he meant. And you? Now I will carry the war into the enemy's country! Were you quite kind – quite right in doing what you did last night? Foolish or no, he was speaking in a very intimate way – of things that he felt deeply. It must have given him great pain to be overheard.'

Her breath fluttered.

'It was quite an accident that I was there. But how could I help listening? I must know – I ought to know – what your Catholic friends think – what they say of me to you!'

She was conscious of a childish petulance. But it was as though she could not help herself.

'I wish you had not listened,' he said, with gentle steadiness. 'Won't you trust those things to me?'

'What power have I beside theirs?' she said, turning away her head. He saw the trembling of the soft throat, and bent over her.

'I only ask you, for both our sakes, not to test it too far!'

And taking her hand by force, he crushed it passionately in his own.

But she was only half appeased. Her mind, indeed, was in that miserable state when love finds its only pleasure in self-torment.

With a secret change of ground she asked him how he was going to spend the day. He answered, reluctantly, that there was a Diocesan Committee that would take the afternoon, and that the morning must be largely given to the preparation of papers.

'But you will come and look in upon me? – you will help me through?'

She raised her shoulders resentfully.

'And you have been to Whinthorpe already! – Why do you go to Mass every morning?' she asked, looking up. 'I know very few Catholics do. I wish you'd tell me.'

He looked embarrassed.

'It has been my custom for a long time,' he said at last.

'But *why?*'

'Inquisitive person!'

Her look of pain checked him. He observed her rather sadly and silently for a moment, then said:

'I will tell you, dear, of course, if you want to know. It is one of the obligations of the Third Order of St Francis, to which I belong.'

'What does that mean?'

He shortly explained. She cross-examined. He was forced to describe to her in detail all the main constitutions of the Third Order; its obligations as to fasting, attendance at Mass, and at the special meetings of the fraternity; its prescriptions of a rigid simplicity in life and dress; its prohibition of theatre-going.

She stood amazed. All her old notions of Catholics as gay people, who practised a free Sunday and allowed you to enjoy yourself, had been long overthrown by the Catholicism of Bannisdale. But this – this might be Daffady's Methodism!

'So that is why you would not take us to Whinthorpe the other day to see that London company?'

'It was an unsuitable play,' he said hastily. 'Theatres are not wholly forbidden us; but the exceptions must be few, and the plays such as a Catholic can see without harm to his conscience.'

'But I love acting!' she cried, almost with a sense of suffocation. 'Whenever I could, I got papa to take me to the play. I shall always want to go.'

'There will be nothing to prevent you.'

'So that anything is good enough for those who are not tertiaries!' she cried, confronting him.

Her cheeks burned. Had there been any touch of spiritual arrogance in his tone?

'I think I shall not answer that,' he said, after a pause.

They walked on – she blindly holding herself as far as possible from him; he, with the mingled ardour and maladroitness of his character, longing and not quite venturing to cut the whole coil, and silence all this mood in her, by some masterfulness of love.

Suddenly she paused – she stepped to him – she laid her fingers on his arms – bright tears shone in her eyes.

'You can't – you can't belong to that – when we are married?'

'To the Third Order? But, dear! – there is nothing in it that conflicts with married life! It was devised specially for persons living in the world. You would not have me give up what has been my help and salvation for ten years?'

He spoke with great emotion. She trembled and hid her face against him.

'Oh! I could not bear it!' she said. 'Can't you realise how it would divide us? I should feel outside – a pariah. As it is, I seem to have nothing to do with half your life – there is a shut door between me and it.'

A flash of natural, of wholly irresistible feeling passed through him. He stooped and kissed her hair.

'Open the door and come in!' he said in a whisper that seemed to rise from his inmost soul.

She shook her head. They were both silent. The deep shade of the 'wilderness' trees closed them in. There was a gentle melancholy in the autumn morning. The first leaves were dropping on the cobwebbed grass; and the clouds were low upon the fells.

Presently Laura raised herself. 'Promise me you will never press me' – she said passionately – 'don't send any one to me.'

He sighed.

'I promise.'

CHAPTER THREE

One afternoon towards the end of Mr Williams's visit, Laura was walking along a high field-path that overlooked the whole valley of the Flent. Helbeck had gone to meet the Bishop on some urgent business; but the name of his Catholic affairs was legion.

The weather, after long days of golden mist, of veiled and stealing lights on stream and fell, had turned to rain and tumult. This afternoon, indeed, the rain had made a sullen pause. It had drawn back for an hour or two from the drenched valleys, even from the high peaks that stood violet-black against a space of rainy light. Yet still the sky was full of anger. The clouds, dark, and jagged, rushed across the marsh-lands before the north-west wind. And the colour of everything – of the moss, the peaks, the nearer crags and fields – was superbly rich and violent. The soaked woods of the park from which she had just emerged were almost black, and from their heart Laura could hear the river's swollen voice pursuing her as she walked.

There was something in the afternoon that reminded her of her earliest impressions of Bannisdale and its fell country – of those rainy March winds that were blowing about her when she first alighted at the foot of the old tower.

The association made her tremble and catch her breath. It was not all joy – oh! far from it! The sweet common rapture of common love was not hers. Instinctively she felt something in her own lot akin to the wilder and more tragic aspects of this mountain land, to which she had turned from the beginning with a daughter's yearning.

Yet the tragedy, if tragedy there were, was all from within, not from without. Augustina – though Laura guessed her mind well enough – complained no more. The marriage was fixed for November; the dispensation from the bishop had been obtained. No lover could be more ardent, more tender than Helbeck.

Why then this weariness – this overwhelming melancholy that seized her in all her solitary moments? Her nature had lost its buoyancy, its old gift for happiness.

The truth was that her will was tired out. Her whole soul thirsted to submit; and yet could not submit. Was it the mere spell of Catholic order and discipline, working upon her own restless and ill-ordered nature? It had so worked, indeed, from the beginning. She could recall – with trembling – many a strange moment in Helbeck's presence, or in the chapel, when she had seemed to feel her whole self breaking up, dissolving in the grip of a power that was at once her foe and the bearer of infinite seduction. But always the will, the self, had won the victory, had delivered a final '*No!*' into which had rushed the whole energy of her being.

And now – if it were only possible to crush back that 'No' – to beat down this resistance which, like an alien garrison, defended, as it were, a town that hated it; if she could only turn and knock – knock humbly – at that closed door in her lover's life and heart. One touch! – one step!

Just as Helbeck could hardly trust himself to think of the joy of conquest, so she shrank bewildered before the fancied bliss of yielding.

To what awful or tender things would it admit her! That ebb and flow of mystical emotion she dimly saw in Helbeck, a life; – all that is most intimate and touching in the struggle of the soul – all that strains and pierces the heart – the world to which these belong rose before her, secret, mysterious, 'a city not made with hands,' now drawing, now repelling. Voices came from it to her that penetrated all the passion and the immaturity of her nature.

The mere imagination of what it would mean to surrender herself to Helbeck's teaching in these strange and moving things – what it would be to approach them through the sweetness, the chiding, the training of his love – could shake and unnerve her.

What stood in the way?

Simply a revolt and repulsion that seemed to be more than and outside herself – something independent and unconquerable, of which she was the mere instrument.

Had the differences between her and Helbeck been differences of opinion, they would have melted like morning dew. But they went far deeper. Helbeck, indeed, was in his full maturity. He had been trained by Jesuit teachers; he had lived and thought; his mind had a framework. Had he ever felt a difficulty, he would have been ready, no doubt, with the answer of the schools. But he was governed by heart and imagination no less than Laura. A serviceable intelligence had been used simply to strengthen the claims of feeling and faith. Such as it was, however, it knew itself. It was at command.

But Laura! – Laura was the pure product of an environment. She represented forces of intelligence, of analysis, of criticism, of which in themselves she knew little or nothing, except so far as they affected all her modes of feeling. She felt as she had been born to feel, as she had been trained to feel. But when in this new conflict – a conflict of instincts, of the deepest tendencies of two natures – she tried to lay hold upon the rational life, to help herself by it, and from it, it failed her everywhere. She had no tools, no weapons. The Catholic argument scandalised, exasperated her; but she could not meet it. And the personal prestige and fascination of her lover did but increase with her, as her feeling grew more troubled and excited, and her intellectual defence weaker.

Meanwhile to the force of temperament there was daily added the force of a number of childish prejudices and dislikes. She had come to Bannisdale prepared to hate all she saw there; and with the one supreme exception, hatred had grown at command. She was a creature of excess; of poignant and indelible impressions. The nuns, with their unintelligible virtues, and their very obvious bigotries and littlenesses; the slyness and absurdities of Father Bowles; the priestly claims of Father Leadham; the various superstitions and peculiarities of the many priests and religious who had passed through the house since she knew it – alas! she hated them all! – and did not know how she was to help hating them in the future. These Catholic figures were to her so many disagreeable automata, moved by springs she could not possibly conceive, and doing perpetually the most futile and foolish things. She knew, moreover, by a sure instinct, that she had been unwelcome to them from the first moment of her appearance, and that she was now a stumbling-block and a grievance to them all.

Was she by submission – to give these people, so to speak, a right to meddle and dabble in her heart? Was she to be wept over by Sister Angela – to confess her sins to Father Bowles – still worse, to Father Leadham? As she asked herself the question, she shrank in sudden passion from the whole world of ideas concerned – from all those stifling notions of sin, penance, absolution, direction, as they were conventionalised in Catholic practice, and chattered about by stupid and mindless people. In defiance of them, her whole nature stood like a charged weapon, ready to strike.

For she had been bred in that strong sense of personal dignity which in all ages has been the alternative to the abasements and humiliations of religion. And with that sense of dignity went reserve – the intimate conviction that no feeling which is talked about, which can be observed and handled and measured by other people, is worth a rush. It was what seemed to her the spiritual intrusiveness of Catholicism, its perpetual uncovering of the soul – its disrespect for the secrets of personality – its humiliation of the will – that made it most odious in the eyes of this daughter of a modern world, which finds in the development and ennobling of our human life its most characteristic faith.

There were many moments indeed in which the whole Catholic system appeared to Laura's strained imagination as one vast *chasse* – an assemblage of hunters and their toils – against which the poor human spirit that was their quarry must somehow protect itself, with every possible wile or violence.

So that neither submission, nor a mere light tolerance and forgetting, were possible. Other girls, it seemed, married Catholics and made nothing of it – agreed pleasantly to differ all their lives. Her heart cried out! There could be no likeness between these Catholic husbands and Alan Helbeck.

In the first days of their engagement she had often said to herself: 'I need have nothing to do with it!' or 'Some things are so lovely! – I will only think of them.' In those hours beside the sea it had been so easy to be tolerant and kind. Helbeck was hers from morning till night. And she, so much younger, so weak and small and ignorant, had seemed to hold his life, with all its unexplored depths and strengths, in her hand.

And now! –

She threw herself down on a rock that jutted from the wet grass, and gave herself up to the jealous pain that possessed her.

A few days more and Mr Williams would be gone. There was some relief in that thought. That strange scene in the drawing-room – deep as all concerned had buried it in oblivious silence – had naturally made his whole visit an offence to her. In her passionate way she felt herself degraded by his very presence in the house. His eyes constantly dropt, especially in her presence and Augustina's, his evident cold shrinking from the company of women – she thought of them with disgust and anger. For she said to herself that now she understood what they meant.

Of late she had been constantly busy with the books that stood to the right of Helbeck's table. She could not keep herself away from them, although the signs of tender and familiar use they bore were as thorns in her sore sense. Even his books were better friends to him than she! And especially had she been dipping into those 'Lives of the Saints' that Helbeck read habitually day by day; of which he talked to young Williams with a minuteness of knowledge that he scarcely possessed on any other subject – knowledge that appeared in all the details of the chapel painting. And on one occasion, as she turned over the small, worn volumes of his Alban Butler, she had come upon a certain passage in the life of St Charles Borromeo: [15]

'Out of a most scrupulous love of purity . . . neither would he speak to any woman, not even to his pious aunt, or sisters, or any nun, but in sight of at least two persons, and in as few words as possible.'

The girl flung it down. Surrounded as she often was by priests – affronted by those downcast eyes of the scholastic – the passage came upon her as an insult. Her cheeks burnt. Instinctively she showed herself that evening more difficult and exacting than ever with the man who loved her, and could yet feed his mind on the virtues of St Charles Borromeo.

Nevertheless, she was often puzzled by the manner and demeanour of the young Jesuit.

During his work at the chapel frescoes certain curious transformations seemed to have passed over him. Or was it merely the change of dress? While painting he wore a long holland blouse that covered the clerical coat, concealed the clumsy limbs and feet, and concentrated the eye of the spectator on the young beauty of the head. When a visitor entered he would look up for an instant flushed with work and ardour, then plunge again into what he was doing. Art had reclaimed him; Laura could almost have said the Jesuit had disappeared. And what an astonishing gift there was in those clumsy fingers! His daring delicacies of colour; his ways of using the brush, that seemed to leave no clue behind; the liquid shimmer and brilliancy of his work – Helbeck could only explain them by saying that he had once taken him as a lad of nineteen to see a loan exhibition at Manchester, and then to the gallery at Edinburgh –

'There were three artists that he fastened upon – Watteau! – I have seen him recoil from the subjects (he was already balancing whether he should become a religious) and then go back again and again to the pictures, feeding himself upon them. Then there were two or three Rembrandts, and two or three Tintorets. One Tintoret Entombment I remember – a small picture. I never could get him away from it. He told me once that it was like something painted in powdered gems and then dipped in air. I believe he got the expression from some book he was reading,' said Helbeck, with the good-humoured smile of one who does not himself indulge in the fineries of language ... 'When we came home I borrowed a couple of pictures for him from a friend in Lancashire, who has good things. One was a Rembrandt – "The Casting-out of Hagar" – I have his copy of it in my room now – the other was a Tintoret sketch. He worked at them for days and weeks, pondering and copying them, bit by bit, till he was almost ill with excitement and enthusiasm. But you see the result in what he does.'

And Helbeck smiled upon the artist with the affectionate sympathy of an elder brother. He and Laura were standing together one morning at the west end of the chapel, while Williams, in his blouse and mounted on a high stool, was painting a dozen yards away.

'And then he gave it up!' said Laura under her breath. 'Who can understand that?'

Helbeck hesitated a little. His face was crossed for a moment by the shadow of some thought that he did not communicate. Then he said, 'He came – as I told you – to think that it was right and best for him to do so. An artist, darling, has to think of the Four Last Things, like anybody else!'

'The Four Last Things!' said Laura, startled. 'What do you mean?'

'Death – Judgment – Heaven – and Hell.'

The words fell slowly from the half-whispering voice into the quiet darkness of the chapel. Laura looked up – Helbeck's eyes, fixed upon the Crucifix over the altar, seemed to receive thence a stern and secret message to which the whole man responded.

The girl moved restlessly away.

'Let us go and see what he is doing.'

As they approached, Williams turned to Helbeck – he seemed not to see Miss Fountain – and said a few troubled phrases that showed him wholly dissatisfied with his morning's work. Beads of perspiration stood on his brow; his lips were pinched and feverish; his eyes unhappy. He pointed Helbeck to the figure he was engaged upon – a strange dream of St Mary of Egypt, as a very old woman, clothed in the mantle of Zosimus – the lion who was to bury her, couchant at her feet. Helbeck looked into it; admired some points, criticised others. Williams got down from his stool, talked with a low-voiced volubility, an egotistical passion and disturbance that roused astonishment in Laura. Till then she had been acquainted only with the measured attitudes and levelled voice that the Jesuit learns from the 'Regulae Modestiae' of his order. But for the first time she felt a certain sympathy with him.

Afterwards for some days the young man, so recently an invalid, could hardly be persuaded to take sufficient exercise or food. He was absorbed in his saint, and in the next figure beyond her, that was already growing under his brush. St Ursula, white robed and fair haired, was springing like a flower from the wall; her delicate youth shone beside the age and austerity, the penitence and emaciation of St Mary of Egypt. Both looked towards the altar; but St Mary with a mystic sadness that both adored and quailed; St Ursula with the rapture, the confidence of a bride.

The artist could not be torn from his conception; and upon Laura too the spell of the work steadily grew. She would slip into the chapel at all hours, and watch; sometimes standing a little way from the painter, a black lace scarf thrown round her bright hair, sometimes sitting motionless with a book on her knee, which she did not read. When Helbeck was there conversation arose into which she was often drawn. And out of a real wish to please Helbeck, she would silence her own resentments, and force herself to be friendly. Insensibly Williams began to talk to her; and it would sometimes happen, when Helbeck went away for a time, that the cold reserve or *mauvaise honte* of the Jesuit would melt wholly before the eagerness of the artist – when, with intervals of a brusque silence, he talked with the rapidity and force of a turbid stream on the imaginations and the memories embodied in his work. And on one occasion, when the painter was busy with the head of St Ursula, Laura, who was talking to Helbeck a few yards away, turned suddenly and found those dark strange eyes, that as a rule evaded her, fixed steadily and intently upon her. Next day she fancied with a start of dislike that in the lines of St Ursula's brow, and in the arrangement of the hair there was a certain resemblance to herself. But Helbeck did not notice it, and nothing was said.

At meals, too, conversation turned now more on art than on missions. Pictures seen by the two friends years before; Helbeck's fading recollections of Florence and Rome; modern Catholic art as it was being developed in the Jesuit churches of the Continent: of these things Williams would talk, and talk eagerly. Sometimes Augustina would timidly introduce some subject of greater practical interest to the commonplace English Catholic. Mr Williams would let it drop; and then Mrs Fountain would sit silent and ill at ease, her head and hands twitching in a helpless bewildered way.

But in a moment came a change. After a certain Thursday when he was at work all day, the young man painted no more. Beyond St Ursula, St Eulalia of Saragossa, Virgin and Martyr, had been sketched in with a strange force of line and some suggestions both of colour and symbolism that held Laura fascinated. But the sketch remained ghostlike on the wall. The high stool was removed; the blouse put away.

Thenceforward Mr Williams — to Laura's secret anger — spent hours in Helbeck's study reading. His avoidance of her society and Mrs Fountain's was more marked than ever. His face, which in the first days at Bannisdale had begun to recover a certain boyish bloom, became again white and drawn. The eyes were scarcely ever seen; if, by some rare chance, the heavy lids did lift, the fire and brilliance of the gaze below were startling to the bystander. But for the most part he seemed to be wrapped in a dumb sickliness and pain; his person was even less cleanly, his clothes less cared for than before. At table he hardly talked at all; never of painting, or of any topic connected with it.

Once or twice Laura caught Helbeck's look fixed upon his guest in what seemed to her anxiety or perplexity. But when she carelessly asked him what might be wrong with Mr Williams, the Squire gave a decided answer.

'He is ill — and we ought not to have allowed him to do this work. There must be complete rest till he goes.'

'Has he seen his father?' asked Laura.

'No. That is still hanging over him.'

'Does his father wish to see him?'

'No! But it is his duty to go.'

'Why? That he may enjoy a little more martyrdom?'

Helbeck laughed and captured her hand.

'What penalty do I exact for that?'

'It doesn't deserve any,' she said quickly. 'I don't think it is for health he has given up his painting. I believe he is unhappy.'

'It may have revived old struggles,' said Helbeck, with a sigh that seemed to escape him against his will.

'Why doesn't he give it all up,' she said with energy, 'and be an artist? That's where his heart, his strength lies.'

Helbeck's manner changed and stiffened.

'You are entirely mistaken, dearest. His heart and his strength are in his vocation – making himself a good Jesuit.'

She shook her head obstinately, with that rising breath of excitement which the slightest touch of difference was now apt to call up.

'I don't think so! – and I have watched him. Suppose he *did* give it all up? He could, of course, at any time.'

Helbeck tried to smile and change the subject. But Laura persisted. Till at last the Squire said with pain:

'Darling – I don't think you know how these things sound in Catholic ears.'

'But I want to know. You see, I don't understand anything about vows. I can't imagine why that man can't walk into a studio and leave his clerical coat behind him to-morrow. To me nothing seems easier. He is a human being, and free.'

Helbeck was silent, and began to put some letters in order that were lying on his table. Laura's caprice only grew stronger.

'If he were to leave the Jesuits,' she said, 'would you break with him?'

As Mr Williams was safely in the park with Augustina, Laura had resumed her accustomed place in the low seat beside Helbeck's writing-table. Augustina, for decorum's sake, had her armchair on the further side of the fireplace, where she often dozed, knitted, and read the newspapers. But she left the betrothed a good deal alone, less from a natural feminine sympathy than because she fed herself day by day on the hope that, in spite of all, Alan would yet set himself in earnest to the task that was clearly his – the task of Laura's conversion.

Helbeck showed no more readiness to answer her second inquiry than her first. He seemed to be absorbed in reading over a business letter.

Laura's pride was roused. Her cheeks flushed, and she repeated her question, her mind filled all the time with that mingled dread and wilfulness that must have possessed poor Psyche when she raised the lamp.

'Well, no,' said Helbeck, dryly, without lifting his eyes from his letter – 'I don't suppose that he would remain my friend, under such strange circumstances – or that he would wish it.'

'So you would cast him off?'

'Why will you start such uncomfortable topics, dear?' he said, half laughing. 'What has poor Williams done that you should imagine such things?'

'I want to know what *you* would do if Mr Williams – if any priest you know were to break his vows and leave the Church, what would you do?'

'Follow the judgment of the Church,' said Helbeck quietly.

'And give up your friend?'

'Friendship, darling, is a complex thing – it depends upon so much. But I am so tired of my letters! Your hat is in the hall. Won't you come out?'

He rose, and bent over her tenderly, his hand on the table. In a flash she felt all the strange dignity, the ascetic strength of his personality; it was suggested this time by the mere details of dress – by the contrast between the worn and shabby coat, and the stern force of the lips, the refined individuality of the hand. She was filled anew with the sudden sense that she knew but half of him – a sudden terror of the future.

She lay back in her chair, meeting his eyes and trying to smile. But in truth she was quivering with impatience.

'I won't move till I have my answer! Please tell me – would – would you regard him as a lost soul?'

'Dearest! I am neither Williams's judge nor any one else's! Of course I must hold that a man who breaks the most solemn vows endangers his soul. What else do you expect of me?'

'What do you mean by "soul"? Have I a soul? – and what do you suppose is going to happen to it?'

The words were flung out with a concentrated passion – almost an anguish – that for the moment struck him dumb. They both grew pale; he looked at her steadily, and spoke her name, in a low appealing voice. But she took no notice; she rose, and, turning away from him, she leant against the mantelpiece, speaking with a choking eagerness that forced its way.

'You were in the chapel last night – very late. I know, for I heard the door open and shut. You must be unhappy, or you wouldn't spend so much time praying. Are you unhappy about me? I know you don't want to force me; but if, in time, I don't agree with you – if it goes on all our lives – how can you help thinking that I shall be lost – lost eternally – separated from you? You would think it of Mr Williams if he left the Church. I know you told me once about ignorance – invincible ignorance. But here there will be no ignorance. I shall have seen everything – heard everything – known everything. If living here doesn't teach one, what could? And' – she paused, then resumed with even greater emphasis – 'and as far as I can see I shall reject it all – wilfully, knowingly, deliberately. What will you say? What do you say now – to yourself – when – when you pray for me? What do you really think – what do you fear – what *must* you fear? I ought to know.'

Helbeck looked at her without answering for a long moment. Her agitation, his painful silence, bore pitiful testimony to the strange, insurmountable reality of those facts of the spirit that stood like rocks in the stream of their love.

At last he held out his hands to her with that half reproachful gesture he had often used towards her. 'I fear nothing! – I hope everything. You never forbade me that. Will you leave my love no mysteries, Laura – no reserve? Nothing for you to discover and explore as time goes on?'

She trembled under the mingled remonstrance and passion of his tone. But she persisted. 'It's because – I feel – other things come before love. Tell me – I have a right to know. I shall never come first – quite first – shall I?'

She forced the saddest, proudest of smiles, as he took her reluctant hands.

And involuntarily her eyes travelled over the room, over the crucifix above the faldstool, the little altar to St Joseph, the worn books upon his table. They were to her like the weapons and symbols of an enemy.

He made her no direct answer. His face was for a moment grave and set. Then he roused himself, kissed the hands he held, and resolutely began to talk of something else.

When a few minutes later he left her alone, she stood there quivering under the touch of power by which he had silenced her – under the angry sense that she was less and less able as the days went by to draw or drive him into argument. The more thorny her mood became, the more sadly did he seem to hide the treasures of the soul from her.

These memories, and many like them, were passing and re-passing through Laura's mind as she sat listless and sad on the hill-side.

When at last she shook them off, the light was failing over the western wall of mountains. She had an errand to do for Augustina in the village that lay half way to the daffodil wood, and she sprang up, wondering whether there was still time for it before dark.

As she hurried on towards a stile that lay across the path, she saw a woman approaching on the further side.

'Polly!'

The figure addressed stood still a moment in astonishment, then ran to meet the speaker.

'Laura! – well, I'm sure!'

The two girls kissed each other. Laura looked gaily, wistfully at her cousin.

'Polly – are you all very cross with me still?'

Polly hesitated and fenced. Laura sighed. But she looked at the stout red-faced woman with a peculiar flutter of pleasure. The air of the wild upland – all the primitive, homely facts of the farm, seemed to come about her again. She had left Bannisdale, choked with feeling, tired with thought. Polly's broad speech and bouncing ways were welcome as a breeze in summer.

They sat down on the stile side by side. Laura gave up her errand; and they talked fast. Polly was all curiosity. When was Laura to be married, and what was she to wear?

'The plainest thing I can find,' said Laura, indifferently. 'Unless Augustina teases me into something I don't want.' Polly inquired if it would be in church. 'In a Catholic church,' said Laura, with a shrug. 'No flowers – no music. They just let you be married – that's all.'

Polly's eyes jumped with amazement. 'Why, I thowt they had everything so grand!'

'Not if you will go and marry a heretic like me,' said Laura. 'Then they make you know your place.'

'But – but, Laura! yo're to be a Romanist too – for sure?' cried Polly in bewilderment.

'Do you think so?' said Laura. Her eyes sparkled. She was sitting on the edge of the stile, one small foot dangling. Polly's rustic sense was once more vaguely struck by the strange mingling in the little figure of an extreme, an exquisite delicacy with some tough, incalculable element. Miss Fountain's soft lightness seemed to offer no more resistance than a daffodil on its stalk. But approach her! – whether it was poor Hubert – or even –?

Polly looked and spoke her perplexity. She let Laura know that Miss Fountain's conversion was assumed at Browhead Farm. Through her blundering though not unkindly talk, Laura gradually perceived indeed a score of disagreeable things. Mrs Mason and her fanatical friend, Mr Bayley, were both persuaded – so it seemed – that Miss Fountain had set her cap at the Squire from the beginning, ready at a moment's notice to swallow the Scarlet Lady when required. And Catholic and Protestant alike were kind enough to say that she had made use of her cousin to draw on Mr Helbeck. The neighbourhood, in fact, held her to be a calculating little minx, ripe for plots and Papistry, or anything else that might suit a daring game.

The girl gradually fell silent. Her head drooped. Her eyes looked at Polly askance and wistfully. She did not defend herself; but she showed the wound.

'Well, I'm sorry you don't understand,' she said at last, while her voice trembled. 'Perhaps you will some day. I don't know. Anyway, will you please tell Cousin Elizabeth that I'm not going to be a Catholic? Perhaps that will comfort her a little.'

'But howiver are you goin to live wi Mr Helbeck then?' asked Polly. Her loud surprise conveyed the image of Helbeck as it lay graven in the minds of the Browhead circle – a sort of triple-crowned, black-browed tyrant with all the wiles and torments of Rome in his pocket. A wife resist – defy? The Church knows how to deal with naughtiness of that kind.

Laura laughed.

'We can but try. But now then' – she bent forward and put her hands impulsively on Polly's shoulders – 'tell me about everybody, and everything. How's Daffady – how's the cow that was ill – how're the calves – how's Hubert?'

She laughed again, but there was moisture in her look. For the thousandth time, her heart told her that in this untoward marriage she was wrenching herself anew from her father and all his world.

Polly rather tossed her head at the mention of Hubert. She replied with some tartness that he was doing very well – nobody indeed could be doing better. Did Laura's eyebrows go up the very slightest trifle? If so the sister beat down the surprise. Hubert no doubt had been upset, and a bit wild, after – well, Laura might guess what! But that was all past now, long ago. There was a friend – a musical friend – a rescuer – who had appeared, in the shape of a young organist who had come to lead the Froswick Philharmonic Society. Hubert was living with him now, and the young man, of whom all Froswick thought a wonderful deal, was looking after him, and making him write his songs. Some of them were to be sung at a festival –

Laura clapped her hands.

'I told him!' she said gaily. 'If he'll only work he'll do. And he is keeping straight?'

Her look was keen and sisterly. She wished to show that she had forgotten and forgiven. But Polly resented it.

'Why shouldn't he be keeping straight?' she asked. No doubt Laura had thought him just a ne'er do weel. But he was nothing of the sort – he was a bit wild and unruly, as young men are – 'same as t' colts afoor yo break em.' But Laura would have done much better for herself if she had stayed quietly with him that night at Braeside, and let him take her over the sands, as he wished to, instead of running away from him in that foolish way.

Polly spoke with significance – nay, with heat. Laura was first startled, then abashed.

'Do you think I made a ridiculous fuss?' she said humbly. 'Perhaps I did. But if – if –' she spoke slowly, drawing patterns on the wood of the stile with her finger, 'if I hadn't seen him drunk once – I suppose I shouldn't have been afraid.'

'Well, you'd no call to be afraid!' cried Polly. 'Hubert vowed to me, as he hadna had a drop of onything. After all, he's a relation – an if you'd walked wi him, you'd not ha had telegrams sent aboot you to make aw th' coontry taak!'

'Telegrams!' Laura stared. 'Oh, I know – Mr Helbeck telegraphed to the station-master – but it must have come after I'd left the station.'

'Aye – an t' station-master sent word back to Mr Helbeck! Perhaps you doan't knaw onything aboot that!' exclaimed Polly, triumphantly.

Laura turned rather pale.

'A telegram to Mr Helbeck?'

Polly, surprised at so much ignorance, could not forego the sensation that it offered her. She bit her lip, but the lip would speak. So the story of the midnight telegram – as it had been told by that godly man Mr Cawston of Braeside to that other godly man Mr Bayley, perpetual curate of Browhead, and as by now it had gone all about the countryside – came piecemeal out.

'Oh! an at that Papist shop i' th' High Street – you remember that sickly-lukin fellow at the dance – they do say at they do taak shameful!' exclaimed Polly, indignantly.

'What do they say?' said Laura in a low voice.

Polly hesitated. Then out of sheer nervousness she blundered into the harshest possible answer.

'Well, they said that Mr Helbeck could do no different, that he did it to save his sister from knowing –'

'Knowing what?' said Laura.

Polly declared that she wasn't just certain. 'A set o' slanderin backbitin tabbies as soom o' them Catholics is!' But she believed they said that Mr Helbeck had asked Miss Fountain to marry him out of kindness, to shut people's mouths, and keep it from his sister –

'Keep what?' said Laura. Her eyes shone in her quivering proud face.

'Why, I suppose – at you'd been carryin on wi Hubert, and walkin aboot wi him aw neet,' said Polly reluctantly.

And she again insisted how much wiser it would have been if Laura had just gone quietly over the sands to Marsland. There, no doubt, she might have got a car straight away, and there might have been no talk whatever.

'Mightn't there?' said Laura. Her little chin was propped in her hand. Her gaze swept the distant water of the estuary mouth, as it lay alternately dark and shining under the storm lights of the clouds.

'An I'll juist warn yo o' yan thing, Laura,' said Polly, with fresh energy. 'There's soom one at Bannisdale itsel, as spreads aw maks o' tales. There's a body theer, as is noa friend o' yours.'

'Oh! Mrs Denton,' said Laura, languidly. 'Of course.'

Then she fell silent. Not a word passed the small tightened lips. The eyes were fixed on distance or vacancy.

Polly began to be frightened. She had not meant any real harm; though perhaps there had been just a touch of malice in her revelations. Laura was going to marry a Papist; that was bad. But also she was going to marry into a sphere far out of the Masons' ken: and she had made it very plain that Hubert and the likes of Hubert were not good enough for her. Polly was scandalised on religion's account; but also a little jealous and sore, in a natural feminine way on her own; the more so as Mr Seaton had long since ceased to pay Sunday visits to the farm, and Polly had a sharp suspicion as to the when and why of that gentleman's disillusionment. There had been a certain temptation to let the future mistress of Bannisdale know that the neighbourhood was not all whispering humbleness towards her.

But at bottom Polly was honest and kind. So when she saw Laura sit so palely still, she repented her. She implored that Laura would not 'worrit' herself about such fooleries. And then she added –

'But I wonder at Mr Helbeck didna juist tell yo himsel aboot that telegram!'

'Do you?' said Laura. Her eyes flashed. She got down from the stile. 'Good-bye, Polly! I must be going home.'

Suddenly Polly gripped her by the arm.

'Luke there!' she said in excitement. 'Luke! – theer he goes! That's Teddy – Teddy Williams! I knew as I had summat to tell you – and when you spoak o' Hubert – it went oot o' my head.'

Laura looked at her cousin first, in astonishment, and then at the dark figure walking on the road below – the straight white road that ran across the marsh, past the lonely forge of old Ben Williams, the wheelwright, to the foot of the tall 'Scar,' opposite, where it turned seaward, and so vanished in the dimness of the coast. It was the Jesuit certainly. The two girls saw him plainly in the strong storm light. He was walking slowly with bent head, and seemed to be reading. His solitary form, black against the white of the road, made the only moving thing in the wide, rain-drenched landscape.

Laura instantly guessed that he had been paying his duty visit to his home. And Polly, it appeared, had been a witness of it.

For the cottage adjoining the wheelwright's workshop and forge, where Edward Williams had been brought up, was now inhabited by his father and sister. The sister, Jenny, was an old friend of Polly Mason's, who had indeed many young memories of the scholastic himself. They had been all children or school-mates together.

And this afternoon, while she was in the parlour with Jenny, all of a sudden – voices and clamour in the forge outside! The son, the outcast son, had quietly presented himself to his father.

'O, an sic a to-do! His fadther wadna let him ben. "Naa," he says, "if thoo's got owt to say, thoo may say it i' th' shop. Jenny doan't want tha!" An Jenny luked oot – an I just saw Teddy turn an spëak to her – beggin her like, a bit masterfu too, aw t' time – an she flounced back again – "Keep yor distance, will yer!" – an slammed to the door – an fell agen it, cryin. And sic a shoutin and hollerin frae the owd man! He made a gradely noise, he did – bit never a word fra Teddy – not as yo cud hear, I'll uphowd yo! An at lasst – when Jenny an I opened t' door again – juist a cranny like – theer he was, takin hissel off – his fadther screamin afther him – an he wi his Papish cöat, an his head hangin as thoo there wor a load o' peät on it – an his hands crossed – soa pious! Aye, theer he goes! – and he may goa!' cried Polly, her face flaming as it followed the Jesuit out of sight. 'When a mon's treated his aan mother that gate, it's weary wark undoin it. Aye, soa 'tis, Mr Teddy – soa 'tis!' And she raised her voice vindictively.

Laura's lip curled.

'Do you think he cares – one rap? It was his duty to go and see his father – so he went. And now he's all the more certain he's on the road to heaven – because his father abused him, and his sister turned him out. He's going to be a priest directly – and a missionary after that – and a holy martyr, too, if he gets his deserts. There's always fever, or natives, handy. What do earth-worms like mothers and sisters matter to him?'

Polly stared. Even she, as she looked, as she heard, felt that a gulf opened – that a sick soul spoke.

'Oh! an I'd clean forgot,' she faltered – 'as he must be stayin at Bannisdale – as yo wad be seein him.'

'I see so many of them,' said Laura wearily. She took up her bag that had been leaning against the stile. 'Now, good-bye!'

Suddenly Polly's eyes brimmed with tears. She flung an arm round the slim childish creature.

'Laura, whatever did you do it for? I doan't believe as yo're a bit happy i' yor mind! Coom away! – we'se luke after you – we're your aan kith an kin!'

Laura paused in Polly's arm. Then she turned her wild face – the eyes half closed, the pale lips passionately smiling.

'I'll come, Polly, when I'm dead – or my heart's dead – not before!'

And, wrenching herself away, she ran down the path. Polly, with her clutch of Brahma eggs in her hand, that she was taking to the Bannisdale Bridge Farm, leant against the stile and cried.

CHAPTER FOUR

'Alan! is it to-night you expect Father Leadham?'

'Yes,' said Helbeck.

'Have you told Laura?'

'I will remind her that we expect him. It is annoying that I must leave you to entertain him to-morrow.'

'Oh! we shall do very well,' said Augustina rather eagerly. 'Alan, have you noticed Laura, yesterday and to-day? She doesn't look strong.'

'I know,' said the Squire shortly. His eyes were fixed all the time on the little figure of Laura, as she sat listlessly in a sunny corner of the bowling green, with a book on her knee.

Augustina, who had been leaning on his arm, went back to the house. Helbeck advanced and threw himself down beside Laura.

'Little one – if you keep such pale cheeks – what am I to do?'

She looked down upon him with a languid smile.

'I am all right.'

'That remark only fills up your misdoings! If I go down and get the pony-carriage, will you drive with me through the park and tell me everything – *everything* –that has been troubling you the last few days?'

His voice was very low, his eyes all tenderness. He had been reproaching himself that he had so often of late avoided difficult discussions and thorny questions with her. Was she hurt? and did he deserve it?'

'I will go driving with you,' she said slowly.

'Very well' – he sprang up – 'I will be back in twenty minutes – with the pony.'

He left her, and she dreamed afresh over her book.

She was thinking of a luncheon at Whinthorpe, to which she had been taken, sorely against her will, to meet the Bishop. And the Bishop had treated her with a singular and slighting coldness. There was no blinking the fact in the least. Other people had noticed it. Helbeck had been pale with wrath and distress. As far as she could remember, she had laughed and talked a good deal.

Well, what wonder? – if they thought her just a fast ill-conducted girl, who had worked upon Mr Helbeck's pity and softness of heart?

Suddenly she put out her hand restlessly to pluck at the hedge beside her. She had been stung by the memory of herself – under the Squire's window, in the dawn. She saw herself – helpless, and asleep, the tired truant come back to the feet of her master. When he found her so, what could he do but pity her? – be moved, perhaps beyond bounds, by the goodness of a generous nature?

Next, something stronger than this doubt touched the lips with a flying smile – shy and lovely. But she was far from happy. Since her talk with Polly especially, her pride was stabbed and tormented in all directions. And her nature was of the proudest.

Where could she feel secure? In Helbeck's heart? But in the inmost shrine of that heart she felt the brooding of a majestic and exacting power that knew her not. Her jealousy – her fear – grew day by day.

And as to the rest, her imagination was full of the most feverish and fantastic shapes. Since her talk with Polly the world had seemed to her a mere host of buzzing enemies. All the persons concerned passed through her fancy with the mask and strut of caricature. The little mole on Sister Angela's nose – the slightly drooping eyelid that marred the Reverend Mother's left cheek – the nasal twang of the orphans' singing – Father Bowles pouncing on a fly – Father Leadham's stately ways – she made a mock or an offence out of them all, bitterly chattering and drawing pictures with herself, like a child with a grievance.

And then on the top of these feelings and exaggerations of the child, would return the bewildering, the ever-increasing trouble of the woman.

She sprang up.

'If I could – If I *could!* Then it would be we two together – against the rest. Else – how shall I be his wife at all?'

She ran into the study. There on the shelf beside Helbeck's table stood a little Manual of Catholic Instruction, that she knew well. She turned over the pages, till she came to the sections dealing with the reception of converts.

How often she had pored over them! Now she pored over them again, twisting her lips, knitting her white brows.

'No adult baptised Protestant ['Am I a Protestant? – I am baptised!'] is considered to be a convert to the Catholic Church until

he is received into the Church according to the prescribed rite
['There! – it's the broken glass on the wall. – But if one could just
slip in – without fuss or noise?'] . . . You must apply to a Catholic
priest, who will judge of your dispositions, and of your knowledge
of the Catholic faith. He will give you further instruction, and
explain your duties, and how you have to act. When he is satisfied
['Father Leadham! – satisfied with me!'], you go to the altar or to
the sacristy, or other place convenient for your reception. The
priest who is with you says certain prayers appointed by the Church;
you in the meantime kneel down and pray silently ['I prayed when
papa died.' – She looked up, her face trembling – 'Else? – Yes once!
– that night when I went in to prayers.'] You will then read or
repeat aloud after the priest the Profession of Faith, either the
Creed of Pope Pius IV.' – ['That's – let me see! – that's the Creed
of the Council of Trent; there's a note about it in one of papa's
books.' She recalled it, frowning: 'I often think that we of the
Liberal Tradition have cause to be thankful that the Tridentine
Catholics dug the gulf between them and the modern world so
deep. Otherwise, now that their claws are all pared, and only the
honey and fairy-tales remain, there would be no chance at all for
the poor rational life.']

She drew a long breath, taking a momentary pleasure in the strong
words, as they passed through her memory, and then bruised by them.

'The priest will now release you from the ban and censures of the
Church, and will so receive you into the True Fold. If you do not
yourself say the "Confiteor," you will do well to repeat in a low
voice, with sorrow of heart, those words of the penitent in the
Gospel: "O God, be merciful to me a sinner!" He will then admin-
ister to you baptism under condition (*sub conditione*) . . . Being now
baptised and received into the Church, you will go and kneel in the
Confessional or other appointed place in the church to make your
confession, and to receive from the priest the sacramental absolution. While receiving absolution you must renew your sorrow and
hatred of sin, and your resolution to amend, making a sincere Act
of Contrition.'

Then, as the book was dropping from her hand, a few paragraphs
further on her eyes caught the words:

'If we are not able to remember the exact number of our sins, it is
enough to state the probable number to the best of our recollection
and judgment, saying: "I have committed that sin about so many

times a day, a week, or a month." Indeed, we are bound to reveal our conscience to the priest as we know it ourselves, there and then stating the things certain as certain, those doubtful as doubtful, and the probable number as probable.'

She threw away the book. She crouched in her chair beside Helbeck's table, her small face buried despairingly in her hands. 'I can't – I can't! I would if I could – I can't!'

Through the shiver of an invincible repulsion that held her spoke a hundred things – things inherited, things died for, things wrought out by the moral experience of generations. But she could not analyse them. All she knew were the two words – 'I can't.'

The little pony took them merrily through the gay October woods. Autumn was at its cheerfullest. The crisp leaves underfoot, the tonic earth-smells in the air, the wet ivy shining in the sun, the growing lightness and strength of the trees as the gold or red leaf thinned and the free branching of the great oaks or ashes came into sight – all these belonged to the autumn which sings and vibrates, and can in a flash disperse and drive away the weeping and melancholy autumn.

Laura's bloom revived. Her hair, blown about her, glowed and shone even amid the gold of the woods. Her soft lips, her eyes called back their fire. Helbeck looked at her in a delight mingled with pain, counting the weeks silently till she became his very own. Only five now before Advent; and in the fifth the Church would give her to him, grudgingly indeed, with scant ceremony and festivity, like a mother half grieved, still with her blessing, which must content him. And beyond? The strong man – stern with himself and his own passion, all the more that the adored one was under the protection of his roof, and yielded thereby to his sight and wooing more freely than a girl in her betrothal is commonly yielded to her lover – dared hardly in her presence evoke the thrill of that thought. Instinctively he knew, through the restraints that parted them, that Laura was pure woman, a creature ripe for the subtleties and poetries of passion. Would not all difficulties find their solvent – melt in a golden air – when once they had passed into the freedom and confidence of marriage?

Meanwhile the difficulties were all plain to him – more plain, indeed, than ever. He could not flatter himself that she looked any more kindly on his faith or his friends. And his friends – or some of them – were, to say the truth, pressing him hard. Father Leadham even, his director, upon whom during the earlier stages of their correspondence on the matter Helbeck seemed to have impressed his own waiting view with success, had lately become more exacting and more peremptory. The Squire was uncomfortable at the thought of his impending visit. It was hardly wise – had better have been deferred. Laura's quick shrinking look when it was announced had not been lost upon her lover. Father Leadham should be convinced – must be convinced – that all would be imperilled – nay, lost – by haste. Yet unconsciously Helbeck himself was wavering – was changing ground.

He had come out, indeed, determined somehow to break down the barrier he felt rising between them. But it was not easy. They talked for long of the most obvious and mundane things. There were salmon in the Greet this month, and Helbeck had been waging noble war with them in the intervals of much business, with Laura often beside him, to join in the madness of the 'rushes' down stream, to watch the fine strength of her lover's wrist, to shrink from the gaffing, and to count the spoil. The shooting days at Bannisdale were almost done, since the land had dwindled to a couple of thousand acres, much of it on the moss. But there were still two or three poor coverts along the upper edge of the park, where the old Irish keeper and woodman, Tim Murphy, cherished and counted the few score pheasants that provided a little modest November sport. And Helbeck, tying the pony to a tree, went up now with Laura to walk round the woods, showing in all his comments and calculations a great deal of shrewd woodcraft and beastcraft, enough to prove at any rate that the Esau of his race – *feras consumere nati*, to borrow the emendation of Mr Fielding [16] – had not yet been wholly cast out by the Jacob [17] of a mystical piety.

Laura tripped and climbed, applauded by his eye, helped by his hand. But though her colour came back, her spirits were still to seek. She was often silent, and he hardly ever spoke to her without feeling a start run through the hand he held.

His grey eye tried to read her, but in vain. At last he wooed her from the fellside where they were scrambling. 'Come down to the river and rest.'

Hand in hand they descended the steep slope to that rock-seat where he had found her on the morning of Easter Sunday. The great thorn which overhung it was then in bud; now the berries which covered the tree were already reddening to winter. Before her spread the silver river, running to lose itself in the rocky bosom of that towering scar which closed the distance, whereon, too, all the wealth of the woods on either hand converged – the woods that hid the outer country, and all that was not Bannisdale and Helbeck's.

To-day, however, Laura felt no young passion of pleasure in the beauty at her feet. She was ill at ease and her look fled his as he glanced up to her from the turf where he had thrown himself.

'Do you like me to read your books?' she said abruptly, her question swooping hawk-like upon his and driving it off the field.

He paused – to consider, and to smile.

'I don't know. I believe you read them perversely!'

'I know what you read this morning. Do you – do you think St Francis Borgia [18] was a very admirable person?'

'Well, I got a good deal of edification out of him,' said Helbeck quietly.

'Did you? Would you be like him if you could? Do you remember when his wife was very ill, and he was praying for her, he heard a voice – do you remember?'

'Go on,' said Helbeck, nodding.

'And the voice said, "If thou wouldst have the life of the Duchess prolonged, it shall be granted; but it is not expedient for thee" – "*thee*," mind – not her! When he heard this, he was penetrated by a most tender love of God, and burst into tears. Then he asked God to do as He pleased with the lives of his wife and his children and himself. He gave up – I suppose he gave up – praying for her. She became much worse and died, leaving him a widower at the age of thirty-six. Afterwards – don't please interrupt! – in the space of three years, he disposed somehow of all his eight children – some of them I reckoned must be quite babies – took the vows, became a Jesuit, and went to Rome. Do you approve of all that?'

Helbeck reddened. 'It was a time of hard fighting for the Church,' he said gravely, after a pause, 'and the Jesuits were the advance guard. In such days a man may be called by God to special acts and special sacrifices.'

'So you do approve? Papa was a member of an Ethical Society at Cambridge. They used sometimes to discuss special things – whether they were right or wrong. I wonder what they would have said to St Francis Borgia?'

Helbeck smiled.

'Mercifully, darling, the ideals of the Catholic Church do not depend upon the votes of Ethical Societies!'

He turned his handsome head towards her. His tone was perfectly gentle, but behind it she perceived the breathing of a contempt before which she first recoiled – then sprang in revolt.

'As for me,' she said, panting a little, 'when I finished the life this morning in your room, I felt like Ivan in Browning's poem[19] – do you recollect? – about the mother who threw her children one by one to the wolves, to save her wretched self? I would like to have dropped the axe on St Francis Borgia's neck – just one – little – clean cut! – while he was saying his prayers, and enjoying his burning love, and all the rest of it!'

Helbeck was silent, nor could she see his face, which was again turned from her towards the river. The eager, feverish voice went on:

'Do you know, that's the kind of thing you read always – always – day after day? And it's just the same now! That girl of twenty-three, Augustina was talking of, who is going into a convent, and her mother only died last year, and there are six younger brothers and sisters, and her father says it will break his heart – *she* must have been reading about St Francis Borgia. Perhaps she felt "burning love" and had "floods of tears." But Ivan with his axe – that's the person I'd bring in, if I could.'

Still not a word from the man beside her. She hesitated a moment – felt a sob of excitement in her throat – bent forward and touched his shoulder.

'Suppose – suppose I were to be ill – dying – and the voice came, "Let her go! She is in your way; it would be better for you she should die" – would you just let go? – see me drop, drop, drop, through all eternity, to make your soul safe?'

'Laura!' cried a strong voice. And, with a spring, Helbeck was beside her, capturing both her cold hands in one of his, a mingled tenderness and wrath flashing from him before which she shrank. But though she drew away from him – her small face so white below the broad black hat! – she was not quelled. Before he could speak, she had said in sharp separate words, hardly above a whisper:

'It is that horrible egotism of religion that poisons everything! And if – if one shared it, well and good, one might make terms with it, like a wild thing one had tamed. But outside it, and at war with it, what can one do but hate – hate – *hate* – it!'

'My God!' he said, in bewilderment, 'where am I to begin?'

He stared at her with a passionate amazement. Never before had she shown such forces of personality, or been able to express herself with an utterance so mature and resonant. Her stature had grown before his eyes. In the little frowning figure there was something newly, tragically fine. The man for the first time felt his match. His own hidden self rose at last to the struggle with a kind of angry joy, eager at once to conquer the woman and to pierce the sceptic.

'Listen to me, Laura!' he said, bending over her. 'That was more than I can bear – that calls me out of my tent. I have tried to keep my poor self out of sight, but it has rights. You have challenged it. Will you take the consequences?'

She trembled before the pale concentration of his face, and bent her head.

'I will tell you,' he said, in a low determined voice, 'the only story that a man truly knows – the story of his own soul. You shall know – what you hate.'

And, after a pause of thought, Helbeck made one of the great efforts of his life.

He did not fully know indeed what it was that he had undertaken, till the wave of emotion had gathered through all the inmost chambers of memory, and was bearing outward in one great tide the secret nobilities, the hidden poetries, the unconscious weaknesses of a nature, no less narrow than profound, no less full of enmities than of loves.

But gradually from hurried or broken beginnings the narrative rose to clearness and to strength.

The first impressions of a lonely childhood; the first workings of the family history upon his boyish sense, like the faint, perpetual touches of an unseen hand moulding the will and the character; the picture of his patient mother on her sofa, surrounded with her little religious books, twisted and tormented, yet always smiling; his early collisions with his morose and half-educated father – he passed from these to the days of his first Communion, the beginnings of the personal life. 'But I had very little fervour then, such as many boys feel. I did not doubt – I would not have shown any disrespect to my religion for the world, mostly, I think, from family pride – but I felt no ardour, and did not pretend any. My mother sometimes shed tears over it, and was comforted by her old confessor – so she told me when she was dying – who used to say to her: "Feeling is good, but obedience is better. He obeys;" for I did all my religious duties without difficulty. Then at thirteen I was sent to Stonyhurst. And there, after a while, God began His work in me.'

He paused a moment; and when he resumed, his voice shook:

'Among the masters there was a certain Father Lewin. He took an affection for me, and I for him. He was even then a dying man, but he accomplished more, and was more severe to himself, than any man in health I ever knew. So long as he lived, he made the path of religion easy to me. He was the supernatural life before my eyes. I had only to open them and see. The only difference between us was that I began – first out of love for him, I suppose – to have a great wish to become a Jesuit; whereas he was against it – he thought there were too many special claims upon me here. Then, when I was eighteen, he died. I had seen him the day before, when there seemed to be no danger, or they concealed it from me. But in the night I was called, too late to hear him speak; he was already in his agony. The sight terrified me. I had expected something much more consoling – more beautiful. For a long time I could not shake off the impression, the misery of it.'

He was silent again for a minute. He still held Laura's hands close, as though there was something in their touch that spurred him on.

'After his death I got my father's leave to go and study at Louvain. I passed there the most wretched years of my life. Father Lewin's death had thrown me into an extraordinary dejection, which seemed to have taken from me all the joy of my faith; but at Louvain I came very near to losing it altogether. It came, I think, from the reading of some French sceptical books the first year I was there; but I went through a horror and anguish. Often I used to wander for a whole day along the Scheldt, or across lonely fields where no one could see me, lost in what seemed to me a fight with devils. The most horrible blasphemies – the most subtle, the most venomous thoughts – Ah! well – by God's grace I never gave up Confession and Communion – at long intervals, indeed – but still I held to them. The old Passionist father, my director, did not understand much about me. I seemed, indeed, to have no friends. I lived shut up with my own thoughts. The only comfort and relief I got was from painting. I loved the studio where I worked, poor as my own attempts were. It seemed often to be the only thing between me and madness . . . Well, the first relief came in a strange way. I was visiting one of the Professors, an old Canon of the Cathedral, on a June evening. The Bishop of the See was very ill, and while I was with the Canon word came round to summon the Chapter to assist at the administration of the last Sacraments, and to hear the sick man's Profession of Faith. The old Canon had been good to me. I don't know whether he suspected what was wrong with me. At any rate, he laid a kind hand on my arm. "Come with me," he said; and I went with him into the Bishop's residence. I can see the old house now – the black panelled stairs and passages, and the shadow of the great church outside.

'In the Bishop's room were gathered all the canons in their white robes; there was an altar blazing with lights, the windows were wide open to the dusk, and the cathedral bell was tolling. We all knelt, and Monseigneur received the Viaticum. He was fully vested. I could just see his venerable white head on the pillow. After the Communion one of the canons knelt by him and recited the Creed of Pope Pius IV.'

Laura started. But Helbeck did not notice the sudden tremulous movement of the hands lying in his. He was sitting rigidly upright, the eyes half closed, his mind busy with the past.

'And as he recited it, the bands that held my own heart seemed to break. I had not been able to approach any clause of that creed for months without danger of blasphemy; and now – it was like a bird escaped from the nets. The snare is broken – and we are delivered! The dying man raised his voice in a last effort; he repeated the oath with which the Creed ends. The Gospels were handed to him; he kissed them with fervour. *"Sic me Deus adjuvet, et Sancta Dei Evangelia."* "So may God help me, and His Holy Gospels!" I joined in the words mentally, overcome with joy. Before me, as in a vision, had risen the majesty and glory of the Catholic Church; I felt her foundations once more under my feet.'

He drew a long breath. Then he turned. Laura felt his eyes upon her, as though in doubt. She herself neither moved nor spoke; she was all hearing, absorbed in a passionate prescience of things more vital yet to come.

'Laura!' – his voice dropped – 'I want you to know it all, to understand me through and through. I will try that there shall not be a word to offend you. That scene I have described to you was for me only the beginning of another apostasy. I had no longer the excuse of doubt. I believed and trembled. But for two years after that, I was every day on the brink of ruining my own soul – and another's. The first, the only woman I ever loved before I saw you, Laura, I loved in defiance of all law – God's or man's. If she had struggled one heartbeat less, if God had let me wander one hair's breadth further from His hand, we had both made shipwreck – hopeless, eternal shipwreck. Laura, my little Laura, am I hurting you so?'

She gave a little sob, and mutely, with shut eyes, she raised her face towards him. He stooped and very tenderly and gravely kissed her cheek.

'But God's mercy did not fail!' he said or rather murmured. 'At the last moment that woman – God rest her soul! – God bless her for ever! –'

He took off his hat, and bent forward silently for a moment.

– 'She died, Laura, more than ten years ago! – At the last moment she saved both herself and me. She sent for one of my old Jesuit masters at Stonyhurst, a man who had been a great friend of Father Lewin's, and happened to be at that moment in Brussels. He came. He brought me her last farewell, and he asked me to go back with him that evening to join a retreat that he was holding in one of the houses of the order near Brussels. I went, in a sullen state, stunned and for the moment submissive.

'But the retreat was agony. I could take part in nothing. I neglected the prescribed hours and duties; it was as though my mind could not take them in, and I soon saw that I was disturbing others.

'One evening – I was by myself in the garden at recreation hour – the father who was holding the retreat came up to me, and sternly asked me to withdraw at once. I looked at him. "Will you give me one more day?" I said. He agreed. He seemed touched. I must have appeared to him a miserable creature.

'Next day this same father was conducting a meditation – on "the condescension of Jesus in the Blessed Sacrament." I was kneeling, half stupefied, when I heard him tell a story of the Curé d'Ars. After the procession of Corpus Christi, which was very long and fatiguing, some one pressed the Curé to take food. "I want nothing," he said. "How could I be tired? I was bearing Him who bears me!" "My brothers," said Father Stuart, turning to the altar, "the Lord who bore the sin of the whole world on the Cross, who opens the arms of His mercy now to each separate sinful soul, is *there*. He beseeches you by me, 'Choose, my children, between the world and Me, between sin and Me, between Hell and Me. Your souls are Mine: I bought them with anguish and tears. Why will ye now hold them back from Me – wherefore will ye die?' "

'My whole being seemed to be shaken by these words. But I instantly thought of Marie. I said to myself, "She is alone – perhaps in despair. How can I save myself, wretched tempter and coward that I am, and leave her in remorse and grief?" And then it seemed to me as though a Voice came from the altar itself, so sweet and penetrating that it overpowered the voice of the preacher and the movements of my companions. I heard nothing in the chapel but It alone. "She is saved!" It said – and again and again, as though in joy, "She is saved – saved!"

'That night I crept to the foot of the crucifix in my little cell. *"Elegi, elegi: renuntio!"* – "I have chosen: I renounce." All night long those alternate words seemed to be wrung from me.

There was deep silence. Helbeck knelt on the grass beside Laura and took her hands afresh.

'Laura, since that night I have been my Lord's. It seemed to me that He had come Himself – come from His cross – to raise two souls from the depths of Hell. Marie went into a convent, and died in peace and blessedness; I came home here, to do my duty if I could – and save my soul. That seems to you a mere selfish bargain with God – an "egotism" – that you hate. But look at the root of it. Is the world under sin – and has a God died for it? All my nature – my intellect, my heart, my will, answer "Yes." But if a God died, and must die – cruelly, hideously, at the hands of His creatures – to satisfy eternal justice, what must that sin be that demands the Crucifixion? Of what revolt, what ruin is not the body capable? I knew – for I had gone down into the depths. Is any chastisement too heavy, any restraint too harsh, if it keep us from the sin for which our Lord must die? And if He died, are we not His from the first moment of our birth – His first of all? Is it a selfish bargain to yield Him what He purchased at such a cost, to take care that our just debt to Him is paid – so far as our miserable humanity can pay it. All these mortifications, and penances, and self-denials that you hate so, that make the saints so odious in your eyes, spring from two great facts – Sin and the Crucifixion. But, Laura, are they *true?*'

He spoke in a low, calm voice, yet Laura knew well that his life was poured into each word. She herself did not – could not – speak. But it seemed to her strangely that some spring within her was broken – some great decision had been taken, by whom she could not tell.

He looked with alarm at her pallor and silence.

'Laura, those are the hard and awful – to us Catholics, the majestic – facts on which our religion stands. Accept them, and nothing else is really difficult. Miracles, the protection of the saints, the mysteries of the sacraments, the place that Catholics give to Our Lady, the support of an infallible Church – what so easy and natural if *these* be true? ... Sin and its Divine Victim, penance, regulation of life, death, judgment – Catholic thought moves perpetually from one of these ideas to another. As to many other thoughts and beliefs, it is free to us as to other men to take or leave, to think or not to think. The Church, like a tender mother, offers her children an innumerable variety of holy aids, consolations, encouragements. These may or may not be of faith. The Crucifix *is* the Catholic Faith. In that the Catholic sees the Love that brought a God to die, the Sin that infects his own soul. To requite that love, to purge that sin – there lies the whole task of the Catholic life.'

He broke off again, anxiously studying the drooping face so near to him. Then gently he put his arm round her, and drew her to him till her brow rested against his shoulder.

'Laura, does it seem very hard – very awful – to you?'

She moved imperceptibly, but she did not speak.

'It may well. The way *is* strait! But, Laura, you see it from without – I from within. Won't you take my word for the sweetness, the reward, and the mercifulness of God's dealings with our souls?' He drew a long agitated breath. 'Take my own case – take our love. You remember, Laura, when you sat here on Easter Sunday? I came from Communion, and I found you here. You disliked and despised my faith and me. But as you sat here, I loved you – my eyes were first opened. The night of the dance, when you went upstairs, I took my own heart and offered it. You did not love me then: how could I dream you ever would? The sacrifice was mine: I tried to yield it. But it was not His will. I made my struggle – you made yours. He drew us to each other. Then –'

He faltered, looked down upon her in doubt.

'Since then, Laura, so many strange things have happened! Who was I that I should teach anybody? I shrank from laying the smallest touch on your freedom. I thought, "Gradually, of her own free will, she will come nearer. The Truth will plead for itself." My duty is to trust, and wait. But, Laura, what have I seen in you? Not indifference – not contempt – never! But a long storm – a trouble – a conflict – that has filled me with confusion – overthrown all my own hopes and plans. Laura, my love, my sweet, why does our Faith hurt you so much if it means nothing to you? Is there not already some tenderness' – his voice dropped – 'behind the scorn? Could it torment you if – if it had not gained some footing in your heart? Laura, speak to me!'

She slowly drew away from him. Gently she shook her head. Her eyes were full of tears.

But the strange look of power – almost of triumph – on Helbeck's face remained unaltered. She shrank before it.

'Laura, you don't know yourself! But no matter! Only, will you forgive me if you feel a change in me? Till now I have shrunk from fighting you. It seemed to me that an ugly habit of words might easily grow up that would poison all our future. But now I feel in it something more than words. If you challenge, Laura, I shall meet it! If you strike, I shall return it.'

He took her hands once more. His bright eye looked for – demanded an answer. Her own personality, for all its daring, wavered and fainted before the attacking force of his.

But Helbeck received no assurance of it. She showed none of that girlish yielding which would have been so natural and so delightful to her lover. Without any direct answer to his appeal or his threat, she lifted to him a look that was far from easy to read – a look of passionate sadness and of pure love. Her delicate face seemed to float towards him, and her lips breathed.

'I was not worthy you should tell me a word. But –.' It was some time before she could go on. Then she said with sudden haste, the colour rushing back into her cheeks, 'It is the most sacred honour that was ever done me. I thank – thank – thank you!'

And with her eyes still fixed upon his countenance, and all those deep traces that the last half-hour had left upon it, she raised his hand and pressed her soft quivering mouth upon it.

Never had Helbeck been filled with such a tender and hopeful joy as in the hours that followed this scene between them. Father Leadham arrived in time for dinner. Laura treated him with a gentleness, even a sweetness, that from the first moment filled the Jesuit with a secret astonishment. She was very pale; her exhaustion was evident.

But Helbeck silenced his sister; and he surrounded Laura with a devotion that had few words, that never made her conspicuous, and yet was more than she could bear.

Augustina insisted on her going to bed early. Helbeck went upstairs with her to the first landing, to light her candle.

Nothing stirred in the old house. Father Leadham and Augustina were in the drawing-room. They two stood alone among the shadows of the panelling, the solitary candle shining on her golden hair and white dress.

'I have something to say to you, Laura,' said Helbeck in a disturbed voice.

She looked up.

'I can't save the Romney, dear. I've tried my very best. Will you forgive me?'

She smiled, and put her hand timidly on his shoulder.

'Ask her, rather! I know you tried. Good-night.'

And then suddenly, to his astonishment, she threw both her arms round his neck, and, like a child that nestles to another in penitence or for protection, she kissed his breast passionately, repeatedly.

'Laura, this can't be borne! Look up, beloved! Why should my coat be so blessed?' he said, half laughing, yet deeply moved, as he bent above her.

She disengaged herself, and, as she mounted the stairs, she waved her hand to him. As she passed out of his sight she was a vision of gentleness. The woman had suddenly blossomed from the girl. When Helbeck descended the stairs after she had vanished, his heart beat with a happiness he had never yet known.

And she, when she reached her own room, she let her arms drop rigidly by her side. 'It would be a crime – a *crime* – to marry him,' she said, with a dull resolve that was beyond weeping.

Helbeck and Father Leadham sat long together after Augustina had retired. There was an argument between them in which the Jesuit at last won the victory. Helbeck was persuaded to a certain course against his judgment – to some extent against his conscience.

Next morning the Squire left Bannisdale early. He was to be away two days on important business. Before he left he reluctantly told his sister that the Romney would probably be removed before his return by the dealer to whom it had been sold. Laura did not appear at breakfast, and Helbeck left a written word of farewell, that Augustina delivered.

Meantime Father Leadham remained as the guest of the ladies. In the afternoon he joined Miss Fountain in the garden, and they walked up and down the bowling green for some time together. Augustina, in the deep window of the drawing-room, was excitedly aware of the fact.

When the two companions came in, Father Leadham after a time rejoined Mrs Fountain. She looked at him with eagerness. But his fine and scholarly face was more discomposed than she had ever seen it. And the few words that he said to her were more than enough.

Laura meanwhile went to her own room, and shut herself up there. Her cheeks were glowing, her eyes angry. 'He promised me!' she said, as she sat down to her writing-table.

But she could not stay there. She got up and walked restlessly about the room. After half an hour's fruitless conversation, Father Leadham had been betrayed into an expression – hardly that – a shade of expression, which had set the girl's nature aflame. What it meant was, 'So this – is your answer – to the chivalry of Mr Helbeck's behaviour – to the delicacy which could go to such lengths in protecting a young lady from her own folly?' The meaning was conveyed by a look – an inflection – hardly a phrase. But Laura understood it perfectly; and when Father Leadham returned to Mrs Fountain he guiltily knew what he had done, and, being a man in general of great tact and finesse, he hardly knew whom to blame most, himself, or the girl who had imperceptibly and yet deeply provoked him.

That evening Laura told her stepmother that she must go up to London the following day, by the early afternoon train, on some shopping business, and would stay the night with her friend Molly Friedland. Augustina fretfully acquiesced; and the evening was spent by Mrs Fountain at any rate in trying to console herself by much broken talk of frocks and winter fashions, while Laura gave occasional answers, and Father Leadham on a distant sofa buried himself in the *Tablet*.

'Gone!'

The word was Laura's. She had been busy in her room, and had come hurriedly downstairs to fetch her work-bag from the drawing-room. As she crossed the threshold, she saw that the picture had been taken down. Indeed, the van containing it was just driving through the park.

White and faltering, the girl came up to the wall whence the beautiful lady had just been removed, and leant her head against it. She raised her hand to her eyes. 'Good-bye,' said the inner sense – 'Good-bye!' And the strange link which from the first moment almost had seemed to exist between that radiant daughter of Bannisdale and herself snapped and fell away, carrying how much else with it!

About an hour before Laura's departure there was a loud knock at her door, and Mrs Denton appeared. The woman was pale with rage. Mrs Fountain, in much trepidation, had just given her notice, and the housekeeper had not been slow to guess from what quarter the blow had fallen.

Laura turned round bewildered. But she was too late to stop the outbreak. In the course of five minutes' violent speech Mrs Denton wiped out the grievances of six months; she hurled the gossip of a countryside on Laura's head; and in her own opinion she finally avenged the cause of the Church and of female decorum upon the little infidel adventuress that had stolen away the wits and con-science of the Squire.

Miss Fountain, after a first impatient murmur, 'I might have remembered!' – stood without a word, with eyes cast down, and a little scornful smile on her colourless lips. When at last she had shut the door on her assailant, a great quivering sigh rose from the girl's breast. Was it the last touch? But she said nothing. She brushed away a tear that had unconsciously risen, and went back to her packing.

'Just wait a moment!' said Miss Fountain to old Wilson, who was driving her across the bridge on her way to the station. 'I want to get a bunch of those berries by the water. Take the pony up the hill. I'll join you at the top.'

Old Wilson drove up. Laura climbed a stile and slipped down to the waterside.

The river, full with autumn rain, came foaming down. The leaf was falling fast. Through the woods on the further bank she could just distinguish a gable of the old house.

A moan broke from her. She stopped and buried her face in the grass – his grass.

When she returned to the road, she looked for the letter-box in the wall of the bridge, and, walking up to it, she dropped into it two letters. Then she stood a moment with bent brows. Had she made all arrangements for Augustina?

But she dared not let herself think of the morrow. She set her face to the hill – trudging steadily up the wet, solitary road. Once – twice – she turned to look. Then the high trees that arched over the top of the hill received the little form; she disappeared into their shadow.

BOOK FIVE

CHAPTER ONE

'My dear, where are the girls?'

The speaker was Dr Friedland,[20] the only intimate friend Stephen Fountain had ever made at Cambridge. The person addressed was Dr Friedland's wife.

On hearing her husband's question, that lady's gentle and benevolent countenance emerged from the folds of a newspaper. It was the 'first mild day of March,' and she and her husband had been enjoying an after-breakfast chat in the garden of a Cambridge villa.

'Molly is arranging the flowers – Laura has had a long letter from Mrs Fountain, and is now, I believe, gone to answer it.'

'Then I sha'n't enjoy my lunch,' said Dr Friedland pensively.

He was an elderly gentleman, with a short beard and moustache turning to white, particularly black eyes, and a handsome brow. His wife had put a rug over his shoulders, and another over his knees, before she allowed him the 'Times' and a cigarette. Amid the ample folds of these draperies he had a Jove-like and benignant air.

His wife inquired what difference Miss Fountain's correspondence would or could make to her host's luncheon.

'Because she won't eat any,' said the doctor with a sigh, 'and I find it infectious.'

Mrs Friedland laid down her newspaper.

'There is no doubt she is worried – about Mrs Fountain.'

'*E tutti quanti,*' said the doctor, humming a tune. 'My dear, it is surprising what an admiration I find myself possessed of for Sir John Pringle.'

'Sir John Pringle?' said the lady in bewilderment.

'Bozzy, my dear – the great Bozzy – amid the experiments of his youth, turned Catholic. His distracted relations deputed Sir John Pringle to deal with him. That great lawyer pointed out the worldly disadvantages of the step. Bozzy pleaded his immortal soul. Whereupon Sir John observed with warmth that anyone possessing a particle of gentlemanly spirit would sooner be damned to all eternity than give his relations so much trouble as Bozzy was giving his!'

'The application is not clear,' said Mrs Friedland.

'No,' said the doctor, stretching his legs and puffing at his cigarette; 'but when you speak of Laura, and tell me she is writing to Bannisdale, I find a comfort in Sir John Pringle.'

'It would be more to the purpose if Laura did!' exclaimed Mrs Friedland.

The doctor shook his head, and fell into a reverie. Presently he asked –

'You think Mrs Fountain is really worse?'

'Laura is sure of it. And the difficulty is, what is she to do? If she goes to Bannisdale she exiles Mr Helbeck. Yet, if his sister is really in danger, Mr Helbeck naturally will desire to be at home.'

'And they can't meet?'

'Under the same roof – and the old conditions? Heaven forbid!' said Mrs Friedland.

'Risk it!' said the doctor, violently slapping his fist on the little garden table that held his box of cigarettes.

'John!'

'My dear – don't be a hypocrite! You and I know well enough what's wrong with that child.'

'Perhaps.' The lady's eyes filled with tears. 'But you forget that by all accounts Mr Helbeck is an altered man. From something Laura said to Molly last week, it seems that Mrs Fountain even is now quite afraid of him – as she used to be.'

'If she would only die – good lady! – her brother might go to his own place,' said the doctor impatiently.

'To the Jesuits?'

The doctor nodded.

'Did he actually tell you that was his intention?'

'No. But I guessed. And that Trinity man Leadham, who went over, gave me to understand the other day what the end would probably be. But not while his sister lives.'

'I should hope not!' said Mrs Friedland.

After a pause, she turned to her husband –

'John! you know you liked him!'

'If you mean by that, my dear, that I showed a deplorable weakness in dealing with him, my conscience supports you!' said the doctor; 'but I would have you remember that for a person of my quiet habits, to have a gentleman pale as death in your study, demanding his lady-love – you knowing all the time that the lady-love is upstairs – and only one elderly man between them – is an agitating situation.'

'Poor Laura! – poor Mr Helbeck!' murmured Mrs Friedland. The agony of the man, the resolution of the girl, stood out sharply from the medley of the past.

'All very well, my dear – all very well. But you showed a pusil-lanimity on that occasion that I scorn to qualify. You were afraid of that child – positively afraid of her. I could have dealt with her in a twinkling, if you'd left her to me.'

'What would you have said to her?' inquired Mrs Friedland gently.

'How can there be any possible doubt what I should have said to her?' said the doctor, slapping his knee. ' "My dear, you love him – *ergo*, marry him!" That first and foremost. "And as to those other trifles, what have you to do with them? Look over them – look round them! Rise, my dear, to your proper dignity and destiny – have a right and natural pride – in the rock that bore you! You, a child of the Greater Church – of an Authority of which all other authorities are the mere caricature – why all this humiliation, these misgivings – this turmoil? Take a serener – take a loftier view!" Ah! if I could evoke Fountain for one hour!'

The doctor bent forward, his hands hanging over his knees, his lips moving without sound, under the sentences his brain was form-ing. This habit of silent rhetoric represented a curious compromise between a natural impetuosity of temperament, and the caution of scientific research. His wife watched him with a loving, half-amused eye.

'And what, pray, could Mr Fountain do, John, but make matters ten times worse?'

'Do! – who wants him to do anything? But ten years ago he might have done something. Listen to me, Jane!' He seized his wife's arm. 'He makes Laura a child of Knowledge, a child of Freedom, a child of Revolution – without an ounce of training to fit her for the part. It is like an heir – flung to the gipsies. Then you put her to the test – sorely – conspicuously. And she stands fast – she does not yield – it is not in her blood, scarcely in her power to yield. But it is a blind instinct, carried through at what a cost! You might have equipped and fortified her. You did neither. You trusted everything to the passionate loyalty of the woman. And it does not fail you. But! –'

The doctor shook his head, long and slowly. Mrs Friedland quietly replaced the rugs which had gone wandering, in the energy of these remarks.

'You see, Jane, if it's true – "ne croit qui veut" – it's still more true, "ne doute qui veut"![21] To doubt – doubt wholesomely, cheerfully, fruitfully – why, my dear, there's no harder task in the world! And a woman, who thinks with her heart? – who can't stand on her own feet as a man can – you remove her from all her normal shelters and supports – you expect her to fling a "No!" in the face of half her natural friends – and then you are too indolent or too fastidious to train the poor child for her work! – Fountain took Laura out of her generation, and gave her nothing in return. Did he read with her – share his mind with her? Never! He was indolent; she was wilful; so the thing slid. But all the time he made a partisan of her – he expected her to echo his hates and his prejudice – he stamped himself and his cause deep into her affections –

'And then, my dear, she must needs fall in love with this man, this Catholic! Catholicism at its best – worse luck! No mean or puerile type, with all its fetichisms and unreasons on its head – no! – a type sprung from the best English blood, disciplined by heroic memories, by the persecution and hardships of the Penal Laws. What happens? Why, of course the girl's imagination goes over! Her father in her – her temperament – stand in the way of anything more. But where is she to look for self-respect, for peace of mind? She feels herself an infidel! – a moral outcast. She trembles before the claims of this great visible system. Her reason refuses them – but why? She cannot tell. For Heaven's sake, why do we leave our children's minds empty like this? If you believe, my good friend, Educate! And if you doubt, still more – Educate! Educate!'

The doctor rose in his might, tossed his rugs from him and began to pace a sheltered path, leaning on his wife's arm.

Mrs Friedland looked at him slyly, and laughed.

'So if Laura had been learned, she might have been happy? – John! – what a paradox!'

'Not mine then! – but the Almighty's – who seems to have included a mind in this odd bundle that makes up Laura. What! You set a woman to fight for ideas, and then deny her all knowledge of what they mean. Happy! Of course she might have been happy. She might have made her Catholic respect her. He offered her terms – she might have accepted them with a free and equal mind.

There would have been none, any way, of this *moral doubt* – this bogeyfication of things she don't understand! Ah! here she comes. Now just look at her, Jane! What's your housekeeping after? She's lost half a stone this month if she's lost an ounce.'

And the doctor standing still, peered discontentedly through his spectacles at the advancing figure.

Laura approached slowly with her hands behind her, looking on her way at the daffodils and tulips just opening in the garden border.

'Pater! – Molly says you and Mater are to come in. It's March and not May, you'll please to remember.'

She came up to them with the airs of a daughter, put a flower in Mrs Friedland's dress – ran for one of the discarded rugs, and draped it again round the doctor's ample shoulders. Her manner to the two elderly folk was much softer and freer than it had ever been in the days of her old acquaintance with them. A wistful gratitude played through it, revealing a new Laura – a Laura that had passed, in these five months, through deep waters, and had been forced, in spite of pride, to throw herself upon the friendly and saving hands held out to her.

They on their side looked at her with a tender concern, which tried to disguise itself in chat. The doctor hooked his arm through hers, and made her examine the garden.

'Look at these Lent lilies, Miss Laura. They will be out in two days at most.'

Laura bent over them, then suddenly drew herself erect. The doctor felt the stiffening of the little arm.

'I suppose you had sheets of them in the north,' he said innocently, as he poked a stone away from the head of an emerging hyacinth.

'Yes – a great many.' She looked absently straight before her, taking no more notice of the flowers.

'Well – and Mrs Fountain? Are you really anxious?'

The girl hesitated.

'She is ill – quite ill. I ought to see her somehow.'

'Well, my dear, go!' He looked round upon her with a cheerful decision.

'No – that isn't possible,' she said quietly. 'But I might stay somewhere near. She must have lost a great deal of strength since Christmas.'

At Christmas and for some time afterwards, she and Mrs Fountain had been at St Leonard's together. In fact, it was little more than a fortnight since Laura had parted from her stepmother, who had shown a piteous unwillingness to go back alone to Bannisdale.

The garden door opened and shut; a white-capped servant came along the path. A gentleman – for Miss Fountain.

'For me?' The girl's cheek flushed involuntarily. 'Why, Pater – who is it?'

For behind the servant came the gentleman – a tall and comely youth, with narrow blue eyes, a square chin, and a very conscious smile. He was well dressed in a dark serge suit, and showed a great deal of white cuff, and a conspicuous watch chain as he took off his hat.

'Hubert!'

Laura advanced to him, with a face of astonishment, and held out her hand.

Mason greeted her with a mixture of confusion and assurance, glancing behind her at the Friedlands all the time. 'Well, I was here on some business – and I thought I'd look you up, don't you know?'

'My cousin, Hubert Mason,' said Laura, turning to the old people.

Friedland lifted his wide-awake. Mrs Friedland, whose gentle face could be all criticism, eyed him quietly, and shook hands perfunctorily. A few nothings passed on the weather and the spring. Suddenly Mason said –

'Would you take a walk with me, Miss Laura?'

After a momentary hesitation, she assented, and went into the house for her walking things. Mason hurriedly approached the doctor –

'Why, she looks – she looks as if you could blow her away!' he cried, staring into the doctor's face, while his own flushed.

'Miss Fountain's health has not been strong this winter,' said the doctor gravely, his spectacled eyes travelling up and down Mason's tall figure. 'You, I suppose, became acquainted with her in Westmoreland?'

'Acquainted with her!' The young man checked himself, flushed still redder, then resumed. 'Well, we're cousins, you see – though of course I don't mean to say that we're her sort – you understand?'

'Miss Fountain is ready,' said Mrs Friedland.

Mason looked round, saw the little figure in the doorway, and hastily saluting the Friedlands, he took his leave.

'My dear,' said the doctor anxiously, laying hold on his wife's arm, 'should we have asked him to lunch?'

His wife smiled.

'By no means. That's Laura's business.'

'Well, but, Jane – Jane! had you realised that young man?'

'Oh dear, yes,' said Mrs Friedland. 'Don't excite yourself, John.'

'Laura – gone out with a young man,' said the doctor, musing. 'I have been waiting for that all the winter – and he's extremely good-looking, Jane.'

Mrs Friedland lost patience.

'John! I really can't talk to you, if you're as dense as that.'

'Talk to me!' cried the doctor – 'why, you unreasonable woman, you haven't vouchsafed me a single word!'

'Well, and why should I?' said Mrs Friedland, provokingly.

Half an hour passed away. Mason and Laura were sitting in the garden of Trinity.

Up till now, Laura had no very clear idea of what they had been talking about. Mason, it appeared, had been granted three days' holiday by his employers, and had made use of it to come to Cambridge and present a letter of introduction from his old teacher, Castle, the Whinthorpe organist, to a famous Cambridge musician. But, at first, he was far more anxious to discuss Laura's affairs than to explain his own; and Laura had found it no easy matter to keep him at arm's length. For nine months, Mason had brooded, gossiped, and excused himself; now, conscious of being somehow a fine fellow again, he had come boldly to play the cousin – perhaps something more. He offered now a few words of stammering apology on the subject of his letter to Laura after the announcement of her engagement. She received them in silence; and the matter dropped.

As to his moral recovery, and material prospects, his manners and appearance were enough. A fledgeling ambition, conscious of new aims and chances, revealed itself in all he said. The turbid elements in the character were settling down; the permanent lines of it, strong, vulgar, self-complacent, emerged.

Here, indeed, was a successful man in the making. Once or twice the girl's beautiful eyes opened suddenly, and then sank again.

Before her rose the rocky chasm of the Greet; the sound of the water was in her ears – the boyish tones of remorse, or entreaty.

'And you know I'll make some money out of my songs before long – see if I don't! I took some of em to the Professor this morning – and, my word, didn't he like em! Why, I couldn't repeat the things he said – you'd think I was bluffing!'

Strange gift! – 'settling unaware' – on this rude nature and poor intelligence! But Laura looked up eagerly. Here she softened; here was the bridge between them. And when he spoke of his new friend, the young musical apostle who had reclaimed him, there was a note which pleased her. She began to smile upon him more freely; the sadness of her little face grew sweet.

And suddenly the young man stopped and looked at her. He reddened; and she flushed too, not knowing why.

'Well, that's where 'tis,' he said, moving towards her on the seat. 'I'm going to get on. I told you I was, long ago, and it's come true. My salary'll be a decent figure before this year's out, and I'm certain I'll make something out of the songs. Then there's my share of the farm. Mother don't give me more than she's obliged; but it's a tidy bit sometimes. Laura! – look here! – I know there's nothing in the way now. You were a plucky girl, you were, to throw that up. I always said so – I didn't care what people thought. Well, but now – you're free – and I'm a better sort – won't you give a fellow a chance?'

Midway, his new self-confidence left him. She sat there, so silent, so delicately white! He had but to put out his hand to grasp her; and he dared not move a finger. He stared at her breathless and open-mouthed.

But she did not take it tragically at all. After a moment, she began to laugh, and shook her head.

'Do you mean that you want me to marry you, Hubert? Oh! you'd so soon be tired of that! – You don't know anything about me, really – we shouldn't suit each other at all.'

His face fell. He drew sullenly away from her, and bending forward, began to poke at the grass with his stick.

'I see how 'tis. I'm not good enough for you – and I don't suppose I ever shall be.'

She looked at him with a smiling compassion.

'I'm not in love with you, Mr Hubert – that's all.'

'No – you've never got over them things that happened up at

Whinthorpe,' he said roughly. 'I've got a bone to pick with you though. Why did you give me the slip that night?'

He looked up. But in spite of his bravado, he reddened again, deeply.

'Well – you hadn't exactly commended yourself as an escort, had you?' she said lightly. But her tone pricked.

'I hadn't had a drop of anything,' he declared hotly; 'and I'd have looked after you, and stopped a deal of gossip. You hurt my feelings pretty badly, I can tell you.'

'Did I? – Well, as you hurt mine on the first occasion, let's cry quits.'

He was silent for a little, throwing furtive glances at her from time to time. She was wonderfully thin and fragile, but wonderfully pretty, as she sat there under the cedar.

At last he said, with a grumbling note –

'I wish you wouldn't look so thin and dowie-like, as we say up at home – you've no cause to fret, I'm sure.'

The temper of twenty-one gave way. Laura sat up – nay, rose.

'Will you please come and look at the sights? – or shall I go home?'

He looked up at her flashing face, and stuck to his seat.

'I say – Miss Laura – you don't know how you bowl a fellow over!'

The expression of his handsome countenance – so childish still through all its athlete's force – propitiated her. And yet she felt instinctively that his fancy for her no longer went so deep as it had once done.

Well! – she was glad; of course she was glad.

'Oh! you're not so very much to be pitied,' she said; but her hand lighted a moment kindly and shyly on the young man's arm. 'Now, if you wouldn't talk about these things, Hubert – do you know what I should be doing? – I should be asking you to do me a service.'

His manner changed – became businesslike and mannish at once.

'Then you'll please sit down again – and tell me what it is,' he said.

She obeyed. He crossed his knees, and listened.

But she had some difficulty in putting it. At last she said, looking away from him –

'Do you think, if I proposed it, your mother could bear to have me on a visit to the farm?'

'Mother! – you!' he said in astonishment. A hundred notions blazed up in his mind. What on earth did she want to be in those parts again for?

'My stepmother is very unwell,' she said hurriedly. 'It – well, it troubles me not to see her. But I can't go to Bannisdale. If your mother doesn't hate me now, as she did last summer – perhaps – she and Polly would take me in for a while?'

He frowned over it – taking the airs of the relative and the counsellor.

'Mother didn't say much – well – about your affair. But Polly says she's never spoken again you since. But I expect – you know what she'd be afraid of?'

He nodded sagaciously.

'I can't imagine,' said Laura, instantly. But the stiffening of her slight frame betrayed her.

'Why, of course – Miss Laura – you see she'd be afraid of its coming on again.'

There was silence. The broad rim of Laura's velvet hat hid her face. Hubert began to be uncomfortable.

'I don't say as she'd have cause to,' he said slowly; 'but –'

Laura suddenly laughed, and Mason opened his eyes in astonishment. Such a strange little dry sound!

'Of course, if your mother were to think such things and to say them to me – every time I went to Bannisdale, I couldn't stay. But I want to see Augustina very, *very* much.' Her voice wavered. 'And I could easily go to her – if I were close by – when she was alone. And of course I should be no expense. Your mother knows I have my own money.'

Hubert nodded. He was trying hard to read her face, but – what the deuce made girls so close? His countenance brightened, however.

'All right. I'll see to it – I'll manage it – you wait.'

'Ah! but stop a minute.' Her smile shone out from the shadow of the hat. 'If I go there's a condition. While I'm there, you mustn't come.'

The young fellow flung away from her with a passionate exclamation, and her smile dropped – lost itself in a sweet distress, unlike the old wild Laura.

'I seem to be falling out with you all the time,' she said in haste – 'and I don't want to a bit! But indeed – it will be much better. You see, if you were to be coming over to pay visits to me – you would think it your duty to make love to me!'

'Well – and if I did?' he said fiercely.

'It would only put off the time of our making real friends. And – and – I do care very much for papa's people.'

The tears leapt to her eyes for the first time. She held out her ungloved hand. Reluctantly, and without looking at her, he took it. The touch of it roused a tempest in him. He crushed it and threw it away from him.

'Oh! if you'd never seen that man!' he groaned.

She got up without a word, and presently they were walking through the 'backs,' and she was gradually taming and appeasing him. By the time they reached the street gate of King's, he was again in the full-tide of musical talk and boasting, quite aware besides that his good looks and his magnificent physique drew the attention of the passers-by.

'Why, they're a poor lot – these 'Varsity men!' he said once contemptuously, as they passed a group of rather weedy undergraduates – 'I could throw ten of em at one go!'

And perpetually he talked of money, the cost of his lodgings, of his railway fare, the swindling ways of the south. After all, the painful habits of generations had not run to waste; the mother began to show in the son.

In the street they parted. As he was saying goodbye to her, his look suddenly changed.

'I say! – that's the girl I travelled down with yesterday! And, by Jove! she knew me!'

And with a last nod to Laura, he darted after a tall woman who had thrown him a glance from the further pavement. Laura recognised the smart and buxom daughter of a Cambridge tradesman, a young lady whose hair, shoulders, millinery, and repartees were all equally pronounced.

Miss Fountain smiled and turned away. But in the act of doing so, she came to a sudden stop. A face had arrested her – she stood bewildered.

A man walking in the road came towards her.

'I see that you recognise me, Miss Fountain!'

The ambiguous voice – the dark, delicate face – the clumsy gait – she knew them all. But – she stared in utter astonishment. The man who addressed her wore a short round coat and soft hat; a new beard covered his chin; his flannel shirt was loosely tied at the throat by a silk handkerchief. And over all the same air of personal slovenliness, and ill-breeding –

'You didn't expect to see me in this dress, Miss Fountain? Let me walk a few steps with you, if I may. You perhaps hadn't heard that I had left the Jesuits – and ceased indeed to be a Catholic.'

Her mind whirled, as she recognised the scholastic. She saw the study at Bannisdale – and Helbeck bending over her.

'No, indeed – I had not heard,' she stammered, as they walked on. 'Was it long ago?'

'Only a couple of months. The crisis came in January –'

And he broke out into a flood of autobiography. Already at Bannisdale he had been in confusion of mind – the voices of art and liberty calling to him each hour more loudly – his loyalty to Helbeck, to his boyish ideals, to his Jesuit training, holding him back.

'I believe, Miss Fountain' – the colour rushed into his womanish cheek – 'you overheard us that evening – you know what I owe to that admirable, that extraordinary man. May I be frank? We have both been through deep waters!'

The girl's face grew rigid. Involuntarily she put a wider space between herself and him. But he did not notice.

'It will be no news to you, Miss Fountain, that Mr Helbeck's engagement troubled his Catholic friends. I chose to take it morbidly to heart – I ventured that – that most presumptuous attack upon him.' He laughed, with an affected note that made her think him odious. 'But you were soon avenged. You little know, Miss Fountain, what an influence your presence at Bannisdale had upon me. It – well! it was like a rebel army, perpetually there, to help – to support, the rebel in myself. I saw the struggle – the protest in you. My own grew fiercer. Oh! those days of painting! – and always the stabbing thought, never again! I must confess even the passionate delight this has given me – the irreligious ideas it has excited. All my religious habits lost power – I could not meditate – I was always thinking of the problem of my work. Clearly I must never touch a brush again. – For I was very soon to take orders – then to go out to missionary work. Well, I put the painting aside – I trampled on myself – I went to see my father and sister, and

rejoiced in the humiliations they put upon me. Mr Helbeck was all
kindness, but he was naturally the last person I could confide in.
Then, Miss Fountain, I went back, back to the Jesuit routine –'

He paused, looking instinctively for a glance from her. But she
gave him none.

'And in three weeks it broke down under me for ever. I gave it
up. I am a free man. Of the wrench I say nothing.' He drew himself
up with a shudder, which seemed to her theatrical. 'There are
sufferings one must not talk of. The Society have not been ungener-
ous. They actually gave me a little money. But, of course, for all my
Catholic friends it is like death. They know me no more.'

Then for the first time his companion turned towards him. Her
eyelids lifted. Her lips framed rather than spoke the words 'Mr
Helbeck?'

'Ah! Mr Helbeck – I am not mistaken, Miss Fountain, in thinking
that I may now speak of Mr Helbeck with more freedom?'

'My engagement with Mr Helbeck is broken off,' she said coldly.
'But you were saying something of yourself?'

A momentary expression of dislike and disappointment crossed
his face. He was of a soft sensuous temperament, and had expected
a good deal of sympathy from Miss Fountain.

'Mr Helbeck has done what all of us might expect,' he said, not
without a betraying sharpness. 'He has cast me off in the sternest
way. Henceforth he knows me no more. Bannisdale is closed to me.
But, indeed, the news from that quarter fills me with alarm.'

Laura looked up again eagerly, involuntarily.

'Mr Helbeck, by all accounts, grows more and more extreme –
more and more solitary. – But of course your stepmother will have
kept you informed. It was always to be foreseen. What was once a
beautiful devotion, has become, with years – and, I suppose, opposition – a stern unbending passion – may one not say, a gloomy
bigotry?'

He sighed delicately. Through the girl's stormy sense there ran a
dumb rush of thoughts – 'Insolent! ungrateful! He wounds the
heart that loved him – and then dares to discuss – to blame!'

But before she could find something to say aloud, her companion
resumed.

'But I must not complain. I was honoured by a superior man's
friendship. He has withdrawn it. He has the right. – Now I must
look to the future. You will, I think, be glad to hear that I am not

in that destitute condition which generally awaits the Catholic deserter. My prospects indeed seem to be secured.'

And with a vanity which did not escape her, he described the overtures that had been made to him by the editor of a periodical which was to represent 'the new mystical school' – he spoke familiarly of great artists, and especially French ones, murdering the French names in a way that at once hurt the girl's ears, and pleased her secret spite against him – he threw in a critic or two without the Mr – and he casually mentioned a few lords as persons on whom genius and necessity could rely.

All this in a confidential and appealing tone, which he no doubt imagined to be most suitable to women, especially young women. Laura thought it impertinent and unbecoming, and longed to be rid of him. At last the turning to the Friedlands' house appeared. She stood still, and stiffly wished him good-bye.

But he retained her hand and pressed it ardently –

'Oh! Miss Fountain – we have both suffered!'

The girl could harldy pacify herself enough to go in. Again and again she found a pleasure in those words of her French novel that she had repeated to Helbeck long ago: *'Imagination fausse et troublée – fausse et troublée.'*

No delicacy – no modesty – no compunction! Her own poor heart flew to Bannisdale. She thought of all that the Squire had suffered in this man's cause. Outrage – popular hatred – her own protests and petulances: – all met with so unbending a dignity, so inviolable a fidelity, both to his friend and to his church! She recalled that scarred brow – that kind and brotherly affection – that passionate sympathy which had made the heir of one of the most ancient names in England the intimate counsellor and protector of the wheelwright's son.

Popinjay! – renegade! – to come to her talking of 'bigotry' – without a breath of true tenderness or natural remorse. Williams had done that which she had angrily maintained in that bygone debate with Helbeck he had every right to do. And she had nothing but condemnation. She walked up and down the shady road, her eyes blinded with tears. One more blow upon the heart that she herself had smitten so hard! Sympathy for this new pain took her back to every incident of the old – to every detail of that hideous week which had followed upon her flight.

How had she lived through it? Those letters – that distant voice in Dr Friedland's study – her own piteous craving –

For the thousandth time, with the old dreary conviction, she said to herself that she had done right – terribly, incredibly right.

But all the while, she seemed to be sitting beside him in his study – laying her cheek upon his hand – eagerly comforting him for this last sorrow. His inexorable breach with Williams – well! it was part of his character – she would not have it otherwise. All that had angered her as imagination, was now natural and dignified as reality. Her thoughts proudly defended it. Let him be rigorous towards others if he pleased – he had been first king and master of himself.

Next day Molly Friedland and Laura went to London for the day. Laura was taking music-lessons, as one means of driving time a little quicker; and there was shopping to be done both for the household and for themselves.

In the afternoon, as the girls were in Sloane Street together, Laura suddenly asked Molly to meet her in an hour at a friend's house, where they were to have tea. 'I have something I want to do by myself.' Molly asked no questions, and they parted.

A few minutes later, Laura stepped into the church of the Brompton Oratory. It was a Saturday afternoon, and Benediction was about to begin.

She drew down her thick veil, and took a seat near the door. The great heavy church was still nearly dark, save for a dim light in the sanctuary. But it was slowly filling with people, and she watched the congregation.

In front of her was a stout and fashionably dressed young man with an eyeglass and stick – evidently a stranger. He sat stolid and motionless, one knee crossed over the other, scrutinising everything that went on as though he had been at the play. Presently, a great many men began to stream in, most of them bald and grey, but some young fellows, who dropped eagerly on their knees as they entered, and rose reluctantly. Nuns in black hoods and habits would come briskly up, kneel and say a prayer, then go out again. Or sometimes they brought schools – girls, two and two – and ranged them decorously for the service. An elderly man, of the workman class, appeared with his small son, and sat in front of Laura. The child played tricks; the man drew it tenderly within his arm, and kept it quiet, while he himself told his beads. Then a girl with wild eyes and touzled hair, probably Irish, with her baby in her arms, sat down at the end of Laura's seat, stared round her for a few minutes, dropped to the altar, and went away. And all the time smartly dressed ladies came and went incessantly, knelt at side altars, crossed themselves, said a few rapid prayers, or disappeared into the mysteries of side aisles behind screens and barriers – going no doubt to confession.

There was an extraordinary life in it all. Here was no languid acceptance of a respectable habit. Something was eagerly wanted – diligently sought.

Laura looked round her, with a sigh from her inmost heart. But the vast church seemed to her ugly and inhuman. She remembered a saying of her father's as to its 'vicious Roman style' – the 'tomb of the Italian mind.'

What matter?

Ah! – Suddenly a dim surpliced figure in the distance, and lights springing like stars in the apse. Presently the high altar, in a soft glow, shone out upon the dark church. All was still silent; the sanctuary spoke in light.

For a few minutes. Then this exquisite and magical effect broke up. The lighting spread through the church, became commonplace, showed the pompous lines of capital and cornice, the bad sculpture in the niches. A procession entered, and the service began.

Laura dropped on her knees. But she was no longer in London, in the Oratory church. She was far away, in the chapel of an old northern house, where the walls glowed with strange figures, and a dark crucifix hovered austerely above the altar. She saw the small scattered congregation; Father Bowles's grey head and blanched, weak face; Augustina in her long widow's veil; the Squire in his corner. The same words were being said there now, at this same hour. She looked at her watch, then hid her eyes again, tortured with a sick yearning.

But when she came out, twenty minutes later, her step was more alert. For a little while, she had been almost happy.

That night, after the returned travellers had finished their supper, the doctor was in a talking mood. He had an old friend with him, a thinker and historian like himself. Both of them had lately come across 'Leadham of Trinity' – the convert and Jesuit, who was now engaged upon an important Catholic memoir, and was settled for a time within reach of Cambridge libraries.

'You knew Father Leadham in the north, Miss Laura?' asked the doctor, as the girls came into the drawing-room.

Laura started.

'I saw him two or three times,' she said, as she made her way to the warm but dark corner near the fire. 'Is he in Cambridge?'

The doctor nodded.

'Come to embrace us all – breathing benediction on learning and on science! There has been a Catholic Congress somewhere.' – He looked at his friend. 'That will show us the way!'

The friend – a small lively-eyed, black-bearded man, just returned from some theological work in a German university – threw back his head and laughed good-humouredly.

The talk turned on Catholic learning, old and new; on the assumptions and limitations of it; on the forms taken by the most recent Catholic Apologetic; and so, like a vessel descending a great river, passed out at last, steered by Friedland, among the breakers of first principles.

As a rule the doctor talked in paradox and ellipse. He threw his sentences into air, and let them find their feet as they could.

But to-day, unconsciously, his talk took a tone that was rare with him – became prophetical, pontifical – assumed a note of unction. And often, as Molly noticed, with a slight instinctive gesture – a fatherly turning towards that golden spot made by Laura's hair among the shadows.

His friend fell silent after a while – watching Friedland with small sharp eyes. He had come there to discuss a new edition of Sidonius Apollinaris,[22] – was himself one of the driest and acutest of investigators. All this talk for babes seemed to him the merest waste of time.

Friedland, however, with a curious feeling, let himself be carried away by it.

A little Catholic manual of Church history had fallen into his hands that morning. His fingers played with it as it lay on the table; and with the pages of a magazine beside it that contained an article by Father Leadham.

No doubt some common element in the two had roused him. –

'The Catholic war with history,' he said, 'is perennial! History, in fact, is the great rationalist; and the Catholic conscience is scandalised by her. – And so we have these pitiful little books' – he laid his hand on the volume beside him – 'which simply expunge history, or make it afresh. And we have a piece of Jesuit *apologia*, like this paper of Leadham's – so charming, in a sense, so scholarly! And yet one feels through it a cry of the soul – the Catholic arraignment of history, that she is what she is!'

'You'll find it in Newman – often,' said the black-bearded man, suddenly – and he ran through a list of passages, rapidly, in the student's way.

'Ah! Newman!' said Friedland with vivacity. 'This morning I read over that sermon of his he delivered to the Oscott Synod, after the re-establishment of the Hierarchy – you remember it, Dalton? – What a flow and thunder in the sentences! – what an elevation in the thought! – Who would not rather lament with Newman, than exult with Froude?[23] – But here again, it is history that is the rationalist – not we poor historians!

'. . . Why was England lost to the Church? Because Henry was a villain? – because the Tudor bishops were slaves and poltroons? Does Leadham, or any other rational man really think so?'

The little black man nodded. He did not think it worth while to speak.

But Friedland went on enlarging, with his hand on his Molly's head – looking into her quiet eyes.

'. . . The fact is, the Catholic, who is in love with his Church, *cannot* let himself realise truly what the Rome of the Renaissance meant. But turn your back on all the Protestant crew – even on Erasmus.[24] Ask only those Catholic witnesses who were at the fountain-head, who saw the truth face to face. And then – ponder a little, what it was that really happened in those forty-five years of Elizabeth . . .

'Can Leadham, can any one deny that the nation rose in them to the full stature of its manhood – to a buoyant and fruitful maturity? And more – if it had not been for some profound movement of the national life, – some irresistible revolt of the common intelligence, the common conscience – does any one suppose that the whims and violences of any trumpery king could have broken the links with Rome? – that such a life and death as More's could have fallen barren on English hearts? Never! – How shallow are all the official explanations – how deep down lies the truth!'

Out of the monologues that followed, broken often by the impatience or the eagerness of Dalton, Molly at least, who worked much with her father, remembered fragments like the following.

'. . . The figure of the Church, – spouse or captive, bride or martyr – as she has become personified in Catholic imagination, is surely among the greatest, the most ravishing of human conceptions. It ranks with the image of "Jahve's Servant" in the poetry of Israel. And yet behind her, as she moves through history, the modern sees the rising of something more majestic still – the free human spirit, in its contact with the infinite sources of things! – the Jerusalem which is the mother of us all – the Greater, the Diviner Church . . . Into her Ursula-robe all lesser forms are gathered. But she is not only a maternal, a generative power – she is chastisement and convulsion.

'. . . Look back again to that great rising of the North against the South, that we called the Reformation, – Catholicism of course is saved with the rest. – One may almost say that Newman's own type is made possible – all that touches and charms us in English Catholics has its birth, because York, Canterbury and Salisbury are lost to the Mass.

'And abroad? – I always find a sombre fascination in the spectacle of the Tridentine[25] reform. The Church in her stern repentance breaks all her toys, burns all her books! She shakes herself free from Guicciardini's[26] "herd of wretches." She shuts her gates on the knowledge and the freedom that have rent her – and within her strengthened walls she sits, pondering on judgment to come. In so far as her submission is incomplete she is raising new reckonings against herself every hour. – But for the moment the moralising influence of the lay intelligence has saved her – a new strength flows through her old veins.

'. . . And so with scholarship. – The great fabric of Gallican and Benedictine learning rises into being, under the hammer blows of a hostile research. The Catholics of Germany, says Renan,[27] are particularly distinguished for acuteness and breadth of ideas. Why? Because of the "perpetual contact of Protestant criticism." –

'. . . More and more we shall come to see that it is the World that is the salt of the Church! She owes far more to her enemies than to any of her canonised saints. One may almost say that she lives on what the World can spare her of its virtues.'

Laura, in her dark corner, had almost disappeared from sight.

Molly, the soft, round-faced, spectacled Molly, turned now and then from her friend to her father. She would give Friedland sometimes a gentle restraining touch – her lips shaped themselves, as though she said, 'Take care!'

And gradually Friedland fell upon things more intimate – the old topics of the relation between Catholicism and the will, Catholicism and conscience.

'. . . I often think we should be the better for some chair of "The Inner Life," at an English University!' he said presently, with a smile at Molly. – 'What does the ordinary Protestant know of all those treasures of spiritual experience which Catholicism has secreted for centuries? *There* is the debt of debts that we all owe to the Catholic Church.

'Well! – Some day, no doubt, we shall all be able to make a richer use of what she has so abundantly to give. –

'At present what one sees going on in the modern world is a vast transformation of moral ideas, which for the moment holds the field. Beside the older ethical fabric – the fabric that the Church built up out of Greek and Jewish material – a new is rising. We think a hundred things unlawful that a Catholic permits; on the other hand, a hundred prohibitions of the older faith have lost their force. And at the same time, for half our race, the old terrors and eschatologies are no more. We fear evil for quite different reasons; we think of it in quite different ways. And the net result in the best moderns is at once a great elaboration of conscience – and an almost intoxicating sense of freedom. –

'Here, no doubt, it is the *personal abjection* of Catholicism, that jars upon us most – that divides it deepest from the modern spirit. – Molly! – don't frown! – Abjection is a Catholic word – essentially a Catholic temper. It means the ugliest and the loveliest things. It covers the most various types – from the nauseous hysteria of a Margaret Mary Alacoque,[28] – to the exquisite beauty of the *Imitation* . . . And it derives its chief force, for good and evil, from the belief in the Mass. There again, how little the Protestant understands what he reviles! In one sense he understands it well enough. Catholicism would have disappeared long ago but for the Mass. Marvellous indestructible belief! – that brings God to Man, that satisfies the deepest emotions of the human heart! –

'What will the religion of the free mind discover to put in its place? Something, it must find. For the hold of Catholicism – or its analogues – upon the guiding forces of Christendom is irretrievably broken. And yet the needs of the soul remain the same ...

'Some compensation, no doubt, we shall reap from that added sense of power and wealth, which the change in the root-ideas of life has brought with it for many people. Humanity has walked for centuries under the shadow of the Fall, with all that it involves. Now, a precisely opposite conception is slowly incorporating itself with all the forms of European thought. It is the disappearance – the rise – of a world. At the beginning of the century, Coleridge foresaw it.

'... The transformation affects the whole of personality! The mass of men who read and think, and lead straight lives to-day, are often conscious of a dignity and range their fathers never knew. The spiritual stature of civilised man has risen – like his physical stature! We walk to-day a nobler earth. We come – not as outcasts, but as sons and freemen, into the House of God. – But all the secrets and formulae of a new mystical union have to be worked out. And so long as pain and death remain, humanity will always be at heart a mystic!'

Gradually, as the old man touched these more penetrating and personal matters, the head among the shadows had emerged. The beautiful eyes, so full – unconsciously full – of sad and torturing thought, rested upon the speaker. Friedland became sensitively conscious of them. The grey-haired scholar was in truth one of the most religious of men and optimists. The negations of his talk began to trouble him – in sight of this young grief and passion. He drew upon all that his heart could find to say of things fruitful and consoling. After the liberating joys of battle, he must needs follow the perennial human instinct and build anew the 'Civitas Dei.' [29]

When Friedland and his wife were left alone, Friedland said with timidity:

'Jane, I played the preacher to-night, and preaching is foolishness. But I would willingly brace that poor child's mind a little. And it seemed to me she listened.'

Mrs Friedland laughed under her breath – the saddest laugh.

'Do you know what the child was doing this afternoon?'

'No.'

'She went to the Oratory – to Benediction.'

Friedland looked up startled – then understood – raised his hands and let them drop despairingly.

CHAPTER TWO

'Missie – are yo ben?'

The outer door of Browhead Farm was pushed inwards, and old Daffady's head and face appeared.

'Come in, Daffady – please come in!'

Miss Fountain's tone was of the friendliest. The cowman obeyed her. He came in, holding his battered hat in his hand.

'Missie – A thowt I'd tell yo as t' rain had cleared oop – yo cud take a bit air verra weel, if yo felt to wish it.'

Laura turned a pale but smiling face towards him. She had been passing through a week of illness, owing perhaps to the April bleakness of this high fell, and old Daffady was much concerned. They had made friends from the first days of her acquaintance with the farm. And during these April weeks since she had been the guest of her cousins, Daffady had shown her a hundred quaint attentions. The rugged old cowman who now divided with Mrs Mason the management of the farm was half amused, half scandalised by what seemed to him the delicate uselessness of Miss Fountain. 'I'm towd as doon i' Lunnon town, yo'll find scores o' this mak' – he would say to his intimate the old shepherd – 'what th' Awmighty med em for, bets me. Now Miss Polly, she can sarve t' beese' – (by which the old North Countryman meant 'cattle') – 'an mek a hot mash for t' cawves, an cook an milk, an ivery oother soart o' thing as t' Lord give us t' wimmen for – bit Missie! – yo've nobbut to luke ut her 'ands. Nobbut what theer's soomat endearin i' these yoong flibberties – yo conno let em want for owt – bit it's the use of em worrits me abuve a bit.'

Certainly all that old Daffady could do to supply the girl's wants was done. Whether it was a continuous supply of peat for the fire in these chilly April days; or a newspaper from the town; or a bundle of daffodils from the wood below – some signs of a fatherly mind he was always showing towards this little drone in the hive. And Laura delighted in him – racked her brains to keep him talking by the fireside.

'Well, Daffady, I'll take your advice. – I'm hungering to be out

335

again. But come in a bit first. When do you think the mistress will be back?'

Daffady awkwardly established himself just inside the door, looking first to see that his great nailed boots were making no unseemly marks upon the flags.

Laura was alone in the house. Mrs Mason and Polly were gone to Whinthorpe, where they had some small sales to make. Mrs Mason moreover was discontented with the terms under which she sold her milk; and there were inquiries to be made as to another factor, and perhaps a new bargain to be struck.

'Oh, the missus woan't be heäm till dark,' said Daffady. 'She's not yan to do her business i' haäste. She'll see to 't aa hersen. An she's reet there. Them as ladles their wits oot o' other foak's brains gits nobbut middlin sarved.'

'You don't seem to miss Mr Hubert very much?' said Laura, with a laughing look.

Daffady scratched his head.

'Noa – they say he's doin wonnerfu well, deän i' Froswick, an I'm juist glad on't; for he wasna yan for work.'

'Why, Daffady, they say now he's killing himself with work!'

Daffady grinned – a cautious grin.

'They'll deave yo, down i' th' town, wi their noise. – Yo'd think they were warked to deäth. – Bit, yo can see for yorsen. Why, a farmin mon mut be allus agate: in t' morning, what wi' cawves to serve, an t' coos to feed, an t' horses to fodder, yo're fair rūn aff your legs. Bit down i' Whinthorpe – or Froswick ayder, fer it's noa odds – why, theer's nowt stirrin for a yoong mon. If cat's loose, that's aboot what!'

Laura's face lit up. Very few things now had power to please her but Daffady's dialect, and Daffady's scorns.

'And so all the world is idle but you farm-people?'

'A doan't say egsackly idle,' said Daffady, with a good-humoured tolerance.

'But the factory-hands, Daffady?'

'O! – a little stannin an twiddlin!' said Daffady contemptuously – 'I allus ses they pays em abuve a bit.'

'But the miners? – come Daffady!'

'I'm not stannin to it aw roond,' said Daffady patiently – 'I laid it down i' th' general.'

'And all the people, who work with their heads, Daffady, like – like my papa?'

The girl smiled softly, and turned her slim neck to look at the old man. She was charmingly pretty so, among the shadows of the farm-kitchen – but very touching – as the old man dimly felt. The change in her that worked so uncomfortably upon his rustic feelings went far deeper than any mere aspect of health or sickness. The spectator felt beside her a ghostly presence – that 'sad sister, Pain' – stealing her youth away, smile as she might.

'I doan't knaw aboot them, missie – nor aboot yor fadther – thoo I'll uphod tha Muster Stephen was a terr'ble cliver mon. Bit if yo doan't bring a gude yed wi to th' farmin yo may let it alane. – When th' owd meäster here was deein, Mr Hubert was verra downhearted yo understan, an verra wishfa to say soomat frendly to th' owd man, noo it had coom to th' lasst of im. "Fadther" – he ses – "dear fadther – is there nowt I could do fer tha?" – "Aye, lad" – ses th' owd un – "gie me thy yed, an tak mine – thine is gude enoof to be buried wi." An at that he shet his mouth, an deed.'

Daffady told his story with relish. His contempt for Hubert was of many years' standing. Laura lifted her eyebrows.

'That was sharp, for the last word. I don't think you should stick pins when you're dying – *dying!*' – she repeated the word with a passionate energy – 'going quite away – for ever.' Then, with a sudden change of tone – 'Can I have the cart to-morrow, Daffady?'

Daffady, who had been piling the fire with fresh peat, paused and looked down upon her. His long lank face, his weather-stained clothes, his great twisted hand were all of the same colour – the colour of wintry grass and lichened rock. But his eyes were bright and blue, and a vivid streak of white hair fell across his high forehead. As the girl asked her question the old man's air of fatherly concern became more marked.

'Mut you goa, missie? – it did yo noa gude lasst time.'

'Yes, I must go. I think so – I hope so!' – She checked herself. 'But I'll wrap up.'

'Mrs Fountain's nobbut sadly, I unnerstan?'

'She's rather better again. But I must go to-morrow. – Daffady, Cousin Elizabeth won't forget to bring up the letters?'

'I niver knew her du sich a thing as thattens,' said Daffady, with caution.

'And do you happen to know whether Mr Bayley is coming to supper?'

'T' minister'll mebbe coom if t' weather hods up.'

'Daffady – do you think – that when you don't agree with people about religion – it's right and proper to sit every night – and tear them to pieces?'

The colour had suddenly flooded her pale face – her attitude had thrown off languor.

Daffady showed embarrassment.

'Well, noa, missie – Aa doan't hod – mysen – wi personalities. Yo mun wrastle wi t' sin – an gaa saftly by t' sinner.'

'Sin!' she said scornfully.

Daffady was quelled.

'I've allus thowt mysen,' he said hastily, 'as we'd a dëal to larn from Romanists i' soom ways. Noo, their noshun o' Purgatory – I daurna say a word for 't when t' minister's taakin – for there's noa warrant for 't i' Scriptur, as I can mek oot – bit I'll uphod yo, it's juist handy! Aa've often thowt so, i' my aan preachin. – Heaven and hell are verra well for t' foak as are ower good, or ower bad – bit t' moast o' foak – are juist a mish-mash.'

He shook his head slowly; and then ventured a glance at Miss Fountain to see whether he had appeased her.

Laura seemed to rouse herself with an effort from some thoughts of her own.

'Daffady – how the sun's shining! – I'll go out. – Daffady, you're very kind and nice to me – I wonder why?'

She laid one of the hands that seemed to the cowman so absurd, upon his arm, and smiled at him. The old man reddened and grunted. She sprang up with a laugh; and the kitchen was instantly filled by a whirlwind of barks from Fricka, who at last foresaw a walk.

Laura took her way up the fell. She climbed the hill above the farm, and then descended slowly upon a sheltered corner that held the old Browhead Chapel, whereof the fanatical Mr Bayley – worse luck! – was the curate in charge.

She gave a wide berth to the vicarage, which with two or three cottages, embowered in larches and cherry trees, lay immediately below the chapel. She descended upon the chapel from the fell which lay wild about it and above it; she opened a little gate into the tiny churchyard, and found a sunny rock to sit on; while Fricka rushed about barking at the tits and the linnets.

Under the April sun and the light wind, the girl gave a sigh of pleasure. It was a spot she loved. The old chapel stood high on the side of a more inland valley that descended not to the sea, but to the Greet – a green open vale, made glorious at its upper end by the over-peering heads of great mountains, and falling softly through many folds and involutions to the woods of the Greet – the woods of Bannisdale.

So blithe and shining it was, on this April day! The course of the bright twisting stream was dimmed here and there by mists of fruit blossom. For the damson trees were all out, patterning the valleys; marking the bounds of orchard and field, of stream and road. Each with its larch clump, the grey and white farms lay scattered on the pale green of the pastures; on either side of the valley the limestone pushed upward, through the grassy slopes of the fells, and made long edges and 'scars' against the sky; while down by the river hummed the old mill where Laura had danced, a year before.

It was Westmoreland in its remoter, gentler aspect – Westmoreland far away from the dust of coaches and hotels – an untouched pastoral land, enwrought with a charm and sweetness none can know but those who love and linger. Its hues and lines are all sober and very simple. In these outlying fell districts, there is no splendour of colour, no majesty of peak or precipice. The mountain-land is at its homeliest – though still wild and free as the birds that flash about its streams. The purest radiance of cool sunlight floods it on an April day; there are pale subtleties of grey and purple in the rocks, in the shadows, in the distances, on which the eye may feed perpetually; and in the woods and bents a never-ceasing pageantry of flowers.

And what beauty in the little chapel-yard itself! Below it the ground ran down steeply to the village and the river, and at its edge – out of its loose boundary wall – rose a clump of Scotch firs drawn in a grand Italian manner upon the delicacy of the scene beyond. Close to them a huge wild-cherry thrust out its white boughs, not yet in their full splendour, and through their openings the distant blues of fell and sky wavered and shimmered as the wind played with the tree. And all round, among the humble nameless graves, the silkiest, finest grass – grass that gives a kind of quality, as of long and exquisite descent, to thousands of West-moreland fields – grass that is the natural mother of flowers, and the sister of all clear streams. Daffodils grew in it now, though the daffodil hour was waning. A little faded but still lovely, they ran dancing in and out of the graves – up to the walls of the chapel itself – a foam of blossom breaking on the grey rock of the church.

Generations ago, when the fells were roadless and these valleys hardly peopled, the monks of a great priory church on the neighbouring coast built here this little pilgrimage chapel, on the highest point of a long and desolate track connecting the inland towns with the great abbeys of the coast, and with all the western seaboard. Fields had been enclosed and farms had risen about it; but still the little church was one of the loneliest and remotest of fanes. So lonely and remote that the violent hand of Puritanism had almost passed it by, had been content at least with a rough blow or two, defacing, not destroying. Above the moth-eaten table that replaced the ancient altar there still rose a window that breathed the very *secreta* of the old faith – a window of radiant fragments, piercing the twilight of the little church with strange, uncomprehended things – images that linked the humble chapel and its worshippers with the great European story, with Chartres and Amiens, with Toledo and Rome.

For here, under a roof shaken every Sunday by Mr Bayley's thunders, there stood a golden St Anthony, a virginal St Margaret. And all round them, in a ruined confusion, dim sacramental scenes – that flamed into jewels as the light smote them! In one corner a priest raised the Host. His delicate gold-patterned vestments, his tonsured head, and the monstrance in his hands, tormented the curate's eyes every Sunday as he rose from his knees, before the Commandments. And in the very centre of the stone tracery, a woman lifted herself in bed to receive the Holy Oil – so pale, so eager still, after all these centuries! Her white face spoke week by week to the dalesfolk as they sat in their high pews. Many a rough countrywoman, old perhaps, and crushed by toil and child-bearing, had wondered over her, had felt a sister in her, had loved her secretly.

But the children's dreams followed St Anthony rather – the kind, sly old man, with the belled staff, up which his pig was climbing.

Laura haunted the little place.

She could not be made to go when Mr Bayley preached; but on weekdays she would get the key from the schoolmistress, and hang over the old pews, puzzling out the window – or trying to decipher some of the other Popish fragments that the church contained. Sometimes she would sit rigid, in a dream that took all the young roundness from her face. But it was like the Oratory church, and Benediction. It brought her somehow near to Helbeck, and to Bannisdale.

To-day, however, she could not tear herself from the breeze and the sun. She sat among the daffodils, in a sort of sad delight, wondering sometimes at the veil that had dropped between her and beauty – dulling and darkening all things.

Surely Cousin Elizabeth would bring a letter from Augustina? Every day she had been expecting it. This was the beginning of the second week after Easter. All the Easter functions at Bannisdale must now be over; the opening of the new orphanage to boot; and the gathering of Catholic gentry to meet the Bishop – in that dreary, neglected house! Augustina, indeed, knew nothing of these things – except from the reports that might be brought to her by the visitors to her sick room. Bannisdale had now no hostess. Mr Helbeck kept the house as best he could.

Was it not three weeks and more, now, that Laura had been at the farm? And only two visits to Bannisdale! For the Squire, by Augustina's wish, and against the girl's own judgment, knew nothing of her presence in the neighbourhood, and she could only see her stepmother on days when Augustina could be certain that her brother was away. During part of Passion week, all Holy week, and half Easter week, priests had been staying in the house – or the orphanage ceremony had detained the Squire. But by now, surely, he had gone to London on some postponed business. That was what Mrs Fountain expected. The girl hungered for her letter.

Poor Augustina! The heart malady had been developing rapidly. She was very ill, and, Laura thought, unhappy.

And yet, when the first shock of it was over – in spite of the bewilderment and grief she suffered in losing her companion – Mrs Fountain had been quite willing to recognise and accept the situation which had been created by Laura's violent action. She wailed over the countermanded gowns and furnishings; but she was in truth relieved. 'Now we know where we are again,' she had said both to herself and Father Bowles. That strange topsy-turveydom of things was over. She was no more tormented with anxieties; and she moved again with personal ease and comfort about her old home.

Poor Alan of course felt it dreadfully. And Laura could not come to Bannisdale for a long, long time. But Mrs Fountain could go to her – several times a year. And the Sisters were very good, and chatty. Oh no, it was best – much best!

But now – whether it came from physical weakening or no – Mrs Fountain was always miserable, always complaining. She spoke of her brother perpetually. Yet when he was with her she thought him hard and cold. It was evident to Laura that she feared him; that she was never at ease with him. Merely to speak of those increased austerities of his, which had marked the Lent of this year, troubled and frightened her.

Often, too, she would lie and look at Laura with an expression of dry bitterness and resentment without speaking. It was as though she were equally angry with the passion which had changed her brother – and with Laura's strength in breaking from it.

Laura moved her seat a little. Between the wild cherry and the firs was a patch of deep blue distance. Those were his woods. But the house was hidden by the hills.

'Somehow I have got to live!' she said to herself suddenly, with a violent trembling.

But how? For she bore two griefs. The grief for him, of which she never let a word pass her lips, was perhaps the strongest among the forces that were destroying her. She knew well that she had torn the heart that loved her – that she had set free a hundred dark and morbid forces in Helbeck's life.

But it was because she had realised, by the insight of a moment, the madness of what they had done, the gulf to which they were rushing – because, at one and the same instant, there had been revealed to her the fatality under which she must still resist, and he must become gradually, inevitably, her persecutor, and her tyrant!

Amid the emotion, the overwhelming impressions of his story of himself, that conviction had risen in her inmost being – a strange inexorable voice of judgment – bidding her go! In a flash, she had seen the wretched future years – the daily struggle – the aspect of violence, even of horror, that his pursuit of her, his pressure upon her will, might assume – the sharpening of all those wild forces in her own nature.

She was broken with the anguish of separation – and how she had been able to do what she had done, she did not know. But the inner voice persisted – that for the first time, amid the selfish, or passionate, or joy-seeking impulses of her youth, she had obeyed a higher law. The moral realities of the whole case closed her in. She saw no way out – no way in which, so far as her last act was concerned, she could have bettered or changed the deed. She had done it for him, first of all. He must be delivered from her. And she must have room to breathe, without making of her struggle for liberty a hideous struggle with him, and with love.

Well, but – comfort! – where was it to be had? The girl's sensuous craving nature fought like a tortured thing in the grasp laid upon it. How was it possible to go on suffering like this? She turned impatiently to one thought after another.

Beauty? Nature? Last year, yes! But now! That past physical ecstasy – in spring – in flowing water – in flowers – in light and colour – where was it gone? Let these tears – these helpless tears – make answer!

Music? – books? – the books that 'make incomparable old maids' – friends? The thought of the Friedlands made her realise that she could still love. But after all – how little! – against how much!

Religion? All religion need not be as Alan Helbeck's. There was religion as the Friedlands understood it – a faith convinced of God, and of a meaning for human life, trusting the 'larger hope' that springs out of the daily struggle of conscience, and the garnered experience of feeling. Both in Friedland and his wife, there breathed a true spiritual dignity and peace.

But Laura was not affected by this fact in the least. She put away the suggestions of it with impatience. Her father had not been so. Now that she had lost her lover, she clung the more fiercely to her father. And there had been no anodynes for him.

. . . Oh if the sun – the useless sun – would only go – and Cousin Elizabeth would come back – and bring that letter! Yes, one little pale joy there was still – for a few weeks or months. The craving for the bare rooms of Bannisdale possessed her – for that shadow-happiness of entering his house as he quitted it – walking its old boards unknown to him – touching the cushions and chairs in Augustina's room that he would touch, perhaps that very same night, or on the morrow!

Till Augustina's death. – Then both for Laura and for Helbeck – an Unknown – before which the girl shut her eyes.

There was company that night in the farm kitchen. Mr Bayley, the more than evangelical curate, came to tea.

He was a little man, with a small sharp anæmic face buried in red hair. It was two or three years of mission work, first in Mexico, and then at Lima as the envoy of one of the most thoroughgoing of Protestant societies, that had given him his strangely vivid notions of the place of Romanism among the world's forces. At no moment in this experience can he have had a grain of personal success. Lima, apparently, is of all towns in the universe, the town where the beard of Protestantism is least worth the shaving – to quote a northern proverb. At any rate, Mr Bayley returned to his native land at fifty, with a permanent twist of brain. Hence these preposterous sermons in the fell chapel; this eager nosing out and tracking down of every scent of Popery; this fanatical satisfaction in such a kindred soul as that of Elizabeth Mason. Some mild ritualism at Whinthorpe had given him occupation for years; and as for Bannisdale, he and the Masons between them had raised the most causeless of storms about Mr Helbeck and his doings, from the beginning; they had kept up for years the most rancorous memory of the Williams affair; they had made the owner of the old Hall the bogey of a country-side.

Laura knew it well. She never spoke to the little red man if she could help it. What pleased her was to make Daffady talk of him – Daffady, whose contempt as a 'Methody' for 'paid priests' made him a sure ally.

'Why, he taaks i' church as thoo God Awmighty were on the pulpit stairs – gi-en him his worrds!' said the cowman, with the natural distaste of all preachers for diatribes not their own; and Laura, when she wandered the fields with him, would drive him on to say more and worse.

Mr Bayley, on the other hand, had found a new pleasure in his visits to the farm since Miss Fountain's arrival. The young lady had escaped indeed from the evil thing – so as by fire. But she was far too pale and thin; she showed too many regrets. Moreover she was not willing to talk of Mr Helbeck with his enemies. Indeed, she turned her back rigorously on any attempt to make her do so.

So all that was left to the two cronies was to sit night after night, talking to each other in the hot hope that Miss Fountain might be reached thereby and strengthened – that even Mrs Fountain and that distant black brood of Bannisdale might in some indirect way be brought within the saving power of the Gospel.

Strange fragments of this talk floated through the kitchen. –
'Oh, my dear friend! – forbidding to marry is a doctrine of *devils*!
– Now Lima, as I have often told you, is a city of convents –'

There was a sudden grinding of chairs on the flagged floor. The
grey head and the red approached each other; the nightly shudder
began; while the girls chattered and coughed as loudly as they
dared.

'No – A woan't – A conno believe 't!' Mrs Mason would say at
last, throwing herself back against her chair with very red cheeks.
And Daffady would look round furtively, trying to hear.

But sometimes the curate would try to propitiate the young ladies.
He made himself gentle; he raised the most delicate difficulties. He
had, for instance, a very strange compassion for the Saints. 'I hold
it,' he said – with an eye on Miss Fountain – 'to be clearly de-
monstrable that the Invocation of Saints is, of all things, most
lamentably injurious to the Saints themselves!'

'Hoo can he knaw?' said Polly to Laura, – open-mouthed.

But Mrs Mason frowned.

'A doan't hod wi Saints whativer,' she said violently. 'So A
doan't fash mysel aboot em!'

Daffady sometimes would be drawn into these diversions, as he
sat smoking on the settle. And then out of a natural slyness –
perhaps on these latter occasions, from a secret sympathy for 'missie'
– he would often devote himself to proving the solidarity of all
'church priests,' Establishments, and prelatical Christians generally.
Father Bowles might be in a 'parlish' state; but as to all supporters
of bishops and the heathenish custom of fixed prayers – whether
they wore black gowns or no – 'a man mut hae his doots.'

Never had Daffady been so successful with his shafts as on this
particular evening. Mrs Mason grew redder and redder; her large
face alternately flamed and darkened in the firelight. In the middle
the girls tried to escape into the parlour. But she shouted imperiously
after them.

'Polly – Laura – what art tha aboot? Coom back at yance. I'll
not ha sickly foak sittin wi'oot a fire!'

They came back sheepishly. And when they were once more
settled as audience, the mistress – who was by this time fanning
herself tempestuously with the Whinthorpe paper – launched her
last word –

'Daffady – thoo's naa call to lay doon t' law, on sic matters at

345

aw. Mappen tha'll recolleck t' Bible – head-strong as tha art i' thy aan conceit. Bit t' Bible says "How can he get wisdom that holdeth the plough – whose taak is o' bullocks?" Aa coom on that yestherday – an A've bin sair exercised aboot thy preachin ever sen!'

Daffady held his peace.

The clergyman departed, and Daffady went out to the cattle. Laura had not given the red-haired man her hand. She had found it necessary to carry her work upstairs, at the precise moment of his departure. But when he was safely off the premises she came down again to say good-night to her cousins.

Oh! they had not been unkind to her these last weeks. Far from it. Mrs Mason had felt a fierce triumph – she knew – in her broken engagement. Probably at first Cousin Elizabeth had only acquiesced in Hubert's demand that Miss Fountain should be asked to stay at the farm, out of an ugly wish to see the girl's discomfiture for herself. And she had not been able to forego the joy of bullying Mr Helbeck's late betrothed through Mr Bayley's mouth.

Nevertheless, when this dwindled ghostly Laura appeared, and began to flit through the low-ceiled rooms and dark passages of the farm – carefully avoiding any talk about herself or her story – always cheerful, self-possessed, elusive – the elder woman began after a little to have strange stirrings of soul towards her. The girl's invincible silence, taken with those physical signs of a consuming pain, that were beyond her concealment, worked upon a nature that, as far as all personal life and emotion were concerned, was no less strong and silent. Polly saw with astonishment that fires were lit in the parlour at odd times – that Laura might read or practise. She was amazed to watch her mother put out some little delicacy at tea or supper that Laura might be made to eat.

And yet! – after all these amenities, Mr Bayley would still be asked to supper, and Laura would still be pelted and harried from supper-time till bed.

To-night, when Laura returned, Mrs Mason was in a muttering and stormy mood. Daffady had angered her sorely. Laura, moreover, had a letter from Bannisdale, and since it came there had been passing lights in Miss Fountain's eyes, and passing reds on her pale cheeks.

As the girl approached her cousin, Mrs Mason turned upon her abruptly.

'Dostha want the cart to-morrow? Daffady said soomat aboot it.'

'If it could be spared.'

Mrs Mason looked at her fixedly.

'If Aa was thoo,' she said, 'Aa'd not flütter ony more roond *that* can'le!'

Laura shrank as though her cousin had struck her. But she controlled herself.

'Do you forget my stepmother's state, Cousin Elizabeth?'

'O! – yo con aw mak much o' what suits tha!' cried the mistress, as she walked fiercely to the outer door and locked it noisily from the great key-bunch hanging at her girdle.

The girl's eyes showed a look of flame. Then her head seemed to swim. She put her hand to her brow, and walked weakly across the kitchen to the door of the stairs.

'Mother!' cried Polly in indignation; and she sprang after Laura. But Laura waved her back imperiously, and almost immediately they heard her door shut upstairs.

An hour later, Laura was lying sleepless in her bed. It was a clear cold night – a spring frost after the rain. The moon shone through the white blind, on the old four-poster, on Laura's golden hair spread on the pillow, on the great meal-ark which barred the chimney, on the rude walls and woodwork of the room.

Her arms were thrown behind her head, supporting it. Nothing moved in the house, or the room – the only sound was the rustling of a mouse in one corner.

A door opened on a sudden. There was a step in the passage, and some one knocked at her door.

'Come in.'

On the threshold stood Mrs Mason in a cotton bed-gown and petticoat, her grey locks in confusion about her massive face and piercing eyes.

She closed the door, and came to the bedside.

'Laura! – Aa've coom to ast thy pardon!'

Laura raised herself on one arm, and looked at the apparition with amazement.

'Mebbe A've doon wrang. – We shouldna quench the smoakin flax. Soa theer's my han, child – if thoo can teäk it.'

The old woman held out her hand. There was an indescribable sound in her voice, as of deep waters welling up.

Laura fell back on her pillows – the whitest, fragilest creature – under the shadows of the old bed. She opened her delicate arms. 'Suppose you kiss me, Cousin Elizabeth!'

The elder woman stooped clumsily. The girl linked her arms round her neck and kissed her warmly, repeatedly, feeling through all her motherless sense the satisfaction of a long hunger in the contact of the old face and ample bosom.

The reserve of both forbade anything more. Mrs Mason tucked in the small figure – lingered a little – said 'Laura, th'art not coald – nor sick?' – and when Laura answered cheerfully, the mistress went.

The girl's eyes were wet for a while; her heart beat fast. There had been few affections in her short life – far too few. Her nature gave itself with a fatal prodigality, or not at all. And now – what was there left to give?

But she slept more peacefully for Mrs Mason's visit – with Augustina's letter of summons under her hand.

The day was still young when Laura reached Bannisdale.

Never had the house looked so desolate. Dust lay on the oaken boards and tables of the hall. There was no fire on the great hearth, and the blinds in the oriel windows were still mostly drawn. But the remains of yesterday's fire were visible yet, and a dirty duster and pan adorned the Squire's chair.

The Irishwoman with a half-crippled husband, who had replaced Mrs Denton, was clearly incompetent. Mrs Denton at least had been orderly and clean. The girl's heart smote her with a fresh pang as she made her way upstairs.

She found Augustina no worse; and in her room there was always comfort, and even brightness. She had a good nurse; a Catholic 'sister' from London, of a kind and cheerful type, that Laura herself could not dislike; and whatever working power there was in the household was concentrated on her service.

Miss Fountain took off her things, and settled in for the day. Augustina chattered incessantly, except when her weakness threw her into long dozes, mingled often, Laura thought, with slight wandering. Her wish evidently was to be always talking of her brother; but in this she checked herself whenever she could, as though controlled by some resolution of her own, or some advice from another.

Yet in the end she said a great deal about him. She spoke of the last weeks of Lent, of the priests who had been staying in the house; of the kindness that had been shown her. That wonderful network of spiritual care and attentions – like a special system of courtesy having its own rules and etiquette – with which Catholicism surrounds the dying, had been drawn about the poor little widow. During the last few weeks Mass had been said several times in her room; Father Leadham had given her Communion every day in Easter Week; on Easter Sunday the children from the orphanage had come to sing to her; that Roman palm over the bed was brought her by Alan himself. The statuette of St Joseph, too, was his gift.

So she lay and talked through the day, cheerfully enough. She did not want to hear of Cambridge or the Friedlands, still less of the farm. Her whole interest now was centred in her own state; and in the Catholic joys and duties which it still permitted. She never spoke of her husband; Laura bitterly noted it.

But there were moments when she watched her stepdaughter, and once when the Sister had left them, she laid her hand on Laura's arm and whispered:

'Oh! Laura – he has grown so much greyer – since – since October.'

The girl said nothing. Augustina closed her eyes, and said with much twisting and agitation, 'When – when I am gone, he will go to the Jesuits – I know he will. The place will come to our cousin, Richard Helbeck. He has plenty of money – it will be very different some day.'

'Did – did Father Leadham tell you that?' said Laura, after a while.

'Yes. He admitted it. He said they had twice dissuaded him in former years. But now – when I'm gone – it'll be allowed.'

Suddenly Augustina opened her eyes. 'Laura! where are you?' Her little crooked face worked with tears. 'I'm glad! – We ought all to be glad. I don't – I don't believe he ever has a happy moment!'

She began to weep piteously. Laura tried to console her, putting her cheek to hers, with inarticulate soothing words. But Augustina turned away from her – almost in irritation.

The girl's heart was wrung at every turn. She lingered, however, till the last minute – almost till the April dark had fallen.

When she reached the hall again, she stood a moment looking round its cold and gloom. First, with a start, she noticed a pile of torn envelopes and papers lying on a table, which had escaped her in the morning. The Squire must have thrown them down there in the early morning, just before starting on his journey. The small fact gave her a throb of strange joy – brought back the living presence. Then she noticed that the study door was open.

A temptation seized her – drove her before it. Silence and solitude possessed the house. The servants were far away in the long rambling basement. Augustina was asleep with her nurse beside her.

Laura went noiselessly across the hall. She pushed the door – she looked round his room.

No change. The books, the crucifix, the pictures, all as before. But the old walls, and wainscots, the air of the room, seemed still to hold the winter. They struck chill.

The same pile of books in daily use upon his table – a few little manuals and reprints – 'The Spiritual Combat,' the 'Imitation,' some sermons – the volume of 'Acta Sanctorum' for the month.

She could not tear herself from them. Trembling, she hung over them, and her fingers blindly opened a little book which lay on the top. It fell apart at a place which had been marked – freshly marked, it seemed to her. A few lines had been scored in pencil, with a date beside them. She looked closer, and read the date of the foregoing Easter Eve. And the passage with its scored lines ran thus:

'Drive far from us the crowd of evil spirits who strive to approach us; unloose the too firm hold of earthly things; *untie with Thy gentle and wounded hands the fibres of our hearts that cling so fast round human affections;* let our weary head rest on Thy bosom till the struggle is over, and our cold form falls back – dust and ashes.'

She stood a moment – looking down upon the book – feeling life one throb of anguish. Then wildly she stooped and kissed the pages. Dropping on her knees too, she kissed the arm of the chair, the place where his hand would rest.

No one came – the solitude held. Gradually she got the better of her misery. She rose, replaced the book, and went.

The following night, very late, Laura again lay sleepless. But April was blowing and plashing outside. The high fell and the lonely farm seemed to lie in the very track of the storms, as they rushed from the south-west across the open moss to beat themselves upon the mountains.

But the moon shone sometimes, and then the girl's restlessness would remind her of the open fell-side, of pale lights upon the distant sea, of cool blasts whirling among the old thorns and junipers, and she would long to be up and away – escaped from this prison where she could not sleep.

How the wind could drop at times – to what an utter and treacherous silence! And what strange, misleading sounds the silence brought with it!

She sat up in bed. Surely some one had opened the further gate – the gate from the lane? But the wind surged in again, and she had to strain her ears. Nothing. – Yes! – wheels, and hoofs! A carriage of some sort approaching.

A sudden thought came to her. The dogcart – it seemed to be such by the sound – drew up at the farm door, and a man descended. She heard the reins thrown over the horse's back, then the groping for the knocker, and at last blows loud and clear, startling the night.

Mrs Mason's window was thrown open next, and her voice came out imperiously – 'What is't?'

Laura's life seemed to hang on the answer.

'Will you please tell Miss Fountain that her stepmother is in great danger, and asks her to come at once.'

She leapt from her bed, but must needs wait – turned again to stone – for the next word. It came after a pause.

'And wha's the message from?'

'Kindly tell her that Mr Helbeck is here with the dogcart.'

The window closed. Laura slipped into her clothes, and by the time Mrs Mason emerged the girl was already in the passage.

'I heard,' she said briefly. 'Let us go down.'

Mrs Mason, pale and frowning, led the way. She undid the heavy bars and lock, and for the first time in her life stood confronted – on her own threshold – with the Papist Squire of Bannisdale.

Mr Helbeck greeted her ceremoniously. But his black eyes, so deep-set and cavernous in his strong-boned face, did not seem to notice her. They ran past her to that small shadow in the background.

'Are you ready?' he said, addressing the shadow.

'One moment, please,' said Laura. She was tying a thick veil round her hat, and struggling with the fastenings of her cloak.

Mrs Mason looked from one to another like a baffled lioness. But to let them go without a word was beyond her. She turned to the Squire.

'Mister Helbeck! – yo'll tell me on your conscience – as it's reet and just – afther aw that's passt – 'at this yoong woman should go wi yo?'

Laura shivered with rage and shame. Her fingers hastened. Mr Helbeck showed no emotion whatever.

'Mrs Fountain is dying,' he said briefly; and again his eye – anxious, imperious – sought for the girl. She came hastily forward from the shadows of the kitchen.

Mr Helbeck mounted the cart, and held out his hand to her.

'Have you got a shawl? – The wind is very keen!' He spoke with the careful courtesy one uses to a stranger.

'Thank you. – I am all right. Please let us go! Cousin Elizabeth!' – Laura threw herself backwards a moment, as the cart began to move, and kissed her hand.

Mrs Mason made no sign. She watched the cart, slowly picking its way over the rough ground of the farmyard, till it turned the corner of the big barn and disappeared in the gusty darkness.

Then she turned housewards. She put down her guttering candle on the great oak table of the kitchen, and sank herself upon the settle.

'Soa – that's him!' – she said to herself; and her peasant mind in a dull heat, like that of the peat fire beside her, went wandering back over the hatreds of twenty years.

CHAPTER THREE

As the dogcart reached the turning of the lane, Mr Helbeck said to his companion –

'Would you kindly take the cart through? I must shut the gate.'

He jumped down. Laura with some difficulty – for the high wind coming from the fell increased her general confusion of brain – passed the gate, and took the pony safely down a rocky piece of road beyond.

His first act in rejoining her was to wrap the rugs which he had brought more closely round her.

'I had no idea in coming,' he said – 'that the wind was so keen. Now we face it.'

He spoke precisely in the same voice that he might have used, say, to Polly Mason had she been confided to him for a night journey. But as he arranged the rug, his hand for an instant had brushed Laura's; and when she gave him the reins, she leant back hardly able to breathe.

With a passionate effort of will, she summoned a composure to match his own.

'When did the change come?' she asked him.

'About eight o'clock. Then it was she told me you were here. We thought at first of sending over a messenger in the morning. But finally my sister begged me to come at once.'

'Is there immediate danger?' The girlish voice must needs tremble.

'I trust we shall still find her,' he said gently – 'but her nurses were greatly alarmed.'

'And was there – much suffering?'

She pressed her hands together under the coverings that sheltered them, in a quick anguish. Oh! had she thought enough, cared enough, for Augustina!

As she spoke the horse gave a sudden swerve, as though Mr Helbeck had pulled the rein involuntarily. They bumped over a large stone, and the Squire hastily excused himself for bad driving. Then he answered her question. As far as he or the Sister could judge there was little active suffering. But the weakness had

353

increased rapidly that afternoon, and the breathing was much harassed.

He went on to describe exactly how he had left the poor patient, giving the details with a careful minuteness. At the same moment that he had started for Miss Fountain, old Wilson had gone to Whinthorpe for the doctor. The Reverend Mother was there; and the nurses – kind and efficient women – were doing all that could be done.

He spoke in a voice that seemed to have no colour or emphasis. One who did not know him might have thought he gave his report entirely without emotion – that his sister's coming death did not affect him.

Laura longed to ask whether Father Bowles was there, whether the last Sacraments had been given. But she did not dare. That question seemed to belong to a world that was for ever sealed between them. And he volunteered nothing.

They entered on a steep descent to the main road. The wind came in fierce gusts – so that Laura had to hold her hat on with both hands. The carriage lamps wavered wildly on the great junipers and hollies, the clumps of blossoming gorse, that sprinkled the mountain; sometimes, in a pause of the wind there would be a roar of water, or a rush of startled sheep. Tumult had taken possession of the fells no less than of the girl's heart.

Once she was thrown against the Squire's shoulder, and murmured a hurried 'I beg your pardon.' And at the same moment an image of their parting on the stairs at Bannisdale rose on the dark. She saw his tall head bending – herself kissing the breast of his coat.

At last they came out above the great prospect of moss and mountain. There was just moon enough to see it by; though night and storm held the vast open cup, across which the clouds came racing – beating up from the coast and the south-west. Ghostly light touched the river courses here and there, and showed the distant portal of the sea. Through the cloud and wind and darkness breathed a great Nature-voice, a voice of power and infinite freedom. Laura suddenly, in a dim passionate way, thought of the words 'to cease upon the midnight with no pain.' [30] If life could just cease here, in the wild dark, while, for the last time in their lives, they were once more alone together! – while in this little cart, on this lonely road, she was still his charge and care – dependent on his man's strength, delivered over to him, and him only – out of all the world –

When they reached the lower road the pony quickened his pace, and the wind was less boisterous. The silence between them, which had been natural enough in the high and deafening blasts of the fell, began to be itself a speech. The Squire broke it.

'I am glad to hear that your cousin is doing so well at Froswick,' he said, with formal courtesy.

Laura made a fitting reply, and they talked a little of the chances of business, and the growth of Froswick. Then the silence closed again.

Presently, as the road passed between stone walls with a grass strip on either side, two dark forms shot up in front of them. The pony shied violently. Had they been still travelling on the edge of the steep grass slope which had stretched below them for a mile or so after their exit from the lane, they must have upset. As it was, Laura was pitched against the railing of the dogcart, and as she instinctively grasped it to save herself, her wrist was painfully twisted.

'You are hurt!' said Helbeck, pulling up the pony.

The first cry of pain had been beyond her control. But she would have died rather than permit another.

'It is nothing,' she said – 'really nothing! What was the matter?'

'A mare and her foal, as far as I can see,' said Helbeck, looking behind him; 'how careless of the farm-people!' he added angrily.

'Oh! they must have strayed,' said Laura faintly. All her will was struggling with this swimming brain – it should not overpower her.

The tinkling of a small burn could be heard beside the road. Helbeck jumped down. 'Don't be afraid – the pony is really quite quiet – he'll stand.'

In a second or two he was back – and just in time. Laura knew well the touch of the little horn cup he put into her cold hands. Many and many a time, in the scrambles of their summer walks, had he revived her from it.

She drank eagerly. When he mounted the carriage again some strange instinct told her that he was not the same. She divined – she was sure of an agitation in him which at once calmed her own.

She quickly assured him that she was much better, that the pain was fast subsiding. Then she begged him to hurry on. She even forced herself to smile and talk.

'It was very ghostly, wasn't it? Daffady, our old cowman, will never believe they were real horses. He has a story of a bogle[31] in this road – a horse bogle, too – that makes one creep.'

'Oh! I know that story,' said Helbeck. 'It used to be told of several roads about here. Old Wilson once said to me, "when aa wor yoong, ivery field an ivery lane wor fu o' bogles!" It is strange how the old tales have died out, while a bran new one, like our own ghost story, has grown up.'

Laura murmured a 'Yes.' Had he forgotten who was once the ghost?

Silence fell again, a silence in which each heart could almost hear the other beat. Oh! how wicked – wicked – would she be if she had come meddling with his life again of her own free will!

Here at last was the bridge, and the Bannisdale gate. Laura shut her eyes, and reckoned up the minutes that remained. Then, as they sped up the park, she wrestled indignantly with herself. She was outraged by her own callousness towards this death in front of her. 'Oh! let me think of her! – let me be good to her!' she cried, in dumb appeal to some power beyond herself. She recalled her father. She tried with all her young strength to forget the man beside her – and those piteous facts that lay between them.

In Augustina's room – darkness – except for one shaded light. The doors were all open, that the poor tormented lungs might breathe.

Laura went in softly, the Squire following. A nurse rose.

'She has rallied wonderfully,' she said in a cheerful whisper, as she approached them, finger on lip.

'Laura!' said a sighing voice.

It came from a deep old-fashioned chair, in which sat Mrs Fountain, propped by many pillows.

Laura went up to her, and dropping on a stool beside her, the girl tenderly caressed the wasted hand that had itself no strength to move towards her.

In the few hours since Laura had last seen her, a great change had passed over Mrs Fountain. Her little face, usually so red, had blanched to parchment white, and the nervous twitching of the head, in the general failure of strength, had almost ceased. She lay stilled and refined under the touch of death; and the sweetness of her blue eyes had grown more conscious and more noble.

'Laura – I'm a little better. But you mustn't go again. Alan – she must stay!'

She tried to turn her head to him, appealing. The Squire came forward.

'Everything is ready for Miss Fountain, dear – if she will be good enough to stay. Nurse will provide – and we will send over for any luggage in the morning.'

At those words 'Miss Fountain,' a slight movement passed over the sister's face.

'Laura!' she said feebly.

'Yes, Augustina – I will stay. I won't leave you again.'

'Your father did wish it, didn't he?'

The mention of her father so startled Laura that the tears rushed to her eyes, and she dropped her face for a moment on Mrs Fountain's hand. When she lifted it she was no longer conscious that Helbeck stood behind his sister's chair, looking down upon them both.

'Yes – always, dear. Do you remember what a good nurse he was? – so much better than I?'

Her face shone through the tears that bedewed it. Already the emotion of her drive – the last battles with the wind – had for the moment restored the brilliancy of eye and cheek. Even Augustina's dim sight was held by her, and by the tumbled gold of her hair as it caught the candle-light.

But the name which had given Laura a thrill of joy had roused a disturbed and troubled echo in Mrs Fountain.

She looked miserably at her brother, and asked for her beads. He put them across her hand, and then, bending over her chair, he said a 'Hail Mary' and an 'Our Father,' in which she faintly joined.

'And Alan – will Father Leadham come to-morrow?'

'Without fail.'

A little later Laura was in her old room with Sister Rosa. The doctor had paid his visit. But for the moment the collapse of the afternoon had been arrested; Mrs Fountain was in no urgent danger.

'Now then,' said the nurse cheerily, when Miss Fountain had been supplied with all necessaries for sleep, 'let us look at that arm, please.'

Laura turned in surprise.

'Mr Helbeck tells me you wrenched your wrist on the drive. He thought you would perhaps allow me to treat it.'

Laura submitted. It was indeed nearly helpless and much swollen, though she had been hardly conscious of it since the little accident happened. The brisk, black-eyed Sister had soon put a comforting bandage round it, chattering all the time of Mrs Fountain and the ups and downs of the illness.

'She missed you very much after you went yesterday. But now, I suppose, you will stay? It won't be long, poor lady!'

The Sister gave a little professional sigh, and Laura, of course, repeated that she must certainly stay. As the Sister broke off the cotton with which she had been stitching the bandage, she stole a curious glance at her patient. She had not frequented the orphanage in her off-time for nothing; and she was perfectly aware of the anxiety with which the Catholic friends of Bannisdale must needs view the re-entry of Miss Fountain. Sister Rosa, who spoke French readily, wondered whether it had not been after all 'reculer pour mieux sauter.'

After a first restless sleep of sheer fatigue, Laura found herself sitting up in bed struggling with a sense of horrible desolation. Augustina was dead – Mr Helbeck was gone, was a Jesuit – and she herself was left alone in the old house, weeping – with no one, not a living soul, to hear. That was the impression; and it was long before she could disentangle truth from nightmare.

When she lay down again, sleep was banished. She lit a candle and waited for the dawn. There in the flickering light were the old tapestries – the princess stepping into her boat, Diana ranging through the wood. Nothing was changed in the room or its furniture. But the Laura who had fretted or dreamed there; who had written her first letter to Molly Friedland from that table; who had dressed for her lover's eye before that rickety glass; who had been angry or sullen, or madly happy there – why, the Laura who now for the second time watched the spring dawn through that diamond-paned window looked back upon her as the figures in Rossetti's strange picture meet the ghosts of their old selves – with the same sense of immeasurable, irrevocable distance. What childish follies and impertinences! – what misunderstanding of others, and misreckoning of the things that most concerned her – what blind drifting – what inevitable shipwreck!

Ah! this aching of the whole being, physical and moral, – again she asked herself, only with a wilder impatience, how long it could be borne.

The wind had fallen, but in the pause of the dawn the river spoke with the hills. The light mounted quickly. Soon the first glint of sun came through the curtains. Laura extinguished her candle, and went to let in the day. As on that first morning, she stood in the window, following with her eye the foaming curves of the Greet, or the last streaks of snow upon the hills, or the daffodil stars in the grass.

Hush! – what time was it? She ran for her watch. Nearly seven.

She wrapped a shawl about her, and went back to her post, straining to see the path on the further side of the river through the mists that still hung about it. Suddenly her head dropped upon her hands. One sob forced its way. Helbeck had passed.

For some three weeks, after this April night, the old house of Bannisdale was the scene of one of those dramas of life and death which depend, not upon external incident, but upon the inner realities of the heart, its inextinguishable affections, hopes, and agonies.

Helbeck and Laura were once more during this time brought into close and intimate contact by the claims of a common humanity. They were united by the common effort to soften the last journey for Augustina, by all the little tendernesses and cares that a sick room imposes, by the pities and charities, the small renascent hopes and fears of each successive day and night.

But all the while, how deeply were they divided! – how sharp was the clash between the reviving strength of passion, which could not but feed itself on the daily sight and contact of the beloved person, and those facts of character and individuality which held them separated! – facts which are always, and in all cases, the true facts of this world.

In Helbeck the shock of Laura's October flight had worked with profound and transforming power. After those first desperate days in which he had merely sought to recover her, to break down her determination, or to understand if he could the grounds on which she had acted, a new conception of his own life and the meaning of it had taken possession of him. He fell into the profoundest humiliation and self-abasement, denouncing himself as a traitor to his faith, who out of mere self-delusion, and a lawless love of ease, had endangered his own obedience, and neglected the plain task laid upon him. That fear of proselytism, that humble dread of his own influence, which had once determined his whole attitude towards those about him, began now to seem to him mere wretched cowardice and self-will – the caprice of the servant who tries to better his master's instructions.

> But now I cast that finer sense
> And sorer shame aside;
> Such dread of sin was indolence,
> Such aim at heaven was pride.[32]

Again and again he said to himself that if he had struck at once for the Church and for the Faith at the moment when Laura's young heart was first opened to him, when under the earliest influences of her love for him – how could he doubt that she had loved him! – her nature was still plastic, still capable of being won to God, as it were, by a *coup de main* – might not – would not – all have been well? But no! – he must needs believe that God had given her to him for ever, that there was room for all the gradual softening, the imperceptible approaches by which he had hoped to win her. It had seemed to him the process could not be too gentle, too indulgent. And meanwhile the will and mind that might have been captured at a rush had time to harden – the forces of revolt to gather.

What wonder? Oh! blind – infatuate! How could he have hoped to bring her, still untouched, within the circle of his Catholic life, into contact with its secrets and its renunciations, without recoil on her part, without risk of what had actually happened? The strict regulation of every hour, every habit, every thought, at which he aimed as a Catholic – what *could* it seem to her but a dreary and forbidding tyranny? – to her who had no clue to it, who was still left free, though she loved him, to judge his faith coldly from outside? And when at last he had begun to drop hesitation, to change his tone – then, it was too late!

Tyranny! She had used that word once or twice, in that first letter which had reached him on the evening of her flight, and in a subsequent one. Not of any thing that had been, apparently – but of that which might be. It had wounded him to the very quick.

And yet, in truth, the course of his present thoughts – plainly interpreted – meant little else than this – that if, at the right moment, he had coerced her with success, they might both have been happy.

Later on he had seen his own self-judgment reflected in the faces, the consolations of his few intimate friends. Father Leadham, for instance – whose letters had been his chief support during a period of dumb agony when he had felt himself more than once on the brink of some morbid trouble of brain.

'I found her adamant,' said Father Leadham. 'Never was I so powerless with any human soul. She would not discuss anything. She would only say that she was born in freedom – and free she would remain. All that I urged upon her implied beliefs in which she had not been brought up, which were not her father's and were not hers. Nor on closer experience had she been any more drawn to them – quite the contrary; whatever – and there, poor child! her eyes filled with tears – whatever she might feel towards those who held them. She said fiercely that you had never argued with her or persuaded her – or perhaps only once; that you had promised – this with an indignant look at me – that there should be no pressure upon her. And I could but feel sadly, dear friend, that you only, under our Blessed Lord, could have influenced her; and that you, by some deplorable mistake of judgment, had been led to feel that it was wrong to do so. And if ever, I will even venture to say, violence – spiritual violence, the violence that taketh by storm – could have been justified, it would have been in this case. Her affections were all yours; she was, but for you and her stepmother, alone in the world; and amid all her charms and gifts, a soul more starved and destitute I never met with. May our Lord and His Immaculate Mother strengthen you to bear your sorrow! For your friends, there are and must be consolations in this catastrophe. The cross that such a marriage would have laid upon you must have been heavy indeed.'

Harassed by such thoughts and memories Helbeck passed through these strange, these miserable days – when he and Laura were once more under the same roof, living the same household life. Like Laura, he clung to every hour; like Laura, he found it almost more than he could bear. He suffered now with a fierceness, a moroseness, unknown to him of old. Every permitted mortification that could torment the body or humble the mind he brought into play during these weeks, and still could not prevent himself from feeling every sound of Laura's voice and every rustle of her dress as a rough touch upon a sore.

What was in her mind all the time – behind those clear indomitable eyes? He dared not let himself think of the signs of grief that were written so plainly on her delicate face and frame. One day he found himself looking at her from a distance in a passionate bewilderment. So white – so sad! For what? What was this freedom, this atrocious freedom – that a creature so fragile, so unfit to wield it, had yet claimed so fatally? His thoughts fell back to Stephen Fountain, cursing an influence at once so intangible and so strong.

It was some relief that they were in no risk of *tête-à-tête* outside Augustina's sick room. One or other of the nurses was always present at meals. And on the day after Laura's arrival Father Leadham appeared and stayed for ten days.

The relations of the Jesuit towards Miss Fountain during this time were curious. It was plain to Helbeck that Father Leadham treated the girl with a new respect, and that she on her side showed herself much more at ease with him than she used to be. It was as though they had tested each other, with the result that each had found in the other something nobler and sincerer than they had expected to find. Laura might be spiritually destitute; but it was evident that since his conversation with her, Father Leadham had realised for the first time the 'charm and gifts' which might be supposed to have captured Mr Helbeck.

So that when they met at meals, or in the invalid's room, the Jesuit showed Miss Fountain a very courteous attention. He was fresh from Cambridge; he brought her gossip of her friends and acquaintances; he said pleasant things of the Friedlands. She talked in return with an ease that astonished Helbeck and his sister. She seemed to both to have grown years older.

It was the same with all the other Catholic haunters of the house. For the first time she discovered how to get on with the Reverend Mother, even with Sister Angela – how not to find Father Bowles himself too wearisome. She moved among them with a dignity, perhaps an indifference, that changed her wholly.

Once, when she had been chatting in the friendliest way with the Reverend Mother, she paused for a moment in the passage outside Augustina's room, amazed at herself.

It was liberty, no doubt – this strange and desolate liberty in which she stood, that made the contrast. By some obscure association she fell on the words that Helbeck had once quoted to her — how differently! 'My soul is escaped like a bird out of the snare of the fowler; the snare is broken, and we are delivered.'

'Ah! but the bird's wings are broken and its breast pierced. What can it do with its poor freedom?' she said to herself, in a passion of tears.

Meanwhile she realised the force of the saying that Catholicism is the faith to die in.

The concentration of all these Catholic minds upon the dying of Augustina, the busy fraternal help evoked by every stage of her *via dolorosa*, was indeed marvellous to see. 'It is a work of art,' Laura thought with that new power of observation which had developed in her. 'It is — it must be — the most wonderful thing of its sort in the world!'

For it was no mere haphazard series of feelings or kindnesses. It was an act — a function — this 'good death' on which the sufferer and those who assisted her were equally bent. Something had to be done, a process to be gone through; and everyone was anxiously bent upon doing it in the right, the prescribed, way — upon omitting nothing. The physical fact indeed became comparatively unimportant, except as the evoking cause of certain symbolisms — nay, certain actual and direct contacts between earth and heaven, which were the distraction of death itself — which took precedence of it, and reduced it to insignificance.

When Father Leadham left, Father Bowles came to stay in the house, and communion was given to Mrs Fountain every day. Two or three times a week, also, Mass was said in her room. Laura assisted once or twice at these scenes — the blaze of lights and flowers in the old panelled room — the altar adorned with splendid fittings brought from the chapel below — the small blanched face in the depths of the great tapestried bed — the priest bending over it.

On one of these occasions, in the early morning, when the candles on the altar were almost effaced by the first brilliance of a May day, Laura stole away from the darkened room where Mrs Fountain lay soothed and sleeping, and stood for long at an open window overlooking the wild valley outside.

She was stifled by the scent of flowers and burning wax; still more mentally oppressed. The leaping river, the wide circuit of the fells, the blowing of the May wind! — to them, in a great reaction, the girl gave back her soul, passionately resting in them. They were no longer a joy and intoxication. But the veil lifted between her and them. They became a sanctuary and refuge.

From the Martha of the old faith, so careful and troubled about many things – sins and penances, creeds and sacraments, the miraculous hauntings of words and objects, of water and wafer, of fragments of bone and stuff, of scapulars and medals, of crucifixes and indulgences – her mind turned to this Mary[33] of a tameless and patient nature, listening and loving in the sunlight.

Only, indeed, to destroy her own fancy as soon as woven! Nature was pain and combat too, no less than Faith. But here, at least, was no jealous lesson to be learnt; no exclusions, no conditions. Her rivers were deep and clear for all; her 'generous sun' was lit for all. What she promised she gave. Without any preliminary *credo*, her colours glowed, her breezes blew for the unhappy. Oh! such a purple shadow on the fells – such a red glory of the oak-twigs in front of it – such a white sparkle of the Greet, parting the valley!

What need of any other sacrament or sign than these – this beauty and bounty of the continuing world? Indeed, Friedland had once said to her, 'The joy that Catholics feel in the sacrament, the plain believer in God will get day by day out of the simplest things – out of a gleam on the hills – a purple in the distance – a light on the river; still more out of any tender or heroic action.'

She thought very wistfully of her old friend and his talk; but here also with a strange sense of distance, of independence. How the river dashed and raced! There had been wild nights of rain amid this May beauty, and the stream was high. Day by day, of late, she had made it her comrade. Whenever she left Augustina it was always to wander beside it, or to sit above it, cradled and lost in that full triumphant song it went uttering to the spring.

But there was a third person in the play, by no means so passive an actor as Laura was wont to imagine her.

There is often a marvellous education in such a tedious parting with the world as Augustina was enduring. If the physical conditions allow it, the soul of the feeblest will acquire a new dignity, and perceptions more to the point. As she lay looking at the persons who surrounded her, Augustina passed without an effort, and yet wonderfully, as it seemed to her, into a new stage of thought and desire about them. A fresh, an eager ambition sprang up in her, partly of the woman, partly of the believer. She had been blind; now she saw. She felt the power of her weakness, and she would seize it.

Meanwhile, she made a rally which astonished all the doctors. Towards the end of the second week in May she had recovered strength so far that on several occasions she was carried down the chapel passage to the garden, and placed in a sheltered corner of the beech hedge, where she could see the bright turf of the bowling green and the distant trees of the 'Wilderness.'

One afternoon Helbeck came out to sit with her. He was no sooner there than she became so restless that he asked her if he should recall Sister Rosa, who had retired to a distant patch of shade.

'No – no! Alan, I want to say something. Will you raise my pillow a little?'

He did so, and she looked at him for a moment with her haunting blue eyes without speaking. But at last she said:

'Where is Laura?'

'Indoors, I believe.'

'Don't call her. I have been talking to her, Alan, about – about what she means to do.'

'Did she tell you her plans?'

He spoke very calmly, holding his sister's hand.

'She doesn't seem to have any. The Friedlands have offered her a home, of course. Alan! – will you put your ear down to me?'

He stooped, and she whispered brokenly, holding him several times when he would have drawn back.

But at last he released himself. A flush had stolen over his fine and sharpened features.

'My dear sister, if it were so – what difference can it make?'

He spoke with a quick interrogation. But his glance had an intensity, it expressed a determination, which made her cry out –

'Alan – if she gave way?'

'She will *never* give way. She has more self-control; but her mind is in precisely the same bitter and envenomed state. Indeed, she has grown more fixed, more convinced. The influence of her Cambridge friends has been decisive. Every day I feel for what she has to bear and put up with – poor child! – in this house.'

'It can't be for long,' said Augustina with tears; and she lay for awhile, pondering, and gathering force. But presently she made her brother stoop to her again.

'Alan – please listen to me! If Laura *did* become a Catholic – is there anything in the way – anything you can't undo?'

He raised himself quickly. He would have suffered these questions from no one else. The stern and irritable temper that he inherited from his father had gained fast upon the old self-control since the events of October. Even now, with Augustina, he was short.

'I shall take no vows, dear, before the time. But it would please me – it would console me – if you would put all these things out of your head. I see the will of God very plainly. Let us submit to it.'

'It hurts me so – to see you suffer!' she said, looking at him piteously.

He bent over the grass, struggling for composure.

'I shall have something else to do before long,' he said in a low voice, 'than to consider my own happiness.'

She was framing another question when there was a sound of footsteps on the gravel behind them.

Augustina exclaimed, with the agitation of weakness, 'Don't let any visitors come!' Helbeck looked a moment in astonishment, then his face cleared.

'Augustina! – it is the relic – from the Carmelite nuns. I recognise their confessor.'

Augustina clasped her hands; and Sister Rosa, obeying Helbeck's signal, came quickly over to her. Mr Helbeck bared his head and walked over the grass to meet the strange priest, who was carrying a small leather box.

Soon there was a happy group round Augustina's couch. The Confessor who had brought this precious relic of St John of the Cross had opened the case, and placed the small and delicate reliquary that it contained in Mrs Fountain's hands. She lay clasping it to her breast, too weak to speak, but flushed with joy. The priest, a southern-eyed kindly man, with an astonishing flow of soft pietistic talk, sat beside her, speaking soothingly of the many marvels of cure or conversion that had been wrought by the treasure she held. He was going on to hold a retreat at a convent of the order near Froswick, and would return, he said, by Bannisdale in a week's time, to reclaim his charge. The nuns, he repeated with gentle emphasis, had never done such an honour to any sick person before. But for Mr Helbeck's sister nothing was too much. And a novena had already been started at the convent. The nuns were praying – praying hard that the relic might do its holy work.

He was still talking when there was a step and a sound of low singing behind the beech hedge. The garden was so divided by gigantic hedges of the eighteenth century, which formed a kind of Greek cross in its centre, that many different actions or conversations might be taking place in it without knowing anything one of another. Laura, who had been away for an hour, was not aware that Augustina was in the garden till she came through a little tunnel in the hedge, and saw the group.

The priest looked up, startled by the appearance of the young lady. Laura had marked the outburst of warm weather by the donning of a white dress and her summer hat. In one hand she held a bunch of lilac that she had been gathering for her stepmother; in the other a volume of a French life of St Theresa [34] that she had taken an hour before from Augustina's table. In anticipation of the great favour promised her by the Carmelite nuns, Augustina had been listening feebly from time to time to her brother's reading from the biography of the greatest of Carmelite saints and founders.

'Laura!' said Mrs Fountain faintly.

Helbeck's expression changed. He bent over his sister, and said in a low decided voice, 'Will you give me the relic, dear? I will return it to its case.'

'Oh no, Alan,' she said, imploring. 'Laura, do you know what those kind dear nuns have done? They have sent me their relic. And I feel so much better already – so relieved!' Mrs Fountain raised the little case and kissed it fervently. Then she held it out for Laura to see.

The girl bent over it in silence.

'What is it?' she said.

'It is a relic of St John of the Cross,' said the priest opposite, glancing curiously at Miss Fountain. 'It once belonged to the treasury of the Cathedral of Seville, and was stolen during the great war. But it has been now formally conveyed to our community by the Archbishop and Chapter.'

'Wasn't it kind of the dear nuns, Laura?' said Augustina fervently.

'I – I suppose so,' said Laura, in a low embarrassed voice. Helbeck, who was watching her, saw that she could hardly restrain the shudder of repulsion that ran through her.

Her extraordinary answer threw a silence on the party. The tears started to the sick woman's cheeks. The priest rose to take his leave. Mrs Fountain asked him for an absolution and a blessing. He gave them, coldly bowed to Laura, shook hands with Sister Rosa, and took his departure, Helbeck conducting him.

'Oh, Laura!' said Mrs Fountain reproachfully. The girl's lips were quite white. She knelt down by her stepmother and kissed her hand.

'Dear, I wouldn't have hurt you for the world. It was something I had been reading – it – it seemed to me horrible! – just for a moment. Of course I'm glad it comforts you, poor darling! – of course – of course I am!'

Mrs Fountain was instantly appeased – for herself.

'But Alan felt it so,' she said restlessly, as she closed her eyes – 'what you said. – I saw his face.'

It was time for the invalid to be moved, and Sister Rosa had gone for help. Laura was left for a moment kneeling by her stepmother. No one could see her; the penitence and pain in the girl's feeling showed in her pallor, her pitiful dropping lip.

Helbeck was heard returning. Laura looked up. Instinctively she rose and proudly drew herself together. Never yet had she seen that face so changed. It breathed the sternest, most concentrated anger – a storm of feeling that, in spite of the absolute silence that held it in curb, yet so communicated itself to her that her heart seemed to fail in her breast.

A few minutes later Miss Fountain, having gathered together a few scattered possessions of the invalid, was passing through the chapel passage. A step approached from the hall, and Helbeck confronted her.

'Miss Fountain – may I ask you a kindness?'

What a tone of steel! Her shoulders straightened – her look met his in a common flash.

'Augustina is weak. Spare her discussion – the sort of discussion with which, no doubt, your Cambridge life makes you familiar. It can do nothing here, and' – he paused, only to resume unflinchingly – 'the dying should not be disturbed.'

Laura wavered in the dark passage like one mortally struck. His pose as the protector of his sister – the utter distance and alienation of his tone – unjust! – incredible!

'I discussed nothing,' she said, breathing fast.

'You might be drawn to do so,' he said coldly. 'Your contempt for the practices that sustain and console Catholics is so strong that no one can mistake the difficulty you have in concealing it. But I would ask you to conceal it, for her sake.'

'I thank you,' she said quietly, as she swept past him. 'But you *are* mistaken.'

She walked away from him and mounted the stairs without another word.

Laura sat crouched and rigid in her own room. How had it happened, this horrible thing? – this break-down of the last vestiges and relics of the old relation – this rushing in of a temper and a hostility that stunned her!

She looked at the book on her knee. Then she remembered. In the 'Wilderness' she had been reading that hideous account which appears in all the longer biographies, of the mutilation of St Theresa's body three years after her death by some relic-hunting friars from Avila. In a ruthless haste, these pious thieves had lifted the poor embalmed corpse from its resting-place at Alba; they had cut the old woman's arm from the shoulder; they had left it behind in the rifled coffin, and then hastily huddling up the body, they had fled southwards with their booty, while the poor nuns who had loved and buried their dead 'mother,' who had been shut by a trick into their own choir while the awful thing was done, were still singing the office, ignorant and happy.

The girl had read the story with sickening. Then Augustina had held up to her the relic-case, with that shrivelled horror inside it. A finger, was it? or a portion of one? Perhaps torn from some poor helpless one in the same way. And to such aids and helps must a human heart come in dying!

She had not been quick enough to master herself. Oh! that was wrong – very wrong. But had it deserved a stroke so cruel – so unjust?

Oh! miserable, miserable religion! Her wild nature rose against it – accused – denounced it.

That night Augustina was marvellously well. She lay with the relic-case beside her in a constant happiness.

'Oh, Laura! Laura, dear! – even you must see what it has done for me!'

So she whispered, when Sister Rosa had withdrawn into the next room and she and Laura were left together.

'I am so glad,' said the girl gently, 'so very glad.'

'You are so dreadfully pale, Laura!'

Laura said nothing. She raised the poor hand she held, and laid it softly against her cheek. Augustina looked at her wistfully. Gradually her resolution rose.

'Laura, I must say it – God tells me to say it!'

'What! dear Augustina?'

'Laura – you could save Alan! – you could alter his whole life. And you are breaking his heart!'

Laura stared at her, letting the hand slowly drop upon the bed. What was happening in this strange, strange world?

'Laura, come here! – I can't bear it. He suffers so! You don't see it, but I do. He has the look of my father when my mother died. I know that he will go to the Jesuits. They will quiet him, and pray for him – and prayer saves you. But you, Laura – you might save him another way – oh! I must call it a happier way.' She looked up piteously to the crucifix that hung on the wall opposite. 'You thought me unkind when you were engaged – I know you did. I didn't know what to think – I was so upset by it all. But, oh! how I have prayed since I came back that he might marry, and have children – and a little happiness. He is not forty yet – and he has had a hard life. How he will be missed here too! Who can ever take his place? Why, he has made it all. And he loves his work. Of course I see that – now – he thinks it a sin – what happened last year – your engagement. But all the same, he can't tear his heart away from you. I can't understand it. It seems to me almost terrible – to love as he loves you.'

'Dear Augustina, don't – don't say such things.' The girl fell on her knees beside her stepmother. Her pride was broken; her face convulsed. 'Why, you don't know, dear! He has lost all love for me. He says hard things to me even. He judges me like – like a stranger.' She looked at Augustina imploringly through her tears.

'Did he scold you just now about the relic? But it was *because* it was you. Nobody else could have made him angry about such a thing. Why, he would have just laughed and pitied them! – you know he would. But you – oh, Laura, you torture him!'

Laura hid her face, shaking with the sobs she tried to control.

Her heart melted within her. She thought of that marked book upon his table.

'And, Laura,' said the sighing thread of a voice, 'how *can* you be wiser than all the Church? – all these generations? Just think, dear! – you against the Saints and the Fathers, and the holy martyrs and confessors, from our Lord's time till now! Oh! your poor father. I know. But he never came near the faith, Laura – how could he judge? It was not offered to him. That was my wicked fault. If I had been faithful I might have gained my husband. But, Laura' – the voice grew so eager and sharp – 'we judge no one. We must believe for ourselves the Church is the only way. But God is so merciful! But you – it *is* offered to you, Laura. And Alan's love with it. Just so little on your part – the Church is so tender, so indulgent! She does not expect a perfect faith all at once. One must just make the step blindly – *obey* – throw oneself into her arms. Father Leadham said so to me one day – not minding what one thinks and believes – not looking at oneself – just obeying – and it will all come!'

But Laura could not speak. Little Augustina, full of a pleading, an apostolic strength, looked at her tenderly.

'He hardly sleeps, Laura. As I lie awake, I hear him moving about at all hours. I said to Father Leadham the other day – "his heart is broken. When you take him, he will be able to do what you tell him, perhaps. But – for this world – it will be like a dead man!" And Father Leadham did not deny it. He *knows* it is true.'

And thus, so long as her poor strength lasted, Augustina lay and whispered – reporting all the piteous history of those winter months – things that Laura had never heard and never dreamed – a tale of grief so profound and touching that, by the time it ended, every landmark was uprooted in the girl's soul, and she was drifting on a vast tide of pity and passion, whither she knew not.

CHAPTER FOUR

The next day there was no outing for Augustina. The south-west wind was again let loose upon the valley and the moss, with violent rain from the sea. In the grass the daffodils lay all faded and brown. But the blue-bells were marching fast over the copses – as though they sprang in the traces of the rain.

Laura sat working beside Augustina, or reading to her, from morning till dark. Mr Helbeck had gone into Whinthorpe as usual before breakfast, and was not expected home till the evening. Mrs Fountain was perhaps more restless and oppressed than she had been the day before. But she would hardly admit it. She lay with the relic beside her, and took the most hopeful view possible of all her symptoms.

Miss Fountain herself that day was in singular beauty. The dark circles round her eyes did but increase their brilliance; the hot fire in Augustina's rooms made her cheeks glow; and the bright blue cotton of her dress had been specially chosen by Molly Friedland to set off the gold of her hair.

She was gay too, to Augustina's astonishment. She told stories of Daffady and the farm; she gossiped with Sister Rosa; she alternately teased and coaxed Fricka. Sister Rosa had been a little cool to her at first after the affair of the relic. But Miss Fountain was so charming this afternoon, so sweet to her stepmother, so amiable to other people, that the little nurse could not resist her.

And at regular intervals she would walk to the window, and report to Augustina the steady rising of the river.

'It has flooded all that flat bank opposite the first seat – and of that cattle-rail, that bar – what do you call it? – just at the bend – you can only see the very top line. And such a current under the otter cliff! It's splendid, Augustina! – it's magnificent!'

And she would turn her flushed face to her stepmother in a kind of triumph.

'It will wash away the wooden bridge if it goes on,' said Augustina plaintively, 'and destroy all the flowers.'

But Laura seemed to exult in it. If it had not been for the curb of Mrs Fountain's weakness, she could not have kept still at all as the evening drew on, and the roar of the water became continuously audible even in this high room. And yet every now and then it might perhaps have been thought that she was troubled or annoyed by the sound – that it prevented her from hearing something else.

Mrs Fountain did not know how to read her. Once, when they were alone, she tried to reopen the subject of the night before. But Laura would not even allow it to be approached. To-day she had the lightest, softest ways of resistance. But they were enough.

Mrs Fountain could only sigh and yield.

Towards seven o'clock she began to fidget about her brother. 'He certainly meant to be home for dinner,' she said several times, with increasing peevishness.

'I am going to have dinner here!' said Laura, smiling.

'Why?' said Augustina, astonished.

'Oh! let me, dear. Mr Helbeck is sure to be late. And Sister Rosa will look after him. Teaching Fricka has made me as hungry as that!' – and she opened her hands wide, as a child measures.

Augustina looked at her sadly, but said nothing. She remembered that the night before, too, Laura would not go downstairs.

The little meal went gaily. Just as it was over, and while Laura was still chattering to her stepmother as she had not chattered for months, a step was heard in the passage.

'Ah! there is Alan!' cried Mrs Fountain.

The Squire came in tired and mud-stained. Even his hair shone with rain, and his clothes were wet through.

'I must not come too near you,' he said, standing beside the door.

Mrs Fountain bade him dress, get some dinner, and come back to her. As she spoke, she saw him peering through the shadows of the room. She too looked round. Laura was gone.

'At the first sound of his step!' thought Augustina. And she wept a little, but so secretly that even Sister Rosa did not discover it. Her ambition – her poor ambition – was for herself alone. What chance had it? – alas! Never since Stephen's death surely had Augustina seen Laura shed such tears as she had shed the night before. But no words, no promises – nothing! And where, now, was any sign of it?

She drew out her beads for comfort. And so, sighing and praying, she fell asleep.

After supper Helbeck was in the hall smoking. He was half

abashed that he should find so much comfort in his pipe, and that he should dread so much the prospect of giving it up.

His thoughts, however, were black enough – black as the windy darkness outside.

A step on the stairs – at which his breath leapt. Miss Fountain, in her white evening dress, was descending.

'May I speak to you, Mr Helbeck?'

He flung down his pipe and approached her. She stood a little above him on one of the lower steps; and instantly he felt that she came in gentleness.

An agitation he could barely control took possession of him. All day long he had been scourging himself for the incident of the night before. They had not met since. He looked at her now humbly – with a deep sadness – and waited for what she had to say.

'Shall we go into the drawing-room? Is there a light?'

'We will take one.'

He lifted a lamp, and she led the way. Without another word, she opened the door into the deserted room. Nobody had entered it since the Orphanage function, when some extra service had been hastily brought in to make the house habitable. The mass of the furniture was gathered into the centre of the carpet, with a few tattered sheets flung across it. The gap made by the lost Romney spoke from the wall, and the windows stood uncurtained to the night.

Laura, however, found a chair and sank into it. He put down the lamp, and stood expectant.

They were almost in their old positions. How to find strength and voice! That room breathed memories.

When she did speak, however, her intonation was peculiarly firm and clear.

'You gave me a rebuke last night, Mr Helbeck – and I deserved it!'

He made a sudden movement – a movement which seemed to trouble her.

'No! don't!' – she raised her hand involuntarily – 'don't please say anything to make it easier for me. I gave you great pain. You were right – oh! quite right – to express it. But you know –'

She broke off suddenly.

'You know, I can't talk – if you stand there like that! Won't you come here and sit down' – she pointed to a chair near her – 'as if we were friends still. We can be friends, can't we? We ought to be for Augustina's sake. And I very much want to discuss with you – seriously – what I have to say.'

He obeyed her. He came to sit beside her, recovering his composure – bending forward that he might give her his best attention.

She paused a moment – knitting her brows.

'I thought afterwards, a long time, of what had happened. I talked, too, to Augustina. She was much distressed – she appealed to me. And I saw a great deal of force in what she said. She pointed out that it was absurd for me to judge before I knew; that I never – never – had been willing to know; that everything – even the Catholic Church' – she smiled faintly – 'takes some learning. She pleaded with me – and what she said touched me very much. I do not know how long I may have to stay in your house – and with her. I would not willingly cause you pain. I would gladly *understand*, at least, more than I do – I should like to learn – to be instructed. Would – would Father Leadham, do you think, take the trouble to correspond with me – to point me out the books, for instance, that I might read?'

Helbeck's black eyes fastened themselves upon her.

'You – you would like to correspond with Father Leadham?' he repeated, in stupefaction.

She nodded. Involuntarily she began a little angry beating with her foot that he knew well. It was always the protest of her pride, when she could not prevent the tears from showing themselves.

He controlled himself. He turned his chair so as to come within an easy talking distance.

'Will you pardon me,' he said quietly, 'if I ask for more information? Did you only determine on this last night?'

'I think so.'

He hesitated.

'It is a serious step, Miss Fountain! You should not take it only from pity for Augustina – only from a wish to give her comfort in dying!'

She turned away her face a little. That penetrating look pierced too deeply. 'Are there not many motives?' she said, rather hoarsely – 'many ways? I want to give Augustina a happiness – and – and to satisfy many questions of my own. Father Leadham is bound to teach, is he not, as a priest? He could lose nothing by it.'

'Certainly he is bound,' said Helbeck.

375

He dropped his head, and stared at the carpet, thinking.

'He would recommend you some books, of course.'

The same remembrance flew through both. Absently and involuntarily, Helbeck shook his head, with a sad lifting of the eyebrows. The colour rushed into Laura's cheeks.

'It must be something very simple,' she said hurriedly. 'Not "Lives of the Saints," I think, and not "Catechisms" or "Outlines." Just a building up from the beginning by somebody – who found it hard, *very* hard, to believe – and yet did believe. But Father Leadham will know – of course he would know.'

Helbeck was silent. It suddenly appeared to him the strangest, the most incredible conversation. He felt the rise of a mad emotion – the beating in his breast choked him.

Laura rose, and he heard her say in low and wavering tones:

'Then I will write to him to-morrow – if you think I may.'

He sprang to his feet, and as she passed him the fountains of his being broke up. With a wild gesture he caught her in his arms.

'Laura!'

It was not the cry of his first love for her. It was a cry under which she shuddered. But she submitted at once. Nay, with a womanly tenderness – how unlike that old shrinking Laura – she threw her arm round his neck, she buried her little head in his breast.

'Oh, how long you were in understanding!' she said with a deep sigh. 'How long!'

'Laura! – what does it mean? – my head turns!'

'It means – it means – that you shall never – never again speak to me as you did yesterday; that either you must love me or – well, I must just die!' she gave a little sharp sobbing laugh. 'I have tried other things – and they can't – they can't be borne. And if you can't love me unless I am a Catholic – now, I know you wouldn't – I must just *be* a Catholic – if any power in the world can make me one. Why, Father Leadham can persuade me – he must!' She drew away from him, holding him, almost fiercely, by her two small hands. 'I am nothing but an ignorant, foolish girl. And he has persuaded so many wise people – you have often told me. Oh, he must – he must persuade me!'

She hid herself again on his breast. Then she looked up, feeling the tears on his cheek.

'But you'll be very, very patient with me – won't you? Oh! I'm so dead to all those things! But if I say whatever you want me to say – if I do what is required of me – you won't ask me too many questions – you won't press me too hard? You'll trust to my being yours – to my growing into your heart? Oh! how did I ever bear the agony of tearing myself away!'

It was an ecstasy – a triumph. But it seemed to him afterwards in looking back upon it, that all through it was also an anguish! The revelation of the woman's nature, of all that had lived and burned in it since he last held her in his arms, brought with it for both of them such sharp pains of expansion, such an agony of experience and growth.

Very soon, however, she grew calmer. She tried to tell him what had happened to her since that black October day. But conversation was not altogether easy. She had to rush over many an hour and many a thought – dreading to remember. And again and again he could not rid himself of the image of the old Laura, or could not fathom the new. It was like stepping from the firmer ground of the moss on to the softer patches where foot and head lost themselves. He could see her as she had been, or as he had believed her to be, up to twenty-four hours before – the little enemy and alien in the house; or as she had lived beside him those four months – troubled, petulant, exacting. But this radiant, tender Laura – with this touch of feverish extravagance in her love and her humiliation – she bewildered him; or rather she roused a new response; he must learn new ways of loving her.

Once, as he was holding her hand, she looked at him timidly.

'You would have left Bannisdale, wouldn't you?'

He quickly replied that he had been in correspondence with his old Jesuit friends. But he would not dwell upon it. There was a kind of shame in the subject, that he would not have had her penetrate. A devout Catholic does not dwell for months on the prospects and secrets of the religious life to put them easily and in a moment out of his hand – even at the call of the purest and most legitimate passion. From the Counsels, the soul returns to the Precepts. The higher, supremer test is denied it. There is humbling in that – a bitter taste, not to be escaped.

Perhaps she did penetrate it. She asked him hurriedly if he regretted anything. She could so easily go away again – for ever. 'I could do it – I could do it now!' she said, firmly. 'Since you kissed me. You could always be my friend.'

He smiled, and raised her hands to his lips. 'Where thou livest, dear, I will live, and where –'

She withdrew a hand, and quickly laid it on his mouth.

'No – not to-night! We have been so full of death all these weeks! Oh! how I want to tell Augustina!'

But she did not move. She could not tear herself from this comfortless room – this strange circle of melancholy light in which they sat – this beating of the rain in their ears as it dashed against the old and fragile casements.

'Oh! my dear,' he said suddenly, as he watched her, 'I have grown so old and cross. And so poor! It has taken far more than the picture' – he pointed to the vacant space – 'to carry me through this six months. My schemes have been growing – what motive had I for holding my hand? My friends have often remonstrated – the Jesuits especially. But at last I have had my way. I have far – far less to offer you than I had before.'

He looked at her in a sad apology.

'I have a little money,' she said shyly. 'I don't believe you ever knew it before.'

'Have you?' he said in astonishment.

'Just a tiny bit. I shall pay my way' – and she laughed happily. 'Alan! – have you noticed – how well I have been getting on with the Sisters? – what friends Father Leadham and I made? But no! – you didn't notice anything. You saw me all *en noir* – *all*,' she repeated with a mournful change of voice.

Then her eyelids fell, and she shivered.

'Oh! how you hurt – how you *hurt!* – last night.'

He passionately soothed her, denouncing himself, asking her pardon. She gave a long sigh. She had a strange sense of having climbed a long stair out of an abyss of misery. Now she was just at the top – just within light and welcome. But the dark was so close behind – one touch! and she was thrust down to it again.

'I have only hated two people this last six months,' she said at last, *à propos*, apparently, of nothing. 'Your cousin, who was to have Bannisdale – and – and – Mr Williams. I saw him at Cambridge.'

There was a pause; then Helbeck said, with an agitation that she felt beneath her cheek as her little head rested on his shoulder:

'You saw Edward Williams? How did he dare to present himself to you?'

He gently withdrew himself from her, and went to stand before the hearth, drawn up to his full stern height. His dark head and striking pale features were fitly seen against the background of the old wall. As he stood there he was the embodiment of his race, of its history, its fanaticisms, its 'great refusals' at once of all mean joys and all new freedoms. To a few chosen notes in the universe, tender response and exquisite vibration – to all others, deaf, hard, insensitive, as the stone of his old house.

Laura looked at him with a mingled adoration and terror. Then she hastily explained how and where she had met Williams.

'And you felt no sympathy for him?' said Helbeck, wondering.

She flushed.

'I knew what it must have been to you. And – and – he showed no sense of it.'

Her tone was so simple, so poignant, that Helbeck smiled only that he might not weep. Hurriedly coming to her he kissed her soft hair. 'There were temptations of his youth,' he said with difficulty, 'from which the Faith rescued him. Now these same temptations have torn him from the Faith. It has been all known to me from first to last. I see no hope. Let us never speak of him again.'

'No,' she said, trembling.

He drew a long breath. Suddenly he knelt beside her.

'And you!' he said in a low voice – 'you! What love – what sweetness – shall be enough for you! Oh! my Laura, when I think of what you have done to-night – of all that it means, all that it promises – I humble myself before you. I envy and bless you. Yours has been no light struggle – no small sacrifice. I can only marvel at it. Dear, the Church will draw you so softly – teach you so tenderly! You have never known a mother. Our Lady will be your Mother. You have had few friends – they will be given to you in all times and countries – and this will you are surrendering will come back to you strengthened a thousand-fold – for my support – and your own.'

He looked at her with emotion. Oh! how pale she had grown under these words of benediction. There was a moment's silence – then she rose feebly.

'Now – let me go! To-morrow – will you tell Augustina? Or to-night, if she were awake, and strong enough? How can one be sure –?

'Let us come and see.'

379

He took her hand, and they moved a few steps across the room, when they were startled by the thunder of the storm upon the windows. They stopped involuntarily. Laura's face lit up.

'How the river roars! I love it so. Yesterday I was on the top of the otter cliff when it was coming down in a torrent! To-morrow it will be superb'

'I wish you wouldn't go there till I have had some fencing done,' said Helbeck with decision. 'The rain has loosened the moss and made it all slippery and unsafe. I saw some people gathering primroses there to-day, and I told Murphy to warn them off. We must put a railing –'

Laura turned her face to the hall.

'What was that?' she said, catching his arm.

A sudden cry – loud and piercing – from the stairs.

'Mr Helbeck! – Miss Fountain!'

They rushed into the hall. Sister Rosa ran towards them.

'Oh! Mr Helbeck – come at once – Mrs Fountain –'

Augustina still sat propped in her large chair by the fire.

But a nurse looked up with a scared face as they entered.

'Oh come – *come* – Mr Helbeck! She is just going.'

Laura threw herself on her knees beside her stepmother. Helbeck gave one look at his sister, then also kneeling he took her cold and helpless hand, and said in a steady voice –

'Receive Thy servant, O Lord, into the place of salvation, which she hopes from Thy mercy.'

The two nurses, sobbing, said the 'Amen.'

'Deliver, O Lord, the soul of Thy servant from all the perils of hell, from pains and all tribulations.'

'Amen.'

Mrs Fountain's head fell gently back upon the cushions. The eyes withdrew themselves in the manner that only death knows, the lids dropped partially.

'Augustina – dear Augustina – give me one look?' cried Laura in despair. She wrapped her arms round her stepmother and laid her head on the poor wasted bosom.

But Helbeck possessed himself of one of the girl's hands, and with his own right he made the sign of the Cross upon his sister's brow.

'Depart, O Christian soul, from this world, in the name of God the Father Almighty, who created thee; in the name of Jesus Christ, the son of the living God, who suffered for thee; in the name of the Holy Ghost, who has been poured out upon thee; in the name of the angels and archangels; in the name of the thrones and dominations; in the name of the principalities and powers; in the name of the cherubim and seraphim; in the name of the patriarchs and prophets; in the name of the holy apostles and evangelists; in the name of the holy martyrs and confessors; in the name of the holy monks and hermits; in the name of the holy virgins, and of all the saints of God; let thy place be this day in peace, and thy abode in the Holy Sion: through Christ our Lord. Amen.'

There was silence, broken only by Laura's sobs and the nurses' weeping. Helbeck alone was quite composed. He gazed at his sister, not with grief – rather with a deep mysterious joy. When he rose, still looking down upon Augustina, he questioned the nurses in low tones.

There had been hardly any warning. Suddenly a stifled cry – a gurgling in the throat – a spasm. Sister Rosa thought she had distinguished the words 'Jesus! –' 'Alan –' but there had been no time for any message, any farewell. The doctors had once warned the brother that it was possible, though not likely, that the illness would end in this way.

'Father Bowles gave her Communion this morning?' said Helbeck, with a grave exactness, like one informing himself of all necessary things.

'This morning and yesterday,' said Sister Rosa eagerly; 'and dear Mrs Fountain confessed on Saturday.'

Laura rose from her knees and wrung her hands.

'Oh! I can't bear it!' she said to Helbeck. 'If I had been there – if we could just have told her! Oh, how strange – how *strange* it is!'

And she looked wildly about her, seized by an emotion, a misery that Helbeck could not altogether understand. He tried to soothe her, regardless of the presence of the nurses. Laura, too, did not think of them. But when he put his arm round her, she withdrew herself in a restlessness that would not be controlled.

'How strange – *how strange!*' she repeated as she looked down on the little blanched and stiffening face.

Helbeck stooped and kissed the brow of the dead woman.

'If I had only loved her better!' he said with emotion.

Laura stared at him. His words brought back to her a rush of memories – Augustina's old fear of him – those twelve years in which no member of the Fountain household had ever seen Mrs Fountain's brother. So long as Augustina had been Stephen Fountain's wife she had been no less dead for Helbeck, her only brother, than she was now.

The girl shuddered. She looked pitifully at the others.

'Please – please – leave me alone with her a little! She was my father's wife – my dear father's wife!'

And again she sank on her knees, hiding her face against the dead. The nurses hesitated, but Helbeck thought it best to let her have her way.

'We will go for half an hour,' he said, stooping to her. Then, in a whisper that only she could hear – 'My Laura – you are mine now – let me soon come back and comfort you!'

When they returned they found Laura sitting on a stool beside her stepmother. One hand grasped that of Augustina while the other dropped listlessly in front of her. Her brow under its weight of curly hair hung forward. The rest of the little face almost disappeared behind the fixed and sombre intensity of the eyes.

She took no notice when they came in, and it was Helbeck alone who could rouse her. He persuaded her to go, on a promise that the nurses would soon recall her.

When all was ready she returned. Augustina was lying in a white pomp of candles and flowers; the picture of the Virgin, the statue of St Joseph, her little praying table, were all garlanded with light; every trace of the long physical struggle had been removed; the great bed, with its meek, sleeping form and its white draperies, rose solitary amid its lights – an altar of death in the void of the great panelled room.

Laura stood opposite to Helbeck, her hands clasped, as white and motionless from head to foot as Augustina herself. Once amid the prayers and litanies he was reciting with the sisters, he lifted his head and found that she was looking at him and not at Augustina. Her expression was so forlorn, and difficult to read, that he felt a vague uneasiness. But his Catholic sense of the deep awe of what he was doing made him try to concentrate himself upon it, and when he raised his eyes again, Laura was gone.

At four o'clock, in the dawn, he went himself to rest a while, a little surprised, perhaps, that Laura had not come back to share the vigils of the night, but thankful, nevertheless, that she had been prudent enough to spare herself.

Some little time before he went, while it was yet dark, Sister Rosa had gone to lie down for a while. Her room was just beyond Laura's. As she passed Miss Fountain's door she saw that there was a light within, and for some time after the tired nurse had thrown herself on her bed, she was disturbed by sounds from the next room. Miss Fountain seemed to be walking up and down. Once or twice she broke out into sobs, then again there were periods of quiet, and once a sharp sound that might have been made by tearing a letter. But Sister Rosa did not listen long. It was natural that Miss Fountain should sorrow and watch, and the nurse's fatigue soon brought her sleep.

She had rejoined her companion, however, and Mr Helbeck had been in his room about half an hour, when the door of the death chamber opened softly, and Miss Fountain appeared.

The morning light was already full, though still rosily clear and cold, and it fell upon the strangest and haggardest figure. Miss Fountain was in a black dress, covered with a long black cloak. Her dress and cloak were bedraggled with mud and wet. Her hat and hair were both in a drenched confusion, and the wind had laid a passing flush, like a mask, upon the pallor of her face. In her arms she held some boughs of wild cherry, and a mass of white clematis, gathered from a tree upon the house-wall, for which Augustina had cherished a particular affection.

She paused just inside the door, and looked at the nurses uncertainly, like one who hardly knew what she was doing.

Sister Rosa went to her.

'They are so wet,' she whispered with a troubled look, 'and I went to the most sheltered places. But I should like to put them by her. She loved the cherry blossom — and this clematis.'

The nurse took her into the next room, and between them they dried and shook the beautiful tufted branches. As Laura was about to take them back to the bed, Sister Rosa asked if she would not take off her wet cloak.

'Oh no!' said the girl, as though with a sudden entreaty. 'No! I am going out again. It sha'n't touch anything.'

And daintily holding it to one side, she returned with the flowers in a basket. She took them out one by one, and laid them beside Augustina till the bed was a vision of spring, starred and wreathed from end to end, save for that waxen face and hands in the centre.

'There is no room for more,' said the nurse gently, beside her.

Laura started.

'No – but–'

She looked vaguely round the walls, saw a pair of old Delft vases still empty, and said eagerly, pointing, 'I will bring some for those. There is a tree – a cherry tree,' the nurse remembered afterwards that she had spoken with a remarkable slowness and clearness, 'just above the otter cliff. You don't know where that is. But Mr Helbeck knows.'

The nurse glanced at her, and wondered. Miss Fountain, no doubt, had been dazed a little by the sudden shock. She had learnt, however, not to interfere with the first caprices of grief, and she did not try to dissuade the girl from going.

When the flowers were all laid, Laura went round to the further side of the bed and dropped on her knees. She gazed steadily at Augustina for a little; then she turned to the faldstool beside the bed and the shelf above it, with Augustina's prayer-books, and on either side of the St Joseph, on the wall, the portraits of Helbeck and his mother. The two nurses moved away to the window, that she might be left a little to herself. They had seen enough, naturally, to make them divine a new situation, and feel towards her with a new interest and compassion.

When she rejoined them, they were alternately telling their beads and looking at the glory of the sunrise as it came marching from the distant fells over the park. The rain had ceased, but the trees and grass were steeped, and the river came down in a white flood under the pure greenish spaces, and long pearly clouds of the morning sky.

Laura gave it all one look. Then she drew her cloak round her again.

'Dear Miss Fountain,' whispered Sister Rosa, entreating, 'don't be long. And when you come in, let me get you dry things, and make you some tea.'

The girl made a sign of assent.

'Good-bye,' she said under her breath, and she gently kissed first Sister Rosa, and then the other nurse, Sister Mary Raphael, who did not know her so well, and was a little surprised perhaps to feel the touch of the cold small lips.

They watched her close the door, and some dim anxiety made them wait at the window till they saw her emerge from the garden wall into the park. She was walking slowly with bent head. She seemed to stand for a minute or two at the first seat commanding the bend of the river; then the rough road along the Greet turned and descended. They saw her no more.

A little before eight o'clock, Helbeck, coming out of his room, met Sister Rosa in the passage. She looked a little disturbed.

'Is Miss Fountain there?' asked Helbeck in the voice natural to those who keep house with death. He motioned towards his sister's room.

'I have not seen Miss Fountain since she went out between four and five o'clock,' said the nurse. 'She went out for some flowers. As she did not come back to us, we thought that she was tired, and had gone straight to bed. But now I have been to see. Miss Fountain is not in her room.'

Helbeck stopped short.

'Not in her room! And she went out between four and five o'clock!'

'She told us she was going for some flowers to the otter cliff,' said Sister Rosa, with cheeks that were rapidly blanching. 'I remember her saying so very plainly. She said you would know where it was.'

He stared at her, his face turning to horror. Then he was gone.

Laura was not far to seek. The tyrant river that she loved had received her, had taken her life, and then had borne her on its swirl of waters straight for that little creek, where once before it had tossed a human prey upon the beach.

There, beating against the gravelly bank, in a soft helplessness, her bright hair tangled among the drift of branch and leaf brought down by the storm, Helbeck found her.

He brought her home upon his breast. Those who had come to search with him followed at a distance.

He carried her through the garden, and at the chapel entrance nurses and doctor met him. Long and fruitless efforts were made before all was yielded to despair; but the river had done its work.

At last Helbeck said a hoarse word to Sister Rosa. She led the others away.

. . . In that long agony, Helbeck's soul parted for ever with the first fresh power to suffer. Neither life nor death could ever stab in such wise again. The half of personality – the chief forces of that

Helbeck whom Laura had loved, were already dead with Laura, when, after many hours, his arms gave her back to the Sisters, and she dropped gently from his hold upon her bed of death, in a last irrevocable submission.

Far on in the day Sister Rosa discovered on Laura's table a sealed letter addressed to Dr Friedland of Cambridge. She brought it to Helbeck. He looked at it blindly, then gradually remembered the name and the facts connected with it. He wrote and sent a message to Dr and Mrs Friedland asking them of their kindness to come to Bannisdale.

The Friedlands arrived late at night. They saw the child to whom they had given their hearts lying at peace in the old tapestried room. Some of the flowers she had herself brought for Augustina had been placed about her. The nurses had exhausted themselves in the futile cares that soothe good women at such a time.

The talk throughout the household was of sudden and hopeless accident. Miss Fountain had gone for cherry blossom to the otter cliff; the cliff was unsafe after the rain; only twenty-four hours before Mr Helbeck had given orders on the subject to the old keeper. And the traces of a headlong fall just below a certain flowery bent where a wild cherry stood above a bank of primroses, were plainly visible.

Then, as the doctor and Mrs Friedland entered their own room, Laura's letter was brought to them.

They shut themselves in to read it, expecting one of those letters, those unsuspicious letters of every day, which sudden death leaves behind it.

But this was what they read:

'Dear, dear friend, – Last night, nearly five hours ago, I promised for the second time to marry Mr Helbeck, and I promised, too, that I would be a Catholic. I asked him to procure for me Catholic teaching and instruction. I could not, you see, be his wife without it. His conscience, now, would not allow it. And besides, last summer I saw that it could not be.

'. . . Then we were called to Augustina. It was she who finally persuaded me. I did not do it merely to please her. Oh! no – *no*. I have been on the brink of it for days – perhaps weeks. I have so hungered to be his again . . . But it gave it sweetness that Augustina wished it so much – that I could tell her and make her happy before she died.

'Then, she was dead! – all in a moment – without a word – before we came to her almost. She had prayed so – and yet God would not leave her a moment in which to hear it. That struck me so. It was so strange, after all the pains – all the clinging to Him – and entreating. It might have been a sign, and there! – she never gave a thought to us. It seemed like an intrusion, a disturbance even to touch her. How horrible it is that death is so *lonely!* Then something was said that reminded me of my father. I had forgotten him for so long. But when they left me with her, I seemed to be holding not her hand, but his. I was back in the old life – I heard him speaking quite distinctly. "Laura, you cannot do it – *you cannot do it!*" And he looked at me in sorrow and displeasure. I argued with him so long, but he beat me down. And the voice I seemed to hear was not his only; it was the voice of my own life, only far stronger and crueller than I had ever known it.

'Cruel! – I hardly know what I am writing – who has been cruel! I! – only I! To open the old wounds – to make him glad for an hour – then to strike and leave him – could anything be more pitiless? Oh! my best – best beloved . . . But to live a lie – upon his heart, in his arms – that would be worse. I don't know what drives me exactly – but the priests want my inmost will – want all that is I – and I know when I sit down to think quietly, that I cannot give it. I knew it last October. But to be with him, to see him was too much. Oh! if God hears, may He forgive me – I prayed to-night – that He would give me courage.

'He must always think it an accident – he will. I see it all so plainly. But I am afraid of saying or doing something to make the others suspect. – My head is not clear. I can't remember from one moment to another.

'You understand – I must trouble him no more. And there is no other way. This winter has proved it. Because death puts an *end*.

'This letter is for you three only, in all the world. Dear, dear Molly – I sit here like a coward – but I can't go without a sign. – You wouldn't understand me – I used to be so happy as a little child – But since Papa died – since I came here – Oh! I am not angry now, not proud – no, no. – It is for love – for love –

'Good-bye – good-bye. You were all so good to me – Think of me, grieve for me, sometimes. –

'Your ever grateful and devoted
'LAURA.'

Next morning early, Helbeck entered the dining-room where Dr Friedland was sitting. He approached the doctor with an uncertain step, like one finding his way in the dark.

'You had a letter,' he said. 'Is it possible that you could show it me – or any part of it? Only a few hours before her death the old relations between myself – and Miss Fountain – were renewed. We were to have been husband and wife. That gives me a certain claim.'

Dr Friedland grew pale.

'My dear sir,' he said, rising to meet his host. – 'that letter contained a message for my daughter which was not intended for other eyes than hers. I have destroyed it.'

And then speech failed him. The old man stood in a guilty confusion.

Helbeck lifted his deep eyes with the steady and yet muffled gaze of one who, in the silence of the heart, lets hope go. Not another word was said. The doctor found himself alone.

Three days later, the doctor wrote to his wife, who had gone back to Cambridge to be with Molly.

'Yesterday Mrs Fountain was buried in the Catholic grave-yard at Whinthorpe. To-day we carried Laura to a little chapel high in the hills. A lonely yet a cheerful spot! After these days and nights of horror, there was a moment – a breath – of calm. The Westmoreland rocks and trees will be about her for ever. She lies in sight, almost, of the Bannisdale woods. Above her the mountain rises to the sky. One of those wonderful Westmoreland dogs was barking and gathering the sheep on the crag-side, while we stood there. And when it was all over I could hear the river in the valley – a gay and open stream, with little bends and shallows – not tragic like the Greet.

'Many of the country people came. I saw her cousins, the Masons; that young fellow – you remember? – with a face swollen with tears. Mr Helbeck stood in the distance. He did not come into the chapel.

'How she loved this country! And now it holds her tenderly. It gives her its loveliest and best. Poor, poor child!

'As for Mr Helbeck, I have hardly seen him. He seems to live a life all within. We must be as shadows to him; as men like trees walking. But I have had a few conversations with him on necessary business; I have observed his bearing under this intolerable blow. And always I have felt myself in the presence of a good and noble man. In a few months, or even weeks, they say he will have entered the Jesuit Novitiate. It gives me a deep relief to think of it.

'What a fate! – that brought them across each other, that has left him nothing but these memories, and led her, step by step, to this last bitter resource – this awful spending of her young life – this blind witness to august things!'

NOTES

Facsimile title page: *. . . metus ille . . . ab imo*: The epigraph reads in full: '. . . metus ille foras praeceps Acheruntis agendus/Funditus humanam qui vitam turbat ab imo' (Lucretius, *De Rerum Natura*, III, 36–7). (. . . 'and that fear of Acheron [i.e., Hell] be sent packing, which troubles the life of man from its lowest depths.')

1 (p. 38). *'pele' tower*: Generally spelt 'peel', originally meaning a fortified dwelling-house, common in the Borders.

2 (p. 39). *spitz*: Any of the various breeds of dog characterized by very dense hair, a stocky build, a pointed muzzle and erect ears.

3 (p. 63). *'Enchanted casements . . . lands forlorn'*: From John Keats's *Ode to a Nightingale* (as again on p. 354).

4 (p. 118). *Manning's*: Henry Edward Manning (1809–92), an English churchman who was originally an Anglican but was converted to Roman Catholicism in 1851 and made Archbishop of Westminster in 1865 and cardinal in 1875.

5 (p. 119). *"Extra ecclesiam nulla salus"*: 'There is no health or good outside the Church.'

6 (p. 125). *'Virgo prudentissima . . . praedicanda'*: 'Most wise Virgin, revered, all-praiseworthy'.

7 (p. 151). *St Philip Neri* (1515–95): Italian priest, founder of the order of the Congregation of the Oratory in 1564.

8 (p. 192). *'he nothing common does nor mean'*: An allusion to the line, 'He nothing common did or mean', from Andrew Marvell's *Horatian Ode on Cromwell's Return from Ireland*, where it refers to Charles I at his execution.

9 (p. 222). *Atreus-threshold*: The curse of the house of Atreus refers to the tragic doom originated by Atreus in a blood feud that encompassed his descendants, including Agamemnon and Orestes.

10 (p. 227). *sub specie peccati*: 'Under the gaze of the sinful': a serious pun on *'sub specie aeternitatis'* ('under the gaze of eternity').

11 (p. 228). *ad majorem Dei gloriam*: 'To the greater glory of God'.

12 (p. 229). *Test Act*: A law passed in 1673 to exclude Catholics from public life by requiring all persons holding offices under the Crown to take the Anglican Communion. Repealed in 1828.

13 (p. 229). *'Domine, exaudi!'*: 'Lord, hear my prayer!'

14 (p. 229). *Domine Deus . . . miserere nobis*: 'Lord God, Lamb of God, Son of the Father, that takest away the sins of the world, hear our prayer. Thou that sittest at the right hand of the Father, have mercy upon us.'

15 (p. 279). *St Charles Borromeo* (1538–84): Archbishop of Milan. A great supporter of the Tridentine reforms, he gave generous help to the English College at Douai.

16 (p. 297). *feras consumere nati . . . Mr Fielding*: This Latin tag (translated by Fielding as 'Born to consume the beasts of the field') is used in *Tom Jones* to describe hunting squires, who are contrasted with those human beings referred to as *'Fruges consumere nati'* ('Born to consume the fruits of the earth') in the line of Horace (*Epistles* I, ii, 27) which Fielding is adapting.

17 (p. 297). *Esau . . . Jacob*: The feuding twin sons of Isaac (see Genesis 25 and 27). Esau was a hunter and Jacob, who was to be father of the twelve patriarchs of Israel, a farmer.

18 (p. 298). *St Francis Borgia* (1510–72): Great-grandson of Pope Alexander IV and Duke of Gandia: in 1565 he became Vicar-General of the Jesuits. He was famed for his extreme asceticism and charitable works.

19 (p. 299). *Browning's poem*: 'Ivan Ivanovich', in *Dramatic Idylls* (1879).

20 (p. 313). *Dr Friedland*: The model in many ways for Dr Friedland was Thomas Hill Green (1836–82), the idealist philosopher, educated at Rugby and Balliol College, Oxford, of which he became a Fellow and Professor of Moral Philosophy. His homely exterior and middle-class radicalism went with a loftiness of character that recalled Wordsworth, of whom he was in some ways a disciple, even in philosophy. He became a cleric despite reservations about the Thirty-nine Articles, and admired the practical aims of Utilitarians like J. S. Mill, while denouncing their philosophy. He lectured on Kant and Hegel and criticized English empirical theories. His own philosophy was that 'the Universe is a single eternal activity or energy, of which it is the essence to be self-conscious, that is to be itself and not-itself in one', and that 'the whole world of human experience is the self-communication or revelation of the eternal and absolute being'. Mrs Ward revered him as the representative of the spiritual and liberating forces of the great college of Balliol, and she closely modelled on him the character Grey in *Robert Elsmere*. In the case of Dr Friedland she drew a more subtle picture, calling on features of Green's life and outlook but fusing them into an independently imagined and distinctive personality. Perhaps the Wordsworthianism of Green is seen in a quite different character, that of the atheistic Stephen Fountain.

21 (p. 316). *ne croit qui veut . . . ne doute qui veut*: '[A man] does not believe through will nor doubt through will.' (From Amiel's *Journal Intime*, translated by Mrs Ward in 1884.)

22 (p. 329). *Sidonius* [or Sidonis] *Apollinaris* (?430–?479): Poet and letter-writer; Bishop of Auvergne.

23 (p. 330). *Froude*: William Froude (1803–36), a friend of Newman, member of the Oxford School and brother of the historian J. A. Froude. He was a Catholic without the popery and a Church of England man without the Protestantism.

24 (p. 330). *Erasmus*: Desiderius Erasmus (?1466–1536), Dutch humanist and the leading scholar of the Renaissance in northern Europe. He published the first Greek edition of the New Testament in 1516 and an attack on the theology of Luther in 1524. He was not literally a Protestant but a precursor of Protestantism.

25 (p. 331). *Tridentine*: Relating to the Council of Trent (1546–63), at which the Roman Catholic Counter-Reformation was formalized.

26 (p. 331). *Guicciardini's*: Francesco Guicciardini (1483–1540), Florentine statesman and author of the most important contemporary history of Italy; he engaged early in the critical use of evidence.

27 (p. 331). *Renan*: Ernest Renan (1823–92), French philosopher, historian and scholar of religion, whose *Vie de Jésus* (1863) was denounced by the church because he attributed the development of Christianity to popular imagination.

28 (p. 332). (St) *Margaret Mary Alacoque* (1647–90): French nun, founder of the devotion of the Sacred Heart.

NOTES

29 (p. 333). '*Civitas Dei*': Saint Augustine of Hippo (396–430), who profoundly influenced both Catholic and Protestant theology, wrote *De Civitate Dei* (*The City of God*) as a vindication of the Christian Church.

30 (p. 354). '*to cease . . . no pain*': See note 3.

31 (p. 356). *bogle*: A dialect or archaic word for 'bogey'.

32 (p. 360). *But now I cast . . . was pride*: From 'Sensitiveness' (1833), by J. H. Newman.

33 (p. 364). *From the Martha . . . to this Mary*: Sisters in the New Testament (Luke 10:38–42). Martha represents good works and Mary spiritual devotion.

34 (p. 367). *St Theresa*: Teresa of Avila (1515–82), Spanish nun and mystic who founded the Carmelite order and seventeen convents. Her writings include a spiritual autobiography and *The Way of Perfection*. The Prelude to George Eliot's *Middlemarch* vaunts her as the example of pure goodness achieved through devotion; the efforts towards goodness and kindly works of the heroine, Dorothea Brooke, are compared with hers. Incidentally, Dorothea is taken to Rome for her honeymoon and experiences a very Protestant sense of revulsion against much of what St Peter's and Catholicism represent.

APPENDIX

ROMAN CATHOLIC RECUSANTS

The term 'recusant' literally referred to anyone who refused to attend the Church of England when it was compulsory, generally speaking from Henry VIII's Act of Supremacy (1534) and Thomas Cromwell's Injunctions to the Clergy (1538) until 1829. It therefore included Puritan dissenters, but came to be applied only to Roman Catholics. On the changing religious and political scene of the seventeenth century, the Catholic Recusants formed a small and scattered rustic nonconformist sect; it was self-conscious, defensive and almost Puritan in its worship, and dominated by its lay aristocracy and squirearchy. The priests were often poorly educated and of low social status (in *Helbeck*, the priest Father Bowles is in that tradition) and Mass might be celebrated surreptitiously in private houses, inn-rooms or even borrowed chapels.

The rebellions of 1715 and 1745 further diminished the confidence and numbers of the native Roman Catholics, but a tiny aristocracy and gentry survived into the early nineteenth century, rarely ceasing to lament that they were a dying breed. Their children might be educated abroad at Catholic schools like the English College at St Omer or at Nantes (as Helbeck's father was) in France, or at Louvain in Belgium, since they were not allowed their own schools in England and any moves to enfranchise them could lead to protests like the Gordon Riots in 1780. Only 150 families of the gentry and seven of the peerage were practising Catholics by 1830, though these were generally well-off and self-assured, the aristocrats having often adopted upper-middle-class attitudes through joining the professions or going into commerce. (Helbeck's comments on this may be seen in Book II, p. 147.) As late as 1851 the heir to the Duke of Norfolk, head of the highest-ranking and most ancient Catholic family, joined the Church of England and sent his sons to Eton.

Yet times were changing: the Prince Regent had said, 'The Catholic Religion is the religion for a gentleman,' and had illegally married the Catholic Mrs Fitz-Herbert. In 1829 the Emancipation Act opened up many walks of life to Catholics and other dissenters and allowed the foundation of Catholic schools (Helbeck attended Stonyhurst). The great Tractarian controversy and the Oxford Movement resulted in Newman's conversion to Rome and the establishment of the High Church in the Church of England, and in 1850 the Catholic hierarchy and new dioceses were introduced under Cardinal Wiseman, who expected the old church to return to the old faith. So English Catholic opinion, which since the eighteenth century had been hostile to monasticism and the Orders, gave way in the 1850s to a more intense ideology, more Continental in tradition, and the large influx of Irish peasants which was settling into the industrial slums increased the number of the faithful and changed their social balance.

By 1900 there had developed in England a Catholic presence that was highly organized, clerically dominated, baroque in form and mostly urban Irish in origin. It was more absolutely separated than had been the case before, when, despite the segregation of Anglicans from others enforced by the law (and some resultant anti-Catholicism), in practice the two sects had lived happily side by side. In these earlier times Catholics might be married and buried by Anglican rites and send their children to Protestant schools and universities, and nuns and priests might wear secular dress (for instance, Mr Donniforth, the priest in *A Simple Story*). Such a relaxed attitude became unthinkable, as the case of Alan Helbeck exemplifies.

FIND OUT MORE ABOUT
PENGUIN BOOKS

We publish the largest range of titles of any English language paperback publisher. As well as novels, crime and science fiction, humour, biography and large-format illustrated books, Penguin series include *Pelican Books* (on the arts, sciences and current affairs), *Penguin Reference Books, Penguin Classics, Penguin Modern Classics, Penguin English Library, Penguin Handbooks* (on subjects from cookery and gardening to sport) and *Puffin Books* for children. Other series cover a wide variety of interests from poetry to crosswords, and there are also several newly formed series – *King Penguin, Penguin American Library* and *Penguin Travel Library*.

We are an international publishing house, but for copyright reasons not every Penguin title is available in every country. To find out more about the Penguins available in your country please write to our U.K. office – Dept EP, Penguin Books Ltd, Harmondsworth, Middlesex UB7 0DA – unless you live in one of the following areas:

In the U.S.A.: Dept DG, Penguin Books, 299 Murray Hill Parkway, East Rutherford, New Jersey 07073.

In Canada: Penguin Books Canada Ltd, 2801 John Street, Markham, Ontario L3R 1B4.

In Australia: Marketing Department, Penguin Books Australia Ltd, P.O. Box 257, Ringwood, Victoria 3134.

In New Zealand: Marketing Department, Penguin Books (N.Z.) Ltd, P.O. Box 4019, Auckland 10.

In India: Penguin Overseas Ltd, 706 Eros Apartments, 56 Nehru Place, New Delhi 110019.

CHARLOTTE BRONTË

SHIRLEY

Edited by Andrew and Judith Hook

At a time when critical inquiry is being focused on the relationship between literature and society, *Shirley* (too often overshadowed by *Jane Eyre*) becomes especially interesting. In it the author charts the forces moulding society in the period of the Napoleonic Wars – from the economic hardship resulting from bad harvests and the British Government's Orders in Council to the oppression of women and the Luddite riots. But, central to all these concerns, accurately documented though they are, is Charlotte Brontë's imaginative grasp of what is common to all these forms of oppression, whether of women or of the poor – the denial of the world of feeling.

VILLETTE

Edited by Mark Lilly
and introduced by Tony Tanner

Published in 1853, *Villette* was Charlotte Brontë's last novel and is often regarded as her most emotionally and aesthetically satisfying work.

As in *Jane Eyre*, the theme is one of passionate personal integrity, the struggle of an individual to preserve an independent spirit in the face of adverse circumstances. Like *Jane Eyre* and *The Professor*, it is deeply autobiographical. It is only in *Villette*, however, that Charlotte Brontë found a narrator such as Lucy Snowe who could explore in a sufficiently complex way the tensions and alterations in her own inner and outer experience. The result is one of the greatest fictional studies in our literature, not of self and society, but of self without society; and of a character who expresses more than any other woman in English fiction the anguish of unrequited love.

and

JANE EYRE

Edited by Q. D. Leavis